YOSEMITE
FAREWELL

YOSEMITE FAREWELL

An Untold Tale from the California Gold Rush

JoAnn Levy

This is a work of fiction based on documentary sources, including quoted diaries, letters, and newspapers relating to actual historical events, locations, and persons. Additional names, places, events, and characters arise from the author's imagination and any resemblance to real people, places, and events is coincidental.

Published by Elzevir House

Cover: 'Indian Woman Panning Out Gold,' from *Hutchings' Illustrated California Magazine*, Vol. III, 1859. Courtesy California State Library. Antique Engraving of Sentinel Rock from the North, Yosemite Valley, Yosemite National Park, Sierra Nevada, California, 1872. Title font is Besley Clarendon ML, created by HiH, and based on the Clarendon font registered by Robert Besley and the Fann Street Foundry in 1845.

Cover, Formatting and Interior Design by Woven Red Author Services, www.WovenRed.ca

Yosemite Farewell: An Untold Tale from the California Gold Rush/JoAnn Levy—1st edition
ISBN ebook: 978-1-7373000-0-7
ISBN paperback: 978-1-7373000-1-4
ISBN hard cover: 978-1-7373000-2-1

for Dan
always for Dan
who believed this is the book
I had to write

and in loving memory of Nancy Jo

Contents

Author's Note

Spanish religionists from Mexico arrived in California in 1769 to find approximately 300,000 native people generally living peacefully with one another as they had for centuries—trapping, fishing, and gathering acorns. At that date, none had ever laid eyes on a mule, a horse—or a European. We can only imagine their surprise.

The Jesuits, establishing missions from San Diego to the future San Francisco, further astonished the coastal natives with mysteries and bells, infected them with smallpox and measles, and essentially disrupted their culture beyond rescue. Inland Indians occasionally met the future when Mexican soldiers on often-brutal expeditions conscripted replacement labor for those dead and dying from initiation into mission life.

After Mexico won independence from Spain, California's missions eventually secularized, officially in 1833. Abandoned Indians with Spanish names wandered into the countryside, some to work for Californios as *vaqueros* or servants, others to rejoin Indian society in the interior. In the 65 years since first encounter, their numbers had declined by a third.

In 1839, John Sutter, a Swiss emigrant, entered California history when the Mexican governor granted him 48,000 interior acres. Naming his grant New Helvetia, Sutter persuaded, often ruthlessly, local Indians to tend his multiple enterprises.

Soon, more emigrants followed, intruding on native lands with belief in their manifest destiny to possess the continent, regardless of anyone already residing there. In 1846, Americans bested Mexico's sovereignty in a brief engagement, raised the stars and stripes, and took over.

By then, California Indians numbered about 150,000. On January 24, 1848, James Marshall, hired by Sutter to build a sawmill on the American

River, unintentionally sealed their fate. The discovery of gold changed everything. Collision between the Americans and the Indians fast-forwarded with one culture living lightly on the land, the other intent on digging it up. When did the Indians realize they would be overrun, their way of life erased, their land and culture lost? Their numbers plummet to 30,000? We can only imagine.

History glamorized Sutter and Marshall, despite their tragic and penniless ends, and generally overlooked the aptly named James Savage, a fun-loving, illiterate, multilingual former mountain man and fur trapper. At the height of the gold rush his name was famous. Few know it now.

Jim Savage arrived in California in 1846, rode with Fremont in the War with Mexico, worked for Sutter, established trading posts on the Merced, Mariposa, and Fresno rivers. To protect his interests as a trader and gold miner, he formed alliances with the Indians residing in the foothills and vast inland valley of tule-rich rivers and streams by learning their languages and marrying the daughters of chiefs. They called him El Rey Tularenos, king of the tulares.

In 1850, Congress invited gold-rich California to join the Union as the 31st state, subjecting the native people to a government unsympathetic to their disrupted culture. As their numbers continued to collapse due to star-vation, disease, and homicide, we can only imagine their desperation at see-ing their land overrun by gold-fevered miners, traders, and settlers. In a final, desperate attempt to discourage white settlement, several hundred attacked a trading post in the southern mines and killed three Americans. Thus began the so-called Mariposa Indian War, in which their one defender, Jim Savage, was charged with bringing them in from the mountains to sign peace treaties and relocate to reservations.

This tragic but commonplace event had one monumental consequence: the discovery of Yosemite Valley.

The extraordinary experiences of California's gold rush pioneers are richly recorded in hundreds of letters, diaries, newspapers, and reminis-cences. The Mariposa Indian War had only one diarist, Robert Eccleston. On April 14, 1851, he wrote:

In the Van rode a young squaw who is acting as guide. She was riding on a large Rowen [sic] horse & sat ast[r]adle & rode without stirrups. She wore a hat under which her black & straight hair hung down gracefully upon her shoulders, which were partially covered with a scarf thrown neg-ligently over the left shoulder, her bodice was white muslin & her skirt of blue fig[ured] calico, & her small feet & ankles showed to advantage. Next to her, Major Savage rode followed by the staff generally, & after

them the whole Battalion in Indian file making a formidable appearance,
each carrying their Red, blue, &c. blankets behind them and our youthful
Guidess would every little while look back & seem proud of her station.

Who was she, this Indian 'guidess'? No one knows. What was she thinking as she led Jim Savage and his ragtag little army into the mountains to pursue Indians? We cannot know. Did she believe she was saving her people? Or betraying them?

We cannot know. We can only imagine.

1847

Coyote said, "I do not like people to die," but Meadowlark told him, "No, it is not well to have too many. There will be others to replace those that die. A man will have many children. The old people will die, but the young will live." Then Coyote said nothing more. So from that time on, people have always died."

—Yosemite Indian Legend

S he must hide. Not yet, he had said, but soon.
Not yet.
For now, she joined the mourners watching smoke drift from the Hachanah *hang'i*. Surrounded by evening shadows and towering pines, the red-cedar roundhouse lay cupped in the earth like an offering to the land.

They had collected together from nearby villages —Cosumnes, Muqueleme, Noma, Omo, Polasu, Yuloni— to grieve together in the old way, burdened by sorrow, bringing spirit gifts for the dead. Since time's beginnings the People had gathered each autumn for their Big Cry.

Breathing deeply the evening air, moccasins softly crushing fallen leaves, she followed the others down the gently declining path into the *hang'i*. In its centered fire pit flames licked darkness remnant with the scent of old smoke and ancient ritual. She pulled her rabbit-fur cape close against the subterranean chill, stepped silently between those already seated, and found a place in the dim outer area, the *et-chat*. Was she practicing hiding? Her father hadn't said when they would leave Yuloni, only that they must.

She dismissed the unhappy thought as she crouched to the earthen floor strewn with incense cedar and pine needles. Sitting cross-legged, she tucked her deerskin skirt around her knees, cradled the gift in her lap, and watched smoke-shadowed silhouettes whispering, weeping, speaking names.

Speaking names. In memory she heard her own again now, the beckoning urgency of the dream voice, insistent as breath: "Di-shi! Di-shi!"

The dream had tugged at her thoughts since morning's first leaked light of dawn gently withdrew the receding vision of a child's moccasins on her feet. Her mother had made them. Even in the dream she wondered that they fit, but the thought fled, dissolved as swiftly as deer disappear between trees.

In the dream she was standing on a rock ledge above a chasm vast and black as inside night sky when moon and stars retreat. She had felt neither dizzy nor fearful, only a strange, sad bewilderment as the echoing voice called, "Di-shi!"

Turning in its direction, she had seen only an unfamiliar landscape, barren and infinite. Where was the village? Where were the People?

"Di-shi!" Plaintive. Demanding.

Di-shi. A People's name. Victoria had said that she had been named Di-shi— Little Blue Jay—for being endlessly curious like that bold, inquisitive bird. Victoria shared many stories about the mission where the long-robes traded prayers and crosses and bells and promises for the People's freedom. Word pictures to collect like grass seed in a gathering basket, tiny bits of this and that. But Victoria rarely spoke about the woman calling from the dream-place, Maria.

Maria. A mission name, like Victoria, Anna. Isabel.

Reluctantly waking this morning, she trailed the dream, a silent hunter of her mother's voice drifting away, windblown as spider silk. Di-shi. Di-shi.

Inside, where thought and dream dwelt, she was Di-shi still, one of the Me'wuk, the People. Inside, she was not Isabel, she was Di-shi, Little Blue Jay. Only her mother called her Di-shi. And so she had known she was in the dream-place again. Because her mother was dead.

"Ain't right," he said, turning his horse from the excitement raising a dust cloud over the corral. "Sight hard and sun hot." Dismounting, he led the chestnut mare into the shade of a convenient oak and tossed the reins over a low-hanging branch. "Girl, this heat 'bout like to flat-iron a man's lungs." He squatted into the cool beneath the tree, plucked a stalk of dry grass, examined it. When had he started talking to his horse? He husked the stem, stuck it in his mouth, and sat, leaning against the tree and itching his sweaty back against its bark.

Never used to talk to his horse before, 'course trappin' was a sight different. Trappin', a man gotta go quiet, keep attention sharp as his knife. This place, made no difference if he talked to his horse or howled at the moon. Fact was, Girl 'bout as good at conversation as most men he'd met in California. Better'n some.

He drew up his knees, rested his elbows on them, stared into the dust-draped distance, then thumbed up the brim of his old slouch hat to better view the scene. Saw the corral fine from here, he did, no need fryin' his head in the sun. View didn't improve none from bein' close up on it. He chewed the grass stalk, itched his back on the oak some more, settled in to watch what Sutter paid him to watch. Paid to watch. Pain to watch. Plain didn't like watchin' it. Paid. Pain. Plain. He glanced up at his horse chomping grass, oblivious to the cloud of investigating insects raised by her intrusion. "Girl, I'm a poet, didn't know it." He slapped at a fly buzzing his ear and turned his attention back to the corral. "Ain't never laid my baby blues on nothin' like this afore." And Jim Savage, in his thirty years on God's good earth, as he'd tell anyone what cared to sit a spell and yarn, had seen many a peculiar sight.

Baby-blues. What Eliza used to say, insisting her favorite flower, baby-blue-eyes, just matched the orbs the good Lord give Jim Savage for gazin' on the world's wonders. He cleared his throat, parched as the heat-shimmered landscape, dislodging the lump that followed memories of Eliza like a faithful dog. No point thinkin' on that.

He tugged his bandana from around his neck and mopped it across his forehead. Pitiful thing to see, them Indians runnin' and hollerin', raisin' all that dust, barely visible in the yellow shroud of rising chaff. He licked his lips, tongued his mouth for enough saliva to spit. Ten years a fun-lovin' free trapper, come to this.

She fondled the faded calico in her lap, crushed by the sadness of absence. Now Victoria, too, was dead. So many mornings together, pounding acorn. In memory she saw Victoria again, straddling her *ho'ya* atop Yuloni's immense grinding rock, *may'tat* in her hand, calico skirt, red as woodpecker's tiny top feathers, bunched above narrow brown knees.

A sudden drumming demanded attention. She looked up. Dancers, remembering the dead, grieving loss, hurried a ragged circle around the fire, fluttered feather plumes to the drummer's beat, rattled clapper sticks. She watched until reverie reclaimed her to the countless mornings she had sat with Victoria, sun warm on her back, the vast granite bedrock cool beneath her. How often she had sat, legs extended each side of her *ho'ya* as she swept it clean with her soap-root brush. How fleeting that treasured time. She remembered the heft of the *may'tat* in her hand, the narrow stone a perfect oblong, remembered thinking one of the First People had left it near the river for her to find. How happily unaware she had been then, scooping acorns from Victoria's shared basket, dropping them into the shallow depression, silently reciting a prayer to acorn as Victoria instructed. "So acorn spirit will know you are happy for the acorn and will come again next year."

Village women and girls, climbing up, coming and going, chatting of one thing or another. When the dream first came, she remembered telling Victoria, as they pounded acorn, "I heard her voice. Maria's voice. I had a dream and I heard her call my name."

Victoria looked sad, said the names of the dead were not spoken, not in the old ways. But sometimes she accepted new ways, the ways of the padres. Only Victoria, among the mission Indians who had followed José Jesús to Yuloni, had lived most of her life with the old ways. She once told how she was seized and taken to the mission when gray already streaked her hair. "Maybe forty snow moons," she said when asked her age, not certain, such things being of no consequence in the old ways.

Hugging the memory now, eyes closed to the shuffling dancers, she could see Victoria's welcoming smile, a crooked blanket seam in her creased face. Could see Victoria's *may'tat* in her left hand, see her right hand scoop the larger bits of broken acorn, the *wassayu,* toward the center of her *ho'ya* and the finer flour to the side. Showing, instructing. Raising and lowering her stone, pounding acorn into meal, saying, "Watch, Isabel. See the right way to make acorn. Your acorn is too thin, Isabel. Add more. Listen to the sound of the *may'tat* in the *ho'ya*. They talk. The pounding starts to ring when the meal becomes too thin, Isabel."

Isabel. Victoria as insistent as her father about the new-ways name. And then Victoria's *may'tat* falling silent when asked to tell the story again. About the massacre.

"Nope, ain't never seen nothin' like this," he said, addressing a particularly persistent fly investigating his face. He flapped his damp bandana at it. "And I been clear to Oregon Territory and back. Ain't mentionin' the Rockies, but practically mapped 'em." He laughed to himself. Talkin' to insects now. But he'd had him some fun then, he had. "Traveled with Pawnee one year, Blackfoot the next. Crow. Sioux. Knew 'em all. Jumped the broom with their women," he told the fly. Never told Eliza, though, not that squaw part anyways.

He veered from that track, circled his thoughts back to Sutter, his eye on the corral, earnin' his pay. Didn't like it, watchin' Indians workin' like that. Couldn't say he liked anything about Sutter's sun-sucked valley. Too hot and too crowded up for a man used to his own company, used to mountains. Still be trampin' and trappin' there if the Utes hadn't got some burr up their butts three years back. He remembered when that dust settled nine free trappers and thirteen company men lay dead in it. Well, he knew an ill wind when it blew through his flaxen hair, he did; his mother raised no fool. Price on pelts gone to nothin' anyway, beaver played out, hardly two hundred pounds of fur from a year's trappin'. Dollar a pound, two for top quality, was all the American Fur Company offered at the rendezvous in 'thirty-nine. Barely enough to pay the traders what he owed for powder, whiskey, and sugar.

In the dust-filled distance, the Indians raced and whooped and hollered. Nearby, his horse nosed deeper into dying grass. "Traders, they made the money, eh, Girl?" he said, watching her. The horse flicked her ears as if to agree. "Tradin'. That's the business for gettin' rich. Traders got the furs *and* the money back they paid for 'em." A lizard skittered up the oak's rough bark, stopped near his shoulder, fixed its unblinking eyes on him. Jim nodded to it. "God's truth, my friend. Trappers give the money right back, buyin' liquor. Yep, tradin', that's the business to be in. And fun, too, I bet."

He mopped his sweated forehead again. Sorely missed solitude, he did. Damn the Utes, the fur company, silk-hatters. Damn 'em all. Not since St. Louis had he seen this many people. More Indians than he could count, and must be near on to three hundred white people crowded in and around the fort, raggedy immigrants like himself, and disbanded soldiers. Seemed like Mormon Battalion boys straggled in every day lookin' for work while they waited for Brigham Young to whistle 'em over the mountain. New York Volunteers, too, a worthless set, not one of 'em any more a soldier than himself, and too late anyways for the little fandango Fremont called a war. Not that the pissant affair might rightly be called a war. Ladies' church society coulda took California from the Mexicans just as easy, and without mussin' their bonnets, anyone cared to know. And come off more respectable in the bargain.

He studied the noisy corral, dust flying from beneath horses' hooves, remembering how it was with Eliza gone, that brief happiness blasted, no money, and no heart for thinkin' what to do next. Hitchin' up with Fremont's amateur army had looked like deliverance. Some army. Ragtag collection of innocents and ruffians all pie-eyed on patriotism, itchy as poison oak. All of 'em more likely to shoot or shout than think. Stuck in his memory like a foot in a boot was the bugler mistakin' the moon for the sun one night, blasted horn rousin' the whole camp from sleep.

He wiped his bandana across his face, feeling hotter just thinking on that idiot. Worse was the greenhorn mistaking a madrone tree for the enemy. Fired enough shots to cripple a forest. Fools on parade. Jim mopped the back of his neck. Fools. Twenty-six grizzly bears killed for sport. And one poor Indian for being the Mexican governor's servant. Saw it again in memory now, the Indian standing silent, tied to a tree, staring into destiny, his executioners noisily vying for the firing squad. A dozen shots and the Indian folded to his knees slow as an old man in church. Not a protest, not a whimper. Jim remembered thinking at the time it was as brave a death as he'd ever witnessed. Poor devil done in by the commanding officer's need to sop bloodlust from fools scratching for a chance to kill someone. Anyone.

Made him ashamed to be of the white-man tribe, it did. Somethin' like watchin' Sutter's Indians. Well, damn the damn Utes and silk-hatters anyway. He sorely missed trappin'. And he sorely missed havin' fun. California so far was servin' up less fun than a funeral.

The horse, suddenly alert, lifted her head from the grass, turned. Whickered.

A loud lamentation startled her from reverie. Around the fire weeping dancers halted, wailed a collective sorrow, turned, faced west, slowly lifted their arms, wailed. The drummer beat a loud, sad tattoo on his log drum and the dancers turned, faced north, raised their arms, rattled their clapper sticks. Old ways.

She stroked the folded calico, remembering how Victoria's mission stories sometimes began with wistful descriptions of orchards, of trees bearing strange fruit, large and white. Pears and apples, sweeter than blackberries, Victoria's old eyes dancing with recollections of their tantalizing taste. So many strange and amazing things Victoria had described: fountains and courtyards, looms and tiles, keys and chains and bells and sundials. The sundial, Victoria explained, pictured people praying, people eating, people herding sheep. As the sun passed overhead its shadow touched the pictures and boys rang bells when the shadow touched the pictures showing what to do. Different bells for prayers and work, other bells for meals.

"The People do not live like that," Di-shi remembered saying, defending old ways. Victoria looking away. At Anna? Then, "No, but we were never hungry."

"What is it, Girl?" Jim hauled himself to his feet and saw a rider approaching. He'd got soft, sure enough, not to notice someone comin' up on him. He brushed dried grass from his pants, put a hand on his horse's warm neck. "There's a good Girl." He could make out the rider now. Bidwell. Sutter's aide-de-fort Jim liked to think of him, when required to think of him, which he rarely felt himself called upon to do. Not his sort, Bidwell. Didn't like his eyes. Could read a man's intention in his eyes. That was the kind of readin' he knew, a practical ability, and considerable more value to it than book learnin', anyone cared to ask. Bidwell's eyes was kinda beady, small and deep-set, maybe worn down from his school-teachin' days, or from scribblin' at Sutter's reports and records and accounts and whatever. A man ought to look up and out on the world, not bury his gaze in paper. Probably why his own baby-blues stood out 'right handsome in his handsome face,' or so Eliza always said. Her memory crowded him this day, he supposed from keepin' company with his other regrets.

Bidwell rode into the oak's thirsty circle of shade, the smell of horse and sweat and heat with him. Jim watched him remove his dusty hat, fan himself with it, wipe his deep-set eyes with his coat-sleeve, then gesture in the direction of the corral with his hat. "How they doing?" He dismounted, not waiting for an answer. "Most are wild Indians, Nisenan, no mission training. Got to keep an eye on them. Run off first chance they get."

Best idea of the day, and me with 'em, Jim thought, not replying. No point rilin' himself further on the lowly situation of Sutter's Indians, nor on his overseer's task neither. Bidwell generally tended to ramble talk anyways. Maybe from bein' a teacher, talkin' all the time and now apparently keepin' his hand in. Yappin' like he knew the answers and was just askin' questions ever' so often to keep the flow up. But now he looked at Jim like it was his turn at the tap.

Jim shrugged. "Can't say as I admire what Sutter's reduced 'em to, but can't fault the results." More than that he felt disinclined to say. One didn't look a gift horse in the mouth. Sutter was practically a bank the way he handed money around, and the only source of it for miles, clear to the coast towns. His own money, what little he'd had of the stuff, had disappeared in the long trek overland—fees for ferry crossings, treats for Eliza at the Fort Laramie sutler, blacksmithin' at Fort Hall. The trip ate money like a cow ate grass, a regular steady consumption. He could use Sutter's sixty dollars a month, sure enough. Maybe outfit for a return East, or have a go at the Oregon Territory again. Didn't rightly know what he'd do, anyone cared to ask, but it weren't watchin' Indians run horses through wheat, that much he knew. Damn, he hated this work.

Bidwell nodded, his gaze on the distance. "Harvesting's something to see, too. Three hundred wild Indians in a grain field, swinging sickles, butcher knives, pieces of hoop iron. Willow sticks if they got nothing else. But this threshing's the wild part."

Jim had watched it some hours now, and agreed. Early that morning, when he'd followed the Indians out, he'd been amazed at the huge pile of wheat heaped up in the immense corral constructed for the purpose. The

Indians knew what to do and went right to it. After driving a herd of horses into the corral, they whooped and hollered, chasing the horses round and round through the wheat. Every now and again one would dash in front to turn the horses and reverse the action. A dangerous maneuver to Jim's eye, but the resulting grain so thoroughly threshed the dry straw was almost chaff.

"Best harvest in the six years I've been here," Bidwell said, waving pestering flies from his face. "I've seen two thousand bushels of wheat threshed in a single hour in that manner. Winnowing, though, that's going to take a month."

For Jim, that cinched it.

Huddled figures nearby whispered and wept. Sorrow hung among them like smoke, collected above the drummer's beat, beneath the dancers' wails. She retreated into memory, recalled Victoria describing her favorite bells, *esquilas.* Glad bells, she had said, rung by turning over and over by boys competing to see who could spin them fastest.

And Victoria telling how José Jesús escaped from the long-robes to ride with the famous horse thieves Cipriano and Estanislao. But later, Victoria said, retelling the story as she often did, he returned to the mission. "For love of Maria," she said, smiling her toothless smile, "for his beautiful Maria. So together they could bring Isabel into the world."

Was her mother beautiful? She herself remembered nothing of her mother or the mission, being but three winters in the world when the long-robes departed with their mysteries and mules. Too young to remember her father leading mission Indians confused by freedom out the opened gates, taking them into the mountains to live in the old ways.

Three winters inside a mission. Thirteen winters in the mountains, living free. Learning to make acorn atop *chaw'se,* sun warming her back. Listening to stories. Imagining one day collecting elder sticks and willow for a baby cradle. Living free in the world as the People had lived since time's beginnings. Free to be Di-shi.

Not Isabel.

Jim wouldn't do it, couldn't sit his horse and watch slave Indians winnow wheat for a month. "Guess I'll be talkin' to Sutter then."

"*Captain. Captain* Sutter," Bidwell said.

Jim snorted. Jumped-up title, self-promoted. Or had the little man advanced himself to general now? And in what army? Pretty good joke, considerin' Sutter's past as a failed trader. American Fur Trade boys at the rendezvous in 'thirty-nine told how Sutter ran out on partners in Santa Fe and St. Louis both. Probably still owed 'em, Jim thought, remembering now how the slick-talking Sutter was said to have got as far as Fort Laramie where Hudson Bay traders took him on to Oregon. And now here the little man was in California, not ten years later, lordin' it over the place, outfitted like a Frenchy king. But hirin' immigrants, Bryant had said, and payin' good wages. Jim rather admired Bryant, had done so ever since the man quit their wagon train halfway from St. Louis. Loaded up mules and announced he was packin' to California. Did it, too. 'Course Bryant didn't have a wife with him.

"I told your *captain* only thing I knew was explorin' and trappin' and Indians. Told him I liked the people, learned their language, comes to me pert easy, understand how they see the world. But I was talkin' regular Indians, not this tamed-up California variety." He jerked a thumb toward the corral. "Anyone with a horse and a behind to sit one can do what's required here. It ain't for me."

The way Bidwell looked him over like he was a specimen of peculiar origin but no particular value made Jim laugh. He hadn't laughed in a long time. It felt good. He laughed some more just for the pleasure of it, and because Sutter was of no account to him anyway and neither was this scribbling truckler. He wanted not to take any man's measure too hasty, liked to get it right, or as near on as a body could, but Bidwell put him off with his observations on the Indians, like they was some kind of perpetual motion machine and not men same as everyone else.

Bidwell was staring at him. "Actually, I rode out expressly to inform you, Mr. Savage, that the captain wishes to see you in his office. I believe he wants to more fully engage your experience with Indians. Their sickness has left us short-handed for the winnowing."

"Sickness?" Jim said, and looked away, studied the yellow dust swirling from the corral. Sickness? As if Bidwell, Sutter, anyone in the valley with ears, didn't hear the ceaseless drumming each night, the desperate wailing from Indian dance houses crying to Great Spirit for cure.

He turned, fixed Bidwell in his sights like he had a gun on him. "I'd say dyin's more like it."

Bidwell slapped at a fly buzzing his ear. "Indians no more trouble than cattle." He squatted down next to the tree, settled himself into watching the Indians, letting Jim Savage know to go.

No more trouble than cattle? Jim shook his head, felt inclined to pity a man who'd never sat down with an Indian, talked, smoked a pipe, shared a meal. He mounted his horse, turned her toward the fort lying white in the distance. Leaned toward her ear. "Must be somethin' worth doin' in this good country 'sides herdin' people."

The wailing grew louder, and she bent beneath it, leaning forward, as if sound had weight, her hair falling long into her lap. Her father's voice in her head now. "Isabel. Isabel. *Su llama* Isabel." Urging her new-ways name, urging the black-robes' language. Instructing. Insisting she needed their words, telling again how language was a special power for seeing the world like those who spoke those words saw it. Me'wuk saw the world through their words, Mexicans and white men through theirs. Different words, different worlds. To survive required learning new ways. "Heed me, Isabel, and you will live long."

José Jesús was brave, wise, a great chief. Everyone respected his counsel. Yet his advice lay heavy on her heart. To be Isabel, to speak as Mexicans spoke? The world she knew and loved, these tree-dressed mountains, this was the great gift of Great Spirit. She loved the softness of old leaves and fallen pine needles beneath her moccasins, the scent of cedar, mornings frosted with grass blinking a sun-startled welcome, the late-day warmth of sun fading from a sky as blue as jays. She belonged where the river sang, exuberantly playing, spraying, splashing, dashing down a mountainside, life blood of her mountain world, Yuloni, a place of the People.

Leave Yuloni? "Heed me, Isabel, and you will live long."

Isabel. Isabel. Drum and bone whistles and clapper sticks echoing her new ways name, intruding on her wandering thoughts, returning her to where old ways were disappearing.

He let Girl set her own pace toward Sutter's fort, ambling past dwellings rough tossed-up by Sutter's ragtag collection of hired hands. He didn't like none of it. Houses sproutin' like weeds in a garden. Wildness dug up, civilization planted. Land once overrun by deer and elk, gone over now to cattle and sheep, wheat, fruit trees, grapevines.

And a fort. Surprised the land with it, Sutter had, along with cannons he fired off now and again to impress guests and astonish the natives. Approaching its entrance, Jim leaned into his horse's neck, whispered into her flicking ear, "Seen some things, ain't we, Girl?"

Sutter had surely forted himself up in style, though against what enemy or to what purpose Jim doubted even the man himself could say. The immense doors, an imposing defense reinforced nearly solid by iron bolts, stood open. Surely loved a show, the so-called captain did. Above the doors a double row of saw-shaped iron arched like grinning teeth. Looked to be sharp enough to sever the ropes of grappling irons. Though who in this land might own or hurl such a possession, or want to, challenged imagination. No California Indian possessed sufficient animosity to put himself to the trouble. A surrounding wall of sun-baked adobes, nearly twenty feet high and three thick, equally confounded him. Who was Sutter thinkin' was comin' to get him? His creditors?

An Indian sentinel guarding the gate saluted. One of Sutter's 'home guard,' tricked out in blue pantaloons, white shirt, and a red bandana around his neck. Jim half raised a hand to acknowledge the man who might once have roamed the mountains a hunter. What a poor bargain he'd made, trading that life for this one. And did he have a choice? José Jesús, now that was an Indian to admire, about the best man he'd met in California. Plenty wary about the way the wind was blowin' white men into his country. No surprise there, already havin' jumped outta the mission frypan. Concerned for his daughter and his band livin' within Sutter's reach. Rightly so, in Jim's opinion.

Bryant's Company H, bad bargain there for José Jesús and his Me'wuk warriors. James D. Savage, too, come to that. None of 'em likely to collect the twenty-five dollars a month promised. Nothin' to show for volunteerin' to fight Mexicans for Fremont 'ceptin' a piece of paper Bryant said could be redeemed for cash when Congress appropriated funds. When pigs fly. Piece of paper, pound of tobacco, and a blue shirt. That'd be it. Jim cursed himself for believin' he'd see seventy-five cents, much less dollars. Government reneged notoriously, ask any Indian it treated with. Ask the Walla Wallas persuaded out of Oregon and into California to fight the Mexicans on Fremont's promise of pay, rations, clothing. None of it delivered. Plenty resentful. Give new meanin' to hostile, the Walla Wallas did, payin' themselves in stolen horses, plunder, and depredation on their way home. Knowing Indians, Jim suspected the Walla Wallas would visit their resentment on whites in Oregon when they got there. Missionaries likely in for a surprise.

She sensed sorrow intensifying in the *hang'i*'s smoke-shrouded shadows. Foot-drummer thumping his hollow log, mourners weeping, dancers with painted faces striped black shuffling sideways, stamping their feet, sending their collected despair to Great Spirit. Singing sadness to stars. The People's Big Cry, mourning together every autumn since time began.

Her thoughts wandered to last year's Big Cry, Victoria anticipating a feast to quiet their crying stomachs, her age-stiffened fingers unraveling each morning another knot from the memory string of twisted milkweed, count-ing the days. Hunger haunting the village. Warriors gone with Americans to fight Mexicans. No one to hunt deer or steal horses for meat. Women and children scratching for the little the earth offered. Old men, hope reduced to habit, trapping birds and squirrels. Anna's eyes glittering from a face thinned by hunger. Victoria suspecting Anna gave her baby her own share of *nuppa*, the thin acorn soup barely sustaining them. Anna in memory now, taking the cradle strap from her forehead, placing the cradle of elder sticks lashed with willow on the ground. Victoria telling the village children old stories of how the People learned to live by watching Great Spirit's creatures.

"*I-Chow,*" Anna had said, *turtle,* watching her infant daughter creeping slowly, cradle on her back, dark eyes staring from a round face fringed by hair black as night.

Anna's baby learning the earth, learning silence.

Learning to hide.

Jim, dismounting, stroked his horse's nose, looked into her huge brown eyes. "Enough commotion here, Girl, to make up a rendezvous and a circus both, eh? And enough left over for a travelin' show."

Inside, where shops, storerooms, and barracks hugged its interior wall, Sutter's fort buzzed with activity. Blacksmiths, sweating over fires tended by Indians, pounded iron into horseshoes and nails. Carpenters sawed and hammered, manufacturing plows. Tanners scrubbed stinking cowhides in-tended for shoe leather and saddles. Coopers shaped oak into barrels. Bakers added heat to the day with ovens in service to bread. Dogs barked. Children ran and played and shouted. Indian women weaving blankets chattered at their looms.

Jim stopped to watch a dozen Indians fashioning adobe bricks from clay and straw, setting them to dry in the sun. They wore cheap cotton trousers he knew cost two weeks' labor. On strings around their necks they wore tin disks stamped by the resident blacksmith with the amount of credit due the wearer at Sutter's store, the only wages paid.

He hurried past the offensive sight of several squatting Indians hungrily scooping into their mouths the smelly porridge of bran and boiled offal Sutter fed them from troughs. How these Indians let themselves get so de-graded puzzled him. The chiefs and warriors who rode with Bryant were proud, fearless men. But here, under Sutter's control, Indians got reduced.

How had that happened?

"*Ha-ha-ha-yah! Ha-ha-ha-yah!*"

Such a cry! She watched the wailing woman unfold from the shadows and stand, bent by sorrow, face smeared black, hair singed short. A widow. "*Ha-ha-ha-yah! Ha-ha-ha-yah!*" the woman cried, pathetically swaying to the thump, thump, thump of foot-drummer pounding his hollow log.

Measles? Had the woman been widowed by the sickness killing the People working for the white man Sutter? José Jesús warned his band, his *nena,* of the sickness too powerful for shaman's sucking cure. And more: soon Indians friendly to Sutter, her father cautioned, would come into the mountains with presents and promises. Sutter needed people to harvest wheat, weave blankets, cure hides. To live in the white man's world. To replace those who had died.

Circling the fire, the principal mourners, *naw-chet-took,* echoed foot-drummer's pounding, shuffling left to right and loudly lamenting the widow's loss. An old man with a tall staff in his right hand rose and shouted, "*Hi-ah-hoo! Hi-ah-hoo!*" Around his head a band of red-shafted flicker feathers, the border black with the bird's tail feathers. Red-tail hawk feathers caped his shoulders.

Was he, she wondered, confused by these unsettling days? Did this old-ways chief see the People disappearing from their land like fading fog? José Jesús wore a red bandana around his forehead, and a blue shirt, gift from a Great White Father for fighting Mexicans. A new-ways chief. No feathers, no wailing, no dancing.

She imagined him racing across the valley now, raiding ranchos, stealing horses. In the old days his father, her grandfather, Chief Te-mi', stole horses to trade with white trappers. Victoria told how white trappers came into her village to trade cloth and knives for horses. "My people had no horses, but your father and Estanislao and Cipriano had run away from the mission and stole horses for them from the ranchos."

How her thoughts wandered! The feather-caped chief was shaking his staff and crying to Great Spirit. Chief Te-mi' had gone to Great Spirit, dying from the white man's shaking sickness. She knew his name only from stories her father told. José Jesús didn't believe speaking the names of the dead risked their return as malevolent ghosts. "New ways. Heed me, Isabel."

She was hearing her father's voice in her head, not the widow's wailing or the old chief's shouts. Victoria's voice, too, telling how Mexican soldiers hunting Indians who ran away from the mission had captured her. "Pretending friendship, they invited us to eat *pinole* and dried meat with them. No one from my village had lived at the mission but when we went to eat, the soldiers made us prisoners with the escaped Christian Indians they had found."

Victoria's voice, vivid still: "Those soldiers carried the padres' great anger for escaped Christian Indians. Forced them to their knees, said because they were Christians, and saved, they could now die and go to heaven. Then the soldiers shot them. When people from my village saw this, we made a great noise, so the angry soldiers decided to shoot us, too. We weren't Christians so a soldier with a flask of water baptized us, then shot everyone except me and two children. We were very quiet, waiting to be shot, so maybe the soldiers decided we would be good Christians and not run away. And that was how I came to live at the mission." Victoria told her story like an old tale descended from the First People, without complaint, simply as how the world was.

Had Victoria learned to see the world like the long-robes and soldiers did, by learning their words?

How her thoughts wandered tonight! So many stories in her gathering basket of collected memories. She remembered old men in Yuloni sharing stories their fathers told about long-robes coming into the land on mules. The People had never before seen mules, they said, and supposed this animal must be father to those they carried on their backs, the way Coyote had made the People. The old men told terrifying stories, too, about Mexican soldiers cutting off the People's ears to give to the padres. And the Mexican commander baptizing a baby with water from his flask, then bashing its head against a rock.

But those who were there, like Victoria, rarely told the worst story. About the massacre.

Jim loosed Girl into the stable's scattered straw. The fort lacked for nothing. When he and other suffering immigrants straggled into Johnson's ranch with the tattered remains of their wagon train, they'd all been sent on to Sutter. Meat to spare and a generous nature, Johnson said. That Sutter had, true enough, although, thinkin' back, seemed like the immigrants had scarcely put themselves to appreciatin' Sutter's hospitality before Bryant collected 'em up like kindling wood and fired 'em into patriotic fervor to fight Mexicans.

That first sight of Sutter in his fancy uniform reminded Jim of the trick pony Eliza insisted on seein' at the St. Louis circus. And didn't she just clap her hands and laugh, and turn to him bright as sunshine, and him laughin' with the pleasure of her.

He thrust the thought away, refused to follow that trail to happier times. What was past was past. He patted his horse's rump and left her to nose a mound of sweet-smelling hay.

In the fort's center was the two-story whitewashed building Sutter used for his office and living quarters. Jim hesitated at the foot of the stairs, waiting while a woman in a faded sunbonnet and dress of patterned blue calico descended with an armful of laundry. He doffed his hat when she glanced at him.

"Why, my sakes!" she exclaimed, stopping on a step above, eyes wide and staring from a tired face. "It's Mr. Savage!"

A sudden shout jolted her from thought. Near the fire, an old man broke from the midst of the dancers, raised his arms high, shouted. *"Hi-ah-hoo! Hi-ah-hoo!"* He looked from side to side, then down. Waited. Then, as if addressing a grave, he told how winter trapped many white people crossing the mountains into the People's land. "Many, many white people coming into the People's country," he repeated. He lowered his arms, looked from one upturned face to another. "These white people caught by early snow, deep snow. Sutter sent Luis and Salvador to rescue the starving snow-stranded people of his white-man tribe." The old man hesitated a moment, looked down again, said softly, "We cry for Luis and Salvador who went to help the starving white people."

She clutched the gift, remembered her disbelief when her father brought the news about Luis and Salvador last winter, how it reminded her of a tale Victoria told about U-wu-lin, the great cannibal giant who roamed the world in the time of the First People. "He collected people to eat," Victoria would say, frightening children, "carrying a hunting sack so large it held an entire village!" Teaching old stories in the old way.

But this was now. And it was true. White people roamed the land. They had killed Luis and Salvador. And eaten them.

"Ma'am?" Did he know this woman, this tired red face beneath a faded blue sunbonnet?

"Jennie Wimmer, Mr. Savage! Me and Peter and our boys was at Fort Laramie when you and your lady come in." She smiled, cocked her head. "Goodness, seems an age ago, don't it? Your missus, she's a purty one. My boys took a shine to her, readin' to 'em like she did."

He stared up at the sunbonneted woman smiling at him, eyes lit with her happy memory, watched her lips moving. "Oh, we sure can use a school teacher here, kids runnin' wild ever'where. I remember her bein' so eager for adventure. Lots of young people like you two headin' for Oregon and California, makin' new starts. How she doin', your missus?"

His expression must have signaled distress like a flapping flag.

"Mr. Savage?" she said, voice apprehensive, smile fading as she hugged the laundry bundle to her bosom. "Oh, dear. She didn't—"

He couldn't look at her, this woman alive and well and clutching laundry, this woman who had made it to California with her husband and children. He stared at the step he stood on. "On the desert—"

"Oh, my, I am so sorry, I am! But the babe—?"

He shook his head, staring at his feet and seeing the sand and the desolation and the burying box he'd cobbled from old wagon boards. Seeing the grave. Seeing Eliza laid in it. Seeing the child wrapped by some woman in the wagon train and placed in its mother's dead arms. And the blowing sand that wouldn't stop, like this Jennie Wimmer, who wouldn't stop.

"Oh, Mr. Savage, I am just so sorry. Right purty your missus was, real nice lady. It's a hardship, your loss. Me and mine, we're sorry for it, truly. I know Mr. Wimmer—"

Jim wanted off the memory, off the scene on the desert, merciless as summer heat, the open grave, the shrouded body, the newborn wrapped in a blanket and laid atop. He wanted off these stairs, away from this woman with her sunbonnet and laundry and sympathy, away from the past.

"Ma'am," he said, not looking at her, covering his face with his hat as he hurried past her up the stairs. He sensed her behind him, watching him go, heard her soft clucking like a hen collecting chicks. Fact was his Eliza weren't strong enough for this country. He needed a woman who wouldn't tear out what was left of his heart. A squaw.

Around the fire, dancers shuffled their sad circle, feather plumes waving, clapper sticks rattling, bone whistles hissing. The widow's dark figure swayed, beseeching Great Spirit. "May his ghost return as Soo-koo-me, great horned owl, in the way of good men!"

When Maximo, the Muqueleme chief, rose to join the dancers, Di-shi wanted to cry out "Ha-ha-ha-yah! Ha-ha-ha-yah!" with the collected voices, but her throat felt thick as wood. More dancers rose with him, relieving those exhausted by circling, shuffling, stamping, weeping into the dark as foot-drummer drummed. Maximo raised his arms, told again the dreaded story she knew too well, how he and his son Raphero had helped Sutter make friends with the Indians. "But Raphero," Maximo shouted, "seeing

Sutter's falseness and bad treatment of our people, attacked the fort to free them. You know what happened! White men killed Raphero! Cut my son's head from his body! Stuck his head on a stick! Put that stick with my son's head up on the wall of his fort! To show what white men may do to the People!" Maximo's great loss. And hers.

"*Ha-ha-ha-yah! Ha-ha-ha-yah!*"

She bent her head, covered her ears, closed her eyes. So many people gone to Great Spirit, murdered by Mexican soldiers, by Sutter, by white people coming into the People's land. Others fallen to illness, weakened by hunger, driven into despair. And Victoria, fading without warning into a final sleep, slipping silently from life into her journey back to Great Spirit. No more to awaken and greet the day, to hear birds sing or wind softly sigh, river laugh. No more to be upon the land, collecting grass seed and digging roots. Leaving *may'tat* abandoned, stories silent, gone. Leaving life. Making a hole in the world.

Finally, at last, shaman and Woochi, the clown, leapt around the fire, dancing the old dance that put the world right again. Then, with the other mourners gathering up their gifts for the spirit world, she rose into the evening's sadness, remembering Victoria telling how the long-robes promised heaven for the good Indians when they died, and a terrible place called hell for bad Indians. "But we talked among ourselves," Victoria had said, "and decided the place called hell was only for white men. Otherwise, the First People would have told of it, and our fathers would have known of it. And so it held no terror for us."

Now, circling the fire, mourners gave the flames the possessions left by the departed — quivers and arrows, stirring sticks, dolls of tule rushes, moccasins, belts of abalone, fish traps, blankets, a baby's cradle. Beautiful perfect baskets went into the flames. Twisted coils of sumac and willow flared briefly, brightly, then diffused softly into smoke, gifts to accompany the dead to the West.

Standing before the fire, she buried her face a last time in the familiar acorn smell of Victoria's skirt, then watched the faded calico burn, weeping anew for the dream voice, her mother's voice, recalling now Victoria's most fearful and dreadful memory, recited only once, never forgotten.

"Maria could not run with you in her arms and an unborn child inside." Victoria's voice, a whisper then, and now. "She handed you to me, crying for me to save you. And we ran, you and I together, into the willows along the valley river. Hid two days before José Jesús found us."

Massacre. Two hundred slaughtered. A Mexican soldier named Amador. Getting even for a stolen horse.

The door stood ajar and Jim didn't knock. After the encounter on the stairs with the laundress, this day weren't better for bein' reminded how little he was enjoyin' it. He thumped into the room without apology, startling Sutter at a table spread with papers and maps. All tarted up in his fancy French uniform, gold braid on his shoulders, brass buttons down his front. In a better mood, Jim thought he might have saluted, had some fun. Not today. Opposite, perched on a stool, a long-faced man with sand-colored hair covering head and chin. Sittin' stiff in a boiled white shirt, like he was waitin' to have his picture took.

Sutter rose, the beginning of a smile forming beneath a draping mustache. The round little man puffed himself up, beaming now like he'd been awarded a medal for lookin' so fine. "Mr. Savage!" he exclaimed and thrust out his hand.

Jim ignored it.

Sutter, pocketing his hand like a kerchief, turned to his seated guest. "Mr. Savage is the man we want!" He withdrew his hand from his pocket and slapped the table, scattering maps and papers. "And here he is!"

Jim looked from Sutter to the seated man. "Ain't roundin' up no Indians." Looked back at Sutter coming from behind the table. "Ain't watchin' 'em do your wheat neither. No taste for it."

Sutter stopped, blinked, clasped his hands behind him, rocked back on his heels. He inhaled deeply, as if to inflate himself to a stature greater than he possessed. "No, no, no, Mr. Savage," he said, Swiss accent thick. "You are explorer, yes?! I need explorer! We get up expedition to hills, yes! Look for good place to make sawmill!"

From obligation, and no wish to re-encounter Mrs. Wimmer's sympathy, Jim heard out Sutter's plan. The man wanted to build a flour mill for his wheat. And to build the flour mill he needed lumber. And to properly site a lumber mill he needed someone to explore up the American River, find a good place for cutting and rafting timber down to the flour mill site.

Sutter had vision; Jim would give him that. But the idea of rafting timber down a wild, twisting river like the American was nigh on to unbalanced. He shook his head in disbelief while Sutter all but danced in his keenness for the project.

"Yes, yes! I make partner to my wheelwright here. He will build my sawmill," Sutter said, waving an enthusiastic hand at his guest. "Forgive I not introduce proper." He puffed himself up, nodded to one, then the other, grinning. "Mr. Savage, Mr. Marshall."

Outside the dance house mourners quietly disappeared into the dark. She stood alone, watched smoke drift among pines and cedars silhouetted against a night sky sprinkled with stars. And heard again, as clearly as she heard a hooting owl, her mother's voice calling from the dream-place.

And silently wept for the message: Beware, strangers are coming. And they will kill you.

1848

'some kind of mettle was found in the tail race that looks like goald'
—Diary, Henry Bigler
January 24, 1848

The first party of Mormons, employed by me left for washing and digging Gold and very soon all followed, and left me only the sick and the lame behind. And at this time I could say that every body left me from the Clerk to the Cook.

—Diary, Johann Augustus Sutter
March 7, 1848

"What a frolic!" Jim said, forking a second serving of pancakes and beefsteak from the platter Mrs. Kittleman held out. He smiled up at her, and then at John Henry Brown, proprietor of San Francisco's City Hotel, sitting next to him at the round table. "Never imagined stayin' in a hotel, sleepin' on a feather bed!"

Brown glanced around the table at his other guests, just finishing breakfast. Sam Brannan and Charley Ross laughed at Jim Savage's high spirits. Leavenworth scowled, no surprise there. And Cump Sherman just looked mystified by the blond-haired Jim Savage wearing buckskins and eating like he'd never seen food before.

"Got four feather beds," said Brown. "Bought 'em from the Mormons." He nodded at Brannan who had sold them to him. He turned to Jim. "And how'd you sleep?"

She rose drowsily from the warmth of her braided rabbit-fur blanket and inhaled her shelter's sweet cedar fragrance. She still half expected to see Victoria sleeping nearby. In the first confused moments of waking, she often imagined she heard the old woman's gentle snoring.

But something had caught her ear. A distinct thump, thump, thump. Not woodpecker drilling an acorn hiding hole. Something else. She closed her eyes, listened. Horses' hooves? Was it horses? Was her father returning?

She slipped into her skirt of dressed deerskin, then out through her shelter's narrow entrance and into the meadow's familiar morning sounds. Leaves skittering, birds chirping, the village nearly deserted now except for those too old to travel. She ducked back inside, found the soap-root brush Victoria had made for her, and headed toward the river.

"Like a king," Jim replied, slicing a chunk of beefsteak and spearing it with his fork. "Twenty dollars to sleep on feathers not unreasonable." Not at all, he thought, given the competition for a decent bed, the city overrun by miners with gold to spend on a spree. What a frolic! Everyone winning the lottery. Even Cump Sherman, sitting opposite, admitting he'd collected a fair share of dust and nuggets storekeeping at Sutter's fort.

"'Course, I am a king," Jim added, chewing enthusiastically. "To the Chauchilas, Potoyensees, all them Yokuts tules Indians." Weren't one to brag, but everyone else raisin' theirselves up. Just natural for a man astonished by good luck to parade it some, let folks admire it.

He chewed, swallowed, grinned. "Called me El Rey Guero at the first," he said, lifting his coffee cup in salute to his royal self, "but I improved the title. Bein' the Blond King didn't fit, I told 'em, there bein' no other blond people to king over. So, I told José Juarez—he's the Chauchilas' chief—I reckoned El Rey Tularenos fit better. King o' the Tulares, that's me. Ask my wives! Eekeno, she's a Nukchu. Or Homut. She's a Chauchila. El Rey Tularenos, that's me."

He laughed, amused by Leavenworth's obvious disapproval and a general expression of surprise on the others' faces. He briefly considered upping the ante by adding he might have a dozen wives, maybe more, wasn't sure, thanks to José Jesús for all the pipe smokin' and promisin'. Then, again, why dilute his rooster strut by admittin' his marital arrangements were mainly treaty agreements, political alliances, mutual insurance. Sort of, 'now that I married your daughter and we're kin, you and me, Mr. Chauchila Chief, and Mr. Potoyensee Chief, wouldn't be right to be raidin' my store or stealin' my stock.'

He speared another chunk of beefsteak, admired it, introduced it to his teeth. Chewed, swallowed, grinned. Billiard balls in the saloon clacked a loud staccato. Someone havin' a frolic.

A pale sunlight sifted through Yuloni's cedars and pines edging the river dancing in its tumble over granite boulders. Laying aside her skirt and moccasins, she waded into a shallow pool, the numbing cold briefly taking her breath. Kneeling, she washed her hair with the soap-root brush, listening to the river's song. Sadly, her father intended still to take her away. Not for fear of labor hunters now, but gold hunters. The old people chose to stay, accepting whatever came. Where her father intended to take her, he hadn't said. But soon he would return and they would go.

On a sun-warmed boulde she sat and tousled dampness from her hair. Then suddenly, again: thump, thump, thump.

She turned in its direction.

Cump Sherman, after a moment, laughed. "One wife is plenty for me. And if the Shawnees want to make me their chief, or king, or whatever, just because my father named me for Tecumseh, here's my answer: If nominated, I will not run; if elected, I will not serve."

He saluted the table with a raised glass of *aguardiente*. "Never too early for the house brandy." He turned to Jim. "Fremont's in need of a post, though, after getting court-martialed out of his military governorship here. Shouldn't he rightly be the Tulares king? You've set up on his land, haven't you?"

Jim shrugged. "Las Mariposas? No particular boundaries there except rivers—the San Joaquin, the Merced—and the mountains. Fremont plenty hot about Larkin's mess up, complained he'd got nothin' but ten square leagues of unfriendly Indians for the three thousand dollars he give Larkin. Wanted a ranch near San Jose. Got Las Mariposas by mistake."

Sherman emptied his glass and slammed it down on the table. "Damned lucky mistake for Fremont, the son of a bitch!"

Jim noticed Leavenworth's frown, man probably disapproved drink and cursing both. Maybe luck, too. Likely against frolic of all persuasions, come to that. On joining the table, Leavenworth had stiffly introduced himself as a druggist, physician, minister, former member of Stevenson's Regiment, and the town's new alcalde. Amused by the man's obvious self-regard, Jim had stood, bowed, then slapped Leavenworth's shoulder. "Howdy do. Jim Savage here. Former trapper turned trader." Laughed at his own joke, didn't figure anyone got it anyway.

"The Good Lord moves in mysterious ways," Leavenworth said now.

Jim laughed. "Larkin, too, I'd say. Fremont plenty steamed at first. Said if I wanted to live with Indians to help myself."

Leavenworth raised an eyebrow. "To the minerals as well?"

Could someone be pounding atop the grinding rock? The few old women remaining in Yuloni usually went out in the morning to dig lily bulbs and collect berries.

Thump, thump, thump. She was certain now. Someone was pounding atop the grinding rock. Making acorn.

Jim, annoyed, shot back. "Two years ago, sir, no one knew what everyone knows now. Except the Indians, who figured it for dirt of another color, and equally useless."

"Now, speaking of land—" said Brown, the hotel proprietor reining in the conversation.

Brown climbin' aboard his hobby horse again, Jim thought, and why not? Makin' a pile in San Francisco real estate, hotel, saloon, gamblin' tables. Miners comin' in from the diggins, after livin' in tents and eatin' flapjacks, well, bees to honey. Buzzin' around the city now with gold in their pokes, drinkin' fine wine, playin' billiards, bettin' on monte, faro, roulette. Gambling tables leased for two hundred dollars a day at his hotel, Brown bragged, and "Everyone makes money."

Or loses it, Jim knew, seeing a young miner surrender his pile to a losing hand. But, no matter, the fellow would head back to the diggins for more withdrawals from nature's great bank. Plenty for everyone. Yes, indeedy. Plenty for Jim Savage and his Indians, too. What a frolic!

"A vacant lot at Montgomery and Washington found no buyers last month for five thousand dollars and sold this month for ten!" Brown said now. "Real estate! Can't lose with all the business coming this way when the news gets delivered. The Kanakas will come when they see the two pounds of the metal I sent to the Sandwich Islands aboard the schooner *Louise*. The store-ship *Matilda* is calling at Valparaiso. More Chileans will come," he said, nodding toward the hotel's front where several of that country's nationals in their native costumes idled on benches, rolling cigarettes and philosophizing. "Oregon is bound to empty into this country. When the courier that left here a month ago, by way of the Isthmus, reaches New Orleans, likely everyone there will be packing up for a trip to California. After President Polk sees that tea caddy full of gold for evidence, well, Katy bar the door. You can bet before long the States will wonder that anyone stays home."

Brannan, next to Brown, slapped the hotelkeeper's back. "Trade's the thing, my friend, trade!"

He turned to Jim. "Bought up all the pans in San Francisco for twenty cents apiece, stocked my store at Sutter's fort. Picks, shovels, bottles, vials, snuff-boxes, anything to hold gold. Moved my merchandise, then moved the populace upriver to buy it."

Jim decided Brannan was somethin' puffed up over his contribution to the gold excitement, repeatin' again his brag on how he rode through San Francisco's streets holding aloft a vial of glitter, hollering, 'Gold! Gold! Gold on the American River!' And how, when the fevered crowd got there, he sold them everything they failed to bring with them.

"Twenty-cent pans went for fifteen dollars apiece," he boasted now. "Made thirty-six thousand dollars in three months."

"San Francisco looked like an epidemic struck the place," Brown said. "Three-fourths of the population took off upriver in any old boat, sloop, lighter, or launch. Others by horse, some on foot. By the end of June wasn't no one left here to get excited."

On the grinding rock a woman pounded acorn, face obscured by the broad brim of a white man's hat. Beside her on the rock pocked with grinding holes a tiny child sat silently watching.

"Anna!?"

From beneath the hat, Anna looked up and laughed. "Isabel! You are still here!" she said, dropping her *may'tat*. She scrambled to her feet and scooped up the child. "See my Little Turtle, how big she is!"

And then they were sitting at the base of the rock chattering like birds, talking on top of each other, eager to hear whatever the other knew of all the excitement. So much had happened since last they'd seen each other. How, when, where, so many questions. Isabel laughed at the tiny girl in Anna's lap, black eyes looking from face to face and back again, tracking the lively conversation.

Isabel asked about Anna's husband, remembering the couple packing baskets and blankets, quiver, digging sticks, arrows, slipping into the forest, watchful as owls, to hide from Sutter's labor hunters.

"Francisco is mining! Traded yellow dirt for this!" she said, taking off the hat, brushing its floppy brim, admiring it.

"Where—" Isabel began but before she could finish the question, Anna, chirpy as a squirrel, said, "Trading post," as she put the hat on. "Traded yellow dirt at trading post." She cocked her head like a strutting quail parading its perky plume. "Many, many things to trade at trading post."

Isabel laughed. "Not the hat. I wondered where Francisco is, wondered how far you traveled."

"A morning walk! Sutter's creek, by Pola-su village!"

"Sutter's creek?"

"Where Sutter's Indian workers dig now. First, though, Francisco and I mined for your father's friend Captain Weber. Did he tell you he saw us?"

Isabel couldn't recall. Her father seemed to arrive and leave like the sun, and nearly as often, checking on her, bringing meat for the old people still in the village, then gone again.

"Valley hot!" Anna continued. "I wanted to come home. Make acorn." She jumped up. "I can show you!"

"How to make acorn?"

"No, not acorn!" Anna said, laughing, then darting away.

Leavenworth nodded. "Our jail-keeper had ten Indian prisoners, two of them murderers. At least he didn't turn them loose to loot the town, but took them with him."

"This city's future is trade, my friends," Brannan repeated. "I predict the building of faster ships. It's all go-ahead, get-ahead. Brown's likely right about the water-lots along Montgomery. Any real estate. I bought a lot up the hill a month ago for ten thousand I could have had a year ago for eight hundred."

Sherman shook his head. "Captain Folsom advised me to buy some lots, but I felt insulted that he should think me such a fool as to pay money for property in such a horrid place as Yerba Buena, as we called this city then. That was 'forty-six, of course, when water-lots on Montgomery sold at auction for twenty-eight dollars." He sighed as he stood to take his leave. "Good day to you, gentlemen. I suspect my future remains with the military. Meanwhile, I have a launch taking me upriver today. Sutter signed over all his holdings to his son to avoid confiscation by his debtors, and the young man engaged me to survey the property for his Sacramento City, as he's calling it."

Jim, watching Sherman depart, said, "I suspect, back in 'forty-six, the Almighty was just settin' up his jokes."

Leavenworth glared at him. "The Good Lord does not make jokes!"

"No offense intended," Jim said, and grinned, pleased at ruffling the feathers of the self-important man who had so solemnly listed his civic contributions to church and school like he'd invented good works. "But I figure God Almighty, or whoever's up there, is havin' himself a mighty fine frolic."

No one spoke for a moment, watching Sarah Kittleman circling the table with her blue-enameled coffee pot, pouring fresh coffee.

"Splendid example right there," Jim said, inhaling the rich roasted aroma and nodding in her direction as she left. "Mormons. All that persecutin' in the States, Smith murdered, Brigham takin' over with a plan to go west into the wilderness. Am I right, Mr. Brannan?" Jim winked at the man. "Musta been a hearty disappointment to leave the States, spend six months cramped up in a cargo ship, and arrive here to find the stars and stripes flappin' in the breeze, eh?"

Jim had Brannan's story from Henry Bigler, one of the Mormon Battalion boys building Sutter's mill. Bigler had been among the Saints heading west out of Missouri who'd got recruited into the U.S. army for the war with Mexico and mustered out in gold-rich California. And now they was supposed to leave glitter behind and join Brother Brigham, waiting in the desert, Bigler had said. Brannan, along with the more than two hundred Saints he'd brought from the East, coming the long way 'round via Cape Horn from New Jersey aboard the ship *Brooklyn,* was expected to go, too. He clearly preferred California's gold over Brother Brigham's sand.

"Something of a surprise," Brannan said, scowling. "But we're making the best of it."

And then some, Jim thought. "See what I mean, Leavenworth," he said, turning to the alcalde. "That's the Good Lord's joke, ain't it? Sail away from the American flag and find it waitin' for you?" He laughed. "Then there's the best knee-slapper of all. As Mr. Brannan here so cheerfully advertised: gold, gold, gold on the American River. How'd the Mexicans miss out on hollerin' *oro, oro, oro?* Ink's hardly dry on that Cahuenga treaty, and my friend Marshall's trippin' over the stuff." He laughed again. "I'm thinkin' the Almighty's got a tricky sense of humor."

A sudden screech turned attention toward the hotel's verandah.

Anna handed Isabel the wide metal dish shaped like a shallow winnowing basket. "Heavy. Not hard to learn," she said over her shoulder, chasing her infant toddling toward a bright-eyed lizard pumping its little gray body up and down on a boulder. Collecting the child into her arms, Anna laughed. "Remember how she crept so slow and quiet with her cradle on her back?"

Isabel nodded. "I do," she said, turning the metal dish one way and then another, remembering Anna bringing her baby in its cradle onto the grinding rock. Hungry times, those days, Anna's glittering eyes, their stomachs crying, Victoria counting milkweed knots. And she remembered a village woman pounding acorn that day saying Isabel was next. "Time for Isabel to make acorn *and* babies." The women laughed, teasing Isabel about having two hungers. She smiled now at her embarrassment. How happy she had been with those women, each at her *ho'ya,* each with her *may'tat,* making acorn together like the First People. The village women were right. She had hungered for a husband, longed to make acorn in the right way with her own daughters and one day the wives of her sons and then their daughters, too.

Nothing had changed. Everything had changed.

"Violin," said Brown. "Or cello. Hard to tell. Dancing Billy hires anyone with an instrument. Doesn't have to be good with it. Billy pays fifty dollars an hour, regardless. Made his pile in dry diggins. Dug out twelve thousand dollars with a butcher knife in six days. Doesn't gamble it, just wants to dance. *Loco*."

Leavenworth shook his head. "More crazies all the time. We've got one in the calaboose now. Cut the tails off five horses and shaved the stumps. When asked what he did it for he said he wanted to send them to England to be made into a brush, to brush the flies off the Queen's dinner table."

"So you know Marshall?" Charley Ross asked Jim.

"Yep, and right there's what I mean about the Almighty havin' a frolic," Jim replied. "A fine carpenter, just wanted to build Sutter a mill. Picked up that shiny bit, showed it around, and, well, once the word got out—" He shrugged, looked at Brannan, who doffed his hat, a performer taking a bow. "But," Jim continued, "weren't no profit in it for Marshall. Sutter neither. Gold hunters run right over the place, ruined Sutter's operations and hounded Marshall to show 'em how to find gold. Got unfriendly somewhat when he wouldn't or couldn't." Jim shook his head. "Like ticks on a dog, just kept at him. Might be he's headed back to Oregon."

"And you, Mr. Savage?" Leavenworth inquired. "What's your story?"

In the creek near the grinding rock, Anna splashed into the water while Isabel sat cross-legged in the grass nearby with Anna's daughter in her lap, the little girl looking up with large dark eyes, reaching a pudgy baby hand to Isabel's face, exploring.

Anna looked back at Isabel. "Watch how I do this," she said. Holding the metal dish with both hands, she dipped it into the creek's bottom, lifted it, and swirled the pan in a circular motion, emptying water over its lip until only sand remained. Squatting, she balanced the dish on her knees with one hand and with the other pushed little stones and pebbles from its edge. "Yellow dirt sinks to the bottom," she said after a while, "but I don't see any."

Isabel hadn't watched. Her eyes were on the little child in her lap, baby hands clutching Isabel's fingers, tiny face with big eyes peering up from beneath a black cap of baby hair. The child smelled like sunshine. Isabel felt a

44

sudden sadness and longing engulf her, imagining that once, in a time before memory, her own mother, Maria, surely held her in this way when she was a baby, a baby she called Di-shi, Little Blue Jay. Had her own tiny hands explored Maria's face, eyes wide? And before that time, Maria had been a baby in her mother's lap, and that woman before her, too, back and back. Mothers and daughters, back and back and back to the First People.

Isabel stroked the cap of black hair, lost in the thought of time's beginning, girls finding husbands, making babies, becoming mothers, having daughters, and daughters becoming mothers. That long, long line from First People to now, to her, to her waiting arms.

Waiting. Nothing had changed. Except everything.

Anna waded from the creek and held out the metal dish. "Do you want to try?"

Jim hesitated, briefly considered how much to brag on, decided to favor fun. Maybe he'd demonstrate. Amuse these folks. "Well," he said, tipping his chair back, hands clasped behind his head, commencing his tale, "soon after the excitement got goin' pretty good on the American, Captain Weber showed up, figured he might find some of the metal on his river." He glanced around, confirmed everyone knew the German who'd settled on the San Joaquin. "Came lookin' for instruction like everyone else. 'Cept he weren't looking for Marshall. He was looking for José Jesús. Heard Sutter'd hired him to keep Indians from stealin' his horses."

Brannan sat forward, slapped his hands flat to the table like he was holding it down. "José Jesús?! I think I met him at Sutter's," he said. "Big for an Indian. About six feet, straight as an arrow. High forehead, penetrating look. Dressed like a Californio. Educated, too. Knew how to read."

"That's him," Jim said. "Considerable influence with his people, all over that area."

Brannan snorted. "Well, didn't Sutter just put the fox in the hen house! Hired a famous horse thief to keep Indians from stealing his horses! That's a good one! And Weber wanted *instruction* from that Indian? For what, how to steal?" He laughed. "Leader of the forty thieves, that Indian!"

Jim was half out of his chair when its front legs thumped the plank flooring. "Captain Weber's friend, *and mine!* As trustworthy a man as I ever met on God's green earth. That Indian says it, he does it." He glared at Brannan. "Unlike some men." He despised sharpers, pegged Brannan for one before he'd met him. Remembered last year, working with the Mormon boys building Sutter's mill, how they'd illuminated him as to the particulars of their strange religion. Weren't clear whether Brother Brannan was collecting but not delivering a portion of their wages to Brother Brigham for what they called tithing. Nor other suspicions the boys had regarding their church's self-appointed representative in California. Didn't matter to Jim. Doubt put paid to the bill. "Any man insults my friends insults me." Jim glared at Brannan, feelin' ready for whatever came next. Enjoyed a tussle now and again, anyone cared to ask.

Brannan, taken aback, looked at Brown, who raised his hands like a preacher silencing a congregation. "Gentlemen."

"Certainly," Brannan said, relaxing, amused now. "I consider myself a gentleman of the first water."

Jim bristled. "You sayin' I ain't?" He was out of the chair, leaning on the table, ready.

Ross placed an arresting hand on Jim's arm. "You were saying about Captain Weber? We here all witnessed his success, you know."

"That nugget weighed eighty ounces!" Brown added brightly, eager to defuse trouble. "Cross and Hobson took it. Paid three thousand dollars for it, three times its value, for being so beautiful. Kind of a kidney shape to it. Sent it to the Bank of England as a specimen for admiration."

Jim, still eyeing Brannan, sat. "Captain Weber, on the advice of his *friend*, José Jesús, put tamed Indians to minin' for him." He looked at Ross, mollified for the moment. "Gold don't mean nothin' much to Indians. Don't use it, don't desire it. Glad to trade it, generously, for food, finery, beads, calico, whatever takes their fancy." He grinned, cheerful again. "In fact, and here I credit John Murphy, my old rival in the tradin' business—" He turned to Brown. "Heard Murphy stayed here recently."

Brown laughed. "He did indeed. I believe I had this story from him."

Jim grinned. "You want to tell it?"

Anna took Turtle and put her down to crawl. She looked at Isabel. "I'm happy to see you."

Isabel watched the tiny girl creeping into high grass, learning the earth. "I'm leaving soon."

Anna retrieved her daughter, sat her in her lap, gave her acorn caps to play with. "Where are you going?"

Isabel shrugged. "I don't know. My father is taking me from here."

"Why?"

"I don't know."

"When?"

"Soon."

For a time, they said nothing, watching Turtle examine acorn caps. Then Anna laughed. Clapping her hands, she said, "Your father chose a husband for you!"

"No, no," said Brown. "Best have it from the horse's mouth—" He looked at Jim. "No offense intended."

Jim nodded. "None taken." He tipped his chair back again, cleared his throat, advanced on his story. "Seein' as the American River got all the gold-hungry diggers necessary to the purpose, and it bein' clear that the metal, had anyone looked, existed just about everywhere—even that pencil pusher Bidwell scurried up to his land-grant rancho and set a passel of Indians to minin' the Feather River. Whole countryside's infected with the fever. Everybody flappin' around like crows, cawin' rumors of more, better, richer, and off they'd fly to some new gulch, stream, or ravine. Well, I'd had about as much company as a man can tolerate. So, there's José Jesús, my old friend—" Jim leveled a dismissive glance at Brannan, who looked to be returning the favor. A sharper, Jim thought again, not worth troubling over. "So, my Indian friend tells me there's a good river to the south, the Merced, river of mercy, no white people and lots of Indians."

Brown laughed. "And butterflies. Las Mariposas. And not so isolated. Murphy was there."

"That's a fact," Jim said. "Came out in 'forty-four, Murphy did, partnered up with Captain Weber for a time. Then, after the flap with the Mexicans, drifted south and set up as a trader with the Indians friendly to Weber because of José Jesús." He looked at Brannan again. "Indians respect agreements."

Brown urged the story. "So, he had a tin cup—"

Jim laughed. "He did. Persuaded the Chauchilas he was a human scale. Blanket held low in one hand, tin cup high in the other. Indians puttin' gold in the cup, Murphy gradually lowerin' it. When the cup's full, there he is, arms evened up. Human scale. And then he'd trade the blanket."

Ross sputtered, "A cup of gold for a blanket?!"

Isabel stared at Anna threading acorn caps onto a milkweed string. What would Victoria think seeing Anna in a white-man's hat? She imagined the old woman's toothless smile, almost heard her saying, "New ways, Isabel, new ways."

A husband? Was it possible? A red-tail hawk circled above Yuloni's old dance house, abandoned now.

Anna dangled the string of acorn caps above her daughter, teasing. "José Jesús *toko hayapo,* chief among chiefs, Isabel. Your father flies far, like eagle, to many villages. In his travels he found a husband for you."

Isabel looked at her, and then away, wondering, remembering. Perhaps there was someone as brave, as noble as the warrior long ago chosen for her, the warrior whose name José Jesús never spoke. A long shadow. Like all the people massacred whose names remained swallowed. Like Maria.

Like Maria. Did her father see Maria's face, the woman he couldn't save, when he looked so protectively at her, Maria's daughter? He was never still, rode like a howling wind chased him. He was everywhere, counseling, protecting, advising. As if a storm was coming. "Hear me, Isabel, and live long. New ways."

She didn't want new ways. She wanted a husband.

"Indians figured themselves winners," Jim said. "Yellow dirt everywhere. Can't eat it or wear it, what's it good for? *Loco gringo* wants to trade a blanket for it, well—" He shrugged. "So, there I am ready to get into the tradin' business and all the custom's goin' to Murphy, the human balance scale."

Brown laughed. "Are you intending to demonstrate?"

Jim looked at the floor, not yet scrubbed from customers' spills and spit, and shook his head. "Naw, I'll just tell it." He turned to Ross, the storekeeper. "Every man understands a bargain, right? So, I figure to undersell Murphy, show the Chauchilas my scale operates lighter. Like I said, Murphy uses hands and arms like a balance, blanket in one hand, tin cup in the other. Indian fills the cup till the blanket comes up even and the trade's made. I show 'em my scale, a better scale. I strap a tin cup to my left ankle, lie down on my back, kick my legs in the air a few times, demonstratin'. I put a blanket on my right foot, and up goes my left foot, tin cup strapped to it. Chauchilas start puttin' gold in the cup, and what do you know, half a cupful and it's even up with that blanket! And I'm in business!"

Brannan scoffed. "The business of cheating Indians."

Jim laughed. Brannan was a sharper, no gentleman, not worth gettin' riled over. A brag, liked talkin' how he was big. "Want to tell us again about those twenty-cent pans you sold for fifteen dollars, *Brother* Brannan?"

Brannan reddened. Ross, shopkeeper and peacekeeper, grabbed Jim's hand, pumped it like they had a deal. "Come down to my place. I can outfit your trading post. Got supplies good as most merchants. Montgomery street at Washington. Northwest corner."

Leavenworth stood. "I chaired a public meeting where we unanimously fixed the price of gold at sixteen dollars an ounce for all business transactions. I'm confident Mr. Ross uses a *standard* scale."

Jim nodded, amused again by the alcalde's starch, guessed he might be off to church.

Brown, standing now as well, said, "I'm heading up to Kittleman's distillery. Join me, Mr. Savage, see our fair city."

Jim looked up at the proprietor, intrigued. "A distillery you say? Kittleman? Would that be your cook's husband? Your *Mormon* cook?"

Brown nodded, Jim laughed, then grinned at Leavenworth. "The Almighty is havin' a fine frolic here."

Outside, Brown announced, "This street's Kearny." He paused to let a mule cart slowly pass with a load of bricks. "From Mission Dolores," Brown explained. Then, ducking his head against a rising wind he led Jim across the dirt road to the plaza on the other side, still talking. "When you came up from the harbor last evening you saw our first brick building," he said. "Mellus and Howard, merchants here for years. Brannan went partners with them at Sutter's place, but Brannan's got no interest in the San Francisco end now that he's resurrected his newspaper. So, besides Ross, a good man, and honest, but short on merchandise compared to Mellus and Howard, you might want to take a look at what they've got. Substantial operation, bought the block bounded by Clay, Sacramento, Sansome and Battery streets last year, used a slip of land about thirty-five feet wide for the building of a wharf. Big shipment of goods just in on the brig *Belfast* out of New York, discharged directly onto the new wharf. Its inauguration. No need for a lighter, straight into the warehouse. It's all go-ahead, get-ahead, for certain. That arrival lowered the price of goods here considerably, Mr. Savage. Probably twenty-five percent. That'll be in your favor."

He slapped Jim on the back. The wind was howling now and sand rising. "And that's why the water-lots doubled in price!" Brown continued, yelling against the wind. "More ships, more wharves. Real estate! Can't lose!"

He took Jim's arm, pulled him from the road as a Mexican *vaquero* galloped past, the horse glittery with silver trappings. "You should have been here for the grand illumination celebrating peace with Mexico, Mr. Savage. A regular whoop-de-do! Cavalcade of citizens on this street! Every ship in the harbor fired its guns, and everyone on shore with a pistol likewise. And that night, every window of any house still occupied lit up with lanterns and candles!" Brown pointed up the rise, left of the adobe customhouse. He raised his voice to new heights, shouting over the wind: "That's Clay street! O'Farrell surveyed the whole town, lots numbered, streets named! That's the new schoolhouse! Doubles as a church for now! Citizens hired a preacher for twenty-five hundred dollars to come over from the Sandwich Islands to help us praise God!"

Jim thought he'd praise God if the Almighty could turn off the tap that was John Henry Brown, shouting something now about the Hudson Bay Company's misfortunes and Russians fur-trading up the coast. Not waiting for the Good Lord to act, he grabbed Brown's hand, pumped it, and hollered into the wind, "Mr. Brown, much obliged, but on a good day I ain't keen on cities, even those with some claim to the verdict!" With that, he abandoned his host, dodged mules, carts, and horses on Kearny, collected his gold from the hotel bartender's safe, confirmed that Washington street was to the right, and headed for it.

Washington street was as unplanked, ungraded, and unformed as Kearny street. Jim hurried downhill against the wind raising whitecaps on the bay where abandoned brigs and schooners swung at anchor, their crews deserted to the mines. He thought the tidal mudflats of Yerba Buena cove looked more swamp of despair than picture of progress. If these so-called water-lots were gaining ground —good one! water-lots gaining ground! — it wasn't apparent to him. Refuse of every description lay half submerged in the mud—bottles and cans in uncountable numbers, garbage, dead animals, discarded clothing, abandoned merchandise, a wreckage of debris no longer identifiable among substances that didn't invite investigation. He suspected only the squawking gulls found the smell attractive.

Montgomery street was nearly as impassable a thoroughfare as its shore-line. A confusion of boxes, barrels, and bales fronted the sheds and shanties of the city's shipping firms and commission merchants, a chaos of off-loaded merchandise looking no more likely to depart than the ships that had delivered it. He maneuvered through the maze to the northwest corner, passed two sick-looking men clumsily loading a dray, found Ross's store, ducked through the entrance, and shouldered the door shut behind him.

"Brown show you the city?" Ross asked, looking up from his plank counter as Jim removed his hat and dispensed sand from its brim.

"You got some weather out there rearrangin' it," Jim said, brushing sand from his shoulders.

"A regular norther," Ross said. "Not unusual. Destroyed a nice little steamboat on the bay last February, the *Sitka*. Owned previously by the Russians. Provided regular service up the Sacramento. All of us sorry to see her lost." He leaned an elbow on his counter. "Summer's a better season. Fog, though."

"Your town's got a short list of advantages."

"But a progressive appearance and a flattering future."

Jim surveyed the merchant's half-empty shelves. "Any of that collection yours out there, those boxes and bales blockin' Montgomery street?"

"Most of it Ward and Smith's, or Mellus and Howard's. Can't find anyone to move it. Before the discovery, you could hire a man for a dollar a day. Prices for everything now constantly on the rise. Higher by tenfold over those ruling in the spring. And that's for commodities. Labor's worse. Anyone successful in the mines won't work, and the rest want twelve or fifteen dollars a day." He shook his head. "Usually too emaciated and weakened by failure to earn it." He brightened. "Did you get up to George Kittleman's tavern, the Rising Sun? Corner of Jackson at Stockton? We've got a bowling alley over on Pacific."

"Guess nothin' necessary's been overlooked then," Jim said. He gestured in the direction of the street. "That's a passel of goods stockpiled out there."

"Shipping's on the increase, that's certain. Customhouse duties generally respectable the second quarter, nearly nine thousand dollars, but this last quarter, well—" Ross threw his hands up like someone had a gun on him. "Swear to God! Seventy-five thousand!"

Jim had heard some whoppers in his time, told more than a few himself. He laughed.

"True as I'm standing here," Ross declared. "You saw the evidence clogging the road. Unfortunately, most of it will likely end up as street paving."

"Well, that'd be a double improvement then." Jim reached inside his coat, withdrew a buckskin bag, plopped it on Ross's counter. "Want to weigh this up, see what business we can do?"

Ross put Jim's poke on his beam scale, added lead weights until it balanced. With a stub pencil he calculated the result on a scrap of paper. "At sixteen dollars the ounce, this is about nine hundred dollars."

"What will you give me for it?"

"Everything in the store."

Jim scratched his head, suspected hotel fleas, considered the offer. Whatever found its way to the wilderness, there'd be some settler, miner, or Indian likely to want it. "No mind to be particular," he said. "Let's see what you got." Early done with this city business suited him. Not inclined to dawdle or chin with storekeeps. Or let the wind skin him alive.

Ross hauled everything off his shelves for Jim's inspection—boxes of bagged coffee and raisins, bottled lemon syrup, molasses, scotch ale, beaver hats, cutlery, bolts of canvas and calico, a collection of boots, shoes, and military uniforms. "I've got a case of hardware here," he said, dragging a box from a corner. "Mainly hinges, doorknobs, keys. Don't suppose you want this stuff?"

Jim glanced at it. "Indians'll make ornaments of most anything," he said, ready to be done. "I'll take it."

"Well, Mr. Savage, it's a pleasure doing business with you," Ross said. "Give me a minute to write up your invoice."

"Only read numbers," Jim said. "You just mark every box and bag with what I paid for it. My guide for pricin'. I'll advance that number tenfold."

Ross considered. "Sure. Anything else? Clothing maybe? I've got a few things in back. Some stuff I agreed to take from a Mexican couple returning to Sonora. Not much."

"Let's see it."

Ross brought out what he had, including a wool serape, striped yellow and orange.

Jim fingered its fringe. "I'll take this for my friend José Jesús. Indian chief. Admirable man. Never met a better."

Ross flipped through the remaining garments. "So you said." He held up a woman's white muslin blouse and a blue-figured calico skirt. "Any use for these?"

"I'll take 'em. Chief 's got a daughter."

Ross laughed. "You marrying her?"

They left after the first rain of the season, on a gray morning unfolding into blue. A packhorse, black and sleek, followed as they walked a trail Isabel supposed deer first made when Coyote first made deer, carpeted now with fallen leaves in burnished colors dulled and dampened by rain from seasons come and gone in their usual order. Leaves greened and grew, faded and fell. The forest dripped, rain-fresh and pungent. Pines, oak, madrone, manzanita, all earthy fragrant with wet. Nothing had changed. Everything had changed.

Isabel wore her rabbit-strip blanket across her shoulders, its fur scented with cedar from all the mornings she'd awakened in her beloved Yuloni. She hadn't looked back. Memory held the village of cedar shelters, the grassy clearing surrounded by towering pines. As she walked, she pictured her favorite oak where she had collected acorns, and the damp place near the river where she had dug lily bulbs, the grinding rock where she had made acorn with Victoria. A memory treasure to visit whenever she wished, wherever her father was taking her.

"South," he said, when she asked.

South. Not north to Hachanah or Omo or Cosumnes, villages whose people she knew. With thoughts as meandering as the damp and leafy trail to the nearest village south, she recalled the morning after last year's Big Cry at the Hachanah *hang-i*. At dawn the low-domed cedar-slab dance house had loomed dark against a pale sky while village women heated stones over a blazing fire, removing them with forked sticks to drop hissing into a water basket woven tight as skin. An old woman and an Omo chief performed the ceremony, standing each side of the basket of heated water, washing the faces of mourners waiting to be freed from grieving. The widow whose plaintive wails filled the *hang'i* with her sorrow declined, protesting. Next year's Big Cry, perhaps, not now, not yet, she had said. And then Isabel's own hesitation, watching while others freed themselves from mourning, wondering what Victoria would advise, what Victoria would want her to do. Deciding at last, wishing she had glad bells to ring, she leaned over the basket while the old woman scrubbed her face with hot water and the chief washed her wrists and hands. The Omo chief recognized her, asked if she was the daughter of José Jesús, asked her name. She had hesitated. Di-shi? Isabel? Both Di-shi and Isabel? Was that possible?

She lost the thought as a runner from Tukupu-su, the nearest village south, greeted them. Villages often lay barely shouting distance one from another. The People had inhabited this land from time's beginning, populating the world until village shouldered village, conical cedar shelters clustering along rivers like berries on vines. Katina, Mona-su, Katuka, Nuchu.

Each village feasted them. And after they had sucked the last shreds of meat from bones and licked their fingers, and children slept, and men had taken up their pipes, her father told his stories. Old news to her, and often others, how the Americans had defeated Mexico, but a story to hear and hear again. José Jesús told it well, elaborating and repeating and circling back in the manner of proper storytelling. In village after village listeners sat rapt as José Jesús, *toko hayapo,* told how he and other Indians had joined American soldiers to fight Mexicans. He described abandoned ranchos, cannons hauled through deep mud and heavy rain, the mission of San Miguel fallen into ruin, the mission of San Luis Obispo collapsing.

At the mission of Santa Barbara, he told them, the rains stopped. "This was the first day of the Americans' new year, by their reckoning," he said. "Indians there paraded, a great procession, from the mission into the town, Americans marching with them singing a strange song, 'Yankee Doodle'.

"Now California belongs to the United States," José Jesús continued, explaining ownership. Explaining California. Explaining. Preparing. Advising.

Talking. Telling about a white man with yellow hair and blue eyes who spoke Indian words, a white man to trust.

The days disappeared. In every village south she and José Jesús were greeted, expected, welcomed. Loyowisa, Tipotoya, Wolanga-su, Pota. "José Jesús coming!" Kuluti, Sukinola, Pangasema-nu. Young boys and barking dogs escorting their arrival. Pasi-nu, Hechhechi, Nochu-chi.

Once, early in their journey, walking on a sunny day, clouds drifting, trees whispering their leaves to a breeze, she mentioned Anna, then Anna's hat, and Anna's mining demonstration and, finally, Anna's supposing José Jesús had chosen a husband for her. Her father stopped, looked long at her. "You will choose." And then approaching boys with barking dogs appeared on the trail to the next village and nothing more was said, not then, not later. She would choose. As time passed, the prospect rooted and grew. Some days she tended it like a crawling child learning the earth. Watchful.

She stopped asking where they were going. The answer was always "South."

In each village, the same story, the good part, the bad part. Isabel, not now expecting her father had chosen her a husband, helped the women cook, played with their babies.

The people always asked: "What does this mean 'belonging to the United States'?"

"It is good," José Jesús told them, intent, commanding attention. "New leaders say Indians are citizens. Same as white men. Many chiefs rode with the white man Fremont, a great leader of the white people, and he gave his word that a Great White Father, in a place named Washington, cared for us as his own children, said we are citizens of the United States now, same as white men, same rights, same laws."

Telling the good news first.

Then this: "*Oro*, gold, yellow dirt," José Jesús said, "makes fever in white men. No shaman can cure this sickness, no sucking or dancing or smoke. This sickness has no cure. White men lose their minds searching for gold, digging for it. They will come for gold, dig our land until animals flee, dig our rivers until fish drown."

"We are many," his listeners often said, disbelieving this news had anything to do with them.

"They are more," José Jesús warned. "Many more. More than you can number. And we must learn new ways or—"

"Or what?" they chorused. Suspicious. Confused.

José Jesús, *toko hayapo*, respected chief among chiefs, solemn then. "Like the animals and fish, we will disappear."

Warning, preparing, cautioning, this was her father's message everywhere. A new sickness. Prepare. New ways. Was this why he took her from Yuloni? To protect her from fevered white men, save her from disappearing?

From village to village, crossing rivers, heading south. Isabel didn't want new ways, she wanted old ways. To make acorn the right way. To watch a crawling child learn the earth. She wanted a husband.

On they went, one village after another, her father talking and talking to the people, feasts and dances, questions and stories. The possibility of a village chief putting forward a son, or a brave warrior offering himself occasionally enlivened her interest in the long journey. None did.

And then one morning, her father unexpectedly mounted the horse and pulled her up behind him. They rode all day, leaving the village trail to follow a low, wide river. The sun was sinking into the horizon when they entered a scrubby clearing. "We stay here tonight," he said.

Even in the generous gilding light of late day it looked to her a poor place. A scatter of tule shelters. Yokuts people peering out at their arrival. An abandoned freight wagon. A large, dusty green tent. A brush corral enclosing a few mules and a chestnut horse.

A white man in buckskins emerged from the tent. "Chief!"

And then there he was, barefoot in buckskins, grinning up at them, lifting a dusty hat in greeting. Beneath it, hair pale as winter. And she stared, still horsed, still gripping her father's back, into eyes blue as sky. And he was grinning at her, looking from her to her father, then back, laughing.

Her father silent, watching. She staring, the white man her father had described, a white man with blue eyes. Like the sky. And yellow hair. Like the sun. She couldn't stop staring.

"Wanna touch it?" he asked, laughing, reaching a hand up, helping her down from the horse. "Go on, touch it," he said. Laughing, looking at her with eyes like sky.

She looked up at her father, into his dark watching eyes, saw him nod. Looked back at the laughing white man, and touched his hair, held a golden curl in her hand. Soft as spider silk.

"Name's Jim," he said, his hand on her hand touching his hair. "I'm Jim."

She looked up at her father, then into the white man's blue eyes, the white man called Jim, and said, without thought or hesitation, "Isabel. I am Isabel." Not Di-shi. Isabel.

New ways.

And then Jim was hooking open the canvas flap of the big green tent, letting in the late light, inviting them inside what he called a store, a tossed-up collection of boxes and bags, barrels and blankets. A pretty Indian woman with a tattooed chin rose from sitting cross-legged on a striped blanket and Jim said something to her in her language, not Me'wuk. She kept her eyes on Isabel as she ducked out the tent flap.

"Nukchu wife," Jim said, looking from Isabel to her father. "Name's Eekeno." He turned to Isabel. "Chief's daughter, like you." He smiled. "She's gettin' us somethin' to eat." Then he looked around the tent as if he'd never seen it before. He waved a hand at the tumble of boxes and barrels. "Got presents here somewheres."

Orange and yellow fringed poncho for her father. For her a muslin blouse and calico skirt that reminded her of Victoria. Omen of new ways?

Eekeno returned with a basket of dried grasshoppers, her dark eyes proud as she offered her food gift, drinking Jim when he spoke to her in her language. So many words, so many people seeing the world with different eyes, different words.

Jim showed off his sale goods. Isabel was amazed. So many strange things to see! And taste! Lemon syrup! He poured a few drops into the palm of her hand, laughed when she touched her tongue to it, made a face, and started to spit, then asked to taste it again. So many things to look at. Did white people need so many things? She lifted a small and oddly heavy metal object from a box and turned it one way, then another, perplexed.

"Door hinge," he said. He took it from her and held it against the leather strap on the hooked-back canvas flap, showed how it worked. "Gonna build me a log store, get me a regular door made and I'll be all fixed for tradin'."

He grabbed a tin cup from a barrel head. "Here, I'll show you." He dropped to his knees on a striped blanket, sat, strapped the cup to his foot. Lying on his back he swung his legs up. "My scale! If'n you wanna buy that door hinge," he said to Isabel, laughing, "drop some nuggets in the cup and we'll make us a bargain!"

Isabel looked at her father. His friend Jim was a clown. Woochi.

Eekeno brought more food, her eyes on Isabel, then left, silently ducking out the canvas flap. Jim dished them up plates of bacon and beans, laughed, said sometimes he varied the meal, ate beans with bacon instead of bacon with beans.

They ate sitting on blankets, fuzzy stripes of red and yellow and green and black. She liked the feel of them. After the meal she curled up on a stack of the striped blankets while her father and Jim lit pipes, smoked, recalled war stories.

"Remember them bugles?! Bugles!" Jim, head back, making a fist, blowing into it a sound like a braying mule. Laughing, always laughing.

And her father laughing. Old friends. New ways. White man in buckskins, Indian in a blue shirt. Talking. Me'wuk words. American words. Spanish words. She grew drowsy wondering if they saw the world with the same eyes from speaking the same words, words traded when they had fought the Mexicans together.

She nestled into the piled blankets, lying on her side, head on one arm folded into the coarse wool beneath her.

"Remember us gettin' to that mission at Santa Barbara! Indians waitin'! Mexicans all vamoosed! And we'd heard reports the Californios would fight us at Santa Barbara!" Voice excited, reliving remembered times. "Exhibited themselves is what they did," Jim said. "Prancin' around on fine horses, wavin' banners and lances. And when we fired our field pieces at them—"

"Run like antelope." Her father's voice, amused. "Yankee Doodle."

"Yankee Doodle!" Jim laughing. "Yankee Doodle went to town, a ridin' on his pony!"

Through eyes half-closed, she saw Jim get to his feet. Arms waving, he danced, singing, "Stuck a feather in his cap—"

Clown. Woochi.

Laughter. "—and called it macaroni!"

Always laughing, this white man with yellow hair, call me Jim. She nestled deeper into the blanket's warmth, burrowed into its scratchy wool, closed her eyes. She had touched his hair. That surprising, unexpected pale winter hair. And she had said her name was Isabel. New ways. Her name was Isabel. She fell asleep wondering what the word *macaroni* meant, and whether her father's target for the arrow aimed south in this long journey had been this big green tent.

Jim glanced at his friend's sleeping daughter. "Long day." He rose, found a lantern, struck a match to its wick, and hooked the lantern overhead on a tent strut. He closed the tent's flap as a moth fluttered in, found the lantern and softly beat against its light. Outside, frogs croaked from the river.

"Fremont's got friendly Indians diggin' gold," he said. "Got the value of the dirt. Women and children, too."

José Jesús nodded. "Fond of raisins. Your trade good?"

"Not much call for door hinges," Jim said, resuming his cross-legged position on his blanket, "but good diggins and Indians takin' to me." He saw the chief slowly shake his head, black hair catching the lantern light, a frown deepening the crevices of his handsome face. Carrying his years good. Respected his opinion, that much certain. "You suspectin' they ain't?"

"Bad place. Rio de Nuestra Señora de la Merced."

Jim laughed. Indians always surprisin' him. "Them mission padres learned you some fine-soundin' words, Chief. And this right purty River of Our Lady of Mercy, with its purty name, this Merced, is a bad river?"

"Mariposa better. For you."

"Well, kinda keen on the mercy idea. Maybe Mariposa, butterflies, ain't bad, but mercy, that might prove useful." He refilled his pipe, tamped it thoughtfully. "Why not the Merced?"

"Teneiya."

"Heard on him. Chauchilas and Potoyensees say he's their enemy." He sucked in smoke, let it out, watched it rise toward his canvas roof in silence. He liked it here, on the Merced. River of Mercy. Teneiya weren't his enemy. Wouldn't brag to his friend here, but, truth bein' true, he reckoned weren't no Indian he couldn't powwow with, get the lingo, smoke a pipe. Weren't no one's enemy, he weren't, and no point takin' sides. And no point arguin' with a friend. He glanced at the sleeping girl curled on blankets. At least their business about her was agreed on.

He contemplated his pipe for a time, then said, "So, I 'spect you heard on Weber's plan?" Best change horses, take another trail from the chief's objection to this location. "Gonna name the town for Commodore Stockton, on account of his bringin' a boat to California for the war with Mexico. Nothin' like havin' the biggest gun in a scrap, is there?"

He, himself, approved Weber's plan to build a town on the San Joaquin. How could he not? Riverboats bringin' in supplies, goods for his store, for tradin' to Indians, supplyin' miners. Gold in his pocket. He tamped his pipe, watched smoke rise, listened to frogs talking in the darkness outside.

"Heard you was gonna help him, Chief."

José Jesús examined his pipe, looked up, nodded. "We talked business."

"You givin' up on—let me think on a word here, Chief— uh, movin' horses, yeah, movin' horses, from one place to another?"

José Jesús laughed. "New business. Labor contractor."

"If'n I could write," Jim said, "I'd get you up what's called a circular, advertise your services." He laughed, sucked his pipe. "Good-lookin', your daughter," he said, changing horses again, nodding in the sleeping girl's direction. "Must be about sixteen now, as I recall. No chin tattoos. Got no objection to 'em myself. Somewhat like 'em on Eekeno."

"New ways."

"I forget what you said about why she ain't married. Remember you sayin'—down in Santa Barbara, I think it was, when we got to talkin'—"

"Chief Maximo's son—" José Jesús said after a long moment. He stared at his pipe.

Jim flinched. Came back to him now, arrowed into him. Felt the twang of it. Raphero. Sutter's bloody answer to Indian revolt stuck on a pike. What could Jim say on that? Shamed to be associated with the white-man tribe? Words not worth the wind to say 'em. Weren't nothin' he could say. Didn't care to think on it neither. World weren't sensible. Lord knew anything was possible, what with James D. Savage himself come to be king of the Tularenos and gold pilin' up like wheat in a harvest. A whole corral of gold to be had.

He studied his pipe, looked up, saw José Jesús lookin' at him like he was takin' his measure. No need to be talkin' around things they weren't sayin'. Nothin' needed sayin' in reply, he saw that, and said it anyways. "You can count on me."

José Jesús nodded. They smoked, listening to the continued staccato conversations of frogs and crickets addressing the night.

Jim waited for the chief to speak, take the talk on a new trail, could see José Jesús had somethin' to say, even before he said it.

"Mariposa better."

Jim shook his head. "Kinda satisfied with this ol' river of mercy, my friend."

"*Uzu'mati*. You know this word?"

"Mebbe heard it. Bear?"

"Grizzly bear. Never runs. Afraid of nothing. Attacks anything."

Jim had heard the word all right, close on to it anyways, not quite the Me'wuk pronunciation. The Potoyensees and Chauchilas had a name for Chief Teneiya and his people something like *uzu'mati*. Said it like it meant more'n bear. Said it like it meant trouble. *Yosemite*.

The next morning, after coffee and Jim's 'flapjacks,' the horse fed and watered, Jim's cheerful goodbyes repeated, the journey resumed. Following again the river that had led to the green tent, Isabel chattered like a little blue jay, telling her father she liked her calico skirt and muslin blouse, possibly lemon syrup, definitely striped blankets. And Jim, too. "Jim is funny, like Woochi. Clown."

Her father nodded. "And friend. Trust him. He has a good heart."

They continued in silence broken only by birdsong and the river singing them into the mountains.

She realized they were no longer heading south.

1849

Innumerable moons and snows have passed since the Great Spirit guided a little band of his favorite children into the beautiful vale of Awani…and here they lived and multiplied, and, as instructed by their medicine men, worshipped the Great Spirit which gave them life, and the sun which warmed and made them happy.

—Yosemite Creation Myth

Her heart ached. Sleepless, she stared up from the warmth of the buffalo robe at a patch of sky visible through the cedar shelter's smoke hole and watched a tiny star fading into morning. Or possibly dimming beneath a passing storm cloud? Earlier that day, or was it yesterday, time confused her now, she and Seethkil had watched a darkening sky gather a storm above the great sliced mountain.

"Winter coming," she had said, and Chief Teneiya's youngest son had said, regret in his voice, "Snow soon."

Snow soon. Snow soon.

Night sounds paused her wandering thoughts. Far from the village a lone coyote howled. Nearby, dry grass whispered. Horse grazing. Sent for her, this horse with a name.

Everything had a name. The sliced mountain had a name. *Tis-sa'-ack*. Who told her *Tis-sa'-ack*'s story? Told how the couple reached Awani after a long journey, tired, footsore, thirsty. *Tis-sa'-ack,* the wife, found the reflecting lake first, quiet water, *ahwei'ya*. So thirsty she drank it all up. Then her angry husband, forgetting his people's customs, beat *Tis-sa'-ack* until she ran from him, pained, humiliated. When her husband followed to beat her again, she hurled her burden basket at him. And the Great Spirit himself, shocked and angered by his children's conduct, turned them into granite. *Tis-sa'-ack*'s tears stained the sliced mountain.

Isabel, watching the graying sky swallow the tiny star, remembered how she had stared on first seeing the sliced mountain. She and her father, after leaving Jim's green tent, followed the river up, into the mountains, where it suddenly, unexpectedly, entered this hidden valley enclosed by towering granite.

"Awani," her father said.

Awani. Great Spirit surely created this secret place for the First People.

She had been stunned by the sight. Such beauty had no words. Granite climbed into the sky. Cliff-top rivers leapt from their heights in shimmering mists. Who could tell of it, this land, surpassing imagination, so beyond ordinary mountains, ordinary waterfalls? She had drunk the sight as greedily as *Tis-sa'-ack* drank the lake.

She had arrived in the gathering season, and Loiya's niece, Tabuce, a gifted weaver fond of wearing roped feathers around her neck and wreaths of tiger lily flowers in her hair, had welcomed Isabel with a beautiful twined-willow burden basket. Tabuce had led her along well-trod trails to favorite black oaks, telling the ancient names and tales of Awani's giant granites and leaping waters.

Wahaw'kee was the three frogs rock, and *toko'ya* was the name of the basket rock to the north. The immense granite mountain looming above the village was *totau'konula*, named for the great cranes, *totau'kons*, that nested near its top.

All the beautiful valley's towering granites and falling waters had names and stories she learned in those first delicious days when Seethkil seemed often nearby, making a new bow, practicing his aim with new arrows. Had she imagined he stood taller, shot straighter than anyone else? Loiya had laughed, catching Isabel watching Seethkil's performance, and Seethkil posturing.

Gazing up through the smoke hole now, watching the fading star disappear, she trailed memory back to the day she and her father arrived, when José Jesús delivered her to Chief Teneiya and said, "My daughter is your daughter."

Her father's premonition? Prediction? Intention? Or her fortunate fate? And now she was indeed Chief Teneiya's daughter, sharing her life with his youngest son, whose mother, Loiya, affectionately confided he was her favorite. Loiya, such warmth in her aging face, so like Victoria who would have envied Loiya's beautiful buckskin belt decorated with dressed woodpecker scalps and fringed with olivella shell disks. Generous, loving Loiya, who gave them the buffalo robe warming winter's approach.

Seethkil, everyone's favorite. Even his two much older brothers, Latta and Till, doted on him. "Made a pet of him," Loiya had said, laughing. "Taught him fun and tricks to amuse everyone."

Seethkil delighted in amusing her. On one of those enchanting early days together, he happily declared, only half-jokingly, that his animal ally was a mouse. "I trapped and tamed him," he'd said, proudly showing her his pet's swift responses to signs and sounds that sent it running and returning to nestle into his hands.

She had been charmed. And not just by the mouse.

She smiled into the darkness, remembering when the green time arrived how Awani burst vibrantly into life with birdsong and lupines and new grass. And how the Awanichees exuberantly welcomed renewal! Such wonder and spectacle in their ceremony honoring *kwi'na*, eagle, everyone feasting and singing, dancing joyously in eagle-feather capes and headbands and arm-bands, swaying and flying like eagles.

And such happiness learning the meadow game played with a buckskin ball filled with soap-root fiber! "Men play with feet, women with hands," Tobuce had explained. "A man takes the ball over the goal only with his feet. A woman can only use her hands. Men can kick the ball, or run with it"— and here Tobuce giggled— "sometimes by catching and carrying a woman holding the ball!" Laughing, explaining, "If a woman doesn't throw the ball fast to another woman, a man can pick her up and carry the ball with her holding it. You see?"

Isabel, watching young men in buckskin breech clouts chasing laughing young women in grass skirts and deerskin dresses, hadn't understood.

Tobuce laughing, adding, "The woman, you see, she throws the ball to another woman, but sometimes she likes to keep the ball to let the man carry her."

Isabel, confused the first time she played, held the ball, unsure whether to run with it or throw it. And then suddenly Seethkil's strong bronze arms were around her, lifting her. She held the ball. He held her. He smiled, eyes laughing, looking at her as if she were a present. And she at once understood the game and laughed as he carried her to the goal at the meadow's end. And beyond.

When Seethkil put his arms around her, and she felt the warmth of his skin, the strength and sinew of him, she understood more than the game. She understood her father's devotion to Maria, Anna to Francisco, Loiya to Teneiya. All the coupling and caring she had only imagined for herself had arrived. And she chose. She chose the handsome, fun-loving, adored young-est son of Chief Teneiya. And he chose her.

Such happy, laughing days making memories together, anticipating those to come. Here, with Seethkil, in this beautiful place Great Spirit had granted the People, was the reason to "live long," as her father had so often admon-ished.

But now? Now? Now that snow was falling and the horse waited?

She dismissed the thought, returned to happy memories of merry games played in the green season's meadow fragrant with sweet clover and wild-flowers, where lofty pines and spreading oaks overlooked the rippling river, banks thick with willow and dogwood and sweet-scented alder. The river had a name. Two names. The Awanichees called it *wahkal'muta.* Her father and his white-man friend Jim called the river Merced, river of mercy.

She pulled the buffalo robe close, watched the fire's dwindling flames send smoke toward the fading star, drifting like memory. Jim. Jim with yellow hair and blue eyes. In the past year she had thought of him often, how he welcomed them with gifts, smoked the pipe with her father. She remembered his playfulness, tin cup strapped to his foot, laughing as he demonstrated his scales. Giving the cup to her after the flapjack breakfast. "Take it, Isabel," he said, laughing. Always laughing. "I got a box of 'em!" Remembered her father advising her, "Trust him. Heed me, Isabel, and you will grow old."

Then, when she and her father reached Awani, José Jesús telling Chief Teneiya about Jim learning the Tularenos' languages, marrying their daughters, protecting their territory from unfriendly white men. They, in turn, protecting his trading post from unfriendly Indians.

And Chief Teneiya's long silence before saying, expression solemn, that the trading post encroached Awanichee territory.

No, not that memory. She wrenched thought back to the present, noticed the fire's reflection from Jim's tin cup hanging next to her stirring stick. She had woven a milkweed rope for its handle. She wanted to remember everything in its place, waiting for her—the seed-beater Loiya showed her how to make, her dipper basket, cooking basket, deer antler for prying out woodpecker's hidden acorns.

She nestled into Seethkil's warmth, softly, not to wake him while she collected into memory the shadowed objects of her life here. There, hanging by his quiver and fish spear, next to his dance ornaments, the sweet alder-wood flute. When had he first wooed her with its sound soft as rabbit fur? She thought a moment, then, yes, after the snow melted in the green time and the trail opened over the mountain to the Mono people. The Awanichees taking acorns, elderberries, manzanita berries, and arrows to trade with their cousins for salt, obsidian, pine nuts—sometimes buffalo skins from Washo people—and especially *kutsavi,* the salty alkali fly Monos collected in shallow water along their lakeshore, so delicious in soups and stews.

Such a lively visit, everyone trading, feasting, running footraces, playing games. She remembered how the Monos, quarrelsomely competitive, played the hand game ferociously, wagered fearlessly, shouted wildly at losses. Several had followed the Awanichees back on the trail, demanding another game at the lake of the shining rocks, *pywe'ack*.

Chief Teneiya's mother was Mono. Teneiya's father, a Me'wuk, had been chief in Awani when the black sickness chased everyone from this valley, pocking the faces of fleeing survivors. No people lived in Awani until Teneiya reclaimed it after finding the sickness gone and the land good again. And then he led Monos, Paiutes, and Me'wuk people into Awani, gathering together a new *nena* for the old land.

The horse whinnied in the whispering grass, interrupting her wandering thoughts. Where had she lost memory's trail? Yes, the trading visit to the Monos, then camping at *pywe'ack*, Seethkil enchanting her with haunting melodies from his alder-wood flute. Tobuce teasing, "He plays for you, Isabel, always wooing."

Always music here. Seethkil's lovely flute. Foot-drums and bone-whistles for festivals and dances. Laughter. Bird song. River rippling. Wind rustling trees. Such lovely contented days collecting redbud, willow, and sumac for weaving baskets with Tabuce, making acorn or tending cooking fires, learning Awani stories. Her favorite was the one about the two bear cubs falling asleep on the rock that grew taller and taller and taller while they slept. And their mother, frantic with worry, begging all the animals to get them down. Gray Fox trying to jump up to them, but unable. Then Mother Deer trying and failing. Even for Mountain Lion, who climbed and leapt the farthest, the wall was too high and too steep. Mother Bear, despairing, wept for someone to save her cubs and then *tutok'ana*, little measuring worm, in his small voice, saying he would try. All the animals laughing at him, but the little worm, curling and stretching, day by day slowly inched his way to the top. The cubs woke up and, frightened by how high they were, cried because they couldn't get down. But little measuring worm showed them the sticky trail he'd made climbing up to them, assuring them they weren't cowards, for they were Mother Grizzly's children, and she was the bravest creature in Awani. Finally convinced, the two fearful bear cubs inch by inch descended the mountain. And so brave little measuring worm saved Mother Grizzly's cubs.

She could be brave, too, do what must be done. She had no choice.

The fire needed tending. She rose silently into the advancing cold, gently stirred dying embers into orange sparks flying brightly into the darkness. I will be like measuring worm, she thought. I know the way. I will go. And I will come back.

No choice, her father had said, only a moon ago now. That memory, bright as a tin cup, returning constant as rain in winter. That day, at first so happily ordinary. She saw it all again, so vividly—women gathering seeds, others fishing or making acorn, children playing, Tabuce fashioning a water basket, Seethkil herding horses and mules from a recent raid into a brush enclosure. She had been building a *chuck'ah* to store acorns, weaving deer-brush branches, tying the ends with willow and grapevines, lining the granary with dry pine needles, incense cedar, and wormwood against insects. And then suddenly a signal runner racing from *cho'lak*, falling water, to *wa-haw'kee*, three frogs rocks. "José Jesús coming! José Jesús coming!"

She had been so happy at first. Her father always brought news, and everyone hurried from whatever they were doing to hear it. And after all the exchanged greetings, the ceremonious pipe-smoking and feasting, everyone gathering into the dance house. In memory she could see him again, rising, so tall, so straight, addressing the people. "Your signal runners have told you of many white people coming into the country," he reminded them. In memory she heard again the strangeness in his voice demanding attention. Everyone had looked, listened intently, as if hearing distant hoofbeats. Something coming.

"You dismiss this news as of no concern to you," he had continued, "supposing these white people cannot disturb you in this place. Their presence in the valleys and foothills means only more horses and mules for your warriors to steal to feed you. That is your thought. Your messengers tell of the yellow dirt these white men dig, and your thought is the white men will dig, and then they will leave. I bring you truth. White people are coming and coming. In the green season they came with tents and made camps. Now they make towns, rancherias too large for you to imagine. They are coming for the yellow dirt, for gold, and coming and coming, beyond counting. They do not respect our ways or our land. You have heard they kill Indians for no cause, and you did not believe. But it is true. And you did not believe when you heard they take Indian children and women for slaves. They do. It is true. And they know you steal their horses and mules and cattle. And that you have no friends among them to object when they kill you. It is true."

Stunned silence, then a torrent of objections and questions and disbelief.

How tall and straight and truthful he stood, cautioning the Awanichees to heed his advice that they might then grow old. "Old ways gone," he insisted. "Miners and settlers coming into this country in numbers countless as flies. One day, know this, they will retaliate against horse raiding. To survive, you must find new ways to live in this new world. The white man called Captain Weber pays wages to Indians to build big rancheria, Stockton. I work for him, find workers for him. You can work for him. Learn new ways to be in the world."

Disagreement and argument had followed, much smoking and long talking. In the end, the Awanichees agreed they did not want to build rancherias for white men. They wanted to live as they had always lived, in this place. They would eat what Great Spirit provided. When the deer fled, they would eat horses, cattle, mules.

But José Jesús was not finished. She remembered him turning to Chief Teneiya and saying, "The white man with yellow hair, Jim Savage—your warriors destroyed his trading post on the Merced river. His friends, the Tularenos, Chauchilas, Nukchus, Potoyensees, are your enemies. They identified your signs and arrows, told him Yosemites attacked his Merced river trading post."

She remembered every word, remembered Chief Teneiya saying, "That white man, Jim Savage, was in our territory, near our hidden entrance. To protect Awani we destroyed his trading post."

Then her father saying, "Jim Savage is my friend," and Chief Teneiya replying, "That is why we did not kill him."

A long silence followed before her father said, "He respects your message. He moved his trading business to the Mariposa. He wishes to unite with the Yosemites as he has united with the Tularenos, who call him king. From the First Times, people sent their daughters to make alliance, an old tradition this uniting with neighbors to prevent warfare. Our daughters are honored to make peace this way." He had paused then, and she remembered now how he looked at her, his eyes speaking to hers. Shattering happiness.

She had stared back, disbelief turning her to granite.

And Chief Teneiya looking at her, saying, "I came to this valley of my ancestors as a young chief many, many years ago," telling the tale everyone knew, repeated especially for her. "Other descendants of the first Awanichees joined me. Also some who fled their own tribes, or the missions, or injustice. A very wise, very old medicine man counseled me in that time. In his last days he foresaw the future. He predicted my band would increase, become powerful while I possessed Awani. If I befriended those who sought protection here, no other tribe would make war with us, or come into this valley to drive us from it. That old patriarch placed a spell on Awani, made it sacred to us alone. No other people would dare make it their home. I was cautioned to guard this place from lowlands people, warned that if they should enter, we would be scattered and taken captive and be destroyed. And I would be the last chief in Awani."

And then her father saying, "Jim Savage wishes alliance with Yosemites. He offers his protection as a white chief and respected king of the Tularenos. To seal these friendship bonds, he sends his horse for my daughter, who is also the daughter now of Chief Teneiya, to go as your promise that you are one with the yellow-hair white man."

Seethkil had leapt to his feet, protesting until Teneiya silenced him. Tobuce wept. And Loiya. But she? She had turned to stone.

Later, she found her tongue, and the courage to bargain for time, begging her father and Chief Teneiya to let her stay until the acorns were gathered and stored for winter. She would go to the Mariposa. At the first snow.

In the days since that promise, she had savored each sweet moment weaving baskets and making acorn with her friends. Building granaries and gathering acorns. And treasuring Seethkil's warmth and cleverness.

"You have the horse," he'd said that first day of decision. Together they had scouted trails to the Mariposa and back, crossing the river at *wawona,* on the southern entrance to Awani. They planned her departure, her return. They assured each other the alliance was temporary. The gold white men wanted must soon be all they could carry and they would take it and return to their homes and families. As she would return to hers. The arrangement was for show. For now.

And now, outside, again the soft whinny. She hung up her stirring stick, ducked through the doorway, went to the horse. She calmed it with a whisper, "Hush, Girl. Hush," and looked up at the morning sky.

It was snowing.

1850

Savage is rather a famous character in the diggings. He exercises a remarkable influence over the Indians, wherever he goes. He subdues them, and they work for him and trade with him.

—*Alta California*
July 3,1850

He is said to have subject to his control fifteen thousand warriors at the present time—at least that is his own estimate, and when we reflect how far his quasi jurisdiction extends, we have no reason to disbelieve him.

—*San Francisco Journal of Commerce*
October 31, 1850

I n the beginning she thought only of Awani, her happiness as rooted in that extraordinary valley as its trees. Her mind wandered there, gathering into her memory basket every face and place and story, every ceremonial dance and song. Among her favorite Awanichee songs was 'the acorn has fallen.' The oldest man in the village each summer deciding which oak to watch. Then choosing a branch on that oak. And finally, on that branch, an acorn. And when it fell, such celebration! Acorn has fallen! Time for singing and dancing the People's gratitude for this food. Such a joyful time, everyone who was away returning for the festivities.

And how she wanted to be back! To be dancing again the big dance for acorn, everyone dressed in the fur and feathers honoring the animals that helped them, circling a blazing fire, dancing and chanting and shaking rattles at the flames, celebrating all Great Spirit's gifts—baskets for collecting acorn, stones for heating fire, the fire itself. Loiya sprinkling acorn four times around the fire, that its smoke might rise in four directions to feed all the spirits of the dead. Such feasting and dancing and singing.

And now, here on the Mariposa, she put the Awanichees' acorn festival into her memory basket and imagined herself an old woman in Awani, making acorn and telling stories to her children's children. She would astonish them with this new story, hers alone, and call it Watching. Tell how one winter on Mariposa Creek she wore calico and sat cross-legged on a striped blanket in the corner of a white man's store watching Americans and learning their words: Boots. Frypan. Matches. Bacon. Flour. Candles. Shovels. Beans. Canvas. Whiskey. Those were her first words, easy words for things on shelves, things white men stomped into the store to buy with their dug-up gold. Many, many Indians traded there, too, she would tell, and like everyone, they grew accustomed to her silent presence on the striped blanket in the corner where she sat, watching.

On one dark day winter rains poured so heavily no customers came to trade. With nothing to watch, she listened to the wind batter the store's thin boards and whistle through its cracks and crevices. She imagined Awani whitening silently beneath drifting snow. Absorbed by thought, she was surprised when Jim knelt to face her, then sat cross-legged on the plank floor and leaned forward, elbows on his knees.

"Isabel, we're in the trading business now, you and me."

She looked away, then stared at the floor. He was in the trading business, shovels for gold, raisins for gold. She wasn't in the trading business, she was the trade, the shovel Chief Teneiya exchanged for the trader's influence with white people.

Jim reached out his right hand to her chin, lifted it, forced her to look at him. "Five," he said, spreading the fingers of his left hand in front of her eyes. He closed it into a fist, then raised one finger after another, starting with his thumb. "One, two, three, four, five." He took her hand, closed it into a fist, opened it as he had his own, asked, "*Mitok'ho?*"

Mitok'ho. Me'wuk for how many. She understood. "*Ma-cho'-ka,*" she said. Five.

"*Ma-cho'-ka.*" Jim nodded. "Five." He repeated his demonstration, one finger at a time, saying, "One, two, three, four, five."

She did the same, repeating.

"Today we're in the tradin' words business," he said. "Your turn."

She nodded. Pointing to her thumb, and then each finger, she counted. "*Keng'a, o-ti'-ko, to-lok'-o, o-i'-sa, ma-cho'ka.*" Trading her words for his. Heeding her father's advice. New ways.

And so her winter of watching became the winter of trading words. When rains pounded the store's roof and winds rattled its slats, and no one threw open the door wanting bacon or a shovel, she and Jim traded and collected one another's words. First, numbers, then body parts—hands, head, nose, feet—then things they could point to outside: trees and rocks and sky and clouds. She learned the names of things the Me'wuk tongue had no words for: ounces, pounds, grams. New words, words that opened a different world, a world seen through a different language. She wondered if the Spanish language contained the secret to why soldiers massacred the People. Or English explained why white people loved gold. She discovered she loved learning, liked having her thoughts stirred with words.

"You s*awa'ja,*" she told Jim one day.

He put on his questioning look, hands open, head tilted.

She hesitated, then smiled and said, "Mush-stirrer." She mimed making acorn mush with an imaginary stirring stick.

He laughed and held out his arms as if addressing a crowd. "Jim Savage, king of the Tularenos and part-time mush-stirrer!"

He danced a little then, on the plank floor in front of her, stomping circles and chanting, "*Sawa'ja, Sawa'ja,*" until she laughed.

"Woochi," she said, appreciating his attempts to soften the hardship of their arrangement. He must have seen how loneliness often overwhelmed her. Her father had said to trust this white man, that he was their friend. Here, on the Mariposa, she had no others.

One rainy day when pride and courage dissolved into longing for Seethkil and Awani, she placed her hand on the store's balance scales that had replaced the tin cup, and said, "Chief Teneiya traded me."

Savage shook his head. "Not Chief Teneiya, Isabel." He hesitated, looking at her, this smart, beautiful daughter of his friend. "Chief José Jesús."

"My father traded me?" She stared at Jim. "My father?"

"To learn to live long is sorta how he put it." He grinned. "Both of us."

She understood the mutual protection of kinship connections with the chiefs of villages surrounding the store, political he called it. She had heard that word, political. Men came to the store talking about California becoming a state, about government, about elections. He did his best to explain the word's several implications. "Wives," he shrugged, "they like me." He smiled. "Eekeno and Homut anyways." He was fond of them, he said, but his true wife was named Eliza. "She died."

Isabel, watching his eyes fill, saw that he had opened his heart to her. After a moment, she said, "Chief Teneiya's son—"

Jim nodded. "I know about your young man, Isabel, and I'm hopin' you get back to him soon as we figure which way the wind's blowin'. Your father wants you to learn new ways, so's you can live long. You're here for your people's survival as much as for me and my store. Your father and me, we talked on it. Figured havin' you here be the best chance any of you got when the country fills up with settlers and miners. No tellin' what kinda trouble might be comin' with 'em."

Remembering Victoria's stories, she asked, "Like long-robes and soldiers?"

"Them padres didn't do your people many favors, but you got their lingo, so that's somethin' useful."

"Knowing their words, I know how they think?"

He studied her. "Mebbe, mebbe. Interestin' idea. I got a friend I'll mention that to. Real smart fella."

A few days later, Jim brought a young man to where she sat in her corner. "Isabel, you got a visitor. Come just to talk to you."

A clean-shaved man in a boiled white shirt beneath a wool coat that matched his trousers nodded at her, pulled up a stool, sat. "Name's Sam," he said, "Sam Ward."

"Sam's got a ferry on the river," Jim said. "But real educated. Wants to learn some Indian words."

Sam took a small notebook and pencil from his pocket. He opened the notebook on his knee, examined the pencil's point, looked at her.

She looked from him to Jim, who joined her on the floor, legs crossed, feet bare, then back at the man named Sam. New ways. If white people learned her words, would they see the world Great Spirit made for the People? The thought made her hopeful.

"I'm tellin' you, Sam," Jim said, "people say Indians is stupid, but look how they learn lingo. Picked up Spanish like they was collectin' acorns. Tossed words in their heads like nuts in a basket." He reached over, tapped the man's paper. "Writin' ain't a bit on the necessary. Me and Isabel's the same. Ain't got writin' and don't need it. Listenin' is what does it."

"Ask her to say her numbers again, slowly, would you? I've contrived my own system for the sounds, a little German, some Greek, occasionally Latin. Takes time to get it down."

She told her words for what Sam asked. Sam made marks in his notebook. Jim watched him, and after a time, said, "I been givin' it some thinkin', Sam, this language business. On why it come easy to me. Figure anybody ain't got readin' and writin' to hold words, got to hold 'em in his head. I'm thinkin' there's some muscle in there gets stronger from usin' it, like an arm swingin' an axe does. Indians got a hundred stories, a thousand, on how the earth got made and who made it and when, and how lizard gave 'em hands, and coyote gave 'em smarts, and what all. Keep it in their heads. I figure they been practicin' this memory business a thousand years."

"Interesting theory," Sam said, writing. "Ask her how she says 'I sleep.' Bautista has it 'tue'ma'. I want to compare her words with his. I'm curious if Potoyensee is similar."

"Bautista's a good one to talk to," Savage said. "Smart, like her." He nodded at Isabel, then looked at Ward. "Seen him ride? Bautista? Like the wind. He's a show, that Indian, wearin' that tall sombrero with the silver band. Ropes cattle like they was standin' still."

"Speaks Spanish like a padre," Sam said, head down, writing, "plays cards like a Mississippi riverboat gambler."

"Don't reckon he picked that up at the mission," Jim said, standing. "Watch him, Sam. Bautista's not a happy man. Too many talents for an Indian these days."

Isabel made the store's corner hers. While Jim's other Indian wives dug gold, gathered seeds, fished, or cooked, she sat in the store. Watching. No one objected; her presence meant the Yosemites would not attack here. And Indians kept their promises.

Isabel wondered if white men kept theirs. Jim had promised the Yosemites his protection from unfriendly white men. But where was his power over white men? She could not see it. White men came into the store, talked, laughed, argued with him. She didn't see the respect and admiration and fear she observed in the Tularenos who trusted him to protect them. How had he achieved this power with the People? Where had it come from? The People had animal allies that helped them in the world. Did white men?

One evening, in the cabin Jim had built for his wives, she asked Homut, his Chauchila wife, how he became El Rey Tularenos.

"White medicine," Homut replied, brushing dust from her skirt, a red calico. "He sent Bautista, chief of Potoyensees, to the West, to Great Spirit. Make Bautista dead." She plopped down on her bedding of blankets, then fell over, to show.

Isabel stared. "Chief Bautista isn't dead."

"After fall down, sit up. Alive again." She sat up. "I saw it."

"I don't understand."

"Great Spirit power come into El Rey from *uzu'mati la'watuh*."

Isabel was confused. "*Uzu'mati la'watuh*?" A grizzly cub's hide, head and claws attached, hung on the wall behind the store's flour barrels.

Homut nodded. "El Rey put bear head on his head, same like Indians wear deer head to hunt deer. One day," she continued, "he send message to chiefs to bring people, see special white medicine man power, great wizard, son of Great Spirit." She raised her arms, waved her hands, as if gathering people. "Yokuts people with many, many villages. Chukchansi, Tachi, Yauelmani, Potoyensee, Siyanti, Yatchicumne. Many come, two hundred, maybe three hundred people see him, bear's head on his head, bear's back on his back, bear's arms on his arms. Roared, roamed around, growled, grizzly head swaying side to side, looking at us, claws swinging." Homut stood, demonstrating. "Then he charged, roaring bear language. Everyone yelled, surprised, fell back, afraid of bear spirit." She pretended surprise, raising her arms, eyes wide.

Isabel imagined the alarm. No Me'wuk medicine man dared assume grizzly bear spirit. Not Yosemites. Not Monos. No animal was more powerful or dangerous. Everyone feared *uzu'mati*'s revenge.

Homut reared back, arms raised, a standing bear. "El Rey's bear spirit," she said, "commanded the chiefs—José Rey, José Juarez, Bautista, many others—come forward to him, feel white medicine man's wizard power. Then, roaring like grizzly bear, El Rey grabbed José Juarez's hands with his grizzly claws." She pantomimed the action. "Chief Juarez hollered! Fell back, eyes wide, hands flapping like bird wings." Homut threw her arms wide, hands jerking. "Then grizzly bear spirit turn on Bautista, growled, grizzly bear arms on Bautista's shoulders." She nodded at Isabel, confirming. "Everyone know Potoyensee chief fearless, talks war against white men. Bautista stand tall, show courage. But grizzly bear claws grab him. Bautista fall down! Body shake! Then stop moving. His people called his name, frightened. Chief Bautista not move, not answer. Dead."

Isabel saw Homut look away, eyes distant, recalling the scene she described. After a moment, Isabel touched Homut's hand, brought her back from memory. "Homut, I saw Chief Bautista in the store. He is alive."

Homut nodded. "White medicine! After El Rey kill Bautista, he throw aside grizzly bear hide, stoop down, stare into chief's dead face. Spoke white medicine words, strange voice, strange wizard-spell words. Touched Bautista's forehead, stroked his face, breathe into chief's mouth with his mouth, rub chief's arms and legs. Talking heavy his wizard words."

Isabel stared. This was no ordinary story, like her Watching story, something to tell her children while she taught them new ways.

Homut's voice a whisper now, urgent. "Bautista open eyes, raise head! El Rey, in white medicine man voice, told chief to stand. Bautista stand! Alive again!" She threw her arms wide, demonstrating.

"You saw this?!"

Homut nodded. "Everyone tell. All Yokuts people know." Voice low, respectful, she said, "Powerful white medicine. El Rey Tularenos."

Isabel was stunned. Did Chief Teneiya know this?

As winter passed, each day of increased sunshine increased the store's customers. Isabel sat in her corner, watched white men get outfitted for mining. Watched Indians trade gold for beads, trinkets, a striped blanket, a red bandana. Five ounces for a blue shirt. Settlers bought nails, writing paper, shared the latest news. "Bowling alley over in Agua Fria now." "Seven mules stole at Woods' diggins. Indians again." "Rich discovery at Quartzberg." "Dry diggins payin' good at Hornitos." "Frenchman at Sonora beat two Mexicans out of their monte bank." "Horses run off over at Harvey's place. Indians."

So many miners and settlers! She should have known. Her father had warned that the white men were coming and coming and coming. One like another—booted, bearded, dusty, stoop shouldered beneath slouch hats. But she would remember a few. Some demanded attention. Like the man who'd stomped into the store, stared at Jim, and shouted, "Well, if'n it ain't the good lord's truth! Heard lotsa talk about an Indian trader over this way callin' hisself Jim Savage. I knowed a Jim Savage, I sez. Bet it be him. And here he is, Jim Savage hisself!"

"Hisself," Savage had said, elbow on his plank counter, looking up, curious. "And you'd be?"

"Ah, you don't know me. I jist remember seein' you somewheres near the Platte, back in forty-six. On accounta that coat you wuz wearin' then!" Laughing. Loud. Slapping his knee. "You still got that old gray coat with the white paint on the back?"

Isabel tensed, alert as a deer hearing a twig snap. She didn't like this man.

Jim, head cocked, eyed him. "You seen me in it?"

"Yep, I did. Big white letters, 'For Oregon'."

Isabel saw Jim's blue eyes soften, visit his past. "Them first five hundred miles," he said, "ever' other man askin' where a body was headin'." He looked at the man. "Got tired of sayin'. Turned my back on folks. Let 'em read it."

The newcomer laughed again. "Them was some times, forty-six."

"My woman painted that coat," Jim said, voice visiting sadness. "God rest her soul, I buried her in it on the desert. Made for California."

"Sorry to hear that. 'Bout your woman, I mean. Hard." The man removed his hat, a gesture Isabel understood showed respect. He slapped his hat back on his head. Looked around, a customer now, looking to buy.

Looking at her. Like a dog finding a bone. "Things on the improvin' way, 'parently," he'd said, grinning, licking his lips. Turned to Jim. Gestured a thumb in her direction. "How much for the squaw?" Looking at her again, grinning, like he was licking peppermint stick from his fingers.

When she remembered this day, she remembered Jim's eyes going dark, his hands gripping the plank, arms tensing. And his roar, "Git outta my store!" *Uzu'mati* roar. "You git! Out!"

Remembering another day, another white man, slapping open the door. Stomping into the store like he owned it, he hollered at everyone, "Campaignin' for judge, boys!" Slick, slippery voice. "Walter H. Harvey is the name! Lookin' to y'all for votes! A vote for Walter H. Harvey is a vote for

California for Americans! Americans, boys!" Strolling around the store, slapping backs. "In Georgia, we knew what to do about Indians, we did! When Georgia found gold on Cherokee land, we kept the gold and kicked the Cherokees out! Sent them *okla-hummas* off to Indian territory!"

Someone asked, "O*kla-hummas?*"

Oily voice laugh. "Choctaw word for 'red people,' friend!" Looking at her, sneering. "Collect these redskins up, ship 'em to Indian territory, name the place Oklahoma!" He'd laughed again, thumped his chest. "I'm your candidate for judge in Mariposa County!" He looked around, proud. Nodded in Isabel's direction. Laughed. "She's your candidate for Oklahoma!"

Jim had snarled, "Git out, Harvey!" Afterwards he'd knelt down by her, took her hand. "Some white men, Isabel, and there ain't no understandin' it, but they hate Indians, got no reason. They'll kill an Indian, any Indian, just for bein' an Indian. No more thought to it than stompin' a snake."

"Stomp a snake?" She imagined white men's heavy, hard-heeled boots stomping a beautiful yellow racer snake. Snake flailing. White man feeling nothing through boots that felt nothing. White men's boots deadened earth's voice. Her people's feet touched earth, felt its life in dusty trails and fallen leaves and forest dampness. The People respected snake spirit, admired the beautiful yellow racer snake, king snake, gopher snake. Stomp snakes? Kill them? Why? Kill Indians? Kill snakes? Why? She didn't understand.

But she was learning. Learning things Seethkil and Chief Teneiya should know. Like the fact that El Rey possessed white medicine power, that he had killed Bautista—and brought him back to life.

And then, as if reading her mind, Jim said, "Like to see Chief Teneiya come in sometime. For trade."

"Awanichees trade with Monos," she said.

"Like to meet the old chief anyways."

Something in Jim's voice said she was free to go. And early one morning, she left.

It is a well-known fact that among our white population there are men who boast of the number of the Indians they have killed, and that not one shall escape.

—Letter, Brig. Gen. Thomas B. Eastland
to Governor Burnett
June 15, 1850

WHILE GIRL NOSED into the tall grass off the trail, Isabel glanced at miners knee-deep in the Mariposa, intently curling water from their pans. Along the shore, more miners diligently shoveled gravel into cradles and long toms. So many miners! Coming and coming. To dig gold, yellow dirt. If the People had need of it their fathers surely would have told them.

Aware now how vulnerable she was, as a woman who might be bought, as an Indian who might be stomped like a snake, she kept her head down. She was a single Indian riding slow, draped in a striped blanket. She was of no more interest to these industrious diggers than the breeze in the trees.

She turned the horse back to the trail toward Awani. Near the big trees, *wawona,* Chief Teneiya's signal runners identified her, welcomed her. Now she urged Girl into a run, felt the horse's power thudding beneath her, racing beneath the lofty canopy of tall trees.

In the meadow, the thirsty horse drank at the river's edge while Isabel drank Awani's glory as if for the first time. She was home. Where rivers poured from granite cliffs, where she could breathe the green-time fragrance of meadow grass, where children ran among its blossoms chasing butter-flies.

Then Seethkil was at her side, leading the horse and looking at her like she was water and he a desert. And then Loiya was putting warm acorn bread into her hands, Tobuce smiling, handing her a gourd of manzanita cider to drink, people gathering around Loiya's cooking fire with greetings and questions.

Throughout the day she unfolded her story, her long, wet winter of watching and learning. Sam Ward. The oily voice man who stomped snakes. She told about settlers buying nails, miners buying shovels, Indians trading for lemon syrup and striped blankets and all the white men, so many white men coming into the country. This part, not being news, held no interest. White men wouldn't find them. Only Chief Teneiya's people knew Awani's hidden entrance. White men? Never.

News that Savage had opened another store, on the Fresno, with hired clerks taking in so much gold they kept it in flour barrels, that interested the Awanichees. But white people's excitement over elections and a state constitution held no meaning for them and Isabel was unable to explain the significance of these words. As she expected, no one was interested in hearing that Jim Savage wanted to trade with Awanichees and meet Chief Teneiya.

Eventually people wandered off, leaving Seethkil at her side, Loiya stirring mush over her fire, and Chief Teneiya smoking his pipe.

Now Isabel told Homut's story. About Jim Savage's white medicine, how he killed Bautista and made him live again.

"*Toloache,*" Chief Teneiya said, refilling his elder-wood pipe from a basket of ground tobacco leaves. "Many names. Moon-flower. Jimsonweed. Mono people drink it green, not so powerful then. Yokuts people make ceremony, drink it to find dream helper, see the future."

He tamped tobacco into his pipe with a twig. "Bautista unhappy with that white trader. Drink too much *toloache* trying to see the future. Dangerous. Sometimes dream seekers lose their trail, lose the way back."

When Isabel said Jim had special grizzly-bear powers, Chief Teneiya laughed. "Fool. Risks *uzu'mati* revenge. That white man crazy."

She said nothing more then. How could her people understand the white man's world, white man's power? White men didn't understand Indians, and her people knew little about the invaders, the things they valued, like the yellow dirt that drew them like flies to a feast. Her father, José Jesús, knew much, learning new ways. And now, she, Isabel, after her winter on the Mariposa, also had a moccasin in both worlds. She wanted to know what white people knew that Indians didn't. She was curious. Di-shi. Little Blue Jay.

But for now, she was simply happy to be home again, making acorn with Loiya, recalling long days with Victoria pounding acorn, hearing Victoria's voice in her head telling children the story of Little Rock Girl, whose name was Nek'naka'tah, a rock herself who lived in rocky places by the river and made people hard like rocks so they could not be cut or shot by an arrow. And the ancient story of how Coyote-man made the world, planting sticks and feathers in the ground where he wished the People to live, and turning those sticks and feathers into men and women. How, when the People woke up, they learned wisdom from the animals and birds—how crane ate fish and cougar ate deer. And how from *uzu'mati*, from grizzly bear, they learned acorn was food.

Awani. How she loved it. She and Seethkil slipping away from curious eyes, climbing a canyon trail to their special place, recalling glad times, repeating them. She loved being with him again on top of the mountain, watching *cho'lak* plunge its waters from the cliff, becoming mist.

"You are Teheneh, the beautiful maiden," he said one day, reminding her of the story attached to the place, "and I am brave Kosookah, hunting deer for our wedding feast."

Isabel knew the story, how Kosookah promised to shoot an arrow from the cliff between *cho'lak* and *le'hamite,* the canyon of the arrow-wood. The number of feathers on the arrow telling what kill he made. In the valley below, waiting for Kosookah's arrow, Teheneh joyfully preparing acorn for their marriage celebration.

Imagining the lovers' happiness pleased Isabel, but not the sad ending, not the part with Teheneh waiting and waiting for the arrow that did not come. Then, in despair, how Teheneh climbed the cliff and found Kosookah dead, killed by a rockslide, his bow in his hand, the arrow lost. How Teheneh, inconsolable, collapsed against him, spirit departing, joining Kosookah. Wailing families and friends making the funeral fire for their bodies, Teheneh embracing Kosookah holding his bow.

"So sad," Isabel said, "how the story ends, how they end."

Seethkil took her in his arms. "But they are together always, and remembered. See," he said, pointing to a granite column, "there is *hum'moo,* the lost arrow, between *cho'lak* and *le'hamite.* Great Spirit placed it in memory of the faithful Kosookah, who died keeping his promise to Teheneh."

"Better to live, hunt, make acorn, make babies," she said. She wanted life, to live long, as her father had wished, to grow old making acorn with her sons' wives, telling stories to her children's children.

Seethkil touched her hair, stroked her face. "This side, that side, the same. Teheneh and Kosookah are together always. Like us. This side, that side. Together forever."

She would always remember that beautiful moment filled with hope and happiness. That last moment before sky dissolved and they were running, the two of them, hand in hand, racing down the trail. Had she imagined she heard wailing? Or had she already succumbed to dread, to knowing something terrible had happened?

She would remember the signal runner racing into the village. Loiya crying out. The runner, shrunken, confirming. "José Jesús!"

Then thought dissolving. And sun falling from sky like a flailing yellow racer snake.

Stomped.

When I first saw him he was traveling in a very unbecoming manner. All he had on was a coarse cotton shirt, which came to his knees, was bare headed and bare footed, with three wives following him...
—Robert Brownlee
Agua Fria, 1850

SAVAGE TILTED AGAINST the counter clutching the bottle like it was some-thing to hold onto if the plank gave way. He put his partner in his sights, best he could. "You know how to read, right?" He thought a moment, then giggled. "Read? Right?" He grinned. "Good 'un, eh? Read! Write!" He gig-gled some more, not sure Ben got the joke, didn't care. Didn't care he, King o' the Tulares, couldn't do neither, read nor write. Didn't care he didn't know what he was drinkin'. Rotgut? French brandy? Whatever it was, it was doin' the job. Felt good to laugh.

Ben looked over from the stool he'd adopted for the duration of Jim's 'frolic.' Coming in, getting the lay of the land, he'd showed customers the door. "Store's closed, fellas," he'd said, then dropped the door's bar in place and himself onto the stool. He glanced at Jim again, confirmed his first look. "Where's your trousers?"

Savage stared at the bottle's label he couldn't read, like it might announce itself if he examined it long enough. "Store's 'bout empty."

"You wearin' some kinda dress or somethin'?"

Savage considered the bottle further. "Reckon you heard about José Jésus." Tipped his head back and the bottle into his mouth.

"Yep."

Savage drank, licked his lips. Assessed the bottle, shrugged. "Well, now that's empty, same's the store." He dropped the bottle, watched it roll off the plank and thud onto the floor. Tried to giggle but it wouldn't come. Weren't much of a frolic. He looked over at Ben again. "Been to Stockton lately?"

"Nope."

"Should go." Dragged a grin onto his face. "Latest in advantages." Tryin' to hold on to the frolic, not wantin' to think on what things had come to. Or where they were goin'. Or where he was goin'. Come all this way and run out of wild, is what it was. Run out of west. Cities sproutin' like weeds. Which weren't the worst of it.

He put Ben in his sights. "Streets sixty feet wide, Ben. Plank sidewalks! Houses two and three stories! Newspaper! Frenchy restaurant! Steamboat regular to San Francisco!"

Heard himself like he was sellin' the place. He flapped at a fly slow-buzzing the liquor spill on the plank. Looked at Ben, considered the fly again. "One of Stevenson's old regiment. No reason, just shot him like he shouldn't a been standin' where the pistol was aimin'. Captain Weber got a doctor, paid for nursin' him but, well—" He shrugged. Near sober as a judge now. Judge, there's a laugh. Slapped at the fly, missed. "Shoot a white man and you got the law to answer to. Shoot an Indian, well, thank you, friend, one less to bother about."

He levered himself half over the plank, fixed his gaze on the bottle lying on the floor. Addressed it. "Law for the white man. That's what you get with a state. A state! Not a territory! A state! Half a continent from here to the next one over but it bein' so rich, Mr. Indian, we'll take it, thank you very much. Don't let the door smack your backside."

"You gonna say what happened to your trousers?"

Savage righted himself. Leaned an elbow on the plank, considered Ben. "Mebbe, mebbe not. How long we been partners?"

"Two years."

"That qualifies, I s'pose." He turned, looked at the grizzly bear hide nailed to the wall. Felt sick, seeing the scene again, Isabel slipping from the back of the lathered horse, her pleading expression. She'd taken his hand, as if his hand had power, pulled him with her and looked desperately from him to the grizzly hide and back. He understood. She knew about Bautista.

He turned back to Ben. "She come in, wild with hope, askin' with that look they got. You know, like they was a hunnert years old and seen things we ain't seen and ain't likely to."

"That bear stunt weren't your best idea."

"Best wizard trick I ever pulled. Shoulda seen it, Ben."

"Heard about it."

"Don't 'spect the report lost much in its travels."

"Nope."

"Thought I was gonna be the dead man there for a time. Huffed and puffed us both back to life. Me and Bautista. They'd a had my skin if'n I'd killed him. Risky device. Retired it."

He'd seen that Isabel understood when he explained the trick. Overwhelmed with grief, she had whispered, "Woochi. Clown." Truth there, he thought, still feeling his helplessness in the face of her sorrow, her disappointment, her loss. Sharing it, he'd gone to the bottle.

"Indians probably figured you ghosted him or somethin'," Ben said, "they bein' regular superstitious."

Jim shook his head, leveled his unfortunately sobering gaze on his partner. "Science professor. One more prospector with no luck, no dimes, and less sense. Called it a 'galvanic battery.' Showed how it worked. Couple a wires, salt water, and you got electricity. Gives a jolt. Said he figured it had 'potential,' his word, as a mining technique."

Ben shook his head. "Good shovel and a strong back, there's your mining technique."

Jim studied the observation, grabbed a memory, forced a laugh. "Yeah, but how 'bout those Frenchies what brought their fancy French rakes?"

Ben grinned. "Didn't want to get their nice shoes wet."

Jim laughed, slapped the counter. "And weren't the best part the wives?! Like they was goin' to a tea party! Little fancy stools to sit on while their men raked the river. Little sugar tongs they brung for collectin' nuggets while they waited! Now there's your minin' technique!"

He ran a finger through the spill. Licked it. "Anyways, I figured it'd be fun for impressin' the natives. White man magic. Traded a mule for it." He studied the spill. "Hard, disappointin' her hope, thin as it was."

Ben snorted. "She had to know you weren't no medicine man."

"Well, where there ain't nothin' else for sale, desperation buys nonsense. Plenty of that from a fool wearin' a bear skin with wires hangin' down the arms. Nothin' to offer her but regret. Plenty of that on tap from the king of the Tularenos."

"Well, what's done is done," Ben said, standing. "Heard the Yosemites was gettin' up some trouble."

"Ain't only Yosemites. José Juárez firin' up the Chauchilas, tellin' em 'too much white man.' Can't argue that. Ask José Jesús, gone to Great Spirit with the news." He watched his fingers explore the liquor spill. Wiped them on the nightshirt. "That sunk-down look on her, hard to take. Told Homut to busy her up fishin' or cookin' or makin' baskets or collectin' seeds, or somethin'." He looked around for another bottle of whatever he'd emptied. Shelves practically bare. "Need supplies."

"Brownlee, over at Agua Fria, got most everything," Ben said, leaning across the counter, looking down. "Trousers, too, case you decide in their favor."

"Agua Fria got a store?"

"Place come up in the world. County seat, you know. Hotel, express office, assayers."

Savage stared at his partner. "Agua Fria?"

"Get yourself over the hill and take a look. Sheriff, judge, jail, court-house."

Jim laughed. "You prankin' me? A courthouse?!"

"Well, more like what your science professor would call 'potential.' Mainly split logs." Ben laughed. "Neatly arranged, though."

"Generous description, courthouse."

"Loosely applied."

Amused now, Jim said, "Jail ditto, I s'pose?"

"Jail's in Sheriff Burney's cabin. Charges the county two dollars a day for their keep. Got a regular bill of fare. Five dollars to arrest a law-breaker. Four to take him to jail. Receive him into jail, another five. Take him to court, over to Judge Bondurant's logs, four dollars. Etcetera. Etcetera."

"Costly business, bringing an outlaw to justice in Mariposa County."

"Fifty dollars to hang one."

Jim thought a moment. "Bondurant got elected judge? Won out over that damned Georgia cracker? That loudmouth braggin' about sendin' Chero-kees to Oklahoma?"

"Harvey? Well, now that California's got a public trough, reckon Har-vey'll be feedin' from it soon's he can find a space to shoulder up to."

"Not much plus to California bein' a state."

Ben nodded. "Sorry business, ain't it? I'm thinkin' on Oregon. Rather not see what's comin' here." Glanced over the counter again. "Rather not see your bony knees, neither."

Jim looked down, studied the subject. "Reckon they ain't no bonier than the next man's." He winked at Ben. "Mighta been a little drunk. Couple In-dians come in, natural, you know."

"Ain't embarrassed by the way God made 'em, are they?"

"Well, these two said they wanted to 'hide themselves' like white men. Store about empty. All I had was what I was wearin'. My old pants and that red-checked shirt I was partial to. Worth twice its weight in gold, that shirt."

"And then some, I bet," Ben said.

Jim laughed. "I liked that shirt. Weren't givin' it away."

"Ain't likely."

"Anyways, one fella bought my trousers, the other one the shirt off my back. Bein' red-checked makin' up for its *shortage* in other departments."

"Indians ain't particular," Ben agreed. "And they ain't stupid. A lot of our crew realizin' they can dig gold on their own account. Quitin' us."

Jim studied the store's depleted shelves. "Plenty profit in tradin' anyway. Sent most everythin' with Greeley and Kennedy to the Fresno store." He spotted a bottle. "Ah, here we go!"

"Ain't had enough?"

"Mebbe, mebbe not." He fetched down the bottle, opened it. "Could use somethin' to eat. You?"

"What you got?"

"Some jerky somewheres, I think." He looked around, noticed a basket, examined its contents. "Grasshoppers. Eekeno roasts 'em up good."

"Ain't nothin' unworthy of an Indian's stomach."

"Mine neither," Jim said, tilting the bottle into his mouth.

Later, sobered sufficiently to walk without staggering, he wandered around the camp, looked for his wives in the shanty he'd built for them, then in his sleeping tent, briefly tempted by his fine log bed. Smelling smoke, he finally noticed a wispy tendril rising gray against trees not far distant. The warm earth of the trail felt good against his bare feet, the sun on his head suckin' up the cold grief from his insides.

Nothin' gained on lookin' back, no fix for it. What was done was done.

He found Homut tending a small fire while Eekeno swept its smoke into an underground yellow-jacket nest with a hawk's feather. Isabel sat folded into herself in the grass nearby, a spiritless sight. Jim squatted down next to her, waited while the smoke numbed the wasps and Homut exchanged her hawk feather for a digging stick and dug out the grubs for boiling or roasting. Not a specialty he favored. Nor the sight of Isabel grieving.

He stood. No help for the past except the future. "C'mon, girls! Let's take a look at Agua Fria!"

Jim watched Isabel rise, stooped by sorrow, Homut and Eekeno helping her up. She'd survive the loss. What choice did she have? For a moment he regretted gold, California, the whole sad business of witnessin' what his baby blues was lookin' out on. A sudden memory came to him, from boyhood, when his dog died, leavin' six pups. Saw his father drownin' 'em. Saw himself cryin', insistin' through his wailin' he coulda taken care of 'em. California startin' to feel like that, too late to take some other direction. Well, nothin' to be done about what's done. Odd, his thinkin' back on Illinois. If his mother could see him now. That'd be a laugh for her, he thought, lookin' down at the nightshirt or whatever it was he'd found on the store shelf to avoid goin' natural like the Indians. Well, what's done is done, and the best fix is a frolic. He turned and sang out, "Here we go, girls!"

He set off enthusiastically, wives single file behind him. He thought about singing them all across hill and dale, tried to remember the words to 'Frog Went A Courtin',' but couldn't. Settled for thinking they made a pretty good parade, wandering among boulders and scrub oak and pines. And didn't the world smell fine! No perfume better'n pine needles and mountain

air. No better music than the chirp and warble of birdsong. He congratulated himself on his fine idea. A ramble, nothin' better'n a good ramble.
'Ceptin' a frolic, of course.

Seemed no time at all, this ramble, Jim decided, cresting a hill and seeing
a cluster of tents and shacks along the creek. Slouch-hatted miners sloshing
and shoveling, bent beneath disappointment and the back-breaking reality
of gold mining. But he surely approved their industry. Some of that gold
bound to find its way into his pockets—when he got some pockets.

He turned to his wives. "Here we go, girls!" Makin' himself bright as
sunshine he was, forcin' cheer into the bitter cup him and Isabel been
drinkin'. Weren't much, better'n nothin'. Gave himself a grin thinkin' those
words were true enough on seein' ahead what passed for the county seat.
"Agua Fria, girls! Somethin' better'n nothin'!"

Between tossed-up shelters and stores strewn along the creek, he spotted
a raised platform of split logs. He turned to his wives, pointed their attention
to it.

"County courthouse!" As if civilization's makeshift advance should interest them. Or himself, come to that.

They dutifully followed him to the log cabin topped with blue drill and
fronted by a clutter of mining merchandise. "Ain't much," he said over his
shoulder, "but it'll do us better'n nothin'!"

Inside, he announced himself to the surprised proprietor. "Jim Savage."
Stuck out his hand. "Don't believe we've met."

"Brownlee," said the man, a long face beneath heavy brows. He shook
Jim's hand, looked him up and down. And down again.

Jim turned, waved his wives in. "Whatever strikes your fancy, girls. Havin'
us a spree."

He noticed Brownlee's gaze. Laughed. "Already been told my knees ain't
my best feature."

Brownlee shrugged, turned to the women examining his merchandise.

Jim saw Homut pick up an item, turn it one way, then another.

"Tinned sardines," Brownlee said.

"Figure she's mostly likin' the color of the can," Jim said. "Partial to red."

Brownlee joined the women, gestured a hand at his well-stocked shelves.
"Got mustard, cigars, pickled walnuts. Lotsa good things."

Jim watched his wives take interest, enlivened by novelty. Even Isabel.
He suspected José Jésus had planted the future in his daughter more than
she realized. New ways, new things. She had a natural curiosity, couldn't help
bein' interested.

"Whatever they want," he told Brownlee. "I'll be waitin' for 'em over there with that gentleman." A Mexican shuffling cards at a gaming table in the back of the store looked up.

"Three-card monte, *senor,*" he said as Jim pulled up a stool opposite and sat.

"Three-card monte, eh? Prob'ly lose my shirt—" He laughed. "Best not lose the shirt, eh?"

The game, Jim knew, was a guaranteed losing proposition. And didn't care. Sorrow to kill and gold to spare. And skill to admire, he thought, watching the Mexican's sleight of hand as every wrong turn of the card cost Jim a pinch of gold from the buckskin bag he wore hanging against his hip like a pistol.

As they played, the man's story drifted out. One of Fremont's old crew, making a living best he could now, he said, since the state decided to tax any miner not a natural-born citizen of the United States. "Tax twenty dollars, *senor,* every month."

"Ain't right," Jim replied, shaking his head. "First lesson in minin' is paydirt's mostly dirt, damned little pay. Government unclear on things out here in the mines. Must be figurin' prosperity'd be a burden on you. Relievin' you of it. Charitable." Stupid law, he thought. Most miners barely made expenses. Add another twenty dollars every month to the cost of the enterprise, the state will lose a miner, gain a gambler. Or worse, a robber. A man couldn't readily dig an extra twenty dollars like early times.

"Most of the easy gold got picked up in forty-eight, the rest in fortynine," he said. "These days, three years into the business, thousands and thousands of prospectors diggin' dirt less and less profitable."

"Si, senor, es verdad."

Jim turned over another losing card. Shrugged. "Government sadly inclined to favor its own people, *amigo.* Tax the foreigners, not the citizens." As if they weren't all of 'em foreigners. Ask any Indian.

"Senor, the French, Chileans, China men, come from other countries. I was born here. How am I a foreigner?"

"Don't let the door smack your backside."

"Senor?"

"Sorry, friend. Bad joke."

When Brownlee pulled up a stool, Jim pulled open his buckskin bag. "Got 'em loaded up?"

Brownlee licked a pencil. "One more of anything likely break the camel's back, as the saying has it. Some red blankets took their eye." He jotted a number. "A few bolts of calico. Several articles of clothing." He laughed.

"Guess they figured you wouldn't object to some trousers." He totaled up the bill. "Also a number of fancy goods, looking-glasses, too, just in from San Francisco. Chinese shipment."

Jim didn't blink at the tab. Seventy-five dollars. Not much of a spree, Agua Fria. Then it struck him. Take 'em to San Francisco! Show 'em a real city! Now, that'd be a frolic!

James Savage, who owned two trading posts on the Fresno and Mariposa, and possessed great influence over the tribes, took some of the chiefs to San Francisco to receive a salutary impression of paleface strength....

—*History of California, Vol. VI*
H. H. Bancroft Co.

ISABEL GRIPPED THE SIDE of the rattling canvas-topped wagon Jim had cheerily announced as Maurison's Express. Homut clutched the wooden slats of the seat they shared. The journey seemed interminable, jouncing and jolting over the rutted road, the heat and dust suffocating. Isabel rolled up the canvas side curtains to catch the breeze, rolled them down to avoid the dust raised by the horses, then up again. She stared unseeing at the bouncing countryside to avoid looking at Bautista and José Juarez sitting opposite. She sensed the two chiefs' injured dignity. Hauled like flour barrels, all of them.

All of them aware fate had entwined them with this one white man.

Jim wanted a good future for her, she believed that. Like her father, Jim wanted her to learn new ways that she might live in the changed world. She trusted him, as her father had. 'He has a good heart.' Her father's voice in memory. The chiefs respected Jim, although she knew they openly suspected El Rey Tularenos possessed less influence with white men than he claimed. And Homut simply wanted to be with him.

Isabel's thoughts wandered. Loss engulfed her. How would José Jesús have counseled his people had he known white men would murder them? Murder him? Why had Great Spirit permitted the People to be slaughtered? Stomped like snakes. What had they done? Again, her father's voice: 'Heed me, Isabel, and grow old.' They can't kill us all. His spirit speaking? Or hers?

Maybe white people could kill them all, with guns and sickness and overwhelming numbers. White people, as her father had warned, continued coming and coming and coming. Miners by the thousands muddied the rivers with their digging, and the fish went away. The people were hungry. Settlers scattered the game, frightened deer from the land.

The chiefs had grown angry and talked war. El Rey Tularenos must help them kill the invading white men before white men killed them. Jim insisted that all the Yokuts tribes together, Potoyensees, Chauchilas, Yosemites, could never defeat the white men. He would show them why. Isabel must see, too, he said, and tell Chief Teneiya.

And now, with no more choice than the horses pulling them, they were going wherever this white man decided to take them.

In Stockton, at the steamboat landing on the San Joaquin, Maurison deposited them into a noisy crowd jostling for berths aboard the two steamboats leaving that evening for San Francisco. "You want the *Sagamore*," he told Jim. "Tickets three dollars cheaper than the *El Dorado* and no fleas."

The huge, river-churning, whistle-shrieking steamboat puzzled Isabel. Why were white people in such a rush to move from one place to another, and make such noise doing it? The People's boats, *kano'wa*, formed from bundles of tule, sat on water as delicately and silent as birds. Why didn't the white men look? See how the People lived gently on the land, respected its spirit? White people didn't know how to live properly. She fell asleep in the noisy belly of the steamboat imagining them leaving.

Next morning, the *Sagamore* chuffed from the river into a huge bay shrouded by fog. Isabel, on deck, peered into the lifting cool gray curtain, stunned by the sight of a slowly rocking forest of masts. Ships beyond counting rolled silent and deserted on the water. So this was how the white people had been coming and coming and coming. On ships, these abandoned ships, these naked masts testimony to the invasion.

The white people weren't leaving.

Overhead, wheeling gulls cried as the dispersing fog revealed the shoreline beyond the ships. Brick buildings came into view, wooden buildings, a crowding eruption of buildings shouldered together at the shore's edge. Beyond them, hundreds more blistered the hillsides.

The white man's rancheria.

Jim appeared suddenly at her side with the chiefs, pointing, directing their attention. "See those roads comin' off the hills, right on down like they was runnin' into the water?"

They did.

"And see those boats with machines on top?"

They did. The loudly pounding machines emitted white smoke, like the steamboat.

"Giant steam hammers," Jim said.

They watched the machines pounding denuded pine trees into the water.

"Extendin' the wharves for more boats, more supplies. More people."

Isabel and the chiefs stared, silent.

Savage drove home the lesson. "For more white people."

At the foot of Montgomery street, the *Sagamore* disgorged its passengers into the noisy, crowded stink of Central Wharf. Rotting debris, floating below on a receding tide, released its stench into the jostling commotion of the shouting, milling throng. Isabel's thoughts flew to Awani's sheltering serenity, to its quiet, to its sweet-scented cedar. Homut looked frightened. The chiefs stared into the distance, impassive. Isabel supposed mission Indians learned early to mask grievance with indifference.

"Mr. Savage! Mr. Savage! Over here, sir! Over here!" A short man in a top hat detached himself from the stream of people to grab Jim Savage's hand and shake it excitedly. "Washington Bartlett, sir! With the *Journal of Commerce*. Copy for you, sir," he said, thrusting a newspaper at Savage. "All the latest celebration plans!"

Jim laughed. "Mister, I don't read newspapers, nor nothin' else, don't know nothin' about a celebration, and don't recall we've met."

Isabel saw a woman wrapped in a grape-colored cape glance from beneath a stiff straw bonnet at Homut, then at her, then each in turn again, quickly looking away. Isabel stared after her. The woman had sniffed, raised her nose, as if she and Homut were the bad smell. Throngs of people looked right through them as if they didn't exist, ignoring even the chiefs. Bautista and José Juarez, not chiefs here. Ghosts. Ghosts. They were all ghosts in this place.

"Oh, we haven't met, no, sir. But everyone's heard about the king of the Indians. You got a reputation, sir, preceding you. Description, too. Recognize you anywhere, especially with your friends here, of course." He nodded at Homut, Isabel, the chiefs. "Yes, sir, you're halfway famous!"

"Halfway, you say?" Jim put one arm around Homut, the other around Isabel, beaming at Bartlett in his top hat while the crowd surged around them.

"Well, now, probably the whole way after I write up your visit," Bartlett said. "Figured you were here for the celebratin' like everyone else."

"Always keen on celebratin'. What kind you got, Mr. Bartlett?"

"Why statehood, sir! Pacific Mail steamship *Oregon* came in last week with the news. Covered in flags, fired her guns. Town went wild, spontaneous jubilation. Pistols and bonfires. Insufficient for the occasion, of course. Officials put their heads together for a proper celebration and today's the day! Festivities commencing in the plaza at eleven o'clock, sir!"

"It's a frolic? That what you're sayin'?"

Isabel felt the pier rock beneath her, grasped Jim's arm. He caught her. "Dizzy," she said.

He smiled, reassuring. "Boat did it. It'll go."

"Yes, sir, you could call it a frolic. Good word." Bartlett took a small notebook from his pocket. "Like to interview you for my paper while you're here, Mr. Savage, if you've time."

"Plannin' on showin' my friends the sights. Come on along! Ask your questions!"

Isabel recognized the signs, the familiar grin, the sudden strut in his step. Homut had noticed, too. They exchanged unhappy glances. A frolic.

"Excellent! Then, first question. Could you say how many Indians are under your immediate jurisdiction?"

"Why, sure thing! Let's say fifteen thousand, Mr. Bartlett. Yep, there you go, fifteen thousand. Give or take." Jim laughed, arms around Homut and Isabel, a nod to the silent chiefs. "Sounds about right."

Bartlett, leading them toward Montgomery street, looked back over his shoulder. "And, Mr. Savage, when did you first go to live with the Indians?"

"Why, I was just a little tucker," Jim replied, stopping to arrange serious thinking on his face. "Indians robbed me from my poor ol' mammy and pappy," he added solemnly. "I'd say, thinkin' on it, Mr. Bartlett, I musta been about six." He paused, rubbed his chin. "Yep, I'd say I was about six years old."

Joining the crowd on Montgomery street, Bartlett directed their attention to the red, white, and blue bunting hanging from every building, American flags fluttering from every staff. Better than a frolic, Jim thought, this huge, noisy crowd. A city celebrating its permanence. Serving his purpose. Showing the chiefs Americans had moved in, claimed the country. Made it a state. Good or bad, a done deal.

"Been some changes since I last seen the place," he said.

"I expect so, sir," Bartlett said. "City keeps burning down. Rises up afterward like the Phoenix from its ashes, improved by each conflagration. You're seeing a revised edition, you might say, new issue."

To Isabel, San Francisco was like nothing ever imagined. Stacked buildings. Bricks. Iron doors. Planked roads crowded by carriages and carts and people, people, people. Everywhere people, hurrying, pushing, shouting. A disturbed wasps' nest of buzzing, swarming people. The white man's rancheria. Jim was showing them the future.

Isabel and Homut, numbed by the noise and activity, stared silently wherever Bartlett led. The chiefs maintained their dignified indifference. Bartlett, an enthusiastic guide, read out the signboards swinging above the boardwalks or nailed to building fronts. He announced them like performances. "Wholesaler! Boardinghouse! Alehouse! Printer and Engraver! City hall!"

In front of an open door, he exclaimed, "Daguerreotypes!" He urged them inside, toured them, to their amazement, through a gallery festooned with pictures of tiny paper people, their staring eyes wide and lifeless and flat.

They examined the miniature scenes, the dead eyes of the camera's captives. "Fancy word, daguerreotype," Jim said. "Frenchy." Downed a complementary drink the proprietor offered. "Pretty good brandy cocktail," he said, wiping his lips. "Enjoyed seein' your dagger-types." Pretty good frolic. Dagger-types.

Back on the street, more signboards. Theatre, haberdasher, bank, post office, oyster house, law offices, grocer, reading rooms, confectionery. "Three stories," Bartlett bragged, pointing to a new brick building as if he'd built it. "You won't see anything else as tall as that in California," he said, turning to Isabel.

She said nothing. No one in this buzzing hive could possibly imagine Awani's towering trees and cloud-crowned granite heights where cranes nested and rivers leapt. How could they?

For the parade, Bartlett elbowed them through people thronging the plaza. "Make room, folks. It's Mr. Savage. Come in special to astonish the natives."

Jim bowed and preened. "Quite a crowd," he said, turning to Bartlett. "City grown some, ain't it?"

"Just had us a census," Bartlett said. "Twenty-one thousand residents."

Jim turned to the chiefs, repeated, "Twenty-one thousand residents." Did they understand the implication? Wooden as trees, both of them.

The military commenced the parade with a loudly bursting artillery salute. Homut and Isabel fell back as if shot. Bystanders laughed at them. Next came the thunderous firing of a cannon. Isabel covered her ears against its roar.

With the cannon's boom still reverberating, the crowd burst into wild cheers as a flag with thirty-one silver stars was run up the giant pole on the plaza. Jim shouted at Bartlett over the din, "Not generally keen on back-pattin', but for puttin' on a show, well, can't beat Americans. Regular whoop-dee-doo!"

Isabel hardly knew where to look. Bartlett provided an eager commentary for the spectacle. "In the blue sash, on the white horse, that's the Grand Marshall," he said, pointing, "and riding behind him are the native Californians, organized themselves at Mission Dolores. Could have turned out seventy-five more had they not been disappointed in horses."

Jim laughed, turned to the chiefs. "Californians short on horses! Figure some misbehavin' Indians was raidin' 'em while they gussied up for a parade?" But then he turned to Bartlett, his voice low, and said, "Friend, the real native Californians, they're standin' right here, ain't they? Ain't in the parade. Ain't never gonna be celebratin' this statehood business, not the real native Californians."

He turned his suddenly sober attention back to the parade. "You go on, Mr. Bartlett. Tell us what we got here, these struttin' fellas in fancy uniforms."

"Well, that's our recently organized California Guards, and marching behind them are various dignitaries, customhouse officers, collector of the port, foreign counsels— representatives from Germany, France, England, Italy, Spain."

"That so?" Savage said, folding his arms and adopting a posture Isabel thought approved the occasion, as if he'd remembered his purpose.

"Need to make notes for my newspaper," Bartlett said, taking his notebook from his pocket, and writing. He looked up a moment later to say the passing division of fifty sailors were from U.S. vessels of war.

Jim turned to the chiefs and solemnly repeated, "U.S. vessels of war." Weren't stupid, the chiefs. Wouldn't be missin' the implication. Lordy, what a day! Regular school in session here for teachin' the hard facts of life. Sorry to be showin' these Indians their future. Forget bows and arrows, fellas. New world. Vessels of war. White man's weapons. He looked back at the parade. Could use another brandy cocktail, he could.

Bartlett identified the passing uniformed officers as members of the police department. Musical bands and more civic dignitaries followed, all the marchers carrying banners. Bartlett scribbled in his notebook and read aloud as he wrote, "The St. Francis Hook and Ladder Company tastefully decorated their carriage with an abundance of flowers, banners, and evergreens." He turned to Isabel. "Very fine, isn't it?"

Isabel stared at the lifeless flowers wilting on the flag-draped carriage slowly wheeling past. She thought of Awani, its meadow alive with flowers. Why did white people put dying flowers on parade and call it fine?

Four horses pulling a carriage with a boat on it came next. Jim looked at Bartlett. "Reckon my friends appreciate you readin' that banner for 'em. A boat on a carriage somewhat confusin'."

Bartlett obliged. "The Watermen of San Francisco—United We Pull More Effective Strokes."

"Don't reckon that'll help none," Jim said, returning his attention to the parade. "And what've we got here?!" he asked, as the crowd burst into applause. Behind a huge crimson banner marched fifty men in silk tunics carrying colorful umbrellas.

"Our Celestials," Bartlett said, scribbling in his notebook. "China boys made a fine turn-out."

"Stole the show," Jim said as a sudden explosion of firecrackers snapped the air. "Ain't likely to get better'n that."

More musicians marched past, and then another fire brigade came into view with a ladder extended above the carriage. Tied to its top rung was a young eagle. "Captured at the mission," Bartlett said. "Imagine that, catching an eagle. Just in time for the celebration. An eagle!" The crowd whistled and hollered and enthusiastically applauded the eagle.

Isabel thought she might be sick. An eagle. Tied to a ladder. Paraded. The chiefs looked away. Jim said, "I think we've seen enough."

They had. Isabel feared the bound, dishonored eagle was an omen.

Bartlett led them into the nearby El Dorado. "More like a palace than a gambling hall," he bragged, pushing open the door into a noisy crowd of dealers and gamblers. "Take a look! Flaming chandeliers gorgeously fitted out. Gilt-framed paintings. Marble-topped bar long as a boat. Fancy mirror big as the wall. And every kind of game! Faro, roulette, thimble-rig, three-card monte!"

"Now we're havin' us a frolic!" Savage said, leading the chiefs to where six smartly outfitted bar-keeps poured from extravagant decanters they fetched from an array behind the bar, the sparkling rainbow of bottled spirits reflected in the gilded mirror. "Me and my friends got dry seein' the sights," he told a promptly attentive barkeep. "Could use us some brandy cocktails!"

Bartlett led Isabel and Homut to chairs at a nearby table, brought them sarsaparillas, continued to praise the room engulfed by cigar smoke and noise. As servers passed with trays of drinks summoned by dealers ringing golden bells, he pointed out the hundred baize-covered tables piled with coins and thronged with gamblers. Musicians bent intent to stringed instruments barely heard. Germans, Bartlett said. The pretty woman dealing cards was from France.

Isabel watched her pick up a stack of coins and casually spill them from one blue-gloved hand to the other and back again. For a moment they caught one another's eye, but the woman looked away, tossed her curls, laughed, measured a stack of coins.

Homut and Isabel heard Jim enjoying his frolic, his voice rising above the din from time to time. The crowd around him applauded when he clambered up on a baize-covered gaming table and loudly, laughingly, drunkenly bet his weight in gold on the turn of a card.

Later, much later, Isabel tried to remember if that was the moment she felt suddenly ill. Or if it was when the boy burst through the door and hollered, "*Sagamore* exploded!"

Bartlett had grabbed his hat and run out the door. Homut had turned to her, alarmed by the tumult of excitement. "Boat explode?! Like China firecrackers?! White man machines kill people?!"

Isabel had felt faint. Was Homut crying, "We are dead! We are dead!" Or was she? Or thinking it when they heard a sudden commotion where Jim was gambling? Terrified, she and Homut joined the crush of onlookers surrounding the scene. José Juarez lay motionless on the floor. Jim stood over him, unsteady, rubbing his knuckles. Chief Bautista, a witness, staring at Jim, stone-silent, stone-faced.

Bartlett got them all to a hotel, and early the next morning they boarded the little sidewheel-steamer *Georgiana*. Isabel and Homut, stunned, kept reliving the scene in the El Dorado. Like seeing an eagle tied and paraded atop the ladder, it seemed unthinkable. No one was saying why Jim hit José Juarez. Did anyone know? A gambling loss? Too much brandy? An insult? A reprimand? It didn't matter. No one hit a chief. The People never struck one another.

The chiefs spoke to no one. Jim, as if the incident hadn't happened, again pointed out the sights, the ships, the machines, the tall buildings and long wharves. He introduced the captain, who assured them of his ship's safety. "No danger aboard the *Georgiana*," he boasted. "Built for the Aspinwall Steam Transportation Line in Philadelphia. Knocked down and sent by sea to San Francisco. Brought her out myself."

"That so?" said Jim, as if this were the most interesting news of the day.

"Yes, sir. Launched her here in April. Pioneered the route from Stockton up the San Joaquin River."

Isabel wasn't listening. What did it matter? They were aboard, captive again. They were going wherever white men took them. What choice did they have? As the steamboat churned away from the wharf, she remembered the *Sagamore* and thought she saw body parts floating in the bay. She leaned over the rail and retched.

Later, downstairs with Homut in the little sidewheel steamer's overheated galley, she stared at the tin plate of food in front of her. Homut urged her to eat, but the stifling steamer's motion and passenger chatter made her ill. Such noise. An incessant clatter of forks against tin plates, cups bumping and banging the wooden table. And the overpowering cloud of food smell.

Her head spun. The steward, a large and smiling man, skin dark as charcoal against the white of his apron, poured coffee while she clutched the table's edge and stared at the plate. "Them's slapjacks, ma'am," he said. "Gots lotsa butter and syrup on 'em. They's good."

She fled up the galley stairs to retch over the rail again.

Eventually the nightmare trip ended wharfside in Stockton, and she, feeling little better, was sitting with Homut once again in Maurison's stage. The impatient driver was tugging at his long gloves, horses restless in their traces, while Jim searched the crowd for the chiefs. They had melted into the mayhem of milling passengers jostling to board, vanishing like night into morning. She had seen them stoic and silent among the bustle and noise, there one moment, gone the next. She understood. She desperately wanted to be elsewhere, home, Awani. With Seethkil, Loiya, and warm acorn soup.

Jim finally clambered aboard and the driver started his horses toward Mariposa. At first, as the stage jolted past the town's bustling enterprises, Jim half-heartedly directed their inattention to various hotels and boatworks, a foundry, a bank. Before long, he lapsed into a morose silence and they all fixed their eyes on the bouncing countryside. There was little to see besides dust drifting across the withered grasses of late summer, the view an unrelieved shimmer of heat, the parched country silent beneath it. No one spoke when they took a quick meal at a stage stop, Isabel sating hunger with salty bacon and half-cooked beans.

When the stage finally delivered them to the Mariposa store, Homut disappeared into the wives' cabin. Isabel went behind a nearby oak and quietly retched. Jim threw open the store's door, said to no one in particular, "Weren't much of a frolic," and proceeded to drink himself into a stupor.

The next morning, seeing Isabel in her corner, Jim hunkered down opposite in their old way. "You seem kinda what my mamma called 'peaky,'" he said.

She could smell the previous night's 'frolic' wafting from him, and his eyes were red. She looked at him a long time, saying nothing, and felt a tear trail her cheek. "I want to go home."

"I seen it," he said softly, "how things are. Seen it afore." He didn't want to remember. But there it was. Again. Eliza in the early days, saying it was no matter, early morning sickness. She would be fine she kept saying, and for a time, when they commenced the journey, with the prairie grass tall and the oxen stout, she was. Not strong enough in the end, though. Too fine a lady, filled with fancies and youth, and keen for a young mountain man with eyes the color of flowers, baby-blue-eyes. He could see her now, leaning against their wagon, laughing, clasping her calico bonnet from a surprise breeze and tying the strings beneath her pretty chin. "Jimmy, I'll be fine, just fine. Don't you worry. Women been doing this birthing business from the beginning of time, most natural thing on earth." And she'd playfully tossed her skirt in a kind of dance, to show him it was nothing, nothing at all. Except the sun got hotter and the trip longer and harder and it turned out that the birthin' business was not 'nothin' at all.'

"I want to go home," Isabel repeated, and reached her hand out to touch his knee and bring him back from the far place she saw he had gone.

He started, as if surprised to find himself where he was, sitting on a plank floor in a ramshackle frontier store with a sad-eyed Indian girl. And not doin' right by her, that was the thing, weren't it, not by a long shot. Her father murdered, and him, her father's trusted friend, thinkin' a frolic to San Francisco some kind of consolation, and how had that gone, there was a question to ask the jury.

Isabel looked at him, and thought, through her tears, he seemed as saddened by circumstance as she was. The two of them, they weren't that different, when she considered it. Both of them simply sharing what fate delivered, hoping for a fortunate future, that was all. Two people trying to 'live long.'

Jim shook his head as if to clear it, and looked at her wonderingly. Who was this girl? What was happening to her? What was she doing here, with him? Did he even know himself? He took her hand in his, and said, "Isabel, I promised your father I'd protect you. Not sure I can do that. Ain't got much history in that regard, and not much conviction on it anyhow. You seen what the chiefs seen. I wanted to put the scare into 'em, show 'em what's what. Ain't good." Why was he telling her this? Like he had thoughts leakin' out his head, and none of 'em useful, and they was flowin' right outta his mouth into her ears. Some kind of protector he was turnin' out to be.

"My father said you were a good white man."

Jim shrugged, half laughed. "Always wanted to be an Indian, you know." He was inclined to tell her how he'd run away as a boy to live with the Sauk and Fox, and why. But it was a long story, and likely only alarm her. Maybe someday. Maybe someday.

"Livin' with Indians when I was a trapper, I learned to sleep little and eat less. I learned from them to run a hundred miles, then sit and laugh for hours over a campfire as fresh and lively as if we'd been takin' a little walk for exercise. I loved it, livin' like Indians, in the real world, not boxed up like white people in houses. I loved the mystery of nighttime, owls hootin', the sudden silence of night creatures disturbed from huntin'. Scamperin' sounds. Somethin' magic about starlight, moonlight, shadowed boulders and trees. Most of all, I liked night trackin', down on my hands and knees sometimes, feelin' the earth, smellin' it."

Isabel nodded. "Learning the earth. *I-Chow.*"

"Turtle," he said.

She felt tears start, bent her head. "I miss my people." She felt bereft beyond telling, missing her father, Awani, Yuloni, making acorn with Victoria, being Di-shi waking from sleep wrapped in her rabbit fur, opening her eyes to the leaked gray light of morning and the tumbling river singing down the mountainside.

Jim stood, pulled her up, looked into her eyes, resisted a sudden surprising impulse to hold her close, hold her hard. She was takin' his heart. "Go home, Isabel. Take Girl, and go home."

Isabel told them all—Teneiya, Loiya, everyone—what she had seen. Described the white man's great rancheria, the war ships, everything.

Only Seethkil believed her.

They had sat on a log together watching children at play in the meadow where one day their child would run. She picked up a twig and drew a large circle in the dirt and scattered a handful of leaves into it. "Water filled with big boats, like forest filled with trees," she explained. With the twig, she drew lines into the circle, next to several leaves. "White men build trails on water, walk from boat to rancheria on top of water."

Seethkil leaned forward, studied her drawing. "Like bridge over river."

She took his hand and held it to her cheek, loving his cleverness, and the touch of him. She loved him for trusting she spoke truth about thumping machines pounding trees into water. He believed her, all of it, believed white men could make war with huge gunships, stack buildings on top of other buildings, parade boats on land, tie an eagle to a ladder.

Bad dreams, the Awanichee women said, with pitying eyes and mumbled misgivings. Captive eagle atop a ladder paraded through a white man's giant rancheria? Gambling palace where a woman with blue hands dealt cards? Bad dream. Crimson banners and gilded mirrors? Marching boat? Exploding boat? Floating body pieces?! They chanted prayers over her, gathered twigs and roots to brew ancient remedies against bad dreams. Sometimes she doubted her own memory. How was it possible to imprison eagle? Eagle was chief of the First People!

One night, soon after she returned to Awani, her old dream came back. Again she felt herself standing on the edge of the world, deserted, desolate. The People gone. "Di-shi! Di-shi!" her mother called. "Di-shi! Di-shi!" Now her dream included three white strangers. Wizards. Coming to destroy the People with wizard power. Wizards carrying magic paper to take the People from their world and put them into boxes. And then time that had been became time yet to come and she saw that a great water covered the place where People had lived, a familiar place, a great valley beyond Awani, and a great sucking from the west drank the water.

"Di-shi! Di-shi!" Not her mother's voice now. Outside, a child's voice, laughing, playing. Outside, a throaty blue jay called and a village child called back. *"Di-shi!"* Little blue jay.

Dreaming again, and now awake, back in the real world. And frightened.

Seethkil, lying beside her, after hearing her dream, soothed her. "Coyote messenger. Sometimes bad message, sometimes good."

She had slept on a coyote skin pillow. She sat up, turned and stared at it, remembering. "Three white wizards taking the People from the land. Or the land from the People, I'm not sure."

Seethkil rose, suddenly angry. "White men take anything they want. Take gold from our land. Why not our land, too?!"

She looked up at him. "Not Awani. No gold here. Why take this land?"

"White men take everything."

"Not all white men," she said. "Remember the white man named Sam I spoke about? He wanted only to trade words, learn our language. And tell me stories of the world he had seen, and long-ago times he read about in books. He told me about my mission name, said Isabel was a queen in a faraway place who sent an adventurer west, a white man named Columbus. The long robes followed him. They gave me her name."

She rose, took Seethkil's hand. "Remember Kennedy? The store agent who invites children to touch his red hair? To show it isn't on fire? And Jim Savage? Jim isn't a bad man."

"You said he hit a chief!"

She wished she hadn't. She had two lives now and, not by choice, moccasins in two worlds. Seethkil wouldn't understand that sometimes she missed the world outside, so different, so filled with things to learn, to understand. And sometimes missed Jim, her Woochi friend in the white man's world. She touched Seethkil's face. How she loved him.

She decided not to share dreams that frightened her and angered him. They were two, together, a child soon joining them in the world. And if white men came into Awani like the long-ago black sickness, they would go to the Monos until Great Spirit returned the People to the land created for them.

That day and those that followed, Isabel chose to keep her own counsel. She gathered acorns, danced with the women, sang to the child within her— and didn't question how often Seethkil and his brothers left Awani. Or where they went. Or why.

He speaks sixteen of their languages, besides English, Spanish, and a little French. Nevertheless, all the tribes have not been willing to recognize his authority…

—Etienne Derbec
Coarsegold, October 1850

ON THE TRAIL from Mariposa to his Fresno store, riding a bad-broke horse on a too-hot day, he heard Eliza saying, "It's the Lord's punishment, Jim Savage, the Lord's punishment." But he'd buried Eliza, didn't give religion much account, and punishment, well, who knew? He'd take a hot day and a bad-broke horse, count himself lucky. Anyone asked, had to say he weren't a man to look back. No point in it. Clocks didn't go backward. Horses couldn't run backwards. And life for sure didn't. What he had in his head, besides Eliza's voice, was guilt, punishment enough. He'd hit José Juarez. Knocked him down. A hundred witnesses. Couldn't say why he done it. Didn't know. Didn't remember anything from that whole El Dorado spree before seeing one chief on the floor and the other one looking at him bad.

His mother would've said, 'Well, what's done is done.' But it weren't, and he knew it.

Horse twitchy, shyin' at every rabbit on the run, spooked. Gave Isabel the good horse, Girl. Isabel in his thoughts, too. Hopin' she'd keep Chief Teneiya and his Yosemites out of this trouble. Missed seein' her in her corner, though. Well, she seen enough 'new ways.' Hadn't they all?

A couple hours' thinkin' along a dusty trail under a hot sun had his head all over the place, and tryin' to get it on straight was comin' to somethin' of a challenge. A bad-broke horse and a hot day weren't no drop in the old oaken bucket. Drop in the bucket, that'd be welcome. No rain in months, none looked to be comin'. Only thing comin', if Eekeno was right, was Indian trouble. Fresno store, she'd said, that's where the talk was comin' from. And skedaddled on account of it. Convincin' behavior on her part, he'd decided. Enough to warrant investigatin' whatever might be happenin' on the Fresno. As if he didn't have enough Indian trouble already. He'd hit an Indian, a chief. Wished José Juarez had hit him. Less trouble in it. Both of 'em too liquored up to stand, truth be told. He'd done some recollectin' on that, come around to rememberin' José Juarez so drunk he'd got himself in a heat over somethin' or another, not that he didn't have cause enough for gettin' riled. Seein' his world comin' apart. A gander at San Francisco not improvin' the view. No way to put things back the way they was.

"Hit José Juarez, I did," he told the horse. "A chief." Nothin' favorable in the observation. Horse still twitchy. Himself the same.

Back-trackin' in his head weren't his way, but here he was hard at it, mind wanderin' all over the place. Somethin' had got him into recollectin' his last trappin' rendezvous. What was it? Some Frenchy word the French trappers used? "Hey, horse!" The horse had shied, like it had seen something, then changed its mind. Twitchy horse, corral full of them, no end to skittish. Half broke, half wild. Like the Indians, come to that. What was that Frenchy word? Name for somethin' familiar as memory, except not a memory, just felt like it. Ah, sure. *Déjà vu.* That was it. *Déjà vu.*

Well, nothin' familiar in him hittin' an Indian. Still couldn't figure how it happened, maybe he just wanted to hit someone and the chief was handy? That would be somethin' to think on. Him no better a white man than the next. But why was he thinkin' hittin' an Indian felt familiar? Not the doin' of it, that weren't it. More like hearin' on it.

Hearin' about an Indian gettin' hit. That was it. What triggered that old memory?

"Kinda feel like we're followin' a trap-line, horse, like the old days, lookin' to find an old memory 'stead of beaver." The bad-broke, no-name horse whickered. "Got any ideas, speak up. But I'm thinkin' mighta been that newspaper fella askin' how I come to live with the Indians. Illinois a long time back but a boy don't forget, you know. That'd be where it come from, I bet. Me and the Sauk. Started one day when the settlers went to fortin' up. 'Indians comin',' Pa said. I asked why. That was me, always askin' why. Pa said a farmer in LaSalle hit an Indian and fired 'em up. I asked why."

The horse prob'ly needed some instruction on that point. "Boys always askin' why. Anyways, Indian broke a hole in the settler's dam. Why? Let the fish through. Why'd the settler stop the fish? Didn't care about fish, wanted to water his crops."

Remembered now how he'd told his pa it weren't fair what happened to the Sauk, and his pa hit him for sassin'. Or for maybe bein' handy. But there it was. Illinois settler dammed a river to water crops, a hungry Sauk Indian opened it to let the fish through. Settler hit the Indian, Indian hit back. Then a lot of people died. And a boy ran away and Indians took him in.

One thing leadin' to another, could lead anywhere. Eliza liked to read aloud from that almanac book she admired. He remembered the bit she used to repeat for most everythin' what took her attention: 'for want of a nail a shoe was lost; for want of a shoe the horse was lost; for want of a horse the rider was lost.'

Truth there, that much certain. Well, thinkin' on Illinois, had that in his head today, he did. "Prairie storms, horse, you shoulda seen 'em. Sky filled to boilin' miles off, black as night, like the wrath of God comin' straight at you and nowheres to hide."

Supposed Black Hawk felt that way when the Illinois militia caught up to him and his band at Bad Axe River. Like the wrath of God had found them, and no place to hide.

Informin' the horse how it was. "Militia put an end to the so-called Black Hawk war with a gunboat. Hundreds of Sauk and Potawatomi men, women, and children killed. Nowhere to run. Tribes already pushed west, just wanted to come home. Galena lead discovered and, naturally, white men wanted it. Push the Indians west. Take their land. Mine the lead."

Well, nothin' new under the sun. Gunboat. Vessels of war. His mind all over the place today.

"Coulda tol' that newspaper man about the Sauk, and Black Hawk, Illinois gettin' settlers, the lead in Galena, come to that. How it weren't fair and I'd run off with the Sauk, learned their ways. Fox, too. Arapaho, Potawatomi, Cheyenne, all of 'em pushed west. Done run out of west. Don't 'spect that would interest folks, though."

The horse didn't seem particularly interested either. And here it was, all over again, only worse. No west to push the Indians to, gold instead of lead, same old story. New country, old story. Enough to wear a body out, thinkin' on how it ain't fair, never gonna get fair. He'd showed José Juarez his future, which ain't fair, ain't got a chance on fair, not with the white man havin' 'vessels of war' and Indians havin' sharp rocks on sticks.

How to make 'em understand they can't win, that it ain't worth their tryin'. Damn, he wished he had a barrel of brandy cocktails, he'd jump in. Some days ain't enough brandy cocktails.

Déjà vu, could be that. Ran off with the Sauk and learned their ways and their lingo and watched 'em lose land, food, face, and future. Chased beaver, chased the west, and what did he catch? Gold fever. Weren't that a kick in the pants, though? All the gold in the world, and nothin' worth gettin' with it except drunk. Hit an Indian. Can't make that right. Couldn't make his own head right either. Couldn't keep this business from blowin' up like a steamboat.

The Fresno store was busy. Indians inside and outside the store today. Indians gathered up all around, looked to Jim Savage, anyone care to ask, that the Indians was just gossipin', smokin', idlin'. Didn't look like no trouble, not far as he could see. Congratulated himself, though, on the prosperous location. Southern mines provin' rich and settlers comin' into the area paid the store's rates, regardless. Saved 'em a trip to Mariposa. Kennedy and Greeley had hired on two new clerks to handle all the business.

Behind the counter, Kennedy, selling a shovel to a new miner, assured Jim everything there was okay. "Only Indian activity we got is just the usual trading. Gold for blankets, shirts, raisins, beads. No problems." He hesitated, scratched his chin under his red beard, thought a minute. "Heard about a little set-to over in Quartzburg, though. Kaweahs confronting some settlers, wanting toll or tribute or something to let them pass through their land. And I suppose you heard a fellow name of Moore got himself killed not far from Mariposa. Nothing out of the ordinary."

Jim considered. It wasn't like Eekeno to pass along a rumor, and then leave. "Looks like plenty of Indians around the store today," he said, still unsure.

"Several chiefs, actually. Ponwatchee's here with some of his Nukchus. José Rey with any number of Chauchilas. Bautista's here. José Juarez. And you must be makin' friends with Isabel's people. Three Yosemites come in. Didn't trade, but looked at those Hudson Bay blankets she likes. Other Indians out there I haven't seen before heard about my curly red mop. Come in to see my hair. Indians can't get enough red. I'm a regular fascination in that department."

"Think I'll have a smoke with 'em."

Outside, Savage squatted under a tree behind the store, filled a pipe, waited. His presence always attracted attention. He was El Rey Tularenos. José Juarez soon joined him, said nothing, squatted down with his own pipe, passed it to José Rey who passed it to Tomkit and Frederico, secondary Chauchila leaders. Others drifted in, enlarged the gathering to Savage's satisfaction. His words would travel back to their villages, and the message advance among them. After a time, he rose, stretched his arms wide, invited listeners in, launched his address.

"My friends, it is good this day to talk. Much to say. I come with friendship to say I hear bad talk about Indians making war. You know I am your brother and speak truth. War is much bad thinking. White men too many to fight. If war comes, they cannot be defeated. José Juarez saw the white man's big city. White men there like ants, beyond counting. If you make war on white diggers their many brothers will come from everywhere against you.

From other mining places they will come. From the big city they will come. They will destroy every tribe that makes war against any white men. Their numbers are great, beyond counting. You must live in peace or you will die. My friend José Juarez traveled there with me. He will tell you what he saw, the white man's great weapons, cannons and vessels of war."

Savage mopped sweat from his neck with his bandana. Ignored the incessant heat. Ignored the silent stares. Rode his message like a bad-broke horse, determined. Pressed forward. Tribal languages required repetition. Indian lore achieved permanence through repetition and so he admonished his silently staring witnesses, cautioned them, repeated the advantages of peace, the dangers of war. Finally, he urged their attention on the chief who had seen with his own eyes the great numbers of white men, the chief who could confirm the futility of war.

He turned to José Juarez, sitting hunkered with his pipe. "Tell the people, Chief, what you saw."

Savage sat. José Juarez stood. After a long silence, he said, "Our brother has told you much that is true. The white man's numbers are great."

He paused, glanced at Savage and said, "But they are many tribes. They are not of the tribe of the white men who dig gold. They will not unite with the tribe here. They will not come to fight against us. Those tribes I saw are many. Their numbers are great, but they are not our enemy. They will not fight us."

Surprised by the chief's misunderstanding, Jim stood. "Whoa! Wait up, Chief!"

José Juarez ignored him, talked over him, past him, raised his voice. "Some white tribes make hair short, some long! Different tribes! Some white men wear blue clothing with gold trim. Numbers few. Different tribe! Small tribe. Some white men wear tall hats. Small tribe! No tribe in the white man's big village is like the tribe that dig gold!"

The chief ignored Savage's protest, repeated his observations, brought them into the center of his listeners' close attention, danced his words forward and around, convincing. "White tribes in big village will not go to war in mountains! They cannot bring their big ships here! They will not bring their big guns here! We have nothing to fear from those tribes. They will not unite with tribe that digs gold. They are enemies with the white tribe here! When white gold-digging tribe go to big village, they give their gold for strong drink and games, and when it is gone, those big-village tribes force them to return here to get more gold for them."

"My brothers—" Savage started.

José Juarez turned on him. "Brother not strike brother!"

Jim flinched. Here's trouble. The blow not forgotten. Nor forgiven. And he'd misjudged the chief's perceptiveness. Mistaken conclusions, but keen observations. A lota fences needin' mendin' fast.

"My brothers!" he said again, waving his arms. "White men all same tribe! Long hair. Short hair. No hair. All same tribe! Blue shirt. Red shirt. All same tribe! Tall hat. No hat. All same tribe! All brothers, all one tribe." He had their attention again. He intensified his remarks, repeated himself, refreshed his argument. "All white men same tribe like white men digging gold. All white men climb mountains, dam rivers. All can come here. And they will! White men will come here to fight Indians! And keep coming and destroy every tribe that comes against them."

José Juarez raised a fist in warning, then his voice. "Speaks with forked tongue! Lies to help his white brothers drive us from our land! Wants gold for gambling with his white brothers! No El Rey Tularenos! El Rey Dinero!"

"Now is the time!" José Rey said, rising, raising a fist. "Now is the time to unite as one people! Potoyensees, Nukchus, Chauchilas, Chukchansi, all the Yokuts peoples, Yosemites, together! Drive gold-digging white men from our land!"

Jim launched another attempt, now drowned out by a Yosemite shouting, "We are many! We will chase white men away! If white men come from their big village, we hide!"

José Rey shouted, "And they will leave!"

A Chauchila chief rose. "If all the tribes make one tribe, white men will run! And leave their things behind!"

A mumbled approval surged through the crowd. Jim Savage knew trouble when he saw it. His mother raised no fool. A storm comin' sure as a boilin' sky rollin' over Illinois. Nothin' he could say was gonna beat the prospect of plunder on top of revenge. Nothin' he could say now was gonna trump these Indians seein' themselves warriors defendin' their land invaded by white men stealin' gold and ruinin' rivers.

This was trouble doubled. Saw himself ridin' that damned bad-broke horse, yellin' at miners and settlers, 'Indians comin'! Indians comin'!' A regular Paul Revere.

Their action seemed preconcerted... driving the miners from the headwaters of the San Joaquin.... Further down settlements and cattle stations were attacked and demolished, particularly on Kaweah and Kern rivers ...attended by massacre and pillage.

—*History of California, Vol. VI*
H. H. Bancroft Co.

SHE WOULD REMEMBER how lovely the day was, a soft breeze whispering, sun warm on her back, her hands slick with oil from making *ko'tca* into the black-seed cakes Seethkil liked with acorn soup. She had gathered the small plants when ripening, spread them to dry on a granite outcropping, waited and watched the proper time, shaken the seeds into her winnowing basket, stored them until they were ready. A long, slow process. Like making the life she felt move in her now.

"I was there!" Seethkil said, suddenly joining her on the log where she knelt over her work.

She would remember his excitement.

"I was there! Said yes with the *wal'lim* chiefs, Bautista and José Rey and José Juarez!"

She would remember a terrible sense then that somewhere a huge tree, very tall, very heavy, was falling, losing its grip on the earth. She felt the weight of it, the enormous unstoppable collapsing crash of it taking breath from her lungs.

"Yosemites say yes! Drive white men away! Chauchilas, Potoyensees, Chukchansi, Siyanti, Tachi—all tribes together!"

Unable to speak from beneath the fallen tree's great weight, she had looked at Seethkil as if he were a stranger. Her husband, the handsome youngest son of Chief Teneiya, a stranger. And she would remember him saying, "We die now or we die later. That is the choice."

In the days that followed, she watched forlornly the gathering of firewood for the sweat house, the preparing of food for the sacred ceremony. Old ways. Seethkil could not be dissuaded from the possibility, the great opportunity, of driving invaders from the land. He spoke only of attack and assault, risk and reward, danger and daring. Into the night and throughout the day, warriors talking and talking, smoking, argument chasing agreement.

In the night, alone in their *o'chum*, she confessed to fear — for him, for them, for the coming child. But Seethkil had become a man grown bold. "If we fail, we go to the Monos," he said. "We will survive."

Dreams haunted her nights. Wizards wandered with fluttering papers and her mother called "Di-shi!" across a darkly barren and abandoned landscape. One night she heard Victoria's voice, resigned to fate. "What is done, is done, Isabel. All of it done, decided, long ago, in the old dream-time. The way the world is, this world, the world that was, the world yet to come. Decided. All of it."

She woke thinking of Victoria, how the old grandmother would have treasured the red blanket from Brownlee's store in Agua Fria. And how distant that day now seemed. The world racing its days. Barely a handful of moons since Jim, funny in a nightshirt, was singing her and Homut and Eekeno over the hill. The wives choosing a red shirt for him. Red, the color of fire, precious fire, providing warmth and defeating darkness.

She woke thinking soon she would teach her unborn child to be grateful to robin for bravely burning its breast to protect fire in the dream-time. And grateful to little mouse for so long ago stealing fire for the Mountain People who lived in the dark. Little mouse playing his flute, its music putting robin to sleep and mouse stealing fire, hiding it in his flute, carrying fire to the top of the mountain where it flew up in the sky and became the sun. And every morning the fire that was the sun rose over the mountain and brought light into the world. Every mother taught every child this story, how the world came into being. She would teach her child to thank robin and brave little mouse and the First People for heat and light, and for all the world's red reminding.

She woke breathless beneath the weight of a fallen tree.

She woke to her mother's voice insisting she was Di-shi, one of the People whose time had come to be in the world. Uncountable as stars, all the mothers, all the children, the long chain from the First People to her own place in the perpetual procession, her time to bring a child into the world. The world continued, like the People, as intended. One mother led to another, one day to the next, inevitable.

She woke to Seethkil warming to war, to revenge.

Was it all decided long ago? when Coyote planted sticks and feathers and grew the First People? set the world in motion? First the one thing, then the next, inevitable as sun rising, wind blowing, winter coming. Trees falling.

She watched Seethkil go into the sweat house, emerge purified for battle.

The Yosemites danced their war dance. Sang their war songs. Fashioned bows. Filled quivers.

Old ways.

She wept.

He rode the bad-broke horse straight to Agua Fria, found Sheriff James Burney in his log cabin, installed in a swivel chair at a rough table, invoicing the county for his recent travels on its behalf. "Four miles from here to Mariposa City, ain't it?" Burney said, glancing up at Savage. "That's about right," he continued, answering his own question. "What's goin' on with you?" Adjusting his spectacles, he returned to his figuring.

"Got bad news," Savage said, wondering how a swivel chair had got to Agua Fria.

Burney licked his pencil end. "Dollar a mile to transport a prisoner," he said. "Beats mining by a few miles, don't it?"

Any other time Savage would have had a little fun with the sheriff over his costs and accounting. Not today, and amusement not a likely prospect soon. "Been over to the Fresno," he said. "Indians rilin' themselves up for some serious trouble. Figured you oughta know, warn folks."

"Indians always getting a burr under their blankets about something," Burney said, turning to look up at Savage. "No point in worryin' up folks with rumors. We got law here now, not like the old days. Indians got to start behaving. Folks ain't gonna put up with their raidin' . Fella come through here not long ago, ruined by Indians. Had a fine spread over by French Camp, cattle worth thousands of dollars. Every head rustled in one night. Went kinda *loco*. Said he was going into the mountains to hunt grizzlies. Name of Adams. You know him? Older fella? Long hair like yours? Big beard?"

Burney frowned, barreled ahead. "Tell your Indian friends we got laws now, Savage. Rules and regulations. Half those Indians don't know how to dress themselves, for cryin' out loud. Women in the towns now! Women don't wanna see some buck wearin' only socks and a hat and thinkin' he's a swell. Any Indian caught loitering or strolling about can be arrested on the complaint of any white citizen. Do they know that? Did you know that?"

"Nope, I didn't," Savage said, thinking a barrel of brandy cocktails not half enough at the moment, wondered how things mighta gone if he hadn't got drunk and hit José Juarez. Or, come to that, hadn't got his big idea to show the Indians the wasp nest that was San Francisco, waiting to be stirred up? And why did all this Indian business feel so familiar?

Déjà vu? He considered. No, not quite that. Not the past repeated. More like the future comin' on like a prairie storm. Cards dealt. Indians all doomed when white men showed up. Our time in the sun, friends. Your time's up.

"Get him arrested," Burney was saying, "and he's for sale to the highest bidder for up to four months. Steals anything of value, a cow, whatever, gonna be fined up to two hundred dollars. He ain't got it, and a white man pays it, well, then he's workin' it off for however long it takes. Ain't specified. Put them all to work, that'll fix your Indians."

Savage felt himself getting riled now. "Thought California got admitted a free state, Burney, not a slave state. Could be some objection to these 'rules and regulations,' don't you think?"

Burney turned back to his invoicing. "Indians entitled to complain to the justice of the peace for ill treatment."

"Generous provision. Sure to be appreciatin' that."

Burney swiveled in his chair, scowled at Savage. "But in no case can a white man be convicted of any offense upon the testimony of an Indian."

"That clarifies, don't it?"

"Signed into law by the legislature of the state of California, Mr. Savage. All official: Act for the Government and Protection of the Indians."

"Sounds like they'll be gettin' plenty of government, maybe not much protection." Doomed. They was always doomed. Sauk, Fox, Winnebago, Potawatomi, Cheyenne, Walla Wallas, Cherokee, Sioux, Arapaho, Chauchilas, Yosemites. Tribes he knew, tribes he didn't. All of 'em doomed. Same old story. Even if it ain't been read yet, it's been written.

Burney turned back to his desk, resumed his invoicing. "We got a government-appointed Indian commissioner now. Name's Adam Johnston. I'll write him about your riled-up Indians and let you know what he thinks. Best I can do."

A pale light seeped a gray morning through the *o'chum* smoke hole. A new day drifting in with women's chatter and the warm aroma of acorn bread baking.

Isabel rose slowly from her bed of buffalo robe, conscious of the increasing weight inside her. Bad dreams again. Seethkil gone again. Inevitable. This day was inevitable. We die now or we die later, Seethkil said. Echoing Homut. We are doomed.

Outside, she let morning wash over her, over bad thoughts. Awani, still here, still the same. Since the beginning of the world, since the First People. Smoke drifting into towering trees, blue jays squawking, women cooking, children chasing pretend prey. The season of retreating green giving way to the color of burnished amber, of acorns. Another day unfolding like countless days gone before, countless days to come. Here was her world.

Tobuce ran over to her. "Isabel, see what Totuya found! Let's make your baby cradle!"

Beloved Tobuce, the gifted weaver, always happy. A fleeting recollection, Victoria warning Anna against fashioning a cradle before the child's birth. Bad luck in the old days of old ways. She pushed the thought away, examined the special willow Totuya had gathered. Cradle-making, baby-making, this was how the world unfolded one day into the next, from time immemorial, from the First People and, before them, Coyote-man and Lizard-man, and Bear Woman, and all the animal spirits that made the People.

She welcomed the cool gray day, the company of Awanichee women fashioning a baby cradle, *choko'nipedeh,* grateful for a morning given to weaving willow and ignoring fear, sharing gossip and laughter. An ordinary day. A right way day.

In the meadow, the women sat chatting in a circle in the late-season grass while Tobuce twined willow for a cradle in the Awanichee manner.

Isabel, carefully kneeling to watch, conscious of the enlarging life within, said, "In Yuloni, in my village, we formed the cradle's back with two lengths of oak and crosspieces of alder wood."

Totuya shyly asked why Isabel had come to Awani. Every child full of why, Isabel thought. Girls and women together, gossiping over basket-weaving, cooking, making acorn, making baby cradles. Life being lived, stories shared, memories made. So often these days her mind wandered back to Yuloni's river, the favorite spot where she washed her hair. Still vivid was the place she gathered soap root, and the grinding rock where she made acorn. Every child full of why. She remembered asking Victoria why acorn was made one way and not another. Why the Mexicans hated them. Why this. Why that. Her mind insisted on traveling. She remembered again Anna's cradle for her little turtle child. Where was Anna now? Mining? Making acorn? Wearing her white-man's hat and making acorn-cap strings for her daughter to play with? Where were Yuloni's people from the village of her girlhood? Vanished.

Tobuce was looking at her. Isabel smiled, admired the cradle's progress. Life's progress. Not long ago she had been an ordinary young woman learning old ways, living old ways. And now who was she? New ways, Isabel. Her father's ghost voice. New ways had snared her like a hunter taking game. She had learned the white man's tongue. Traveled on a steamboat. Slept in a hotel. She had become a woman no longer ordinary. She had seen a parade with a crimson banner and marching men carrying umbrellas and tossing firecrackers. And eagle tied to a ladder.

Jim Savage had seen the eagle atop that ladder, too. White-man power on parade. To show her, the chiefs, Homut, all of them. To warn them. Beware, Indians.

And now Indians drummed and danced, filled quivers. Beware, white man.

It was hard work; the watching for Indians, who were very troublesome, kept us from being lonesome. It was unsafe to go far away from our camp alone. Many miners were killed by Indians....

—Daniel A. Clark
Mariposa, September 1850

SHERIFF BURNEY LEANED back in his swivel chair, hands clasped behind his head. "Well," he said, looking pleased at Savage's arrival, "just the man we're waiting for. Colonel Johnston here has got some news. Plans you should approve."

Jim had news of his own, somewhat of a pressin' nature, in his opinion, but he was all ears for whatever the Indian commissioner cared to share. Johnston, a tall man with a wide smile, lifted his length from the stool opposite Burney's desk, stuck out a hand. "Mr. Savage, a pleasure to make your acquaintance, sir. Heard quite a bit about you."

"Some of it good," Burney said, disengaging his heft from his chair to drag a second stool from behind the nearby stove warming the cabin.

Jim shook the tall man's hand, took his measure. They was gonna get along.

Snoring and the smell of stale whiskey drifted from the next room. "Jail patron," Burney said, pushing the stool toward Savage. "And he's got some opinions on Mariposa City, too."

Jim grinned. "Besides that noisy endorsement for the local rotgut?"

Burney looked confused.

Jim saw Johnston repress a grin. "I'm guessing Mr. Savage is referring to your reluctant guest, not me."

Got the joke. Firm handshake, too. Yep, they'd get along. "Kinda enjoy keepin' the sheriff here amused, when the mood strikes," Jim said, laughing. "Plus, while gettin' here to Agua Fria I got my own opinions passin' through Mariposa. Couldn't hardly hear myself think, what with Fremont's damned steam engines pounding quartz into muck. Extractin' gold a regular mechanical operation there. Costly business, Fremont's monster machines, six of 'em bangin' away day and night. Thump. Thump. Thump."

Another day he might have said a whole camp of Indians could whoop their departin' and who'd hear? Which didn't seem appropriate at the moment.

"Miners glad for the noise, prob'ly," he added. "Evidence the town's comin' up in importance." He turned to Burney who had resumed his swivel chair. "Mariposa likely stealin' the show from Agua Fria soon, takin' what glory there is in bein' a county seat. Heard the citizens there gettin' up some handsome plans for a courthouse. With regular chairs. And a roof."

"You gonna sit?" Burney asked, indicating the stool.

"I spent the night in that fair little city," Johnston said. "Came away impressed by the general enterprise afoot. I was just telling the sheriff here about the latest entertainment there."

"Always keen on entertainment," Jim said, sitting, nodding at Burney. "Fond of a frolic myself now and then." His news would keep. Liked Johnston already, seemed a decent sort, might as well be sociable for a moment. "You stop in on Mariposa's premier gamblin' hall by any chance? I hear it's now so come up in grandness it boasts artistic attractions."

"I did, actually," Johnston said, resuming his seat, learning back, grinning. "Walls inside painted to represent the four seasons. I'm inclined to think a broom may have stood in for a brush. But the effect does arrest the eye."

Jim laughed, turned to Burney. "What's it gonna cost the county when you decide to arrest the eye?"

"Colonel Johnston's come here about Indians, Mr. Savage," Burney said gruffly, "not your amusements."

"Ah, amusements," Jim said, "no end of 'em in Mariposa City. Got cheated outa three dollars last month for a hollered-up show advertisin' pantomimes, character dances, dangerous jumps, feats of strength, balancin' stunts, and tightrope dancin'. Frenchy clown doin' shrieks and contortions, pure humbug. Townspeople agreed. A second performance gulled no one into buyin' a ticket, even—"

"Colonel Johnston's been over to your Fresno store," Burney interrupted. "Maybe you'd like to hear his report on the Indians."

"All ears," Jim said, pushing his hair back with both hands, demonstratin'. Any report likely better than the one he had to share. Maybe if he hadn't been drunk he coulda talked 'em down off whatever high horse they'd climbed up on. Not like they wasn't entitled.

"Unless," Burney continued, "you prefer informing us further on Mariposa City's attractions."

Jim looked at him, thinking any other day he might have said Mariposa City's gambling halls were about as much town as needed. Could write a book on towns, he could, if he could write, which he had no mind to, and if he favored towns, which he didn't. But he had some experience with the fine art of chance. Had done some thinkin' on faro, monte, roulette wheel, poker.

Johnston interrupted his thoughts. "Fact is," the Indian agent said, "the best evidence of a town intent on permanence is how quickly it peels off its canvas. Stores fashioned up from old ship's sails nailed to trees advertise a camp. You want a town, you need planks and nails, nails and planks. Floors. Walls." He paused, looked from Burney to Savage, and back at Burney. "And fact is, California is moving in that direction, and unless we deal with the Indian problem, it will not be amusing."

"Colonel Johnston proposes to give them Christmas," Burney said.

"Start the civilizing process," Johnston added.

Jim considered this proposal in light of his own news. "You got a plan, do you?"

Burney said, "Wants to arrange a big powwow for the local tribes next week. Colonel Johnston visited all the area's rancherias, as well as your Fresno store."

"I took presents as well as promises," Johnston said. "Assured the chiefs that as representative of the Great White Father in the country's capital, I was a messenger of good will and peace."

"And?" said Jim.

"And they unanimously professed friendship for the Great Father and all his white children."

"Believe 'em?"

"Not a word."

Him and Johnston, they'd get along, but it made a body weary, all this talkin' and predictin'. And bone-tired just thinkin' on this morning's discovery. Couldn't rightly blame 'em. No idea who or what got 'em goin'. First thought he'd had was to wish Isabel had been there. Smart girl, Isabel. Seen a real city, not a jumped-up camp. Seen the future. Knew hopeless when she saw it. She coulda talked the women outta this bad idea anyway. Whatever it was. Weren't good, that much sure. He'd inspected the entire area around the store where Indians had made a village. Bein' somewhat likkered, took another look. Staggered around a second time, he had. Or a third? He couldn't recall. Recollectin' not his keenest skill at that hour.

"Well, then, I got somethin' of interest for you," he said, finally, leaning forward and fixing his gaze on Johnston.

"And what might that be?" Burney asked, eyebrows raised like he was waiting to be amused.

"My Indians are gone. Ever-gol-dang-blasted one of 'em," Jim said, looking at his own hands, as if they were somehow responsible, then up at Burney, then Johnston.

"What do you mean 'gone'?" Burney asked. "How gone?"

"I mean gone," Jim said, looking at him. "All gone. Disappeared. Even Homut. Bad sign, her gone. Not a single one of my wives anywheres. No one anywheres." He turned to Johnston. "Big encampment around my store, y'know. Whole dang place deserted. Skedaddled, every man, woman, and child."

Johnston stood, concerned. "Your Indians intending to join up with the hostiles, you suppose?"

Jim sighed. "Need to find 'em 'fore they do. I can track 'em but won't look persuasive, y' know, one man tellin' two hundred to go home and be good little Indians."

Excitement prevails throughout the Mariposa region, in consequence of the difficulties that are apprehended with the Indians. Savage, the white chief, had entirely failed in his efforts to
pacify them, and they had on the contrary commenced hostilities.

—*San Francisco Journal of Commerce*
December 31, 1850

WARRIORS, REHEARSING SILENCE, crept from the village before dawn,
soundless as smoke, faces charcoaled, horses' hooves soft as heartbeats. Isabel sensed their departure more than heard it. She snugged the red blanket
close around her shoulders and joined Loiya at her cooking fire.

"He will return safely," Loiya said, offering a fragrant acorn biscuit. "My
youngest son. All of them. Make war like they make dance. For show."

Isabel sat clutching the warm bread in both hands, unable to eat. Loiya
must know warriors in fearsome paint and feathers wasn't pose and posture.
Not now. In some gone time, dancing and chanting instilled terror into enemies. Not now. New ways.

Loiya stirred the fire, flames leaping into morning's fading darkness.
"The People have lived in peace with their neighbors since time beyond telling," she said. "No one made war foolishly or lightly, over dishonor or insult.
To do so endangered everyone needlessly, threatened survival." She lay aside
her stirring stick, looked at Isabel. "Nothing's changed," she said.

Everything's changed, Isabel thought.

Loiya touched Isabel's shoulder. "Daughter," she said, "the People killed
rarely. Only in revenge."

But they believed devoutly in revenge, Isabel wanted to say. If a man
failed to avenge the killing of a relative or friend, he would not receive
friendship in the spirit world, nor protection from ill-tempered ghosts. And
the spirit world was forever.

Loiya surely knew this war was not for show. The women consoled themselves with hope, avoided speaking their fears, but they knew. Invading white
men intent on gold had met the People's friendship with gunfire, igniting
the ancient necessity of retribution. And the People's vengeance had already
leapt its surprise on unsuspecting settlers and wandering prospectors. Ran-
dom death, seemingly without reason, confused white men. Isabel had heard
their alarmed talk of friends killed who never harmed an Indian, never

exchanged a hard word with an Indian. But white men didn't know the ways of the People, that Indian vengeance required only someone be killed. Anyone. It was the killing that counted.

She felt her unborn child moving within her. Was she frightening it with her thoughts? Her fear? She wanted to assure the child waiting to join the world that all would be well, that its father was the brave youngest son of Teneiya, chief of the feared Yosemites. That no one had ever invaded Awani. That the People were safe here. And white chiefs had promised this land belonged to the People. Forever.

The sun lifted itself from darkness, shone down on Awani, lent shadows to towering granite as it crossed the sky. Old men smoked. Women, saying little, tended children, cooked. Waited. Throughout the long day Isabel's mind traveled, thought unraveled. The world felt upside down. When the child within her moved, she told it tales, whispered assurances, made promises that might be lies.

Evening approached, ending long hours of chasing fear, of pretending an ordinary day. Then, suddenly, alarmingly, shouts. A runner shouting. The runner racing through the village, raising dust, raising hope, shouting. Women ceased weaving and cooking and making acorn. Children ceased chasing. Blue jays listened. And then a great ground-shaking rumble of horses' hooves. Horses coming. Warriors returning. Warriors coming. Warriors whooping. Horses pounding. Coming closer.

Isabel felt suspended by hope as whooping warriors astride thundering horses pounded closer. A dust-cloud of horses drumming the earth exploded into view. Behind them, stolen horses and mules laden with trappings and spoils. Wildly shouting warriors, quivers empty, feathers fluttering, circled the village flourishing their plunder. Blankets. Guns. In the vanguard, three riders, exhilarated with conquest and glory, yelping and whooping, brandishing poles fluttering victory. Like flags, Isabel thought, transfixed. But not flags. Not flags. Scalps.

Three scalps.

Isabel stared. Scalps. Three scalps. One *red. Curly and red.*

She felt the world spin, and she with it. Felt the world collapsing and she into it. Felt her child shrinking, retreating. Heard sky-piercing shrieking. Hers. Then wailing. Hers, as her lifeless child spilled from between her legs in a flood of red.

"Plenty men around Agua Fria got guns and grievances," Jim told Adam Johnston. "And keen for a chance to chase Indians."

Within an hour they'd collected a dozen enthusiastic volunteers from the mining camp's saloons and gambling halls. Jim led them to his store on the Mariposa where they dismounted and followed him around the deserted encampment, examining cold campfires and empty tents and cedar dwellings. They peered where he pointed. He knelt, brushed leaves aside, showed them tracks Indians had left.

Behind him someone quietly assured the others. "No dog can follow a trail like he can."

"Might depend on the dog," one said.

Jim stood, wiped his hands on his pants. "A child could track 'em. Gone up into the mountains."

"Rough country," Johnston said.

Jim nodded. "Like as not we'll be trackin' into the night."

Trackin'. He loved it. But trackin' Indians? What turn in life's trail had got him trackin' Indians? And what choice was there but to talk 'em down and bring 'em back? Johnston was the man to do that, tell 'em it weren't only Jim Savage's truth on how things was now. Had to keep 'em from joinin' some uprisin' that, truth be told, might be bitin' him on his backside. His doin'. For hittin' a chief. Dammit. For want of a nail a shoe was lost. Well, had to get on with gettin' on, wherever that was goin'. He looked at the men. "Night trackin'. You men good with that?"

They were.

It was a long night of climbing, halting, listening, waiting, moving on. Finally, just at dawn Jim spotted Bautista standing on a hilltop. The Potoyensee chief, back to the rising sun, stood watching the volunteers approach. Jim shielded his eyes from the sun's glare, definitely Bautista. Couldn't miss that big sombrero with the silver band. Jim raised a hand in greeting.

Johnston, at his side, asked, "You know him?"

"Bautista."

"That's not good."

"Maybe, with luck," Jim said, "we'll have us a parley."

Johnston looked doubtful. "Let's hope it's only threats and demands."

"Stay here with the men. Get 'em to show their rifles, just for display, nothin' threatenin', while I parley us some negotiatin'." He advanced up the hill alone.

Jim Savage admired Indians, always had. How they lived, natural, with the earth more than on it. Wanted to be one when he was a boy, always told anyone cared to ask. But now, in this place and time, bein' Indian weren't what any white man might call a good idea. And when all was said and done,

Jim Savage belonged to the white-man tribe. And what needed doin' right now was preventin' warfare between his tribe and Bautista's.

Some four hundred yards distant from the silently watching chief, Jim raised a hand in greeting. "Bautista, my brother!"

Bautista waited.

"Brother!" Jim repeated.

"No white man brother!" Bautista abruptly raised his arms, an arrow gripped in one hand, bow in the other. "White man kill my people! Kill my father!"

Savage glanced back down the hill where Johnston stood surrounded by the dismounted volunteers who'd tracked all night, and whose enthusiasm for chasing Indians was likely dissipating with daylight. Did Johnston know that a white rancher had killed Bautista's father for stealing horses? Or that Bautista was bound to avenge the death? Maybe on the second part, not likely on the first. Did Johnston, or any volunteer clutching pistol or rifle, understand Indian vengeance? That killing any white man served the purpose? Any white man. Soberin' news, prob'ly.

He looked uphill, across the distance between himself and Bautista. Bad business, this. What was there to say? What Indian hadn't had family killed? Wonder was their delayed response. Indians entitled to credit on their forbearance, truth be told. If every Indian with a festering grievance retrieved his injury, well, nobody safe from the consequences.

"Bautista, you are a great leader! Lead your people to safety! To their rancheria!"

"And wait for white man to kill them?! Or starve?!"

"Bautista, your people can dig enough gold for food! For everything they want!" Needed to talk the chief down, he did. He was Jim Savage, King of the Tularenos! He launched himself into exhorting like a preacher loves Sundays.

Bautista studied his bow, and then his arrow, while Jim hauled up his old arguments embellished with pretty promises, knowing his talk was hollow as a tule reed whistle. Weren't surprised Bautista did, too.

"Digging gold hard way to live!" the chief hollered.

Savage shouted back, "White men dig gold!" Not much of a rejoinder, that one, he thought. After a season of hard digging in the mines, most white men with a decent fall-back skill fell back like they'd been shot.

"White man dig gold! Indian steal it!"

Shoutin' the consequences for Indians stealin' from white men not likely to win friendship on a good day, Jim knew, and this weren't comin' on to bein' a good day. Remindin' Bautista that white men outnumbered leaves on trees and more comin' was another used-up speech, but he tossed it up the hill anyways. No surprise Bautista wasn't impressed.

"Lies! White man lies!"

"Bautista, we are friends and friends do not lie!"

"Enemies!"

Another Indian joined Bautista on the hilltop. Savage recognized José Rey.

The Chauchila chief raised a defiant fist. "We will kill and plunder until no white face is left in our country! Fresno store robbed! Men dead!"

"What about the Fresno store?" he shouted. Had he heard right?

The only answer was the sudden appearance of more Indians joining the chiefs. Many more. Jim shielded his eyes, guessed maybe two hundred, rough guess, but considerable.

He rejoined Johnston, surrounded by alarmed volunteers. "More hostility than we bargained for."

"Looks like," Johnston said. "What was that about the Fresno store?"

"Hard to say, maybe a trick to get us outta here. We got guns and they don't. Not a fight they can win. Indians want the first encounter decisive in their favor. In order to commit the other tribes, get 'em believin' they can beat us."

"Looked decisive to me!" said a mounted volunteer, turning his horse. "Those Indians want to kill us!"

"Hold on," Jim said, still thinking. "This might be the trick, right here." He looked at Johnston. "They need to win the first engagement. Only sure bet on winning the first engagement is to attack men not expectin' trouble. We were expected."

Johnston considered. "Are you thinking—"

"My Fresno store."

Drumming. Would the drumming never stop? Her head hurt. Her heart hurt. How long had she lain here, alone on the buffalo robe wet with her tears? Where was Seethkil?

"Isabel?" Loiya's voice, soft, sad, soothing. "I am here."

When had Loiya left? When had she returned? Would the drumming never stop?

Rising slowly, heavily, sitting now, she saw Loiya crouched by the buffalo bed. In her hands a tiny bundle swaddled in rabbit fur. Loiya held it out and Isabel reluctantly, sadly, took it. So tiny, barely there at all. Barely there at all.

"Seethkil? Where is Seethkil?" she whispered, holding the tiny bundle that was barely there at all.

"I'm here, I'm here." His voice husky. He wrapped the red blanket around her shoulders, helped her stand, led her outside.

Drumming, the incessant drumming. How long must warriors celebrate their enemies' death? Was this the second day? the third?

Seethkil holding her, she holding the little bundle. Almost nothing, barely there at all.

Loiya quietly asking, "Cave of the old woman?"

Her heart hurt. Cave of the old woman? An old woman, alone, no family. Isabel remembered taking acorn soup to her. Would the drumming never stop?

Seethkil saying, "Yes," leading Isabel away from the pulsating drumming of the dance house.

Seethkil, gentle Seethkil. Funny and gentle, Seethkil with his little mouse. She wanted that happy time back, the playful time, the laughing time. Gone. Drowned by drums, by chanting warriors dancing their ghost dance, warning off the ghosts of the slain. Old ways. Ghosts? They were all ghosts.

She felt night's cool dampness caress her face. She looked up. Snow-shadowed stars. Snow. Too late to cross to the Monos. Too late. Wizards coming. White man wizards.

An owl called and a sudden wind snatched withered leaves, scattered its whispering harvest into the night as Seethkil led her into the old woman's cave. Inside, he offered the old woman roasted horse meat. She grabbed it, retreated to a dark corner, away from her fire, didn't speak. Rarely spoke, made no sense when she did, Isabel remembered. She felt a strange kinship now. Imagined herself silent here one day, alone, waiting for Great Spirit to take her to the West.

Seethkil added dried pine needles to the old woman's fire. Sparks leapt red and bright, danced against the darkness. Isabel stroked the rabbit-fur bundle, felt tears gather and spill. Remembered Loiya saying the season was wrong, that winter opposed life's beginnings. The People joined the world in the green time, in the time of buds and blossoms, when the sun warmed the earth and grass grew.

Isabel, weeping, gave the little bundle to the flames. She and Seethkil watched their son's spirit leave on its lonely journey to the West.

In his time, Jim had seen some sights. But nothing like this. At first, neither he, nor Adam Johnston, nor any of the thirty-five men with them, said a word. They sat their horses, and silently stared. A dense tule fog softened the view with an eerie unreality, but the scene was real. Several yards from his destroyed tent-store lay the skeletal remains of a man evidently feasted upon by wolves or coyotes. In the store's wreckage, two naked bodies. Scalped. One partially dismembered, the other thickly arrowed. Jim knew the markings. Yosemite arrows. Someone dismounted, ran for the trees, another followed. The sound of retching broke the silence.

Dismounting, he surveyed the disaster. Greeley, Stiffner, and Kennedy murdered. Worse. Butchered. Anthony Brown missing, probably dead. Corral empty. Horses, mules, and cattle gone. Store stripped of everything valuable. He found shovels among the ransacked remains. Indians didn't want shovels. Bautista's taunt: 'Better to steal gold.'

No sooner said than done, Jim thought, examining the store's dismantled safe. He knew it held about eight thousand dollars in gold before the attack. Hinges beat off. With an axe? Took some doing, that did.

He passed the shovels out to a half dozen willing men and they began digging the graves, jabbing the earth and cursing Indians.

"If words could kill—" Johnston started to say. The thought hung in the air, unfinished.

Words couldn't, Jim wanted to say, but arrows did. Greeley was going into his grave bristling with twenty.

Not Kennedy. Indians had retrieved their arrows from his punctured body, leaving massive wounds of torn flesh. Jim stared at the man's scalped, naked remains. "Blankets stole. Nothin' to cover the body," he said to no one in particular.

A volunteer began snapping fir boughs and small cedar branches. "Better'n nothin'," he said.

When the grisly task was done, someone said a prayer. The men chorused a quiet "Amen."

Not much of a ceremony, Jim thought. But what was there to say? Well, friends, here ends your California adventure. Goodbye.

And, truth be told, goodbye to his own adventure. Goodbye, El Rey Tularenos, your kingin' time's over, you been deposed. Your subjects want you dead, that's the message. You talked Indian, parleyed and posed and palavered, but under your grizzly bear costume, you're a white man. And this here's payment for your betrayal.

Back in Mariposa City, he hauled Johnston into the first saloon they came to, ordered the barkeep to bring a bottle of whatever was handy. The horrific deaths of Kennedy, Greeley, and Stiffner sat hard. He hadn't suspected things could go so bad so fast. "On me," he told Johnston, raising his glass, "ain't been my best day. Attack on my store aimed at me, you know."

Johnston nodded. "Trouble only begun. Bautista and Jose´ Rey have no idea what they started."

Jim emptied his glass. "Or what they're up against." Fact was, despite the gruesome Fresno deaths, he devoutly wished his Indians better than the grinding down and rounding up sure to come. Fact was, drunk or sober, he was a white man, not the Indians' king, or brother. He was a white man who hadn't taken their side against the invaders. His influence with Indians was spit in a river now.

"Well, so much for giving them Christmas," Johnston said, lifting his glass. "There goes my plan to start them on the merry road to civilization."

Jim looked at the Indian agent. "Ain't gonna be no Christmas party? Too bad. Good excuse for another bottle. Not that I need one. Excuse, that is." He tossed back another glass, and said, "I better talk to Sheriff Burney. Again. Figure this time he'll give the threat some of his official attention. County's full of prospectors wanderin' around exposin' their scalps. Ain't enviable."

"I'm going to the governor, report the situation," Johnston said, pushing his empty glass across the bar, and getting up. "Bottle's all yours."

Jim had it half empty when he declared drunkenly to anyone who cared to listen, "Well, no sense in lookin' back at shouldas or couldas. What's done is done. Best bury regrets with the dead and get on." He slammed the glass down on the bar, picked up the bottle and waved it at the barkeep. "Gonna be needin' another, mister! This one don't seem to be workin'!"

He looked around the saloon, declared, "Bein' king to them Indians, that was some fun!" He raised his empty glass to their bemused stares. Turning to the barkeep, he said, "Fill 'er, friend, to the top!"

He lifted the refilled glass to his reflection in the bar's mirror. "Bein' king, reg'lar frolic!" He turned back to the room. "Salutin' myself for bein' a king!"

He emptied the glass, called to the barkeep. "Another, brother!" He laughed. Saluted himself again. For bein' a poet.

1851

[The chief] also said to Savage he must not deceive the whites by telling them lies; he must not tell them that the Indians were friendly; they were not, but on the contrary were their deadly enemies; and that they intended killing and plundering them so long as a white face was seen in the country.

—Letter, Adam Johnston
to California Governor Peter H. Burnett
January 2, 1851

That a war of extermination will continue to be waged between the races until the Indian race becomes extinct must be expected. While we cannot anticipate this result but with painful regret, the inevitable destiny of the race is beyond the power and wisdom of man to avert...

—California Governor Peter H. Burnett
State of the State Address
January 6, 1851

A fragrant smoke wafted the warm, early-morning smell of baking acorn bread. She carried a piece in one hand, snugging the red blanket around her shoulders with the other. A path of fallen pine needles and frost-crisped leaves led to a clearing, a refuge where she loved watching the sun rise, scatter a glittering gold across snow-topped mountains, ignite morning into day. She sat down on a mossy fallen cedar, ate the bread, pulled her blanket close. Distantly she heard women chattering, preparing a feast to celebrate another raid. She should join them. The intention drifted, then disappeared. Again, as she had yesterday and days before that, she lost herself in wandering thought. She gazed up into winter-bare trees, twigs and branches a sky-scribble. Like pencil markings white men left on paper.

This had once been the season of old men mending nets, women making mushroom stew, children collecting acorns from oaks with antler horns, disappointing woodpeckers.

Would such a time come again? A time without warriors painting their faces? sweat-house smoke adding gray to each day? Seethkil insisting he must go, that he was a man, a Yosemite, fearless.

She started, feeling a hand on her shoulder. Looked up. Tabuce.

"Isabel, see what I have brought you," she said, joining her on the cedar log. She held out a small white bone awl, a coil of bunchgrass, bundled maple shoots, willow, buckbrush, redbud. "Bring your eyes back from the mountain. Make a cooking basket, Isabel."

Had she confided in Tabuce the wish to escape over the mountain with Seethkil to join the Mono people? Confide her dream of three wizards? She couldn't remember.

"White people cook in kettles," Isabel said, her gaze distant. Indestructible, she thought, and wondered if she meant kettles. Or white people.

Later, Seethkil found her still staring toward the now-risen sun, a coil of redbud in her lap. She sensed his approach, lowered her eyes to the bone awl she held in one hand and the thin black strand of bracken fern root in the other. "Old ways," she whispered over the basket's beginnings, as if she might be overheard. The task required concentration. Yosemite designs differed from those learned from Victoria. She eased the awl into the coil, pulled the fern root through to wrap around the redbud.

"We will drive them away!"

Pride in his voice. Excitement, like winning a race on the meadow. A new kind of game. She was beyond tears, beyond fear.

He sat down by her, hands on his knees, as if to keep his legs from leaping into imagined battle. "Kaweahs warned the white men trespassing on their land at Four Creeks."

The Yosemite method of twining was, to Isabel's eye, superior.

"Told them ten days to leave!"

She liked the unpeeled winter-gathered young shoots of creek dogwood, its red bright against the black bracken.

"Those white men are dead now!"

She had heard the story already, perhaps twice, all the wives had heard how the Kaweahs killed several cattle-raising settlers with their arrows. In return, a white man, a survivor with a gun, killed seven Indians before the Kaweahs— was it only the Kaweahs?— avenged their deaths by flaying one of the settlers alive and nailing his skin to a tree.

She remembered those men, when they bought supplies at the Mariposa store. Had Jim told those men the Kaweahs were friendly? She couldn't remember. They weren't bad men, just men with white skin. She stared at the dogwood shoot in her hand. Had it lost color when Tabuce soaked it?

"Today we took seventy-two mules and horses from a ranch near Agua Fria!"

Perhaps it was only a game to Seethkil, and soon he would tire of it. She would finish the basket, snow would melt, the trail to the Monos open. Six moons, maybe seven.

"Chief Jose´ Rey and Chief Jose´ Juarez sent messengers to us, to the Chauchilas, Chukchansi, Potoyensee, Nukchus. Five hundred warriors! Uniting!"

She looked at him, her handsome Seethkil, too gentle to harm a mouse. Felt a tear drift slowly down her cheek.

Seethkil brushed it away. "I must go," he said. "I am Chief Teneiya's son."

Jim Savage, hearing there was Indian trouble on the San Joaquin, at Cassady Bar, a mining camp Cassady had progressed into a trading post, rode up to investigate. He found a dozen miners hauling stones from the river, a dozen more stacking them, building a wall, others digging a moat.

"If you men think fortin' up gonna discourage the natives," he told them, "I got bad news. It ain't."

"We got bad news, too," a miner replied. "In Cassady's cabin."

Inside, Savage saw an unconscious man on a cot, one arm fallen to his side, a whiskey bottle on the floor, and Lewis Leach on a low stool bandaging the stump of the other arm.

Jim looked back at the whiskey bottle. Empty. Disappointin'. Could use a swallow. Or two. "You doctorin' again, Leach? Thought I'd outfitted you for minin'."

"My fall-back occupation," Leach replied, tying off the bandage and standing. He pulled Jim from his patient's earshot, nodded in the cot's direction. "Only survivor of an attack at Four Creeks. Took half a dozen arrows in his arm, couldn't save it." He lowered his voice further. "This isn't the best place for that fellow, or any of those miners out there. Cassady told them all they need is a wall, a moat, and a guard at night."

Jim shook his head. "Cassady's a fool. We got an Indian agent, name's Johnston, gone to tell the governor things here is bad, more'n we can handle."

"Try to convince Cassady of that. Maybe he'll listen to you, the famed El Rey Tularenos."

"Kingin' days over. Indians changed their minds."

"Sorry to hear it."

"Came to say folks ain't safe here. Paul Revere." Also a poet, anyone care to ask.

"Not news to me." Leach looked in his patient's direction.

"The Paul Revere part?"

"Help me get him into my wagon before he wakes up."

That night, local miners smelling of dust and sweat crowded into Cassady's cabin, sitting or standing wherever space permitted, sharing rumors and drinking whiskey by lantern-light.

Jim leaned against a log wall cracking his knuckles until it was the loudest sound in the room and everyone was looking at him. Everyone knew him, the Indians' friend in buckskins, their defender with the long, blonde hair.

He folded his arms and looked around the room, getting their attention. "Come to tell you fellas Indians gettin' united up. Which ain't news to folks in Four Creeks, as you seen. Welcome mat ain't out here neither, and fortin' up not your best plan. Till this Indian trouble blows over, you boys might be thinkin' on a visit to Mariposa."

Cassady, a big man thoughtfully tugging his bushy beard, looked Jim up and down." These Indians ain't nothin'."

"That right?" Jim asked, head cocked as if impressed.

Cassady laughed. "I'm a Georgia man! We know Indians!"

Jim shook his head. Puffed-up braggin' Georgia man. Another Harvey. Tiresome.

One of the miners spoke up. "Trouble been over at Four Creeks, not here. We got that wall and trench, switch off standing guard every night."

Someone said, "Hey, Cassady. It's your turn tonight."

Cassady hooted. "Not me! I ain't staying out in the cold lookin' for Indians!"

"Well, as it's you that's got the property here," the first miner observed philosophically, "and you can risk it, I guess we can."

Jim left the men squabbling and spent the night in an abandoned covered wagon inside the enclosure. The next morning, he found an arrow in its canvas, pulled it out, showed it around the camp. "I'm for Mariposa, boys. My ma didn't raise no fool."

Cassady snorted. "I ain't afraid of no Indians."

Days later, back in Mariposa, Jim sat waiting at his favorite saloon for Johnston's return, commiserating with whoever wandered in to report his cattle driven off, cabin burned, neighbor murdered. Lewis Leach found him there, joined him at the bar. "Indians got Cassady."

Jim dipped a finger in his drink, licked it. "Ain't surprised." Not a bad brandy cocktail. Becomin' somethin' of an expert on the subject of brandy cocktails, anyone care to ask. "Indians identified?"

"General conclusion is Kaweahs."

"That'd put 'bout all the Yokuts people at war now." He drank off the glass. Knew how it would go. Same old story, same old winners and losers. Just a matter of time. "Another one, barkeep!" He slapped a gold coin down next to his empty glass, turned to Leach, "Rather be drinkin' than thinkin'." A poet.

He examined the refilled glass, visiting the memory of how he'd smoked with Bautista, José Juarez, all the valley tribes. Early days on the Merced, tin cup strapped to his ankle. "Keep it comin', barkeep," he said, raising the glass high. "Here's to the Chauchilas and Potoyensees, and their languages. And their daughters." Emptied the glass. "Somethin' of a frolic for a time."

"Good times gone to glory now," Leach said, reaching for the bottle. "Took a few men up to Cassady's place." He filled his glass, took a long swallow, wiped his mouth with the back of his hand. "Found Cassady dead on the riverbank near his trading post. They cut off his legs." He emptied the glass, poured another. "Sliced out his tongue and pinned it with an arrow over the region of his heart. We buried what was left of him."

Jim clinked glasses with Leach.

"To Cassady," Leach said.

"Restin' in pieces!" Jim said.

He wanted to laugh but couldn't remember how.

So many people! She clutched the red blanket against the chill as Seethkil led her horse into the crowds thronging the rancheria. She recognized Potoyensees, Nukchus, Chukchansi, Chauchilas, Yokuts arriving in bands, uniting in this immense village. So many winter-frosted cedar shelters! Sixty? Seventy? Strings of jerked mule meat draped the shelters' sides. Baskets of acorn flour hung from tree branches. An enormous corral of restless mules and horses. Children everywhere, chasing and playing. Dogs scampering. Women roasting horse-meat, the good smell drifting on the breeze. Such plenty in the midst of winter. No one's stomach cried this day.

"Jose' Rey's celebration!" Seethkil said, helping her down from her horse, looking around. "Victory feast!"

How tall and proud Seethkil stood now, raised up by his part in the raid, all the warriors enlivened by their daring, their success. She thought of her father, missing him still, always. Her father, honored among the People, famously raiding horses. She understood the triumph in it, taking what white men valued. Feasting on their loss.

And Seethkil blind to the consequences, his ears deaf to her fears. Her words wind. What more could she say? What else could she do? Where Seethkil would go, she would go, one foot following the other, one day following the next.

"Isabel!"

She and Seethkil turned.

"Isabel!"

"Homut?!"

Seethkil said something about the dance house, left her embracing her old friend. She and Homut held one another's hands, looked into each other's eyes while crowding people eddied around them, two stones in a stream. So many questions, so much to say. Where to begin?

"How did you come here?" Isabel finally asked, wanting to know so much more. A flutter of questions. Where to start? Why had Homut left the Mariposa store, left Jim?

As if hearing Isabel's thoughts, Homut sighed. "This rancheria was my home," she said, glancing left and right as though to confirm her claim. She shrugged, corrected herself. "Is my home."

They spoke through their eyes, silently acknowledging what they had shared, and seen. Was Homut also remembering San Francisco? The white man's immense rancheria shown them for a warning? A warning ignored by José Rey. Did Homut, who had loved Jim, fear for him? As she herself did, hearing now his name spat from the tongues of passing warriors who once called him brother.

She silently held Homut's hands. What was there to say? What purpose did words serve? The past was past. Happiness gone before it was recognized, never to come again. Not surrounded as they were now, by warriors welcoming the future—with something like glory.

Sheriff Burney burst into Jim's Mariposa store. "Need your help," he said, half out of breath, the door banging behind him.

"Howdy to you, too," Jim said, looking up from figuring the cost of whiskey versus champagne for a customer examining labels.

Burney dropped into a chair by the stove, inhaled. "Recruiting volunteers," he said, taking another deep breath, "to go after the Indians."

Jim set his elbows on his plank counter, laced his fingers, propped his chin on them, and looked thoughtful. "This where I'm s'posed to say better late than never?"

Burney ignored the jab. "That rancher near Agua Fria? Howard? Indians took his entire herd, more than seventy horses, headed up into the mountains with them."

"Darned be my stockings," said the customer buying whiskey. "Them Injuns be purty considerable tiresome."

"The general consensus," Burney agreed. "A lot of men keen to go after Howard's horses." He sighed. "At first, anyway."

Jim laughed. "Till they realized the Indians might prefer to keep 'em?"

Burney nodded. "A lot of them decided they had more pressing commitments," he said, getting to his feet. "But I've got sixty men actually mustering themselves instead of their intentions and I could use your help."

"Help? What kinda help would that be?" Jim asked, amused at the possibilities.

"Well, recovering the horses, dammit!" Burney hollered. He stood, took a breath. "And—"

"And?"

"Talking the Indians out of objecting, of course."

Jim scratched his chin, grinned. "Oh, they'll be objectin'. Kinda bought into 'finders-keepers', y'know."

"My men are armed!"

"Well, that'd be some persuasion, I guess." Jim considered. Store business down to nothin' much since miners was quittin' the diggins on account of injuns bein' considerable tiresome. He was bored. And reasonably sober. He shrugged. "Alright. Let's do it."

Tracking continued through a full day and into the evening before Jim sensed the Indians not far ahead. Around midnight he called a halt and told Burney to alert the line to make camp and unsaddle their horses. "From here on, men gotta be on foot, and silent," he told Burney. "Choose some to stay back with the animals, the rest to follow us." He sniffed the night air. "Campfires not far. Indians havin' a feast, I can smell it. And I hear 'em singin'."

Burney snorted. "Singing? I don't hear any singing."

"Keep your voice down," Jim said. "You doubtin' on me? We goin' forward here?"

Burney nodded, walked back to advise the volunteers. After some minutes, he returned. "Left seventeen men to watch the animals. We got sixty to go ahead," he whispered.

Jim, satisfied, led them cautiously forward for the next three hours. With no light but the stars, he urged the men down rugged ravines and up a mountainous incline patchy with snow. When he judged they were within half a mile of the Indians, he whispered to Burney, "Take your boots off. Feel the way with your feet and follow me."

Some two hundred yards from the Indians' camp, Jim gestured to Burney to stay back. He crept forward alone now, slow, an inch-worm, belly-crawling through the brush. At the edge of the encampment noisy with laughter and singing, he felt the hair on the back of his neck rise when he peered up. This was no raiding party! Maybe a hundred and fifty Chauchilas, as many Chukchansi. Yosemites, too. Kaweahs, Potoyensees. He heard Chauchilas talking, his name mentioned.

He crept back to where the shivering volunteers waited. Before he could report, a terrifying yell announced a swarm of howling Indians rushing from their camp toward the volunteers, bows at the ready, arrows flying. He'd been spotted! Standing, he hollered the men to their feet.

Burney yelled, "Engage, men! Engage!"

They rose, firing pistols and rifles. Bullets tore into the advancing Indians. The volunteers, encouraged, charged up the incline to the rancheria, killing several Indians and wounding more. The Indians turned, fled, disappeared.

Jim signaled a stop to the gunfire. In a silence as unexpected as the assault, he and Burney looked around, uncertain. Suddenly a rifle shot sounded. The men looked from one to another, confused, and then one of them, a young Texan, stumbled, stared down at red spreading across his shirt, and fell.

Another rifle shot shattered the silence. Burney shouted, "The Indians got guns!" Frightened men looked wildly in every direction as another volunteer fell. Someone yelled, terrified, "Guns?! They got guns?!"

In a shower of bullets and arrows, the volunteers ran.

Jim yelled, "Stop, men! Stop!"

Burney hollered, "Form up! Form up!"

"Raise your rifles, men!" Jim shouted, watching the volunteers run. "Raise your rifles!"

Chasing after them now, he sensed an arrow finding the spot where seconds before he had stood. A shout followed the arrow. "*Por el rey dinero!*"

A familiar voice. Bautista.

Isabel, sitting alone in the dark outside her *o'chum,* gazed toward the pass to the Monos. Moonlight calmed her fears for Seethkil. He'd assured her of his swift return from wherever the warriors were raiding now, drunk on victory and resurrected pride. She wanted to share his conviction that white men would leave the land. The Indians' recent triumph had enlarged Seethkil's confidence. How brave and beautiful he was. And how she wanted to share his certainty.

If only she dared to believe.

If only she hadn't seen San Francisco.

Not wanting to cast a shadow on Seethkil's fearlessness, she spoke no more of the white man's great rancheria, vessels of war, captured eagles. No one listened now, not even Seethkil. But he promised, and she trusted, they would go to the Monos when passage permitted, to resume life in the old ways. To live long.

Now, gazing into the cold white distance bathed by the moon, she let memory visit past happiness, heard Seethkil's flute and laughter wooing her. So long ago those days seemed now. How had time dashed so swiftly from then into now? those glad days turn into ash? into shots and shouts and speeding arrows? In memory, she heard again the death cries from the battle, saw Homut terrified, women and children fleeing.

And Jim's name shouted.

Burney swiveled in his chair, looked up at Jim standing behind him. "I'd say our seventy-seven men had bravely engaged with about four hundred Indians." He returned to his search for a pen. "And you, Mr. Savage, appeared to be the object of particular attention. Called your name, got you in their sights, fired in your direction."

Jim watched the sheriff uncap an ink bottle with the seriousness of an official act. "Favored me some, they did. Can't say I fancy the partiality." Fact was he'd never been worse frightened in his life. "Situation somewhat more serious than I figured."

"Time the governor knew how things are going here with all this Indian unrest."

"Right," Jim said.

"I am writing," Burney said, dipping his pen. "Today the 13th?"

"January is all I know. Ain't that enough?"

"Don't think so." Burney wrote the date, hesitated. "How's a governor addressed? Sir? Your Excellency?"

Jim thought a moment, decided 'El Rey' probably not worth mentioning. "Use 'em both. Ain't the important part. Tell 'im several men been killed over on the San Joaquin, too. Not sure of the numbers. And some over at Bear Valley." He frowned. "Tell him what we've done so's he knows it ain't nothin'. How we tried to drive the Indians back with the few volunteers we could get."

Burney read aloud as he wrote: "*In order to show your Excellency that the people have done all that they can do to suppress these things, to secure the quiet and safety in possession of our property and lives, I will make a brief statement of what has been done here.*"

Jim supposed a man given to calculating miles ridden and outlaws arrested weren't likely to short a report to the governor, but it weren't brief so far, not to his ear. Damned bad-broke horse could mosey over to Stockton and back before Burney'd finish writing.

"When was it we raised up the company, the 6th?" Burney asked.

Jim shrugged. The day, how'd that matter? Number of guns, that mattered. Indians musta had eight or ten rifles. Comin' up in the world. Gettin' civilized.

Burney inched his account forward, confirming details, recalling events, scratching his pen across another sheet of paper while Jim imagined the bad-broke horse learning a few circus tricks before ambling back from Stockton to Agua Fria.

Burney read aloud again. "*The Indians are watching our movements, but we can keep them back until I can hear from your Excellency.*" He turned to Savage. "How's it sound?"

"Like you're writin' a book."

At length, Burney blotted the final page, read it out: "*If not authorized and commissioned to do so, and furnished with some arms and provisions, or the means to buy them, and pay for the services of the men, my company must be disbanded, as they are not able to lose so much time without compensation.*" With a final flourish of his pen, he added: "*Very respectfully, your obedient servant, James Burney.*"

Jim acknowledged the letter was masterful in clarity, if not brevity. Arms and provisions and compensation and authorization. Couldn't make the case clearer than that. Full might of the state certain to come down on the Indians. Damn, he needed a brandy cocktail. Or two. Or ten.

She loved the mountains at night, sitting in the dark beneath moon and stars. She longed for Seethkil's return, for escape to the Monos she imagined peacefully sleeping now, safe in the distant stillness. She longed for escape from the memory of rifle fire and flaming torches. From that night of senseless death and destruction Seethkil called a victory.

Why? Because more had not died? Because none were captured? Because the enemy retreated?

Or because Jim fled? Seethkil telling how he and Bautista followed Jim down the mountain, calling his name, taunting, spotting him, aiming, missing. "He lives," Seethkil told her when he returned. "Bautista says white medicine."

White medicine. She remembered, from her watching and waiting time, the grizzly cub's hide nailed on the store wall. She'd been saddened by the sight, imagining the capture, the killing, its mother's loss. And Homut, hands fluttering, voice growling, describing Jim draped in the skin, taking Bautista's life, restoring it. Now, in his escape down the mountain, Jim had confirmed Bautista's belief in his wizardry. She almost believed it herself.

'Snow soon' she had said on that long-ago morning when she so reluctantly left Awani and rode Girl down the mountain to the Mariposa. To watch and wait. Two winters gone now, time melting like snow. Once she had been Di-shi, loving old ways like blue loves sky. Her girlhood as lost to her now as Yuloni, as her mother, as Victoria, her father. And the tiny soul refusing life, returning to Great Spirit.

Nothing served by grief. She wanted not to think of loss, of how few moons had climbed the heavens since her father declared new ways, new days. Had he lived, would he be astonished by the daughter she'd become? Learning new ways, ideas, words, seeing parades, steamboats. Learning from Jim, with eyes like sky, hair like sunshine. Her friend. Her teacher. Trading words. She missed those days now, her corner, that time. She missed his laughter, his prancing and dancing. "*Sawa'ja, Sawa'ja.*" Mush-stirrer! "Woo-chi!" Clown! Heard his voice. "Damn, that was fun!" A frolic.

She stood, brushed snow from her hair, breathed in the cold clean night air, gazed east to where the Monos waited.

In the distance, a coyote howled.

Jim Savage was still trying not to be sober when Burney's deputy found him in a Mariposa saloon wetly lamenting his fall from Indian affections.

"The governor's authorized a battalion!" declared the deputy, a youth, excited. "To be organized immediately! By you, sir, Mister Savage, I mean, Major Savage! Sheriff Burney sent me to tell you you're in charge, you're a major now, Mister Savage!" The boy fumbled an awkward salute. "Major Savage, sir!"

And now here he was, Jim Savage, deposed king of the Tularenos, standin' on a stump in Agua Fria, organizin' a so-called battalion to chase Indians. His head ached.

"Robert Eccleston, sir!"

The eager volunteer held up a little leather diary for Jim to see. "Keeping a record of the adventure, sir! Making my first entry, sir! February 12!"

"At ease, Private," Jim said. Hoped that was all the military lingo he'd need for this business. It was all he knew. Him a major, there's a joke. Laughs few and far between these days. Take 'em where you find 'em. Today that was in Agua Fria, in front of Whittier's hotel. A hee-haw right there, Whittier callin' his slapped-up shanty a hotel. Beds were chalk marks on the floor and a blanket Whittier pinched for the next customer when the first one snored.

Biggest laugh was on himself, anyone care to ask. Burney shoulda been in charge. "Press of business," Burney had said. "Big county, and I'm its sheriff."

Also landlord to outlaws at four dollars a day, as Jim recalled, and escort at a dollar a mile for bringin' 'em in, and takin' 'em to court, and wherever else it paid to haul 'em. Then, of course, it cost to summon witnesses. And to escort them to court, too. He understood why the sheriff couldn't afford to neglect his duties. Ditto the former Texas Ranger now tax collectin' from the county's foreign miners. Proceeds provided his livelihood, the fellow said. Jim understood. No sense chasin' Indians when dollars was in chasin' Chinese and Chileans.

Half a knee-slapper, though, the governor authorizin' this fandango with no funds to pay for it. Representative gone off now to San Jose to persuade the legislature to ante up. Jim figured his own reward for drawin' the short straw to head up this circus likely the same pay he got ridin' with Fremont on the tiff with Mexicans five years back. What the little boy shot at. Nothin'.

Still, what did he have to lose? Same answer. Nothin'. No trade anyways. Indians weren't diggin' gold. Too busy persuadin' prospectors outa that profession, too. Miners likely find more profit in huntin' Indians instead of gold anyways. Collect some government dollars for roundin' up the natives. Most men joinin' up had lost animals or friends or both in recent months. Gettin' paid for gettin' even somethin' of an attraction, Jim supposed, surveying the ragtag collection of settlers, miners, prospectors, down-and-outers, and assorted no-accounts milling around the stump he stood on.

Fact was, and he weren't admittin' on it out loud, he didn't trust nobody else to do this job. Least of all—worst of all—Walter H. Harvey. Out struttin' his rooster walk now, recitin' objections to Jim's 'credentials' to anyone who cared to listen. Crowin' again about sendin' Cherokees to Oklahoma. Couldn't get himself elected judge on that platform, so here he was campaignin' for this job.

And what job was it? Nothin' much. Just make the country safe for white men to move into, dig up, and take over. Just a simple matter of relievin' Indians of life, liberty, and the pursuit of whatever happiness they once had a chance at.

Jim groaned at the sight of Harvey coming toward him, pushing the diary keeper aside.

"*Mister* Savage," Harvey bellowed, "any gentleman can see the obvious error in giving the rank of Major to a civilian!"

Jim studied the insult. "Harvey, I'm takin' some exception to your insinuatin'. Consider myself a gentleman of the first water, I do. Inclined to defend the opinion if I weren't otherwise occupied. Busy here, bein' a *Major*, musterin' two hundred men into somethin' passin' for a militia."

Truth be told, Harvey weren't worth the bother of a fight. More fun in returnin' the annoyance. Jim grinned, raised a stiff hand to his forehead to shield his baby blues, adopted a look-out pose and surveyed the crowd. "Been keepin' an eye out for gentlemen all mornin', Harvey. Sad shortage."

"Listen, Savage, I am a military man! I was at West Point, for god's sake!"

"For god's sake?!" Jim said, looking Harvey up and down, as if impressed. "That right? Thought the Good Lord quit recruitin' after Joshua took Jericho."

"You are not qualified to put an end to this Indian business, *Mister* Savage!"

"*Mister* Harvey, you are testin' my good nature. I aim to see Indians don't get themselves exterminated."

"You merely delay the inevitable," Harvey retorted, turning. He took two steps and looked back. "Our business is not finished."

What was finished, Jim supposed, feeling sunk down by responsibility he didn't care to examine, was the Indians. Dared fate bravely, they did, anyone care to ask. What white man could face subjugation or extermination with more courage? Or any? Some choice. Kill a man fast with a bullet. Or watch him die slow from despair.

The Commissioners...will proceed... to Fremont's old camp... to meet the sachems and warriors. Savage is encamped...with a portion of his command. His men are patiently awaiting the action of the Commissioners.

—*Daily Alta California*
March 8, 1851

FEBRUARY FADED INTO MARCH while Jim felt increasingly disinclined for his assignment. A downhill business was his opinion on the matter, and he supposed he'd had all the fun he was likely to see. Of the two hundred men mustered into his so-called army, only seventy-five owned a gun. A black-smith hired to repair old rifles purchased for the rest declared most of them only a hair less dangerous to the shooter than the target. No one in the company, after moving out from Agua Fria to a camp with good grazing, thought to post a guard. Indians came in the night and stole fifty horses.

The legislature, meeting in San Jose, continued to haggle the funding. Brownlee, the Agua Fria storekeeper, on the government's promise of payment, provisioned the men with boots, ammunition, flour, beans, pork, coffee, canned goods, and assorted liquors. Jim suspected Brownlee more likely to collect the nothin' the little boy shot at than government reimbursement.

And, to his relief, it appeared the so-called Mariposa Battalion might share the nothin'-to-shoot-at target when in mid-March three Indian commissioners from Washington arrived with an extensive military escort bringing supplies to Agua Fria for the battalion.

"Makin' quite an addition to the encampment," Jim said, watching the military arrive behind the three commissioners dismounting their government-issued horses in front of his tent. "I'm Savage," he said, extending his hand. "Name, not an inclination." He shook hands offered as they introduced themselves. McKee, Wozencraft, and Barbour. Government men in city clothes. All of 'em wearin' white boiled shirts, city hats. Alike as peas in a pod.

He couldn't keep 'em straight, the three men in his tent now, perched on whatever stool, box, or barrel was handy, talkin' like they was readin' reports. He leaned forward, concentrating. Wozencraft? or maybe Barbour? —was going on about encountering four hundred Indians waiting for them at Dent's ferry. "Their leader or chief, we're not certain who spoke for them," he was saying, "but we understood them to be already disposed to peace and treaties."

Jim nodded. "Ain't surprised. José Rey, the Chauchila chief feverin' allied uprisin', got himself killed attackin' armed settlers. 'Spect his passin' somewhat reduced Indian enthusiasm for war." Too many gone too early to the Great Spirit. Maybe some glory in it. Couldn't see it himself.

McKee—or maybe Wozencraft—he'd figure 'em out soon enough, said, "We understand that the Indians of this country are extremely ignorant, lazy and degraded, yet generally harmless and peaceable in their habits until actually goaded to seek revenge for injuries inflicted upon them. Their very imbecility and poverty should with enlightened and liberal white men entitle them to commiseration and long forbearance."

Jim bristled. "Might take exception to bein' called imbeciles."

The commissioner, ignoring the objection, continued. "It is essential to the character of the state and indeed of the United States as a civilized and Christian nation, that a stop should be put to the shedding of blood. If, hereafter, depredations are committed by the Indians, upon either the persons or property of the whites, and you will apprise us of the facts, we will use all proper exertion to bring the offenders to justice, by the military force of United States."

"Well, the road ain't runnin' in one direction, fellas," Jim said, looking from one to the next and back. "Whites been shootin' Indians like they was in season, just for bein' Indians." He hesitated, remembering José Jesús, cleared his throat, resumed. "Indians was the original owners here. This was their fishin' and huntin' grounds, their acorn orchards. Now, I ain't sayin' I ain't partial to gold, but Indians bein' treated like they was the intruders? That ain't right."

"The shooting in cold blood of a white man by an Indian is murder," said one commissioner. "Punishable by death."

"So likewise if an Indian be killed by a white man, the crime is the same," said another.

"Your name again?" Jim asked him.

"Wozencraft."

"Got it. Wozencraft." Good eyes and a heavy beard lookin' for a chin, Jim thought, the way it climbed down to his jaw, then up and over his mouth to drop down again. Good eyes, mouth and chin kinda lookin' out from behind a hair hedge. Wozencraft he'd remember.

"The safety and security of every community demands that equal and exact justice is made out to all alike," Wozencraft continued. "The punishment should be the same."

Jim sighed. "Should be, but ain't. You fellas might want to check the law on that."

The commissioners stood. "It will be our earnest endeavor, Mr. Savage, to quiet the difficulties which now exist," Wozencraft said, "and afford to both whites and Indians such justice as their good conduct may entitle them to."

Jim shook the man's hand. Couldn't fault good intentions. "Care to say what treaty terms you offered the Indians waitin' at Dent's ferry?"

Barbour, or maybe McKee, Jim wasn't sure, replied, "For a promise to live in peace and friendship with white men, we advised them they'd get food, animals, and clothing."

"And we explained that their Great White Father loved them," said Wozencraft, "and would send them teachers so they could learn to read and write, and instructors with seeds and equipment to show them how to farm."

"Seems a generous exchange for peace and friendship," Jim said.

"And quit claim deeds to their land, of course."

Jim sighed again. Regular real estate transaction. Felt inclined to ask what they had on offer in the way of water-lots. He looked at each man in turn. Just doin' the government's business. Shook his head. "And where exactly did you gentlemen figure all these Indians get themselves into the farmin' business?"

"I can show you," Wozencraft said. "Map's in my saddlebag." He ducked out of the tent, and returned with a map he unfolded on Jim's cot.

Jim looked at the drawing, colored patches with black block numbers and lettering he guessed were names. Wozencraft traced a finger around the largest patch, colored yellow. "Mariposa is a huge county," he said, "and we understand it's sparsely settled by whites. Plenty of room for everyone. We're drawing up plans for the immediate establishment of large land tracts reserved special for the Indians."

Reserved special. A reservation. Jim imagined Indians herded up like cattle, led into their special corral. Like Sutter's Indians racin' horses and threshin' wheat. Seemed a lifetime ago. Looked bad to him then, like good old days now.

"You fellas identify the Indians you met who'd decided not to fight? Get any names?"

McKee, or maybe Barbour, said, "Cornelius. Said he was chief of the Tuolumnes and promised to bring his people in within two weeks."

"We presumed," said the other, "that the tribes apprehended the government's intentions."

"A general disinclination to engage," said Wozencraft.

"Fact is, fellas," Jim said, "I expect most tribes'll be linin' up to avoid war. Most of 'em peaceable by nature. Abundantly supplied with 'general disinclination.'"

General disinclination. When he was done bein' Major Savage, maybe promote himself to General Disinclination.

Despite the military's arrival and commissioners making treaties, Jim's men wanted to hunt Indians. He put their restless energies into scouting, setting up tents, posting lookouts. One afternoon, so engaged, he heard his name shouted.

"Major Savage! Major Savage!"

Eccleston again, wavin' his diary. Only volunteer keepin' a record of the adventure. Always wantin' details of the commissioners' progress.

"A few minutes, sir! To make sure I got it right, Major."

Jim listened while Eccleston read: "March the first. The commissioners are doing their best to make a treaty with the Indians and have given them eight days from today to bring in their families and all they possess."

She woke terrified, heart pounding, clutching the buffalo robe, staring into the dark, her dream still vivid. Trembling, she woke Seethkil. "Three wizards!" she cried. "Here! In the land! They are here!"

Seethkil pulled her close, cradled her into his warmth, calming her, stroking her face. He murmured into her ear that the familiar dream vision meant nothing. They would go to the Monos he told her. Soon. Together. Always together. "Teheneh the beautiful maiden and fearless Kosookah," he said, soothing her. "Together."

When the snow melted.

"They propose the Indians shall come down into the plains," Eccleston said, reading from his diary, "and settle, allowing them ten years' provisions and a pair of pants, shirt and blanket every four months to each Indian. They also give them one farmer, a carpenter, a schoolmaster and preacher, and a blacksmith."

"That's the promise," Jim said. He imagined Chief Teneiya and his warriors smokin' pipes and laughin' over an offer of preachers and pants. Sayin' thanks but no thanks, we been fine a few thousand years without either.

That the terms looked good to the peaceful Tuolumnes was no surprise. They were hungry. If they had to live where white men told them to, at least they would eat. Good as his word, Chief Cornelius brought the Tuolumnes in, smoked a pipe with the commissioners, put his mark on the treaty paper, promised to persuade hostile tribes along the Merced and Mariposa rivers to do the same.

In less than two weeks six tribes came in, small parties at first, hesitant and fearful. Hundreds of Indians soon followed. The commissioners distributed presents, hosted feasts, explained treaty terms, told chiefs to make their marks. Jim translated, assured the commissioners the Indians were willing. What choice did they have, he wanted to ask. What else is on offer? What the little boy shot at, that's what. Indians weren't stupid, never had been. Brave, for a fact, and foolish maybe, but not stupid. They understood negotiations. This deal meant agreein' to whatever the Great White Father chose to give 'em. If that was a preacher and a pair of pants, well, better'n a bullet in the back.

And what about him? Jim Savage, former king of the Tularenos? Felt gut-punched seein' his old friends makin' marks on treaty papers. Bautista humiliated, a proud man reduced, pledging docility. Jim put a hand on the chief's broad shoulder, praised his bravery, recalled to him their friendship. Bautista, rigid, silently walked away. What was done was done.

The Mariposa Battalion, with little else to do, amused themselves with footraces and dances. In camp one night, Jim watched a few come-in Indians put on a dance, a small show for the volunteers and soldiers. Not a shadow on the feathered ceremonials and spirited dancin' he'd participated in, clapper-rattles shakin', foot-drums poundin'. No heart in it now. How could there be? Indians with heart weren't comin' in. And when they eventually did, as they must, they'd leave heart behind.

While waiting for more tribes to come in, the commissioners counseled military regulars to restraint and patience. Jim's Mariposa Battalion men waited more or less impatiently until rain drenched the camp for several days and spirits sagged. Then they grew restless.

"Give us somethin' to do, Major!" a volunteer begged. "This sittin' around waitin' is makin' us crazy!"

Makin' him crazy, too, anyone care to ask. After some thought, he realized Chief Ponwatchee's small Nukchus band hadn't come in. His fidgety men didn't know Nukchus wouldn't fight. A fifteen-mile uphill slog through mud was bound to take the itch off the desire to shoot anyone but him.

His order galvanized the troops into a flurry of activity, packing mules, saddling horses. Under a darkening sky in an intermittent rain, he hollered, "Let's move out, men!"

Within a few miles they were splashing through rising canyon creeks, scaling slippery ridges, grappling with reluctant animals. It rained steadily. Mules lost their footing, then their packs. Men lost their footing, or the trail. Or both. Some turned back. Jim called a halt after a fatiguing six or seven miles, the company relieved to stop and take shelter beneath dripping trees.

At daylight he roused them again. Spirits sodden as their gear, they pushed on beneath a steady downpour. At dawn on the third day of complaining, swearing, collapsing, and quitting, the thinned ranks finally surrounded the Nukchus' rancheria and surprised the Indians into placid surrender.

If any of his exhausted men expected an exciting confrontation, Jim suspected they were relieved to be wrong. All they wanted was rest and dry boots.

Chief Ponwatchee, an old friend, invited Jim to sit by his fire, share a pipe. Jim sat, accepted the pipe, assured the chief he came in friendship. Those white men surrounding the rancheria? Friends. Everyone friends. He expressed his admiration for the Nukchu people. And then he reminded the chief of old tribal tales, omens that white men would overcome his people one day.

Damn, he hated this business. He shook his head. "This is that day, Chief. In the valley three wizards got presents for your people. Sent by the white men's Great Wizard. The Great Wizard wants Indians to live like white men, on the plains. Wants you all honest. Peaceful. Good Indians."

Weren't no way to pretty the picture. No preachin' and teachin' or elaboratin' details, no repeatin' and recitin'. Give it to 'em straight. He sighed, looked up from the pipe bowl warming his hands, and said, "Here's how it is, Chief. You don't do what the Great Wizard wants, these white men out there gotta kill you and your people. Gotta kill you now if your people don't agree to be good Indians."

A persuasive argument.

Ponwatchee rose without a word, left his fire and gathered together his mystified people watching the surrounding white men slapping their arms against themselves for warmth. Jim stood at his side while the chief explained that wizards sent these white men to take them all to a new place to live, would give them presents when they got there.

No one objected. What choice did they have?

Jim told his men to set up camp while the Nukchus prepared a reluctant departure. "Make tents with your blankets," he told them. "We're halfway into the mountains. Snow's likely."

Halfway into the mountains? He considered the possibility, conferred with Ponwatchee. The chief said yes, he could send a runner up the mountain to the Yosemites.

"Simple message," Jim said. "Tell Chief Teneiya to come in. Tell him he has no choice."

She stirred the fire, lifted a hot stone from flames with a forked stick. Slid it into her simmering acorn soup. Watched steam rise grayly into another gray day. Glanced at Seethkil, bearskin blanket over his shoulders, hunched over his whittling. Silent. Another gray day. Like the one before. And days before that. One day like the next. Rain. Snow. More rain. Fog. Gray.

Awani lay silent beneath a gray sky. No drums, no dancing, no laughing. Children huddled quiet inside shelters. Women silently stirred acorn mush at their fires. Warriors silently stared into the distance, or smoked, or whittled pipes with sharpened obsidian. A few scraped hides. Others fashioned buckskin moccasins they lined with shredded cedar bark and stitched with milkweed fiber. Waiting.

Waiting for what was to come. Waiting for snow to stop, to open the pass to the Monos. Waiting for returning runners to report. Had the Chauchilas surrendered? Muquelemes?

Waiting. Waiting for Chief Teneiya to decide.

Waiting for Teneiya, Jim watched a gray sky release a light snow, silently whitening trees and cedar shelters. When a late-afternoon sun emerged to glitter the landscape, clouds glowed peach, then gold. As twilight dissolved into an inky nightfall, stars winked above treetops stretching skyward.

Late into the night he sat with Chief Ponwatchee, content. This was a life he'd known well. Preferred it, anyone doubted enough to ask. Waiting. Abiding. The Indian gift of how to be in the world.

On the second day, the sky blue and bright, a band of Pohonochees cautiously approached. He greeted them, assured friendship, advised them their future had been determined by three wizards. With the Nukchus, now slowly packing baskets and blankets and dismantling their shelters, they must leave the mountain. The wizards had decreed the destruction of their villages.

He saw his men, initially puffed up by their sham conquest, deflate at the sight of their charges. The Indians accepted their fate with submissive dignity, although the treaty terms were, Jim knew, a mystery to them. Not that it mattered. What choice did they have?

Late on the third day of waiting, a chestnut horse with a rider appeared in the distance, slowly approaching through the forest. Jim waited in the stillness, alert, curious. Teneiya? Chief of the Yosemites coming in alone?

The horse drew closer, its rider's red blanket collecting snowflakes. The horse lifted its head and whinnied.

Jim drew a deep breath. "Hello, Girl," he said to himself, "been missin' you."

When she rode into camp, he reached up, offered a hand. She took it. Head bowed, she dismounted. When she looked up, grief-ravaged eyes met his. Chief Ponwatchee mumbled a few words of welcome and his wife led Isabel into a shelter. Jim followed, ducking through the narrow entrance.

The chief's wife brought bowls of warm acorn porridge she placed in their hands, left them sitting cross-legged on blankets, looking at each other across a small fire.

Jim stared at her. Where was the girl from those long-gone days on the Mariposa? Did she remember how they sat, like this, learning each other's words, beginning to talk?

She held the porridge bowl in her lap. Looked up. He hadn't changed. Blue eyes. Yellow hair. How the days had fled since last she saw his familiar face. Only six moons. Time rushing like Yuloni's river.

He saw sadness, trouble doubled. Belatedly realized no cradled infant clung to her back. Her sorrow visible. Heart heavy. Familiar to his own, the image indelible: burying box, desert sand. He sighed, shook his head. No end to loss. He mumbled an awkward sympathy.

"He decided against this world," she whispered. "I sent his cradle basket on smoke that he might remember the People."

He looked at her, this sad girl-woman. "Nothin' gained in lookin' back, Isabel, for none of us. Future comin' at us fast."

She nodded. And then, as if collecting alms, she held the porridge bowl out in two hands. "I come to beg," she said. "Jim, friend of my father, my friend, Chief Teneiya's people belong where Great Spirit intended. Awani is our home."

He sighed. "This trouble ain't got no fix to it, Isabel. Your people got to come in."

"Chief Teneiya fears for Awani—" She started to say more, how Teneiya wandered the village as if lost, mumbling to himself, repeating the ancient prediction of the People's land lost, the People no more.

"Ain't my decision, Isabel. Yosemites got to come in."

She looked from him to the fire's dying flames. "We will be ghosts."

"Whole blasted world populated with ghosts." He shook his head, overwhelmed. Sauk ghosts, Fox ghosts, Cherokee ghosts, Choctaw ghosts. Made a body wonder how there was room in the world for livin' people. Made a body angry, this business. Couldn't do nothin' about any of it. Not her distress, not Teneiya's fear. Indians brought down to poverty, and worse. Proud past disappearin' into a forlorn future. World just a pot full of troubles.

He took a deep breath. Well, he weren't the one stirrin' it. He was just Jim Savage, mountain-man promoted into leadin' this sorry round-'em-up business. Gone downhill from bein' a king to bein' a Major. That right there, that was the Almighty havin' a joke. Except there weren't no hoot in it. What a world. He was losin' his sense of humor.

"Isabel, look at me. You gotta hear me. Yosemites got to come in."

Her eyes pleaded, her voice broke. "I come begging for Awani!"

"Teneiya know you come in?" Was she here on her own? Got her father's blood in her, sure thing. Had to admire the gumption.

"I speak for Awanichees." Her eyes filled. "Jim, El Rey, let us live."

He winced. There's the joke again. King of the Tularenos. A spree, a lark. A fraud. He knew it. She knew it. Those days gone. And here he was with this sad chapter in a book he couldn't write, wouldn't if he could. No hero in it. Herdin' Indians, people he admired. A lousy story. He wished he'd never heard of California or its blasted gold.

"Teneiya don't bring his people in, Isabel, army of white men gonna come down on 'em like an avalanche. You know that word? Avalanche?"

"Snow mountain," she said. "Crash down. Bury everything." She gestured one hand sweeping over the other.

No point hidin' the facts. He told her the treaty terms. 'Reserved' lands. Explained quit-claim deeds. Watched her eyes widen. Heard her breath quicken. Saw he'd stunned her.

"You were there! When the Americans promised!" She rose, stood staring at him. "My father was promised, when he fought the Mexicans with the Americans, our land was ours forever! Promised! Remember that treaty?! You were there!"

He remembered.

Early days. Before gold.

He stood, faced her, shook his head. "Americans generally mean what they say when they say it." He wondered if that was true. Or maybe they just put the best face on what looked like two faces. "Unfortunately, not reliably," he added. That much he knew was true. "These commissioners got new treaties."

"I tell them!" she declared.

Jim sighed. Her father's daughter. Weren't runnin' from this avalanchin' future. Brave. Hopelessly brave.

He instructed half his company to escort her and the few Nukchus prepared to go, and watched them leave in a lightly falling snow. Later, to his surprise, where only trees had been a moment before he saw a tall, very straight figure appear beyond the encampment. He took a deep breath. No mistakin' authority.

For a long minute, he stared at the Indian caped in bearskin. The Indian stared back, waited.

Jim went out to meet him. Looked up into the creased brown face, nose pierced by a shell stick, earlobes ornamented with bird bone tube, hair thick beneath a beaded net. Older than expected, maybe sixty or so.

"Teneiya," the chief said.

Jim nodded. "Yep."

Chief Ponwatchee left them sitting at his fire to parley privately and Jim honored the expected formalities, offered a pipe, his respect, a lengthy welcome, and then his assurance.

"This comin' in," he told Teneiya, "is not a trick to put your people under my power." He placed his hand on his chest, gestured sincerity. "If Yosemites go to the commissioners, like other tribes, and agree to live in peace with white men, there will be no more war." He explained the terms of the treaty.

Teneiya sat silent a long time before saying, "My people do not want to leave."

Jim wanted to say 'Right, heard all about your mountain fortress, Chief. Yosemites tucked away tight as ticks up there. But old times, they're gone, ain't comin' back. What's more, got my own grudgement, Chief, case you want particulars. Ain't forgot my friends was butchered. And now here I am, a trumped-up major in a trumped-up army, which might give you a laugh, same as me, but all the fire power's on my side. And right here, right now, I'm the white man and you're the Indian, and we ain't gonna have us a parley about what your people want or don't want. They ain't got a choice.'

What he said was, "Here's the deal, Chief," and gave his spiel. Spelled out the commissioners' promised inducements, all the things the Great White Father wanted to give his Indian children.

Teneiya listened with an expression that said he was waiting for an offer worth hearing. After a long silence, he spoke. "My people do not want anything from the Great White Father you talk about. The Great Spirit is our father, gives us everything we need. We do not want anything from white men. Go! Let us remain in the mountains where we were born, where the ashes of our fathers were given to the winds. I have said enough!"

Jim bristled. Go?! You have said enough!? I been waitin' four days to hear Go?! You have said enough!? He stared at the chief. Felt like shoutin' he was losin' his good nature, and plenty keen on quittin' this man's army anyways. And you, Mister Teneiya, can tell Mister I-was-at-West-Point to 'Go!' He's got news for you from Oklahoma he's sure to mention. Cherokee ghosts, friend.

He took a deep breath, then another, let the moment pass. Sucked his pipe. Looked at the chief. Sucked his pipe some more, then said, "Chief, if your people have all you need, why do your warriors rob miners? Why do they murder white men and take their belongings and burn their houses?"

Now Teneiya smoked. Jim saw him thinking, considering, then slowly examine his pipe, turning it one way, then another. At length he looked at Jim. "To steal from an enemy is not wrong. We believed white men digging gold were our enemy. Now we know they are not. We will be satisfied to live in peace with white men. But my people do not want to go to the plains. We have enemies with some tribes, and they will make war with us there. We can defend ourselves in the mountains."

Jim sighed. "Chief, that is not what we can call a realistic proposal." He looked at Teneiya and shook his head. Tired now, he knocked ash from his pipe, ready to be done. "Fact is, Chief, things ain't gonna go that way. If your people stay in the mountains, they're gonna steal horses and mules and kill white men. Ain't no secret your people robbed my stores and murdered my men. I am the last person you want to appeal to. I mean that. The last person." Well, maybe not the last person, probably next to last. He imagined Walter H. Harvey, a grin on his fat red face, informin' Teneiya about Oklahoma.

The chief frowned. "If the Chauchilas do not boast about who killed your men or burned your store they are cowards. They came to us to unite against white men."

Jim stood, ran his hands through his hair like he was ready to pull it out. "Who did what or why ain't the point here! You and me can palaver and smoke and trade grievances until summer comes and blisters our heads. Arguin' ain't changin' nothin'. Done dancin' around, Chief. I ain't here to persuade. I'm here to say you got no choice. You gotta bring your people in, and go to the commissioners, and make terms with 'em or your people gonna get killed. That's a fact. Not one of 'em gonna be left alive."

Teneiya rose, hands in fists he held to his chest. "My people are few upon the earth and soon shall be no more. I am old. Kill me if you want."

"Go get your people. Bring 'em in."

They stared at one another. Neither moved. Jim understood Teneiya had to make his stand. For pride. For show. "Need you to say it, Chief. Need you to give me your word."

At length, Teneiya gave it.

Jim watched the old man leave, and prepared to wait. He waited three days.

No one came.

Article 3. The said tribes or bands hereby jointly and severally relinquish and forever quit claim to the United States all the right, title, claim, or interest of any kind, they or either of them have, or ever had, to lands or soil in California.

—Treaty, Made and Concluded
Camp Barbour
April 29, 1851

SUCH DUST AND NOISE! Everywhere she looked, soldiers erecting tents or directing confused Indians this way or that, sutlers packing and unpacking bawling mules and creaking wagons. Hammers pounding, saws rasping, men hanging canvas, making a canvas town. She remembered canvas sails furled against the masts of abandoned ships at anchor in San Francisco's bay, crews gone for gold. White men coming and coming, and now here they were, covering the country with canvas.

From a passing young man in uniform she learned the camp had a name, Fremont. She knew the name. Her father fought against the Mexicans with Fremont, the white man who made the treaty that promised the Indians their land forever. The white man she needed to see.

"Where?" she asked.

The soldier, confused, said, "What? Who?"

"Fremont."

He laughed. "Fremont ain't here. Ain't gonna be here. Fremont's the name commissioners gave the place."

She understood. The People named the places they lived, visited, traveled. Rivers, canyons, mountains, lakes, boulders, ravines, villages: Cosumnes, Muqueleme, Yuloni, Awani. Names passed down from time beyond imagining. And now white men had come with new names.

She found the commissioner's large blue tent where the soldier directed her, and waited impatiently until another soldier said, "You can come in now."

Inside the tent a bearded, dress-coated man in spectacles sat hunched over papers piled atop a board balanced on barrels.

"We were promised our land forever!" she declared, fists gripping her calico skirt. Right was on her side. The law. White man's law.

He glanced up at her, removed his spectacles. "You speak pretty good English, young woman."

"I know your words, many words," she said. She had watched and waited one long winter on the Mariposa learning them. They tumbled from her now, a river of words insisting, demanding, reminding. Awani was the People's home, their land, promised to the People forever by Great Spirit and by the Americans defeating the Mexicans. The People belonged to Awani. And Awani belonged to the People, and there they would live in peace with the white man.

The commissioner was looking at her like some curious specimen unexpectedly brought to his attention. He nodded agreeably.

"I have good news for your people from their Great White Father when they come in," he said. "Flour and plows and axes and seeds and shirts and pants, and more."

Had he heard her? Were his ears stopped? Was he deaf?

She watched him install his spectacles, take a paper from his board table. Clearing his throat, he read a list of promises. Hatchets, hoes, iron, steel, grindstones. On and on. How did white people breathe, how did the earth breathe, under such a mountain of things?

When he concluded, he looked up and smiled.

She shook her head. "Awanichees have all we need. We do not want your things." She explained how the People lived, how little they needed, how the land provided for them. "And when the People die," she said, "we send their things with them, in smoke." How to explain, in all this noise, that sending useful and familiar possessions with the departed provided a place upon the earth for new baskets and blankets and fish-hooks and flutes for new people. Victoria's red calico skirt, gone from the earth as smoke, all the People's belongings, gone with them to the Great Spirit, smoke.

She wanted to tell him more, much more. How after death the People became ghosts, returned as cougar or crane, elk or owl. That if Awani was not theirs, where would they roam, where would they fly?

The commissioner was shuffling papers, no longer looking at her, and she had so much to say! About how white men destroyed rivers, cut trees, trampled the land that was Great Spirit's gift to the People. She wanted him to hear her. How could he hear? This place was so noisy. The bustling activity outside the blue canvas sounding louder and louder. Hammers and saws and shouts for more nails, more canvas. The shouting, it hurt her head. She was getting confused. Was she repeating herself?

The commissioner was staring at her, elbows planted in the sprawl of maps and papers on his makeshift desk, hands folded.

She stared back. Had he understood anything she'd said, this white man who had come from the Great White Father in a place named Washington?

She felt suddenly exhausted, overwhelmed by noise and odd memories crowding her thoughts.

"Your people will have a new home," he said. He shuffled papers, extracted one, turned it toward her, and pointed a stubby finger at a penciled map. "Here. Parcel 273." He looked up at her. "Good farming land. On the Fresno River."

This white man must be deaf. "The People are not farmers!" Had she shouted? Or only imagined she had? Seethkil a farmer? Chief Teneiya a farmer? She said again, barely a whisper. "The People are not farmers."

The commissioner smiled, stood. "You learned English. Your people are clever. They'll learn to farm. We'll send a farmer to teach you. Everything will be fine once your people come in, sign a treaty, and get settled. Don't worry."

"Chief Teneiya won't sign! Awani is our land!" This man had no ears!

"They'll come in, young woman." He sat, looked up at her, then back at the map. "Major Savage has his orders."

A soldier led her out of the tent.

So much noise, bawling mules, shouting soldiers. She couldn't think. Her head hurt. She looked around at the bustling construction of the dusty tent camp. Where to go? What to do? She needed to think. She crouched under a nearby tree and pulled her red blanket up to her ears. What would her father do? or Jim? Seethkil? Chief Teneiya? She didn't know. One thought chased the tail of another. She couldn't think. Her head hurt.

The commissioner's voice drifted from the tent, reciting the Great White Father's promises to someone… "one hundred head of steers and one hundred sacks or barrels of flour, ten brood mares and one stallion, twenty-five cows and a bull, ten plows, ten sets of harness, one hundred axes, ten picks, a year's supply of seeds…."

She covered her head with her arms, thoughts racing. The Yosemites weren't farmers. Losing Awani would kill them. If they didn't come in, white men would kill them. They must come. To farm, to be fenced, enclosed. Leave Awani. Come in. Come in. Come in. That's what the commissioner said. "Come in." She heard him now, reciting promises—

"—one hundred chopping axes, one hundred hatchets, three hundred garden hoes, eight hundred pounds of iron, two hundred pounds of steel, fifteen grindstones, two flannel shirts and two pairs of coarse pants for each man and boy…."

Echoes. They must come in. They must come in. Live on Parcel 273.

"—three thousand yards of brown sheeting, three thousand yards of calico, thirty pounds of Scotch thread, assorted needles, one gross of thimbles, six dozen pairs of assorted scissors...."

What was she doing here?! Where had her life gone? Oh, to be sitting with Victoria once more in the sunshine on the grinding rock making acorn, forest fragrant with cedar and pine, listening to scolding jays, watching Anna's infant daughter crawling, silently learning the earth.

What was she doing here, huddled beneath a red blanket next to a blue tent? Who were these passing strangers, soldiers leading bewildered Indians obediently going this way or that, wherever soldiers directed? Team after team of plodding mules hauling creaking wagons through swirling dust. She couldn't think. So much din and confusion. She couldn't think, couldn't think.

Today about noon Major Savage started for the Yoosemita Camp with 57 men

—Diary, Robert Eccleston
March 27, 1851

"YOU'RE ISABEL, RIGHT? Red blanket. Figured you must be Isabel."

She looked up. A white man, trimmed beard, kind eyes. Fringed red scarf around his neck. She didn't know him.

She nodded. Yes, Isabel. She was Isabel.

He held out a hand. "Bunnell, Lafayette Bunnell. Doc. Everyone calls me Doc."

She stared at his extended hand, confused.

"Major Savage sent me to find you."

To find her? Where was she? She looked around. Blue tent. How long had she been here? Had she slept beneath this tree? Had she eaten? A tin plate. Scraps of food. Someone had fed her.

Bewildered, she took the offered hand, stood.

"Come with me, Isabel. This way."

She followed.

Another blue tent, canvas chairs. Jim. Here was Jim. Jim? Confusing. How long since they talked? Her mind was a tangle. Jim was standing, looking at her, talking at her. What was he saying? She was so tired. Her head ached.

"Isabel? Look at me."

She looked at him. How did eyes borrow the sky? She shook her head, tried to understand. What was sky eyes saying? Something about Chief Teneiya? Treaty conditions? Something about the land between the rivers.

"From the Merced to the Tuolumne, Isabel. For the Yosemites. Forever. For all time. Commissioners promise—"

Promise. For all time. Her mind wandered. White people waved promises like flags, folded them up, forgot where they left them. Forgot they existed. She looked at him. How did hair take color from summer grass?

"Isabel, listen to me. The Yosemites must come in. They have no choice."

No choice, no choice. Her head hurt.

"Isabel, listen to me. José Jesús understood times was changin'. What did your father want for you, for Teneiya's people? New ways, remember? You know what he'd say."

José Jesús. She concentrated. What would José Jesús want for Teneiya's people? She looked around. Blue canvas, so much canvas. Outside, braying mules, shouts, laughter. Soldiers. How did she get here? Why was she here?

"Isabel, listen to me. Yosemites gotta come in. Ain't no choice but the reservation."

Reservation? Her people? Yosemites? On a reservation?

Her voice, asking, "How will they live on a reservation?"

"I don't know, Isabel, but they'll live."

José Jesús. Her father's voice in her head, "Heed me, Isabel, and live long." She wanted to live. To live long with Seethkil. What choice did she have? She nodded. Yes, life.

"You understand what you gotta do?"

She nodded.

"You ready?"

She nodded.

Beneath gray clouds obscuring a darkening sky, pack mules brayed. Shouting men steadied horses. Somehow, she was astride, the horse's warm flesh against her legs, its large life impatient. Jim, mounting his horse next to hers, turned in his saddle, looked back. She turned, too. Behind them a column of mounted men, red blankets and blue blankets rolled behind their saddles, rifles by their sides. On her shoulder something soft, red, fringed. A scarf. She lifted an edge, examined it. Where had it come from?

"Brownlee."

Had she spoken?

"You remember Brownlee? Sutler in Agua Fria?" Jim talking, looking at her as if she didn't know him. "He got in some things from China. Doc gave it to you. Remember?"

She didn't. Was she a ghost? She must be a ghost.

The company set off in a light rain. She was a ghost going home, to Awani. Jim on the chestnut horse. Girl? Jim watching her, she watching the distance, the company moving into it, horses whinnying, men shouting, clouds shifting, sun shining, the day advancing, the great life of the horse beneath her splashing through rivers, crossing ravines, ascending winding trails between pines and past oaks, into the hills.

Time passing, daylight fading, a biting wind swirling fallen leaves, whistling into trees, whispering snow from branches. Cold nipped her face. She wasn't a ghost. She knew the country, recognized the trail, realized where she was and, suddenly, what she was doing. She was leading white men to Awani. To the Yosemites' hidden place. White men with guns! What was she thinking? She hadn't been thinking. Was she saving her people? Or betraying them?!

Jim, on the horse at her side, the chestnut, Girl. Was he saying something? She looked at him. He was looking at her, talking. "Need to stop, Isabel. Set up camp." He called the company to a halt.

She stood apart, watching through the slowly drifting flakes of a late-day snowfall. White men rowdily intruding on the forest, on *wawona*, planting tents, hobbling horses and mules, disturbing the vast forest silence with shouts and laughter. She felt ill.

Jim caught Bunnell's attention, waved him over. "Keep an eye on her, Doc. Looks about to collapse." He gestured toward Isabel, her red blanket bright against the snow.

"Look at that tree!" Doc exclaimed, pointing. "Must be two hundred feet tall! The base looks thirty feet in diameter!"

"Tell her how proud her father would be," Jim said. Anyone care to ask, he wasn't sure whether he felt relieved to have got her this far or not. Didn't know his own mind, come to that. Wanted this sad, bad business over, that's what he wanted. And best get it done. Get done findin' Teneiya and his band and bringin' 'em in. Get the best men on it and get it goddamned over with.

He grabbed Doc's shoulder. "Listen, Doc, admire trees later. Let's finish this Indian business. Chasin' Indians ain't easy. Gonna be slowed up by snow from here on. Best bet in this game gotta be on the quickest men."

Bunnell looked at him. "You mean actually fast? Running fast?"

"Right! A foot-race!" Jim turned, shouted for attention. "Men, listen up! Gonna have us a foot-race! See who's gonna chase Indians!"

Isabel huddled in the dry needles beneath a tall tree, pulled the red blanket close, watched men run, holler, shatter the forest silence with jeers and cheers. She imagined them racing into her village, terrifying women and children, alarming warriors. Arrows flying. Guns firing. How had she not realized what she was doing? Her head ached. Her people weren't Nukchus, Potoyensees, Yokuts surrendering and signing treaties. What had she done? Yosemites wouldn't surrender. Die now, or die later, Seethkil had said. Where was he now?

"Major! Major!"

She looked up. A sentry running towards Jim. "Major! Major!"

Everyone turning, staring. The sentry hollering. "Major! Look! Indians!"

She stood, disbelieving. There they were! Coming through the forest, into the camp! Chief Teneiya! Her People! Carrying baskets and blankets and children. Bowed down by exhaustion, coming in! Coming in! She had not betrayed them! They had chosen! They would live, they would all live!

She hurried toward them, toward Jim greeting Chief Teneiya, heard Chief Teneiya saying deep snow delayed them, made travel difficult. But they had come. As promised.

"Everyone? All your people?" Jim's expression doubtful, looking around, telling someone to get a count.

Now everyone crowded around, staring at one another, white men at Indians, and Indians at white men. No one looked at her. She searched faces, wandered among them, unnoticed. Someone was shouting numbers, counting.

Jim yelled, "Count 'em again!"

She watched old people, women, children, herded into groups. More counting and shouting.

"Seventy-two, Major!"

Jim, voice exasperated, saying, "Expected more than what you got here, Chief."

Chief Teneiya protesting, declaring his people had come in.

"Gotta be more, Chief." Jim, shaking his head. "All gotta come in. Not just a sample."

She knew not everyone had come in.

Unnoticed, she slipped silently into the trees.

She found Seethkil sitting on the broad outcropping of their special place, watching her climb the trail, waiting for her where they agreed. Wrapped in the buffalo robe, bow by his side, arrows quivered.

"Like Kosookah," she said, tears filling her eyes at the sight of him.

The sun was briefly out. Melting snow dripped from tree branches, dimpling drifts.

"White men coming," she said, going to him. He opened his arms, took her in to the buffalo robe and the rich warm animal smell of him. "To bring the people in," she said, burying her head against his shoulder.

He knew, he said, his voice soft, all the warriors knew. "Women, children, old people, slow people go in." He held her, looked at her, touched her face. "For now."

"For now?"

"Awani is our land."

She held his dear face in her hands, looked at him. "Seethkil, white men are coming. With guns. Guns." Did he understand?

He nodded. "We know."

"They are coming. Here. Into Awani."

"We hide," he said. "White men have no eyes to see our trails, our caves. Ours. Since First People."

She knew he didn't understand. But they were together on this day of pale sun brightening snow-dusted trees far below. And below, for now, Awani lay resplendent in winter white. And silent. No drumming, no singing. Silence disturbed only by birdsong and cedar branches releasing snow.

Three moons, perhaps two, if Great Spirit willed it, until passage to the Monos.

The date of our discovery and entrance into Yosemite was about the 21st of March 1851. We were afterward assured by Ten-ei-ya and others of his band, that this was the first visit ever made to this valley by white men.
—Lafayette Bunnell

JIM TURNED HIS HORSE, headed back along the treacherous snow-heavy trail, nodding to each man of the company as he passed. No sign of Doc. Where had he gone off to? Like tryin' to herd butterflies, this business. People flittin' off in all directions. Isabel gone, no surprise there. No surprise where. Ha! Still a poet!

Rough trail, this. Enormous trees and boulders, heavy brush. He leaned forward, patted Girl's neck, whispered, "Doc out here somewhere, keep an eye out." He sat back, saddle leather creaking, scanned the landscape. Teneiya swearin' seventy-two was all of 'em. Balderdash. He knew it, she knew it. Sure as shootin' rapids and rabbits, prob'ly that many more still up the mountain. Isabel with 'em, knowin' the commissioners want 'em all. Lock, stock, and barrel.

What a business. Teneiya finally admittin' maybe some renegades, maybe some Paiutes and Monos, stayed back to cross the mountain. Seein's believin', Chief. Let's go see. Teneiya gatherin' up his pride like it was somethin' fine to wear, agreein' to show Jim the trail back to his village. Started off ramrod straight, like he was headin' a parade. Hardly gone a mile before complainin' he was old, tired, and goin' back to wait with his seventy-two friends and family, leavin' a sullen, foot-draggin' old mission Indian, Sandino, for guide.

And now Doc had flitted off somewhere. Doc, who understood Indians. Inclined to their ways, telling how his family had been Indian traders in Detroit. "Learned our customers' language, habits, and character," he'd said. "After which all subsequent attempts to civilize me failed."

But where was he? Tirin' business this trail, snow three feet in places. The men good at trail-breakin', though, each one leadin' for a time, then droppin' to the rear where the snow was packed and the ride easier.

Jim squinted, seeing Doc's horse tied to a madrone, and Doc atop a rocky outcrop gazing into the distance. "Doc, you better wake up from that dream up there! We're huntin' Indians, remember? Might be some lurkin' around studyin' on that hair I'm thinkin' you'd like to keep!"

Bunnell glanced in his direction, then back into the distance. "If my hair is now required, I can depart in peace, for I have seen the power and glory of a Supreme Being."

Dismounting and tossing Girl's reins over a manzanita branch, Jim started up the rise. "You havin' visions?" he hollered. "Get into the whisky at breakfast?"

Doc shook his head. "Back in the winter of forty-nine, I was mining near the Merced and—"

"Not a lonely occupation, even in forty-nine," Jim said, grabbing a spruce branch and hauling himself around a large boulder. "Reckon I outfitted half the county. Before it were a county. I'd be mighty grateful to the Good Lord or Great Spirit or whatever supreme being could bring those fine times back. Gold blowin' in like rain on a storm. Indians happy with a blanket. Wives happy with raisins. That frolic all gone to hell." He scrambled the final few yards to where Doc sat.

Eyes locked on the distance, Doc continued. "As I was saying, there was one day I was climbing a trail up from Ridley's ferry and spotted some stupendous rocky peaks, just a glimpse, but I was, I confess it, dazzled by the scene. Made such an impression I inquired around, asked if anyone knew the locality so I could get a closer look. No luck. Until now." He pointed. "Jim, just look. Honest to God, it's unlike anything you've ever seen, anything I've ever seen, maybe anyone's ever seen."

Jim nodded, studying the distant granite cliff. "Fine sight, Doc, but natural wonders not on the schedule. Gotta go. Devil of a trail."

The trail, to their eventual surprise and relief, descended into a grassy meadow nearly free of snow. There they found John Boling, second-in-command, fashioning a tent from blankets. "No snow and good grazing for the horses and mules," Boling said as the late arrivals dismounted. "Got the men setting up camp."

Doc whistled, pointed. "My God, Jim, look at that mountain! And the waterfalls!"

Jim ignored him. "Still got some day left," he said to Boling.

"Tried to get Sandino to move on," Boling said, gesturing toward the mission Indian looking morose on a log by the river, "but he poured out a volley of Indian lingo nobody could understand. Made all kinds of signs, got me to follow him. River's the problem. Village is on the other side and water's too high to cross."

"Teneiya and his people crossed it," Jim said, annoyed. "Must be a ford somewhere, upriver or down. Anybody look?"

"Tunnehill took off on his mule to see. Said he didn't believe the Indian."

"Somewhat on the doubtin' side myself," Jim said, looking over at Sandino studying his knees. "What did Tunnehill find?"

Boling gestured a thumb. "That's him, by the campfire, drying off. Boys razzed him on getting baptized."

"Don't start Doc on religious stuff. Says he's seein' the face of God Almighty."

Bunnell looked at them. "I admit I'm devoutly astonished at the grandeur here. And see over there!" He turned, pointing. "That cliff is the very captain of mountains. Overwhelms the senses, doesn't it?"

"Yep," Jim said, "fine fortress. Perfect for hidin' Teneiya's renegades and refugees." And Isabel.

As evening advanced, he posted guards. The men made a sparse meal of dried meat from the short rations they carried, smoked their pipes, relaxed by campfires. They were laughing and chatting in the darkness when Bunnell shouted, "Hey, boys!" and surprised them into silence.

He stood. "You might think this is sentimental, but I'm guessing some of you feel the mysterious magnificence of the scenery here." He looked around at the silhouetted granite. "It's amazing, isn't it? We should name this place." He scanned fire-lighted faces. "Tunnehill, you're the first white man ever to receive baptism here. Why don't you baptize the place with a name?"

Tunnehill laughed. "If you're providing whiskey for the ceremony, Doc, I'll participate. But if it's another cold-water affair, I've done enough in that line."

Jim joined in the general laughter and the men returned to their lively chatter. Bunnell, disappointed, resumed a silent contemplation of the shadowed scenery until one of the men hollered, "I like Doc's idea. Let's name this place."

Suggestions followed. When a particularly fanciful foreign name received laughter, Bunnell stood again. "This is an American landscape, men," he said, eyes on the blackly silhouetted mountains towering toward the stars, "and I'll wager it's the grandest ever looked upon. Why go to some foreign country to name it? Why not name it for the tribe who occupied it? I propose we give this valley the name Yosemite. It is certainly suggestive of the place, and it's American!"

"Devil take the Indians!" hollered Tunnehill. "Why honor these marauding murderers?"

"I'm with Tunnehill!" someone shouted. "Who knows what Yosemite means, anyway? If you wanna give it a name for bein' so grand, let's call it Paradise Valley!"

Jim, seeing Doc's disappointment, stood. "Yosemite ain't Teneiya's band. Means grizzly bear. Some tribes say '*oo-soom-ity*' or '*uzu'-mati*'."

Bunnell nodded. "I've heard it pronounced even differently from that."

Jim looked around at the men. Always approved havin' an audience, he did. Particularly enjoyed talkin' on his talent for language, anyone care to ask. "When I first come here and learned the lingo," he said, "it all sounded sorta like the Kaweahs talk. But if you got an ear for it, it's sorta just a shift in dialect, kinda how a Swede differs from a Norwegian, or Danes from Swedes."

"Exactly," Doc said, on his feet again. "I learned Chippewa as a boy, but an Indian whose dialect differed said I was speaking French Chippewa while hers was old Chippewa. Useful distinction."

Jim began again. "Matter of fact—"

"Hear ye! Hear ye! Hear ye!" hollered Tunnehill. "A vote will now be taken to decide what we're gonna call this valley!"

The men cheered.

Jim looked at Doc. "Guess your namin' idea trumps my lingo lecture." He shrugged. "Thought folks ought to know somethin' about the people gettin' booted out of this place and down the mountain."

"Might be curious someday," Doc said, looking up at the stars. "If any Indians survive to tell the tale."

Or talk their own tongue, Jim thought.

Votes counted, the decision went to Yosemite.

The next morning Jim spotted a faint plume of smoke curling into the leaden sky. That settled the question. Indians still here. Likely Isabel and her man out there somewheres. Damn sorry business. He directed Sandino's attention to the smoke, saw the Indian glance up and quickly away. Looked jumpy, ready to run given half a chance. Insisted the river too fast to cross.

Jim shook his head. "Ain't too tricky for folks actually wantin' to cross it."

He ordered the men to fall in and started Girl into the water, signaling the column to follow. They splashed through to the north side without incident, and followed a trail towards an enormous rock cliff. As the expedition approached it, Bunnell craned his neck. "Hard to guess its width or its height," he said to Jim, riding by his side. "Cliff might be fifteen hundred feet, maybe more. Difficult to assess its sheer perpendicularity."

"Forget what's over your head, Doc," Jim said. "Look what we got in front of our noses."

In a clearing ringed by cedar shelters and acorn caches, he dismounted. Squatting by a fire pit, he held a hand above the ashes. "Still warm. Teneiya's men here somewhere." Isabel, too. Somewhere.

He stood, shrugged, looked at the men. "They're expectin' us but it ain't bad or we'd a seen arrows invitin' a fight. They're hidin'. Let's find 'em."

Search parties followed tracks disappearing into cliffs, crevices, canyons and inaccessible ledges no one dared climb. "Major," one discouraged tracker declared after several hours of fruitless pursuit, "them Indians gotta be part mountain goat. Or maybe they got some ghost power to give 'em wings and spirit 'em away. They just plumb vanished."

As the gray day wore on, searchers found only footprints, deserted shelters, caches of acorns, stored nuts and seeds and dried grasshoppers. Jim investigated an apparently terminating trail, imagined himself one of the Yosemites slipping into a rocky ravine or canyon, elusive as a mountain lion. Fact was, anyone cared to ask, he admired how Indians perfected silence. Probably laughin' as soundlessly as they disappeared. A prey superior to its hunters.

Then one of the men hollered, "Major! Over here!"

Jim backtracked in the direction of the repeated shout to a cave's narrow entrance. Inside, an ancient Indian woman crouched, hissing curses as Jim approached. Well, that's somethin' anyways, he thought, seeing the red, fringed scarf draped over the old woman's thin shoulders. Isabel been and gone, and good luck to her, wherever she was. Old woman likely too feeble to travel, he guessed, seeing scattered animal bones, evidence these famous horse thieves had been eating their captures. He told the men to leave her be, collected kindling for her fire, and returned to the village where he found Doc exiting a cedar shelter.

"Not much in there except baskets," Doc said, "although many are large and beautifully made. I'd say that compared to the Eastern tribes, their property is meager. Some horn ornaments mainly, and rabbit blankets."

"Indians don't require much," Jim said.

"Some Indians here apparently inclined to civilization's inventions, though."

Jim, eying a distant waterfall, asked, "Pistol? Rifle? Ain't slow in adoptin' advances in that direction." Wondered still how he escaped Bautista's surprise attack. Had things gone different, well, what then? But things didn't go different, just one way. White man's way.

'No. No guns. Nothing valuable. A tin cup." He held it up.

Jim stared. Memory washed over him. Her laughing, him laughing, dancing, mush-stirrer. He sighed. No one laughin' now. Old days gone, and best be gettin' on with this one. Get these Indians down to sign the damned treaty before soldiers convinced 'em with rifles that worked. Isabel knew how the wind was blowin'. Likely out here somewheres tellin' 'em about it. Any luck, she'd be bringin' in the rest of 'em. Be glad to see her back, and that was a fact. Seein' her scarf, the tin cup, well—

Bunnell tossed the cup back where he found it. Inspecting another cedar shelter, he called out, "Not much to lose here."

Only everything, Jim thought. "They're hidin' up in those rocks," he said, gazing now at the surrounding granite cliffs, "and we ain't likely to find 'em. Need 'em to come in voluntary."

He wandered around the village, imagined Isabel living here, examined a well-filled acorn granary.

There's the answer, he thought, right there.

He found Boling, gave the order. "They'll come in when they got nothin' to eat. Burn everything."

That evening, camped in the meadow while smoke drifted from torched acorn caches and shelters, the men voiced frustration. They'd explored the length and breadth of the valley and found nothing.

"Nice scenery, though," Boling said, picking his teeth.

"Amazing waterfalls!"

"In case Tunnehill's river baptism didn't suit 'im!"

Doc laughed. "Those granite domes. There's something to write home about."

"How 'bout that one split clean through?"

"Neat as sliced bread!"

Jim interrupted. "Men, we ain't tourists. Come to collect Indians. What we got in that department, not countin' our worthless guide and one old squaw in a cave, is *nada,* zero. Storm headin' in gonna make this a hell of a gloomy hole if it traps us. Ain't got enough provisions to sit it out, barely enough to see us back to base camp. Need to head back before we get hungry. Yosemites gonna need to eat, too. What with their grasshoppers and seeds and acorns all burned up, they'll be comin' in soon. We're done here. Pack up at daylight."

Damned bad business this. He hoped she'd understand what he'd done. And why.

The long, difficult trail back drained strength and morale. Worse, when they finally reached base camp, the young man Jim left in charge, Eccleston, said he had no provisions.

"Nothing left, Major. Indians et everything and then went to feedin' themselves," he said, gesturing toward Teneiya's people gathered around their fires.

"Made theirselves to home, ain't they?" Jim said, sniffing the air. Stew of some kind. Maybe squirrel.

"Yes, sir. Kept themselves busy making lodges, collecting stones and kindling for their cooking baskets. Appear satisfied to stay, don't they?"

"They do."

Jim wandered among them until he found Teneiya, enjoying a pipe. "First thing tomorrow, Chief, get these folks movin'. Rest of your people comin' along soon, count on that."

Teneiya silently contemplated his pipe.

The next morning, Jim watched the Indians leisurely prepare for departure. Children, gone exploring, had to be collected, fed, and collected again. Mules and horses rounded up. Baskets and blankets organized. No one in a hurry except his men, chafing at the delay, complaining. They were cold and hungry and impatient and remained so throughout the slow progress of starting the Indians down the mountain. Teneiya and his people, indifferent to haste, ignored curses and pleas.

Jim didn't blame them. This was not an enterprise of their choosing. But his men were hungry, anxious to get going. Boling, standing at Jim's side, watching, said, "At this rate, we'll be days on the trail. The men are hungry and tired and bored. Mostly hungry."

"Noticed several squaws offerin' 'em food," Jim said.

Boling grimaced, scratched his nose. "Some of us sampled their grass-seed mush and acorn jelly. Only thing we could stomach was piñon nuts. Devoured those. Regret their scarcity."

Jim shrugged. "Roasted grasshoppers ain't bad when a man's past bein' particular. Get hungry enough, folks'll eat 'bout anything what runs or flies." Felt bad now over burning up Isabel's acorn caches. Come down in the world, for a fact, from sellin' Indians raisins and door hinges to burnin' their food. Three years, and everythin' gone catawampus.

Boling cleared his throat. "I can't see these particular Indians needing all of us for an escort. Their boys go out hunting for rabbits and squirrels and come back, you know. And they all seem contented with the idea of the Fresno destination."

"Told 'em they'd feast big when they get there," Jim admitted. "Been delightin' their imaginations with descriptions of the presents commissioners promised 'em."

"Why not let most of the company go ahead? You take them down the mountain, get them fed. Leave me a few to help guard, and I'll bring Teneiya and his people in."

The snow was melting, not quickly, but soon they could cross to the Monos. She'd rescued scorched acorns from the burned village, not many, but they would eat. Seethkil and his brothers, all the hiding people, had prepared for the expected siege with hidden caches of smoked meat and insects, acorn mush in water-tight baskets.

White men had come into Awani. And found no one. White men had come into Awani, and left. Outwitted. Outwaited. And soon melting snow would permit passage. She gazed into the snowy distance, imagined crossing, imagined the future. She and Seethkil living long. Soon.

At the Fresno camp Jim reported to Wozencraft. "Yosemites comin' in. Captain Boling's got Chief Teneiya with about seventy of 'em. Rest comin' soon as their stomachs cry."

"How long?" asked the commissioner.

"Three days, maybe four. That's for Boling's portion. Can't tell for certain when the others will show, but they will. Got nothin' to eat and nowhere to go."

While waiting, Jim talked with the commissioners about reservation boundaries and settlement procedures and then with Tredwell Moore, the military commander, about plans for a fort to protect the boundaries from encroachment.

Three days had passed since Jim and most of the Battalion had arrived. The men had set up camp, satisfied their hunger, and returned to waiting further orders once Boling showed up with Chief Teneiya's people. Jim waited, confident.

On the fourth day, Moore, with youthful impatience and, like most of the military, resentful of Savage and his volunteered battalion, demanded, "Let's see your Indians! Where are they?"

"Slowed up some by women and children," Jim said, defensive, disliking the challenge and the challenger both. Already figured him and Moore not goin' to be happy neighbors on the Fresno reservation.

"Ought to be here by now," Moore said, frowning, suspicious.

On the fifth day, Jim mounted Girl and rode back a few miles expecting to encounter Boling's procession. Nothing. No one. He kept riding. Nothing. No one.

He finally found Boling at a deserted campsite, frantic when Jim rode up and dismounted.

"Captain Boling," he said, snapping his fingers in Boling's distraught face, "you're lookin' like you lost the trick of breathin'."

Boling waved his hands distractedly in the air, shook his head. "Major, it seemed useless to require men to stand guard."

"Clarify me some, Captain Boling," he said, looking around and disbelieving his eyes. Not an Indian in sight. And were Boling's men looking behind trees?!

Boling took a deep breath, exhaled. "As you said, it seemed the Indians could scarcely be driven off, they were so anticipating their feast and presents."

Jim stared at him. "Where's Teneiya?"

Boling started to speak. Closed his eyes. Shook his head.

Jim snapped his fingers again. "Captain!"

Boling opened his eyes, looked away. "You see, Major, after a couple of nights, I didn't think it necessary for my men to keep a watch—"

"You sayin' you failed to post a sentry!?"

"Well, what with the Indians being mostly women and children and old people, and Chief Teneiya cooperating the way he was—" Boling shrugged. "Guess they fooled me."

Jim imagined Teneiya and his people flitting like butterflies into the trees, disappearing like smoke. "Guess they did."

"Apparently they can be quick and silent when they want to."

Jim sighed. "Seems we got us a foopaw here of impressive proportion."

"Foopaw?"

"Frenchy word. Learned it at rendezvous. I'd say this here's a major foopaw."

General Disinclination, meet Major Foopaw. He studied the mortified Boling. "You lost 'em, Captain. Go find 'em."

You are aware that I know this old fellow well enough to look out well for him, lest by some stratagem he makes his escape.... if you will send me ten or twelve of old Ponwatchee's best men I could catch the women and children and thereby force the men to come in.

—Letter, John Boling to Major Savage
Merced River, Yosemite Village
May 15, 1851

A ROCK. A rock, the right rock. So tired. So tired. Hands, knees, so sore. Throat dry, so dry. Crawling. Searching. What was it she wanted? A rock? A rock. Tired. Dirty. Throat hurts. Hard to breathe. Head hurts. Look. Don't think. Eyes open. Don't think. Find the right rock. Eyes open.

Where was she? She looked around, knew the place. *Wahaw'kee.* Three frogs. Loiya dug roots here. Roots. Hungry, so hungry. Hiding. Crawling. Hiding. Creeping. Someone following. Two rocks. She needed two rocks.

Wailing. Such noise. Shouting, shooting, wailing.

Two rocks. Crawling. Dirty hair in her eyes. Knees bleeding. A man following. Shouting.

Shouting. Whose voice? Teneiya? Chief Teneiya? Yes. Teneiya shouting. "Kill me, captain, as you would kill my people if they were to come to you! You would kill all my race if you had the power!"

Chief Teneiya. Everyone back. Children frightened. Hiding. Hungry. Silent. Like turtles. *I-chow.* No crying. Indian children never cried. Turtles. Anna's baby learning the earth.

What was she doing? Yes. Looking for a rock. Two rocks.

People running. Teneiya shouting. "When I am dead I will call to my people to come to you! My spirit will make trouble for you and your people, as you have caused trouble to me and my people!"

Wailing. Such wailing.

"Isabel!?"

That white man again. Following her. So many white men. Too many white men. Coming and coming. Like wasps.

On her hands and knees, crawling. She needed the right rock.

"Isabel!?"

Coming and coming. Coming into Awani.

Tired. She was so tired. Running, hiding. Such noise. Shooting. Shouting. Wailing.

Teneiya shouting again. "You may kill me, sir captain, but you shall not live in peace! I will follow your footsteps! I will not leave my home! I will be with the spirits among the rocks and waterfalls, in the rivers and with the wind!"

Wailing. Wailing.

"Isabel?!"

Two rocks! Right rocks! Old ways. She picked them up, held them close against her chest. Concentrated. Thought what to do. Her head hurt. Concentrate. Strike one against the other. Stone splinters. Like that! She hit the stones against each other. *Crack! Chip!* Make sharp, like arrowhead. Sharp edge. *Crack! Chip! Crack! Chip!*

People running. Teneiya shouting. "You will not see me but you will fear the spirit of the old chief and grow cold!"

Wailing.

"Isabel? You remember me, Isabel?"

Sharp-edged rock in one hand. Pulling her hair with the other. Dirty, hair so dirty. Where was her soap-root brush? Victoria's soap-root brush. Washing her hair in the river. Yuloni's river. Her head filled with pictures. Yuloni. Making acorn.

Wailing.

"Lafayette Bunnell, Isabel. Doc. You remember me."

Good rock. Sharp rock. Old ways.

"Here, take my hand, Isabel. I'll help you up. We're going in. Everyone's going in. Quiet now. No more wailing."

Leaning against a boulder, she raised the sharp rock in one hand. Pulled her hair tight with the other. And began to cut.

The inquiry was made of those unfortunate people if they were then satis-
fied to go with us; their reply was they were more than willing, as they could
go to no other place....
—Letter, Captain John Boling, Mariposa Battalion
to Col. George W. Barbour, Commissioner
May 29, 1851

GETTIN' ITCHY IS what he was, Jim realized, strolling the nearly abandoned camp littered with empty bottles, tossed cans, and sardine boxes. A few sway-backed mules corral-crowded a slender shade, grass used up and trod down. Mules and men all waitin' around for this Indian business to get itself got through. About done, thank the Lord or Great Spirit or whoever or whatever. Only Boling and his men still to come in, most the rest gone to town with their pay. Likely musterin' theirselves out of this so-called battalion and into a saloon is what they was. Gettin' started on whatever the future was sendin' next.

Itchin' for it himself, what with him and John Marvin, the quartermaster, goin' partners on the twelve hundred dollars for the tradin' license for the Fresno reservation. Store under construction. Supplies ordered: cotton trousers and woolen shirts, Panama hats, handkerchiefs, pipes, tobacco, molasses, cooking utensils. Agreed to give the custom to Brownlee, what with him still waitin' reimbursement from the government for supplyin' the battalion. Likely gettin' what the little boy shot at, Jim suspected, way things was lookin'. Well, they'd all start recoupin' soon as Boling got the Yosemites in. Damned Chauchilas finally in, braggin' on scarin' Teneiya's seventy-two friends and family, tellin' 'em Boling was takin' 'em to be killed so white men wouldn't have to pay 'em for their land. As if killin' 'em was required. As if payin' 'em was required. Chauchilas, damned trouble makers.

He strolled past a few men lazing in shade, eating, joking, enjoying themselves.

"Hey, Major! We got oysters over here! Y'want some?"

"Full up," he said, continuing his inspection, hand lifted to acknowledge. Oysters. Provisioners doin' a bang-up business. Mariposa Battalion, word had it, cost the state more than two hundred thousand dollars. Eccleston crowin' around he'd got six hundred dollars for his services, plus ninety for his horse.

Continued his stroll, kicking cans. Anyone with somethin' to sell showin' up for a share of the payout, gettin' a piece of the pie. Picture-taker in his long black coat, tall hat, lookin' like an undertaker. Send home your likeness starin' flat-eyed into the future. Dagger-type. Writer roamin' around camp showin' off fancy letter paper with a dancin' elephant scarin' the hair off the head of a terrified miner. Ten dollars to scratch out a letter to your sweetheart. Lonely feller sayin', "Tell Matilda, for god's sakes, write!"

Jim paused, watched a blue jay hop among empty cans and bottles like it was lookin' for a souvenir. Camp a regular rendezvous now, everyone lookin' to sell or buy. Bookseller delightin' Lewis, the adjutant the commissioners appointed to do Jim's readin' and writin'. "Oliver Twist!" Lewis exclaimin', goin' on about someone named Martin Chuzzlewit, other odd names. Lewis, fresh from college in the East, couldn't get enough readin' in him. Collected newspapers like they was worth somethin'.

Gettin' assigned an adjutant turnin' out good. Might use Lewis when this Indian business got done. Almost was. Windin' down anyways. Four thousand Indians on their reservations— Merced, Stanislaus, Fresno, San Joaquin, Kaweah— waitin' for the Great White Father's promises to show up.

Half glad the commissioners needed him here to translate treaty terms whenever another tribe came in. Kaweahs signed. And he'd persuaded the commissioners to let José Rey's brother, Chief Poholeel, treat for the Chauchilas. So that was done. Chauchilas in. Boling bringin' Yosemites in, redeemin' his foopaw. Somethin' in Boling's letter had bothered him. What was it?

He found Lewis's tent, flap entrance open. Inside, Lewis lay stretched out on his cot, reading a book.

"That letter from Boling," Jim said, leaning in, one hand on the canvas. "Let's hear that again."

Lewis jumped to his feet. "Yes, sir. From the beginning?"

"The part about findin' the Yosemites," Jim said, coming in and pulling up one of Lewis's canvas camp chairs.

Lewis retrieved the letter from the wooden box he kept for the Battalion's official correspondence, shuffled the pages. "Here it is," he said, and began: "*My command then set out to search and found the rancheria at the head of a little valley, and from the signs it appeared that the Indians had left but a few minutes. The boys pursued them up the mountain on the north side of the river, and when they got near the top, helping each other from rock to rock on account of the abruptness of the mountains, the first intimation they had of Indians being near was a shower of huge rocks which came tumbling down the mountain, threatening instant destruction. Several of the men were knocked down, and some of them rolled and fell some distance before they could recover, wounding and bruising them generally. One man's gun was knocked out of his hand and fell seventy feet before it stopped, whilst another man's hat was knocked off his head—"*

Jim slapped his knee, laughed. "Give Boling's letter to the newspapers, Lewis. Folks over in Sacramento and San Francisco oughta know how serious things is up here, men droppin' their guns and losin' their hats makin' the country safe for white men."

"Newspapers? Yes, sir! Good idea, sir!"

Jim laughed again, the image of lost hats and dropped guns in his head. "Keep readin', Lewis."

"Yes, sir," Lewis said, finding his place. "*The men immediately took shelter behind large rocks, from which they could get an occasional shot, which soon forced the Indians to retreat, and by pressing them close they caught the old Yosemite chief, whom we yet hold as prisoner. In this skirmish they killed one Indian and wounded several others.*"

Jim snorted. "Guns for white men, rocks for Indians. Not what anyone would call a fair fight."

"No, sir. But at least Boling caught Chief Teneiya."

"He'll bring him in this time, bet on that. Bring 'em all in." Isabel, too. A worry. Somethin' in Boling's letter stuck in his mind. What was it?

Just then, outside the tent, horses, a shout. "Major Savage?!"

"In here!" Jim shouted, standing, recognizing the voice.

Boling threw back the tent flap. "We got them, Major, all of them!" He took off his hat, fanned himself with it. "Left the weakest, women and children and old people, camped a few miles back." He dropped onto the remaining camp chair.

"Let's have the particulars," Jim said, sitting opposite and learning forward, elbows on his knees, hands clasped.

Boling nodded. "So, the morning after the train of pack animals and provisions arrived with Chief Ponwatchee and his twelve warriors, we discovered tracks in the direction of the Monos' country. We followed the trail, and after some difficulty eventually found the Yosemites had taken refuge at a large lake, completely frozen over, where I guess they expected they were secure from the intrusion of white men."

"Nukchus any help?" Jim asked.

"Absolutely. All the men with me witnessed their good conduct and service in trying to bring the Yosemites to terms. If the government delivers on its promises, and bad-disposed white men are kept from among them, I'm confident the Indians will maintain the peace."

"Write that up in a letter to the military," Jim said. "Indians don't get half the credit they should for tryin' to get along with whites." He shook his head. "Frankly, I don't trust Moore's sympathies."

"Moore?"

"Tredwell Moore. In charge of the state's militia buildin' Fort Miller on the Fresno reservation." He stood. "Bunnell come in with you?"

"Left him at the corral."

Jim found Doc watering his horse. "So, you're back from the mountains."

"I am, but my god, Jim, they're glorious!"

"What's glorious?"

"The mountains! Like I told Isabel, such cliffs and waterfalls I never saw before. I doubt if they exist in any other place."

"Where is she?" Jim wanted to see her, tell her— tell her what? That she was safe? Had a future?

"Back at the temporary camp with Teneiya," Doc said. "They'll be coming in after they get fed. Plenty hungry. I heard you bought Fremont's beef for them."

"Sorta usin' my new license as Indian subagent," Jim said. He'd worry later about paying Fremont. "She okay? Isabel?"

"Can't say exactly how she is. Not good. Not talking much," Doc said, turning back to his horse. "Told her we're calling that big granite mountain El Capitan. She said it already had a name."

"Wouldn't expect Spanish names to sit well with Indians, Doc. They got reason to hate Mexicans."

"I think El Capitan was the only Spanish name we used. You remember that extraordinary rock with one side split off? We decided a good name for it was Half Dome."

"Indians likely not keen on white men namin' their country," Jim said, not saying what he thought about white men taking it and making it theirs. And him a part of it, maybe lookin' back when his future got used up. Old, maybe a family man, lookin' back at all this. Tellin' tales. Lookin' back. Him and her, lookin' back. Whoa, he thought, catching himself.

Doc, still talking, said, "and we discovered a lake on the trail to the Monos. Named it Lake Teneiya. The chief was with us, showing us the trail, told him we named it in his honor, but he wasn't pleased. Said his people long ago named it." He patted the horse's rump. "We named it Lake Teneiya anyway."

"What happened up there, Doc? Boling said two Indians was tied up for hostages, tried to escape and got shot."

"A cause of regret to nearly the whole command. A guard let the two Indians untie themselves. When they ran, he shot and killed them. The guard, expecting praise, was accused of murder. Sorry to say, no punishment followed."

"Not astonished. Anything else?"

"Well, there was the one Indian killed during the skirmish at the lake, and the whole camp was saddened by the sight of Chief Teneiya carrying the body up a steep ravine for burial. We decided to call it Indian Canyon. Isabel cried out the canyon had a name, and something about a lost arrow. Pretty upset, got to wailing."

"Wailing!? Isabel?"

"Chief in a frenzy, too. Interesting. In his excitement, Teneiya made a correct use of many Spanish words, showing he was more familiar with them than he had ever admitted, shouting in a style of language and manner of delivery which took us all by surprise. He accused Boling of permitting the killing, cursed him, truly cursed him, burst forth in lamentations and denunciations, yelling that Boling should kill him, Teneiya. Words to that effect, went on in that vein, very dramatic. Cursed all of us. Said his spirit would follow us, make us fear him. Claimed we killed the child of his heart."

"The child of his heart?"

"His youngest son."

The major is in town for the purpose of closing up the business of the Indian battalion… he has the contract for furnishing the Indians, under the late treaty, with beef and other edibles to keep them from devouring the miners' mules.

—*Stockton Journal*
July 9, 1851

"SOLD!"

Jim looked up. Gone wool-gatherin' again while Marvin was up in front of the boys conductin' a bang-up public offerin' of commissary goods. Everything stacked up for sale and gettin' auctioned off. Boys steppin' up with their pay, outfittin' theirselves with horses, mules, and clothing, becomin' civilians again.

And here he was, sittin' on the same stump where he'd enlisted these men six months ago. Gettin' 'em mustered out. Finally over. All of it over. The battalion. The bringin' in. All the Indians on their assigned reservations. 'Ceptin' Yosemites. Come in and then gone home, and good luck to 'em. Couldn't say just how that happened, whether he let Teneiya and his kin go or maybe suggested they leave? Or encouraged 'em? Or hadn't prevented 'em leavin'? Weren't sure. Didn't matter. No one missed 'em. No one cared Teneiya and his family after a month on the Fresno reservation drifted off like ghosts. Pretty much what they'd turned into. Chief Teneiya—a mighty oak fallen. More child than chief now. Dignity drained outa him like water out a busted dam. Sorry sight. Empty old man grousin' about reservation food, complainin' the Nukchus was tauntin' his downfall, grumblin' about the valley heat. Sorry sight. Discouragin' business seein' Teneiya reducin' down to a sad, grouchy old Indian.

Isabel on his mind, too. No surprise. Hauntin' him, her grief-ravaged face and chopped hair. Pained him more'n he had words for in her language, in any language. Told her so. Told her she'd endure it, her loss, outlive it, survive it, knew that truth from personal experience. Knowed he was ramblin' on and on. Talkin' to himself as much as her, sayin' what came into his head, surprisin' himself how he felt about her.

Now here he was watchin' a lively sale of military goods underway in a last hurrah, and still thinkin' on her. Understood loss, both of 'em. Only good thing about loss is it fades. Still there, but not so blindin' bright after a time. Life was long. Future comin', that's what counted. Told her so. Told her how him and her knew old ways was past. Shared the past, they did. Could share what lay ahead. Why not? Get on with gettin' on. Survive. Told her that. Told her she'd get her grievin' done, and he'd be plannin' the future. Remembered how she stared like she was seein' but she weren't. Right through him like he was a window. But maybe she heard what he was sayin', that he'd be waitin' to look out for her, like he'd promised her and her father. She could count on that. Count on him. Told her so. Future full of possibilities.

Possibilities, that's the ticket. He stood, stretched his back, rolled his shoulders. Feelin' good, feelin' like the sun just got sunnier. Polished itself up for a brighter future. He had plans, he did. He'd get crackin' on 'em soon as this day's official musterin' out was over.

Following the auction, Adjutant Lewis officiated over the formalities and Brownlee rolled out half a barrel of whiskey and another of port wine, with a sack of sugar to make the drink palatable.

Jim drank a cup, nodded. "Got to hand it to you, Brownlee," he said, piling a tin plate with roast beef, bread and cheese, walnuts. "You got up a real feast for the boys."

Brownlee sliced more beef, forked it onto Jim's plate. "Everyone's glad to see the end of this Indian war."

"Weren't no war, anyone care to ask," Jim said, spooning more sugar into his wine. "Just a long, drawn-out corralin' up is what it was. But I suppose the boys is entitled to braggin' rights for their troubles."

After the meal, in a general call for speeches, Sheriff Burney climbed up on an empty supply box and defended himself against rumors questioning his conduct. To Jim's amusement, no one seemed to know what the sheriff was talking about. When the sheriff finally sat down, a volunteer took his place on the box to announce his candidacy for the legislature. Huzzahs of support greeted his list of promises of what he would do for everyone should he be elected. The next speaker mounted the box to say he had no plans but should he be a candidate for any office in the future, he'd like their vote, too. Big applause.

And now, Jim saw, they were all looking to him.

"Speech, Major Savage! Speech!"

He supposed he had to say something. Hadn't thought much on it but he stepped up on the box and for a moment silently surveyed the faces of the men who had followed him into canyons and ravines and mountains, across rivers, through rainstorms and snow, stood by one another, stood by him. He held up his hands, let the foot-stamping and hollering die down.

"Well, men, these six months ain't been much of what I'd call a frolic. Reckon you'll agree we had our ups and downs."

"Up one mountain and down another!"

Jim joined the laughter. "We been through a lot together. Good times and bad. We been cold and we been wet—"

"And baptized!" Tunnehill hollered.

"And hungry!"

"Not hungry enough to eat roasted-up grasshoppers!"

"I ate 'em! They ain't bad!"

Jim laughed with the men while they exchanged humorous recollections, and when they settled down, looked expectant, he launched a recounting of their bravery, their trials, their steadfast loyalty to the trust placed in them by the citizens of California. Some of this praise was even true, he said, and got more laughs. He had them now. "You got stories you'll be stretchin' the rest of your lives, men." They quieted, waiting. "You chased Indians. Likely the last to do it."

He paused, watched them considering. "Surely do hope so. Six months ago, enlistin' in this operation, you prob'ly thought an Indian a dangerous animal to be destroyed. You mighta thought killin' one was a useful and praiseworthy deed. But now you seen 'em hungry, just people tryin' to stay alive. You seen 'em in their villages, with their children and old people, givin' up. You led Chief Ponwatchee's people down the mountain, saw those Nukchus was gentle, inoffensive people. Yosemite squaws offered you food. Chauchilas, Chukchansi, Kaweahs, Potoyensee, Tuolomnes. Just people. Different ways of livin', of seein' the world, but people. Maybe you think different about 'em now, see it's fear and not knowin' 'em is what brings on arrows and bullets. Maybe see it's kinda a habit, this judgin' without knowin' each other. And I just wanna say it's beneath you, as gentlemen, to fear and hate these people."

Jim sensed the men growing restless, heard murmurs of opposition, but he couldn't stop himself. "You may grow rich. I hope you do. And I hope you grow old. But regardless of your fate, you can and must be gentlemen. In the end, that's what counts—bein' respected as a gentleman. Your integrity, your honor—all wrapped up in bein' a gentleman. Don't never let no one say you're not a gentleman."

Thought it weren't bad speechifyin', anyone care to ask. Didn't think anyone would. Fine by him. No plans on bein' a candidate for judge or sheriff, out pumpin' hands and slappin' backs.

But he had plans, he did, anyone care to ask.

They wanted to go home. Home drew them like thirst to water. Was Loiya the first to beg? Chief Teneiya beyond speech? She couldn't remember if she begged for release on their behalf? Words drifted away, lost to mind and tongue. All she recalled now was yearning. Yearning for home. For life as it had been, as they remembered it. Before. Before the long slow stumble out of the forest, down to the hot, dry valley. Stomachs crying, hearts crying. Herded like cattle onto throat-parching plains to see the future. They would die on the reservation.

On their return, she had fallen to her knees in the meadow, buried her face in fading late-season clover, inhaled its familiar fragrance. Kneeling at the river's edge, she confronted the dark devastation of her reflection. Hair shorn ragged, face black with pine pitch. She was one with the scorched village.

They wandered among the wreckage, dazed, like smoke-dulled wasps listlessly circling a destroyed nest. Wordlessly, they picked forlornly among charred remains, finding a fish hook here, a bone awl there, looking for anything remaining from before their world turned upside down.

She knelt in the ashy debris of her *o'chum*, sifted through the burned scraps, found only the tin cup, blackened but whole. Indestructible. Like white men's power.

In those first days of listless return, no one spoke of the horrific running, hiding. Of being chased. Hunted. Captured. Driven onto the reservation, taunted by enemies, humiliated. No one needed to. Disgrace and death hung in the air they breathed. Men's eyes grew vacant, disheartened by defeat and the reservation. Warriors no more. Ghosts.

Some, a few, crossed the mountain to the Monos and Paiutes. Others simply disappeared, to hide or survive, Isabel supposed, as Great Spirit willed. She watched Chief Teneiya withdraw into his vague bewilderment. What was he thinking? That the ancient prediction had been fulfilled? Or had he, like her, collapsed beneath the unimaginable?

And yet they lived.

And living required attention. Numbly, women resumed the necessary tasks that filled days. They rescued half-burned cedar from old shelters to erect new ones, gathered acorns, commenced a minimal existence in a world no story predicted. In the time of harvest, they dutifully thanked acorn for the food that meant survival. It was a spiritless celebration. Isabel could not remember the words to the songs.

When the time for the Big Cry arrived, they wept loudly into the night, and through the next day, and the following night, and the next. Mourners shuffled an endless circle, danced a new dance beseeching the spirits of the dead to return, to fight the intruders on their behalf, make the white men leave. Woochi did not dance to put the world right. No one believed it possible. Half-burned baskets and quivers rescued from the destroyed village went into the fire, completing earthbound usefulness, rising into smoke memories for the dead. Isabel had searched forlornly for something of Seethkil's to send to his spirit, and offered the flames a charred remnant she supposed had once been a flute played soft as rabbit's fur by the handsome youngest son of Chief Teneiya courting her at the lake of shining rocks.

Everyone gave the fire what they could, mourned, wept, danced. Remembered. No one prepared the washing ceremony, there being no relief from sorrow so profound. They did not know what to do with grief so immense. They had no stories from when Coyote made the First People, no guidance from Great Spirit, no warnings from animal spirits for these times.

Leaves dried and curled and drifted from trees. Skies darkened. Clouds gathered atop the mountains. Winter arrived. Frost rimmed cedars and firs. Birds and deer and earth's little creatures hid. Stomachs cried. Children weakened. Old people died. Survivors subsisted frugally, hunger sharp as arrows. Some abandoned hope and crept away, down the mountain to the white men's mining camps. To beg.

Isabel slept, often and long, through dark nights and into gray mornings, dreaming. She dreamt of spring, collecting seeds in her gathering basket. She dreamt of remembered laughter, chasing a ball in the meadow. And of waiting and watching and trading words on the Mariposa while rain lashed a canvas roof. Of old ways. And dead people.

Regretted waking.

"No leaks," Jim said, dragging a chair to the blazing pot-bellied stove. He glanced up at the rafter-rattling sounds of gusting winds and pounding rain of November's heavy downpour. "Good roof. A good sign." He sat, tamped his pipe, watched Lewis open a recently delivered crate.

"Could be a bad winter," Lewis said, prying off the crate's top.

Jim felt inclined to good signs, not bad winters, his future chuffing along on its intended track. Hopeful. "What did our good commissioner send us?"

Lewis held up a length of cloth for inspection.

Jim snorted at the sight. "What's that s'posed to be?"

Lewis rummaged through the crate, removed a paper, examined it. "Invoice says 'blankets', sir."

"Might serve for a window."

"Sir?"

"Noticed what you got there has a peculiar advantage."

"Sir?"

"Holdin' it up to the light, our Indians'll be admirin' both front and back at the same time, without the bother of turnin' it over."

"A bit thin," Lewis agreed.

"Gotta consider the convenience, though."

"Sir?"

"Regular blankets likely be hinderin' movement when our Indians go huntin' their own rations. Feedin' theirselves often as not."

"The Government promised—"

"Promises somethin' of a failure I'd say. Bad flour one week, no beef the next." He sucked at his pipe, then looked at it. "And now we got see-through blankets for 'em. Window blankets!" He tapped his pipe against the stove's side. "If it ain't one trouble, it's ten." He looked up at Lewis. "White men operatin' a ferry on Indian land. That's another. And Tredwell Moore over at Camp Miller or Fort Miller, or whatever he's callin' his militia these days, ignorin' it."

He tamped his pipe again, gestured it at the newspaper Lewis had been reading earlier. "Anything in there for your collection?"

To Jim's amusement his adjutant had indeed given over to the San Francisco newspapers the letter Boling had written from Yosemite Valley. After seeing it printed in the *Daily Alta,* Lewis made a regular hobby of combing newspapers for articles on local matters.

Lewis nodded. "Quite a long article on Rootville."

"Rootville?"

"That's what they're calling the tent town by the fort."

"What's it say?"

"You won't like it," Lewis said, abandoning the crate. He unfolded the paper, flattened it out on the counter, found the article, scanned it. "A good deal of self-congratulation in it. Starts out praising the soldiers for building the fort, goes on from there."

"Let's hear it."

Lewis adjusted his spectacles, ran a finger down a column of type, cleared his throat. "*This Military Post of itself, sirs, renders additionally attractive, and enhances much in value, our little city; for whilst the privates of the command spend in our midst all their pay—individually but little, tho' in the aggregate, a respectable sum—*"

Jim looked up from his pipe at his adjutant. "Mighty high writin', ain't it? Words like 'whilst' and 'aggregate' showin' off, would you say, Lewis?"

"I would."

"Go ahead. Let's have the rest."

Lewis found his place. "*—they afford that protection and security to life and property, which the occasional threatening aspect of Indian affairs so imperatively demands; and at the same time our citizens are enabled to encourage and foster an exceedingly lucrative trade with the Indians themselves.*"

"Sellin' 'em whiskey."

"I expect so."

"And guns maybe. Indians gettin' 'em somewheres and know how to use 'em. If they don't get the provisions they been promised, might be dispatchin' their own dinner soon. Fond of mule meat, as I recall. Or maybe dispatchin' miners again, come to that, if white men keep encroachin' what little territory we give 'em from what was theirs before we took it. Reckon some folks like to keep pushin' 'em west 'til they drown."

Lewis nodded, continued. "*These are indeed advantages, and such as are only enjoyed at Rootville. The Indians, of whom there are large numbers, dwell conveniently near us—*"

"And ain't happy about it."

Lewis looked up. "And the citizens know it. Listen to this," he said, turning the page. "*Within a few days past the Indians have disclosed unmistakable evidences of growing dissatisfaction; their land, which was solemnly guaranteed to them by a late treaty, is now overrun with miners, both Americans and foreigners, and the richest holes in the river wrested from them by the strong arms of the invaders. This river is without doubt pregnant with the glittering ore, beyond all previous conception of its wealth; and on this account it is that miners cavil so at the terms of a treaty which withholds from them a free access to its banks.*"

Jim sighed. "Miners find out those treaties ain't been ratified, it's gonna be 'Katy, bar the door'. What else does it say?"

Lewis found his place. "*Whether, on this account, an Indian war is to be projected, lies hidden in the bosom of an unrevealed future. Meantime, our youthful Rootville is rapidly attaining to its maturity, and before long, I expect to hear of its 'west end' and 'uptown' lots finding a ready sale in the San Francisco market. This is the age of wonders!*"

Jim shook his head, imagined water-lots advertised for sale on the river. "Indians remarkable for patience, ain't they?"

"Maybe not so patient," Lewis said, removing his spectacles. "The San Joaquin paper mentioned Judge Marvin's visit to the Four Creeks area. Says Pasqual's band is —let me think, how did he put it? —dissatisfied. That's the word. Dissatisfied."

"Pasqual's band ain't received one thing the treaty promised 'em, nothin'. Get dissatisfied enough, folks gonna see a few thousand Indians headin' back to the mountains. Ain't gonna be persuaded to come in again. Ain't stupid. Can't fool 'em twice."

Lewis, adjusting his spectacles, said, "Your name's mentioned in the article. It said you were well fortified for the winter, that your Indians were out gathering acorns."

Jim knocked his pipe against the stove. "Squaws wanderin' farther and farther from the reservation for their acorns. Goin' home." Like the Yosemites, he thought, tamping his pipe. He wondered about her, liked to think maybe this rain was washin' pitch from her sad face. He imagined her up in her big mountain valley now, doin' her grievin' like she needed to.

"Barley's coming up," Lewis said. "That will help."

"A little, for a time anyways." Two hundred reservation acres planted to barley. His Indians learning how to farm. Learning how to live like white people. Schoolhouse built. Imagined her in it, the way she took to learning when they traded words on the Mariposa. Only two years ago? Rain pounding and wind blowing like now. Two years. Hard to believe. Imagined her sittin' in the corner of this new store. He missed her, anyone care to ask.

Lewis unfolded another newspaper, the crackle of it startling Jim from his wool-gathering. He looked up to see his former adjutant glance at a first page, turn to the second, study it. Newspapers. California a regular printin' press these days, every little town puttin' out a newspaper. Might think about learnin' to read someday himself, somethin' for his old age. Old dog. New tricks. Why not? Life's possibilities. Settlin' in here, good climate, good future.

"This will interest you," Lewis said. "Some Mexicans over at Bear Valley struck serious ore a couple of weeks ago. Apparently the richest find in the Mariposa area. Took out two hundred and fifty thousand dollars in two weeks."

"Bear Valley? That'd be near Fremont's operations." Jim laughed. "You know, Lewis, that story just keeps gettin' better. First, Fremont wants a ranch near San Jose, and mad he gets Las Mariposas instead. Discovers gold, gets over his mad. Then he can't get his grant's boundaries defined, so no one's recognizin' he's got legal right to the richest damned dirt anywheres. S'posed to be his, and everybody and anybody diggin' it up." He laughed again. "Mexicans found it, you say?"

Lewis read a moment, nodded. "They're calling the place New Mexican Camp." He ran a finger under the print, shook his head, looked up. "Harvey's taking it over."

"That damned blow-hard! What's he got to do with it?"

"Guess he stepped in to organize the miners. Called a meeting to adopt rules, make everything official." Lewis read to himself for a moment. "Got himself appointed president."

"President?! Of what?"

"Ain't exactly clear. Camp, maybe, or the miners. Or the meeting."

Jim laughed. "Finally got somethin' to West Point over! A minin' camp meetin'! Maybe with any luck that'll keep 'im outta my hair."

With any luck.

He filled his pipe, listened to the whipping wind and lashing rain.

1852

...treaties were made in which the various tribes were promised a great many valuable presents, which of course they never got. There was no reason to suppose they ever should; it being a fixed principle with strong powers never to ratify treaties made by their own agents with weaker ones, when there is money to pay and nothing to be had in return.

—J. Ross Browne
California Inspector of Indian Affairs

S he kept apart from the others, was avoided in return. Had she been heard murmuring Seethkil's name? Did they fear she might conjure his ghost? Risk ill will? Bring more misery upon them? How was that possible? Would a drowned man dread rain? Neither Chief Teneiya nor Loiya spoke Seethkil's name. Were their memories as silent as their tongues? For her, whispering his name kept alive the memory of past happiness. She welcomed his ghost, all the ghosts. Seethkil. Victoria. José Jesús. All of them.

Winter passed and the green time arrived, bringing sun-warmed mornings and birdsong. She climbed the old trail alive with the spirits of boulders and trees, air fragrant with pine and incense cedar, *cho'lak*'s falling waters singing to her. Here, witness to Great Spirit's grandeur, the sun in its place at the top of the sky, she watched the illuminated valley renew itself, green again with clover and new grass. The People were home. Great Spirit provided. They survived.

When sentinels reported one morning eight white men prospecting along the river, their river, Awani's river, *wahkal'muta,* alarm roused them to old excitement. Enlivened by the trespassing, Chief Teneiya gathered his people. Awani was theirs. Invasion again? Not permitted. Never again. Men smoked, talked of reprisal, attack, the chance to be men again. Yosemites.

Distressed, Isabel reminded them they'd promised peace, urged the women to opposition. "War will make us all dead!"

Sentinels relayed the slow progress of eight white men coming into Awani. Chief Teneiya and men who once were warriors recalled former triumphs and entered their sweat house. Emerged renewed. Impatient.

"White men want gold, not war!" Isabel cried. "Let them dig! They will leave!"

Her plea fell on deaf ears.

Men drummed, sang, danced.

Isabel implored Tobuce, Loiya, all the women, to protest more pointless killing. Be no part of it, she begged.

When a runner reported the prospectors crossing the river, warriors filled their quivers.

Isabel left, retreating across the valley with a little band of six men and fifteen women and children.

The threatened confrontation arrived in a terrifying thunder of war-whoops, the shouts of a hundred outraged warriors echoing among the valley's granite cliffs, rending the sky, stopping the throats of birds, the hearts of deer.

Isabel saw, on a distant rise, Chief Teneiya, surrounded by warriors in paint and feathers, proudly raise an arm. Finding his old voice, he yelled for attack. Howling their war cries, the Yosemites raced toward the river.

Before long, Isabel and her small band of defectors heard nearby a frantic, thrashing chase. Yelling and terrified screams followed, then rifle shots. Lutario, Tobuce's husband, turned frantically first one way, then another, stopped, listened. Unable to resist the excitement longer, he bolted in its direction.

Tobuce wailed, "Lutario! No!" as he ran into the brush.

Hours later he returned, grinning, holding high a glinting gold watch on its chain. He took it from a miner's pocket, he bragged, sauntering among them, unfolding the story, the glory, the sweet taste of victory. To Isabel's horror, he swung the watch back and forth, like a scalp. Laughing, he said, "How he ran! How they all ran! We surprised them and chased them and they ran like rabbits!"

Adding suspense to his tale, he looked around at his listeners. "One white man had an axe, for cutting wood for his fire," he said, dramatically raising his arm with an imaginary weapon. Then he laughed. "Killed with his own axe! A second killed by arrows! A third man ran away with an arrow in his arm! Terrified! Screaming! Another ran with an arrow in his neck. How he ran! Terrified! Like rabbit!"

To show how it was, Lutario raced excitedly in one direction, turned on his heel, reversed, his hands frantically dancing the story he breathlessly recounted. "We crossed the river, chasing, chasing! The white men fired rifles and did not hit us! Up the trail, away they ran. How they ran! Rabbits! We surprised them, cut off their escape! They hid themselves on a rock ledge! We went above. Rolled rocks down on them!"

Lutario beamed. A good day. Two white men killed. Their trapped friends terrified. Warriors victorious. Renewed. Lost pride and dignity revived. Yosemites again.

Isabel urged Lutario to hide his plunder. He refused. He was proud. A warrior.

Fearing a storm cloud of consequences, she argued that the past belonged to the Awanichees. The present belonged to white men. White men who would retaliate as surely as wind blew and grass grew.

No one listened.

In the village, victorious Yosemites danced and drummed, celebrating, their blood still up.

Until trackers reported seeing more white men.

Coming into Awani.

We are likely to have another Indian war, many of the Indians on "the reserves" have fled.... the Yeosemotys are the most hostile and warlike; they have always refused to treat with the Commissioners....

—*Daily Alta California*
June 18, 1852

HOOFBEATS, PRETTY SURE he was hearin' hoofbeats. More'n a few. "Keep readin', Lewis," he said, opening the door and letting sunshine splash yellow on his store's plank floor. Fine day. Sunshine warmin' barley fields and vegetable patches. Indians busy makin' adobe bricks, 'ornamenting the plain with a stately pile," one newspaper reported about his plans for a house 'two stories high and surmounted by an observatory.' Comin' right along, it was. Better'n a pumpkin shell. All his plans, comin' along.

"Listen to this," Lewis said, "from the San Joaquin *Republican. Indeed, we all blush for our idle habits, compared to his energy, and what he has accomplished with his Indians.*" He folded the newspaper, looked up. "Everybody's astonished at the work you've got from the Indians."

Jim cocked an ear. Hoofbeats, definitely. "Can't figure what's a surprise there. A hungry man gets uncommon roused over the prospect of eatin'. Downright cheerful at doin' it steady. No trouble persuadin' Indians to farm after a winter listenin' to their stomachs cry."

"No thanks to the government's promise to send a farmer," Lewis said, stowing the newspaper below the counter.

"Government breaks promises like cows break wind," Jim said from the open doorway, waiting. Hoofbeats. Lots of them.

Indians farmin'. That was somethin', alright. Thanks to his hired hand. Fella glad to work land so fertile in a climate so mild. Joined right in helpin' him and twenty-five reservation Indians dig an irrigation ditch from the river. Cleared twelve acres. Planted corn, beans, peas, potatoes, squashes, pumpkins, tomatoes, beets, onions, carrots, cabbages, and parsnips. Everythin' practically leapin' outa the ground to yell boo. Yep, kinda proud. Three hundred and fifty acres in grain now, every adult male Indian with a patch his own, and enough surplus vegetables for sellin'.

Yep, hoofbeats. "We're gettin' us some company, Lewis." Fact was, he liked plantin' seeds with the squaws and kids. School teacher he'd hired liked it, too. Taught the kids English while they was droppin' seeds. Old nursery rhyme: *Peter, Peter, pumpkin-eater, had a wife and couldn't keep her. Put her in a pumpkin shell, and there he kept her very well.*

"Don't look like a social call." More like his winnin' streak was 'bout to run out. "Tredwell Moore," he added, leaving the door open and joining Lewis behind the store counter. "With about thirty soldiers."

Lewis looked toward the open door, sighed. "Things going too good too long, I guess."

"Got to go the other way from time to time," Jim said, watching the riders dismount to water their horses at the trough. "Keeps up variety."

Lewis nodded. "Might be some rule of nature."

"Could be that," Jim said.

Moore appeared at the open door, stomped across the planks, and slapped gloved hands on the plank counter. "Two white men killed, Mister Savage!"

"Unfortunate rumor, Lieutenant."

"What!?"

"As you see, I ain't dead."

"This isn't funny, Savage!"

"I can see you ain't amused." Weren't but a few months since he'd ridden over to Fort Miller and confronted Tredwell Moore with his own mad, planted his hands on Moore's desk, stared into the hooded eyes glaring at him now.

"Eight miners left Coarsegold Gulch to explore the Merced's south fork," Moore growled. "None of them, of course, expecting trouble. Not from Mister Savage's Indians!" He cocked his head. "Apparently they were wrong, Mister Savage!" Voice rising, he spit, "Dead wrong! Two dead miners, Mister Savage! Your Indians, Mister Savage! You let the Yosemites off the reservation to go back to killing the state's citizens!"

Jim waited for Moore to get said what he had to say. Weren't gonna be anything he wanted to hear, that much certain.

Moore glowered. "I had your word, *Mister* Savage. Remember?"

Jim sighed. "I do." He vividly remembered their recent exchange at Fort Miller, Moore saying, "There have to be rules and regulations for these Indians. They need to understand that appropriate punishment follows crime. That Indian of yours was caught stealing from a miner, took that good citizen's provisions."

Jim had his own mad up. "Tyin' a hungry Indian to a tree, floggin' 'im for tryin' to feed himself, that your idea of 'appropriate punishment'?! Indians got rights! Signed treaties for 'em!"

Moore reminding him California's treaties weren't ratified. Jim smacking Moore's desk. "Best you don't try explainin' such particulars to the Indians! Commissioners told 'em their Great White Father loved 'em! How about we let 'em believe it awhile!"

He remembered it all. Remembered he'd said, "Leave misbehavin' Indians to me! Save you regrettin' on yourself, Lieutenant. You got my word on it." Stuck out his hand. Moore had stared at it, clearly not keen on his so-called jurisdiction being challenged. Shrugged, shook. Handshake slack as rope.

Now Moore was fuming. "You're responsible, Savage! As you have repeatedly asserted your authority in that regard, I am advising you that we— you and me and those soldiers out there—will bring those murdering Yosemites in. You realize that's why I'm here?"

Chickens home to roost, for a fact. He'd showed Moore how to handle Indians when some boys stole and killed a horse. Took hold on that problem by taking three chiefs into custody until the guilty boy came in. Pretty good solution. The boy got turned over to the sheriff and whipped in the presence of white men, an Indian doing the whipping. Everyone seemed satisfied, including Tredwell Moore.

Weren't no point arguin' the Indians was hungry and the horse was food. And now, here they was, those same Indians harvesting so much barley the first crop got sold, at Stockton prices, to Tredwell Moore himself, for the soldiers at Fort Miller. What a world. Made a body's head spin.

He looked at Moore now, shook his head. "Naw. Didn't s'pose you come for vegetables."

Might be timely, Moore's demand, given how he'd been thinkin' lately. About Isabel. A year up in the mountains, bound to got her grievin' done. She'd like the school, fifty or sixty students showin' up regular. Indian kids learnin' songs in English, singin' Indian songs for visitors. Teacher sayin' the Indian children impressed him with their fondness for books, and impressed visitors with their —what was the word, Jim liked it, liked learnin' new ones— yeah, 'teachability.' Kinda thought that meant the teacher's ability. Maybe it went both ways. Unexpected.

Unexpected. Like shaking a hand slack as rope and making a pact with the devil.

"Mister Savage, I repeat, *Mister* Savage, the law will not allow these murders to go unpunished. Those Indians must be chastised and returned to the reservation. I have thirty-two infantrymen horsed and waiting. This is an authorized military operation."

Jim sighed. *Déjà vu.* "Had myself a military authorization once."

"You think being a *Major* implied distinction!"
"Nope. Advanced myself."
"What!?"
"General Disinclination."

Capt. Moore's Company of U.S. Infantry, stationed at Fort Miller, on the San Joaquin, is now en route for the scene of the murders. Major Savage will also accompany the command...
—*San Joaquin Republican*
June 15, 1852

"HAD ME A TRADIN' POST somethin' near here," Jim said, leaning against a tree while watching Moore's soldiers set up camp on the Merced. "My first store. Brush poles and canvas."

He missed those early days on this River of Mercy. Bacon and beans. Beans and bacon. Tin cup. An old man now by California standards, tellin' how it was in the old days. "Back in 'forty-eight it was. Yosemites burned me out. I took the hint. Let 'em be."

Moore glanced at him. "This isn't 'forty-eight, Savage. It's eighteen hundred and fifty-two. Different world."

"It is," Jim agreed. "Wonder is the Indians don't fall down from everythin' goin' all catawampus on 'em practically overnight." He sighed, looked at Moore. "Yosemites opposed my locatin' in these parts. Ain't got any friendlier, I guess." Teneiya, that old warrior, gone back to old ways.

"So it appears," Moore said tersely, "considering they murdered this man's brother and his friend."

The miner, a survivor from the prospecting party, arm wrapped in a dirty bandage, cocked his head and looked at Savage sidewise. "Wonder is they didn't kill you."

Moore nodded. "Isn't it."

Jim laughed. "Indians can't kill me, Moore. You wasn't here for that little fandango when the Chauchilas tried it. Called me out in battle. By name. Couldn't kill me. Couldn't touch me. Then, with me headin' up the battalion and defeatin' all of 'em, well, they figure I got supernatural powers. Willin' to credit me some continuin' wizard wisdom on account of it." He grinned. Strutting again. Old rooster.

The next day, he led Moore and a scouting party into the granite-bound valley surrounding the Awanichees' village, sat his horse while Moore dismounted, peered inside a few deserted shelters and cursed.

"Where are they?!" he demanded, staring up at Jim.

Jim shrugged. "Could be anywheres. Got us in their sights, though. Teneiya woulda posted lookouts. You can count on that."

Moore glowered. "Find them!"

Jim sighed, shook his head. "Might be gone over the mountain to the Monos, or holed up around here somewheres. Indians skilled at disappearin'."

"Find them!"

Jim dismounted, agreeably strolled around the abandoned village. "Ain't far. Some of 'em anyways," he said, casually pointing out tracks to Moore's scouts. He followed a faint trail some distance, Moore at his heels. "Women mainly. And kids. Nothin' worth followin'," he said, turning back.

All that day, and the next, Moore and his soldiers followed trails and tracks Jim showed them. Failing to find a single Indian, Moore's patience grew thin, then thinner. On the third day it snapped when two arrows, seemingly out of nowhere, killed one of his sentries. "If bloodshed is what they want," he yelled, "bloodshed is what they will get!"

Enraged, he sent a dozen patrols in a dozen different directions, shouting, "Bring me an Indian! Dead or alive!"

He turned on Savage. "Let's see where those tracks go, *Mister* Savage, the ones you declared weren't worth following!"

"Women and children," Jim said, shaking his head.

"Let's see!"

Later, in the heavy silence that followed the final echo of five rifle shots leaping between granite cliffs, Jim, stupefied, stood rooted while his mind reeled. When something resembling sensible thought returned, his brain searched for a word it finally found. *Aftermath*, he thought. Or did he say the word out loud? His mind still trying to make sense of it, the word, all of it, any of it. What he'd just seen, what they all had witnessed, the image searing hot as a cattle brand. Odd word, *aftermath*. School teacher, admiring the reservation's barley, predicting a second crop, a second mowing, *after-mowth*.

Aftermath. Result, consequence. Odd thought. It disappeared. He had once prided himself on his ability to sense what lay ahead, animal or ambush, friend or foe. Not this day. Never saw how this day would go, could go, so wrong, so bad. Didn't see this day's fork in the road. Was it him? Gone soft from baskin' in newspaper fame? From plantin' beans and peas and pumpkin seeds in the sun? Maybe. Or maybe some days defied prediction.

Seemed ordinary enough at the outset, the day had, showing Moore the nothing trail to nowhere important. Children's tracks, women's tracks. A nothing trail. He remembered leading Moore and maybe ten or twelve infantrymen, some mounted, some tracking on foot. And then a scout hollering discovery, riding back, excited. "Found them, Lieutenant! A dozen Indians! Maybe more!"

A nothing encampment, brush shelters in a rocky canyon. No lookouts, the little band surprised. Curious children, a dozen unsuspecting men and frightened women. And Isabel. Isabel. He had stared. She stared back.

He'd barely registered the fact of her, the sight of her, when an Indian ran at Moore, yelling. Events avalanching. Moore demanding Jim translate what the Indian was saying. The prospector riding with the company dismounting, running toward the Indian, hollering, "That's my brother's watch!" Indian backing away, grasping the pocket watch hanging from a string around his neck, shouting. Jim looking from Isabel to Moore and explaining. "He's sayin' he's objectin' to white men comin' into the Indians' territory." Looking from Moore to Isabel standing motionless, carved from granite. Moore accusing the Indian of murdering the prospectors, declaring the pocket watch clear evidence.

Jim shaking his head, looking from Isabel to Moore to the Indian protesting his innocence. "Says he didn't take part in the killin'. Admits he saw it. Says no white men got the right to enter their land without consent."

Was that the unforeseen turn taken? Had Moore's already frayed rope broken just then? If so, Jim had to admit he missed the moment.

Moore had slowly surveyed the little band of cowering Indians, cocked his head, and said, very calmly, "Mister Savage, tell this man and these people they have no claim here. Tell them their chief signed a treaty of peace and agreed that the Yosemites would live on the reservation provided for them."

Had Jim himself corrected Moore or had he interpreted the Indian's confident assertion that Teneiya had not agreed to treat? that Teneiya had never made his mark, that no other chief was authorized to speak on his behalf? that the Yosemites never recognized the commissioners' authority? And had that argument been at all important to what happened next?

He couldn't recall. What he recalled vividly was Moore's unexpected order, issued with no more emotion than 'dinner's served, time to eat': "By the authority of the United States Military I am arresting this man for murder. The punishment is hanging."

And then to everyone's surprise an infantryman was suddenly binding the protesting Indian's hands behind his back and a woman was screaming, "Lutario!" and Jim was staring from the screaming woman and protesting Indian to Isabel. And Isabel was looking frantically from the woman to him, like he was a white medicine man wizard and where was his magic?

A chaotic confusion unreeled rapidly before his disbelieving eyes, each scene more vivid than the last, instantly framed, like pictures. One picture after another. Pictures. What were they called? A fancy, Frenchy word. He knew French words. Learned 'em at rendezvous. Right. Yes. The photographer's studio. In San Francisco. Pretending he couldn't say French words. Too many brandy cocktails. Remembered thinking himself clever, saying *dagger-type* for daguerreotype, grinning while the man showed his framed pictures, wanting to make some of Jim and his Indians on their city tour. And now here he stood, mind racing, remembering the photographer with his polished sheets of silver-plated copper, jabbering about light and time and his displays of paper people, exact as themselves, made small. Heads rigid as death, eyes staring straight off the paper, out of the past and into the present. Dagger-types.

Before him now, motionless as a photograph, an Indian on his knees, hands tied, staring into the distance. Dagger-type. Isabel and the women and children and five men, still as stones, staring out of the past and into the present. Dagger-type.

And then the sudden, wild commotion as the captive broke free and ran. Ran as if shot. And wasn't. Ran for his life. Escaped.

And before anyone got the meaning of it, Moore's outraged order. The confused infantrymen finally getting the intention, grabbing the five Indian men, lining them up like fence posts. No one understanding, not even Jim clear until Moore gave the order. Not believing, even then. Seeing, but not believing.

Not believing until five soldiers pointed five rifles at five silent, terrified Indians. Not until five rifle shots echoed off the valley's granite cliffs. Not until five wide-eyed Indians fell over dead.

She didn't speak. And he had no words for what they had seen, not then, not later. What was there to say? On the trip back to the Fresno, she rode behind him on the horse, arms around his waist, head against his back. It seemed to him that she breathed only because she didn't know how not to.

In the first days that followed, he hoped only for a sign that she inhabited her body, that sense had not departed with speech. She followed listlessly when he led her through the unfinished adobe house. Peter, Peter, Pumpkin Eater. He brought her food which eventually she ate, absently, dutifully. He showed her the store. She chose a corner, sat, said nothing, expression vacant. She rose when he asked her to. She followed where he led. Fields. School. She looked wherever he pointed, but he sensed no connection. She seemed not to see or comprehend. And she remained mute.

He trusted time to blunt her memory, and his. Trusted time to ease her from the past into the present, release her from silence. He talked to her about the farm, about the school. About the future. Waited for her to attach attention to the sound of his voice. Anyone's voice.

One morning as she sat, a silent fixture in the store's corner, he took newspapers from a shelf and dropped them with a thud on the counter in front of Lewis. "Read her somethin', anything you can find what might take her interest."

Lewis glanced at Isabel, shook his head, whether at the spiritless sight or his own uncertainty Jim didn't know.

Lewis installed his spectacles, adjusted them, leaned against the counter, thumbed through the papers. "Saw something about a new stage service a few days ago," he said, "in the *Republican*, I think." He looked at Jim. "Indians call stages a 'rolling house,' did you know that?" He turned back to the newspapers, not waiting for an answer. "Article had to do with Sam Ward. I remembered you said he used to come and talk with her at your Mariposa store."

He opened a newspaper, turned a few pages, silently scanned a column of type. "Here it is. Doesn't come to much. Just says Sam Ward welcomed the stage at Belt's ferry by preparing a meal for the stage driver. Biscuit, ham, and horse-hash."

Jim nodded. "Belt's gonna profit from that stage goin' through regular. Passengers, freight, ferryin' fees. Easy money. Next thing you know, anyone with a rope and a boat will get himself into the ferryin' business."

"Reminds me," Lewis said, folding the newspaper and looking at Jim. "Remember John Poole? On the King's River?"

"Poole's been haulin' that old whaleboat of his across that river more'n two years. Wonder it still floats."

"Seems to. Bill Campbell's gone in with Poole now, set up a trading post at the ferry, hired a clerk name of Edmunds. Chief Watoka's not happy about it. Came here looking for you while you were gone with Lieutenant Moore."

Jim glanced at Isabel. Had she heard? "Count it a personal favor, Lewis," he said, leaning in, his voice lowered, "you don't mention Moore's name in her hearin'. Mine neither, come to that. Expect we've seen the last of him anyways."

Lewis flinched. "Of course. Sorry. Won't happen again."

Jim, eyes still on Isabel, voice quiet. "Him discoverin' gold up there while chasin' Indians, abandonin' the military, takin' up prospectin'." He shook his head. "Joke in there somewheres, Lewis," he said, looking up at the rafters now, "if I can remember where I left my laugh."

"Fort's new commander seems a better man."

"Ain't much of a contest." Jim looked at Isabel again. No reaction.

Lewis said, "About Watoka—"

"What's his problem?"

"Near as I could understand, he's mainly unhappy Edmunds isn't you."

"Edmunds? Who's Edmunds?" Lewis lookin' at him now like he was deaf. "Oh, yeah, you just said. Poole's new clerk." His mind lately wanderin' like a lost dog.

Lewis nodded. "Watoka said when you came into his country and set up a trading post, you gave his people blankets."

"He wants blankets from us?"

"No, that's what he wanted from Edmunds. You know, presents, respect. From you he wants something official he can show Poole and Campbell they're on reservation land belonging to the Indians by treaty."

"Poole's ferry and Campbell's old store was there before the signin'. Anything in the newspapers about those treaties?"

"Still not ratified."

Jim considered. He looked over at Isabel, back at Lewis. "Them treaties don't ratify, we'll be goin' to hell in a handcart. Until that sorry day, let's try keepin' up some appearance of justice." He drummed his fingers on the plank counter, thinking. He slapped the counter. "Got it! Let's give Watoka a real official declaration!" He grinned. "Write him up somethin' official soundin'. The more official, the better!"

By the time they'd finished, anyone care to ask, Jim felt right proud to be actin' on behalf of Watoka, the commissioners, why, even California, come to that. "Read it out, Lewis," he said, "like you was the Great White Father himself."

Lewis squared his shoulders, rattled the paper importantly, and read:

"Greetings: Know all men by these presents, that the holder of this, Watoka, is the chief of the Chonemne tribe, and has treated with the Commissioners for the lands which he now occupies, which said land, he, the said Watoka, is resolved to hold and occupy with his people, apart, and alone, entirely free from white men and their settlements. He, the said Watoka, desires me to say that no molestation or hindrance will be given to white men traveling through this country, but that he is determined to prevent all encroachments on his peoples' lands."

Jim glanced over at Isabel, thought he detected interest, wasn't sure. "How we gonna sign it? Barbour? Wozencraft?"

Lewis shook his head. "Only name Chief Watoka believes has any authority is James D. Savage."

Jim sighed. "Well, then, put that."

Lewis dipped his pen in its ink-pot, scratched it across the bottom of the paper, looked up. "You could take this to Chief Watoka when you go to Poole's to supervise the polling there."

"What polling? Remind me." Lately he couldn't remember anything.

"You agreed to collect votes at Poole's. John Boling's collecting at Woodville."

"Woodville? Where's Woodville?"

"Wood's old log cabin. Legislature named it the county seat."

"Wood's cabin?"

"It's the new county's courthouse."

"Why there?"

"It's the only structure in the new county not canvas."

"Got a roof?"

"I believe so."

"One-uppin' Agua Fria anyways."

"Progress."

"What they callin' our new county?"

"Tulare. Harvey's on the ticket for judge. He was the prime mover in getting the legislature to approve dividing Mariposa County in half."

Jim looked over at Isabel. Somethin' in her eyes, not sure what. "Harvey'll campaign for any office got a vacancy," he said, watching her closely. "Ain't no office, he's campaignin' anyways."

She was in there, he saw it. Harvey's name? Did she remember that old blowhard?

Sitting inside Poole's makeshift store, Jim started to sweat. "Hot enough in here to bake bread," he said, looking at Edmunds behind the counter, half asleep from the heat.

"Movin' the votin' outside."

"Ain't my business," Edmunds said, eyes closed.

Storekeepin' weren't neither, Jim thought, carrying the collection box and blank ballots outside, kicking the store's door closed behind him. Too green for these parts, Edmuds was. Twitchy with Indians. Surprised Poole and Campbell took the man on.

Jim squatted in the dry grass under a large oak and admired the view. A fine clear day it was, even the distant coast range visible. Mountains up to his left still white on their tops, snow not yet done meltin' into rivers. He scratched his itchy back against the tree's warm rough bark, swatted a fly from his ear, and settled into waiting. Had a momentary feeling of something repeated, not quite a *déjà vu*, just a sense of the familiar.

Well, Edmunds weren't his worry. Fact was, didn't have no worries except Isabel, and she'd be comin' around. So here he was, a regular citizen, seein' a new county gettin' its organizin' done, settin' up for business. Kinda liked it. Not what anyone would call a frolic, just miners and settlers takin' a day from their work, makin' their marks and lookin' serious, handin' over their ballots like they was bank deposits. Stayin' to gossip some or drink Campbell's whiskey. Jawin' about prospectin' or some big plan or other. A fine day, he thought. Even the sight of Harvey comin' toward him now was no more annoyin' than flies. Part way amusin', seein' Harvey in his black frock coat in this heat, paradin' himself like he'd already been elected judge.

"So, Mister Savage," Harvey said, flapping a bandana from a coat pocket and wiping sweat from his forehead. "Got yourself appointed commissioner of our county elections, I see."

Jim laughed, handing up a ballot. "Harvey, I been holdin' office in these parts since I showed up. You musta missed hearin' 'bout me bein' king."

Harvey snorted, marked and folded his ballot, and dropped it in the box. "Indians don't count."

"Why, Harvey," Jim said, grinning, "sure they do. Indians plenty smart. They can count."

Harvey, scowling, departed stiffly. Jim laughed. Edmunds weren't his worry. Harvey weren't his worry. And it was a fine day for starin' at the distance and rememberin' fine times, like bein' king of the Tularenos. Had him some frolics since that first summer at Sutter's place watchin' Indians thresh wheat the way they done. Had some adventures, he had. Seen Marshall discover gold, seen San Francisco strip itself of tents like they was rags, dress itself up in bricks. Bested old Murphy at the scales game, on his back, blanket on one foot, tin cup strapped to the other, waggin' his legs in the air. Laughed now at the memory.

"Somethin' funny, Major?"

Jim grinned up at a late-comer. "Just thinkin' on old days. How you doin'?"

"Damned hot is what." The man mopped his face with a white handkerchief.

"Lookin' at that kerchief you got reminds me of a trick I used to do," Jim said. "Had some fun with the Indians in the old days. I'd tack a handkerchief like that to a tree. Take aim and put six holes in it every time. Good shot. Decent distance, too. Impressin' the Indians, I was. Then I'd reload usin' empty cartridges, hand the gun to some unsuspectin' buck and tell him to shoot me. 'Aim right at me,' I'd say. Stand close up.'"

Jim laughed, remembering. "'I'm a white medicine man,' I'd say. 'Can't kill me. Shoot me with bow and arrow, I live. Shoot me with pistol, I live.' Lotta Indians didn't know, in them early days, about six-shooters firin' empty cartridges. Guns just a big noise to 'em then. Anyways, had me a secret handful of bullets and after I'd get someone to shoot, I'd reach out quick after each shot like I was catchin' the bullet. Amazed everyone, 'specially the kids, when I showed those bullets I'd caught. Convinced 'em I was a white wizard. Fine times. King of the Tularenos."

The man marked his ballot, handed it over. "Them days gone."

Jim nodded, took the ballot, dropped it in the box, and looked toward the distant mountains. "Yep, them days gone."

Indians on King's River…threatened to kill the ferrymen….
Major Harvey left this evening with some eighteen or twenty
men. A fine chance for the boys to have a frolic….

—*Daily Alta California*
July 13, 1852

BACK AT HIS TRADING POST, Jim counted the ballots with Lewis. "Well," he
said, "Harvey'll be happy now."

"Maybe," said Lewis, dipping a pen in an inkpot to write the Secretary of
State that one hundred and nine voters had elected Tulare County's first slate
of officers.

The following day Jim watched Isabel silently go into the fields to pick
peas. He trailed after her. Felt good, sun on his back, earth warm on his bare
feet, the smell of summer. Never imagined himself a farmer, could see it
now. He watched Isabel pull a slender green pod from a vine, examine it as
if it were a discovery. Woman had grit, he thought, survivin' what she seen,
what she'd lost. Come to that, enough loss for both of 'em, for a lifetime.
He looked up, shielded his eyes from the white sun overhead. Sun rollin'
around, bumpin' one day into the next, beamin' down now on James D.
Savage plantin' and pickin'. Weren't that a hoot?

When a rumor of massacre reached the reservation, Jim ran his hands
through his hair, imagined he smelled sunshine clinging to his fingers.
Wanted to be in the fields with Isabel, that's what he wanted. Not burdened
by this new problem.

After riding over to Fort Miller and back, he told Lewis, "Shoulda known
there'd be trouble at Poole's, what with that clerk bein' twitchy and Watoka
gettin' his patience used up. Fracas is the way it started, no more'n a squab-
ble. Watoka and half a dozen Indians come in complain' or threatenin' Edmunds, got him so afraid he asked some men in the store to watch the place,
'defend it against hostilities' is what he said, while he went for help. That
man don't understand all the posin' and pretendin' Indians do, how they
make a show to solve problems, not start 'em up. If Poole had been there
when Watoka come in, the two of 'em woulda had theirselves a smoke and
a little council. Poole woulda give the chief somethin', save face all around."

A few days later a newspaper reported the event and Lewis clipped the
article.

"What's it say?" Jim asked, standing in the doorway watching Isabel out in a field, picking peas.

"Headline says 'Difficulty with the Indians'."

Jim shook his head, watched her slowly, steadily filling a basket. "More like Indians got difficulty, anyone care to ask." He saw her hesitate a moment, look around, then continue along the row, picking peas, putting them in her basket. "Let's hear it."

"It's dated from the San Joaquin River. Says, and I quote, '*The people here are expecting every day to have the devil to pay with the red-skins. A few days ago, a man keeping a store and ferry on Kings River came into our camp, stating that he had been warned by a body of some six or eight chiefs, of the Kings River tribe, to leave immediately—that the next time they warned him they would kill him. Very soon there was a party numbering twenty-eight men, mounted, and armed to the teeth, who left here for that river, to investigate the affair. Had they confined themselves strictly to this object, there is no doubt but the whole affair might have been settled to the satisfaction of all parties; for I believe it to be the desire of the Indians to preserve the treaty. But instead of making any inquiries regarding the threat, the whole party rode into the rancheria, and after a few words had passed, the import of which I did not understand, they commenced firing upon and killed about twenty-five or thirty of them. There has been a great deal of discontent among the Indians here at Fort Miller. They have been holding council with each other all day; in fact they do not look like the same Indians. They are sulky, and do not leave their camp.*'"

"Well, that 'sulky' part's right anyway," Jim said. "Watoka reported the whole thing to Fort Miller's new commander—what's his name?"

"Patten."

"Yeah, Patten. Patten told me eight of Watoka's people got killed outright, and ten wounded."

"From the sound of this article, it seems the writer was there."

Jim shrugged, lit his pipe. "Well, if so, he ain't clear on what he seen. Weren't twenty-five or thirty Indians murdered. Not that eight don't count. They do. Patten's got the particulars in a signed statement made by the men involved. Watoka's demandin' their arrest."

"You said Edmunds was twitchy."

"That greenhorn high-tailin' off to get help — 'save the place from attack' is what he claimed — and found Harvey, of all people. Harvey always keen to rile men up, give a bunch of hot-heads a chance to make trouble."

"Harvey's been acting the big-shot since getting elected judge."

Jim chewed his pipe stem. "Been braggin' West Point in ever'body's face since he come to California."

"Bragging without credentials," Lewis said. "I have it on good authority he didn't finish his first year."

Jim knocked his pipe against the stove. "Gettin' tired of Harvey and his kind, always lookin' to make trouble, any excuse to puff theirselves up, be bigger'n some other feller. Any other feller. Indians easiest. S'posed to be gentlemen, them West Pointers."

Lewis returned the newspaper to its shelf. "There's talk about arresting Harvey over the attack."

"Might happen," Jim said. "Wozencraft's gone to San Francisco to see if he can get a U.S. Marshall to investigate it. Told Patten to arrange talks with the Indians. Gonna be a council at Four Creeks, fifteenth of August. Patten's sent to Benicia for a detachment of dragoons to meet us there. More military the better, he thinks."

"Meanwhile?"

Meanwhile? Meanwhile, all he wanted, truth be told, was to smell sunshine on his hands, bring some life back to Isabel's eyes, watch her pick peas, and feel the earth's warm dirt under his feet. Well, get this thing all settled and that's what he'd do.

He sighed. "Patten wants me to see if I can calm things down with the Indians. I'm gonna talk to 'em, invite 'em to the council, all of 'em what wants to come see if they're ever gonna get a fair shake. Ain't certain myself, and that's a fact."

[T]hey would not be quiet one week was it not for the influence of Major Savage....

—*San Joaquin Republican*
July 3, 1852

DURING THE NEXT FEW DAYS, he visited a dozen Indian villages around Four Creeks, meeting with more than a hundred Kaweahs solemn as church-goers at a sermon. He forced as much confidence into his voice as he could haul up from wherever it had sunk to. He knew it was old talk with old words the Indians had heard before. Even to him it sounded hollow as a tule-reed whistle.

The Kaweahs' chief had looked at him sadly. "What shall we do? We try to live on these lands the commissioners gave us. We want friendship with the white man. But we have no peace on the lands the commissioners gave us. And if we flee to the mountains, they hunt us and kill us. Where shall we go and what shall we do? When the commissioners gave us the U.S. flag, and our papers, they told us that it would protect us, but now the flag is all stained with our blood, and our papers are all bloody, and who shall wash it off? We are poor and weak. The whites are rich and strong and we pray for mercy."

Jim had no answer. What could he say? "We'll be talkin' on it, Chief, at the council."

Back on the Fresno, he pulled up a stool near Isabel's corner, watched her examining her basket of peas. Lewis, behind the counter reading newspapers, said, "Harvey's circulating a signed statement saying he would leave it to the public to determine whether the party under his command 'transcended propriety,' he says. Says he does not 'feel the tongue of slander.'"

"Ain't slander when it's true," Jim said. "Indians more'n willin' to live alongside white people that honor treaty obligations. Only need protectin' from miners and settlers encroachin' on their land. No need preachin' 'em peace, it's all they want."

Isabel was methodically opening the pods, carefully removing peas to a smaller basket, placing empty pods in another.

"Four Creeks could be fine farm land," Jim said, watching her. "Get this bad business done, maybe me and Marvin and our farmer should talk to the

Kaweahs about plantin' pumpkins and beans and peas and such. Grow eve-rythin' in that rich soil they got. Maybe we should invite the chiefs over here, show 'em what they could do. Grow crops, sell 'em to the settlers."

"Worth a try," Lewis said, watching Isabel shell peas.

Jim watched her, too. "That's somethin' new, ain't it?" he asked.

"Still hasn't said a word, but I think she's getting better," Lewis replied. "While you were gone that farmer you hired to oversee the crops noticed her picking peas. He told her we needed to save some for seed, to plant next year. Didn't know anything about her, who she was, or anything, just gave her some instructions, put her to it. She seems content with the task."

Jim nodded. "Good. Give her some belief in the future. Next year, a new crop, and the year after that another crop. The world gettin' on with gettin' on. Sun rollin' around the sky, comin' up and goin' down."

No frolic needed, he thought, only peace and peas. That would be enough, peace and peas. Smiled to himself. 'Peace and peas.' A poet.

….a few restless spirits in Mariposa county have fomented this state of things, by not only disregarding the treaties made with the Indians, but by also trampling on their acknowledged rights, and setting at naught every principle of justice and humanity.
—*Daily Alta California*
August 12, 1852

WATCHING AND WAITING. Listening. Words. Drowning in words. The People's words, saved, forgotten, found, lost. Words, rivers of words, awash in her head. White man's words, in the air, everywhere, invisible as wind, finding her ears, stealing her thoughts, catching in her throat, stopping her tongue. So many words. Too many words. She liked the green smell of peas and beans. Their sweet taste. The warmth of sunshine. The familiar comfort of her corner, here in the store, safe. The man called Lewis reading newspapers. And the sight, the fact, of her friend, her one friend, her only friend, more than friend. Blue eyes and yellow hair. She watched him now, looking at her. Sensed his concern. Was grateful. More than grateful. An old feeling filling the empty place inside. Like sunshine. A feeling more than she had words for. If she had those words. She should look for them.

She had once thought if she learned the Mexicans' words, she would see the world as they saw it, and in that way learn why they hated the People and murdered them. When the white men came, she learned their words, too. And still she didn't know why so many people wanted Indians dead. Words were worthless. She watched her friend examine his gun.

"Better give me some extra bullets," he told Lewis. "Patten thinks there could be trouble."

Lewis took a box from the shelf. "With the Indians?"

"With Harvey. Heard he's afraid he's gonna get arrested by that company of dragoons Patten sent for. Should be. Should be hanged. Or shot. Or somethin'. Won't be. But maybe he don't know that."

"You shouldn't travel alone."

"John Marvin's goin' with me and Patten is meetin' us near Poole's place. We'll be goin' to Four Creeks with him and the dragoons. Ain't expectin' trouble, but ain't no harm preparin' for it." He took six bullets from the box Lewis held out.

She watched him feed bullets to his gun. And then, sudden as an avalanche, she tasted ashes. Heard ghosts whisper warnings. Secrets. Secrets she should tell. Her head filling with secrets to tell. She needed to find words, speak the secrets. Where had she put her words? So many words, and she couldn't remember where she left them. He was staring at her.

"Did she say somethin'? You hear her say somethin'?"

Lewis looking at her. "I don't think so." Lewis looking away, closing the box of bullets, putting it back on the shelf.

"I thought I heard her say somethin'."

He came to her. Sat cross-legged on the floor, looking at her. Old days. Old ways. He took her hand in his. Smiled. He took her fingers, one by one, softly speaking the numbers in Me'wuk. He touched her face, stroked it. "Isabel?"

She was hearing Victoria's ghost voice. A whisper. 'What is done is done.' He stroked her face. She touched his in return. She liked looking at him. Hair like sunshine. Eyes like sky.

His death is a matter of great importance, inasmuch as his influence over the Indian tribes, for weal or for woe, was very great.

—*Sacramento Daily Union*
August 21, 1852

"SPARIN' THE HORSES will slow us some, won't matter. Plenty of time," Jim said. The horses' hooves barely lifted dust from the road.

Marvin nodded. "Hot one," he said, holding his horse's reins loose, eyes half-closed against the sun's brightness.

Jim looked from John Marvin up at the cloudless sky. Not a whisper of breeze in the parched-up oaks, alders, and cottonwoods. Day hardly started and him and Marvin both sweatin'. Birds retired early from their chirpin'. August heat hangin' lead-heavy. Nothin' stirrin' 'cept insects, circlin' slow, spiritless, like they was makin' their rounds more from habit than interest, he thought. Hills scorched, grass fried up. Somethin' to look at, though, this country, blond with wild oats. Elk and wild horses grazin' far off, makin' a shadow on the distance. Man might maybe could hear geese honkin' if he listened good. All that tule marsh collectin' ducks and waterbirds. Whole great valley practically a garden, just waitin' to grow crops. Some country. But blisterin' in summer, that much certain.

"Day headin' for stove-hot," he said after a time.

"Feels like it," Marvin replied. "I assume Patten will wait for us at Poole's ferry."

"Plannin' on meetin' us near there. Prob'ly ain't keen on crossin' the river and facin' Watoka until I get there to translate. He won't be rushin' now that Wozencraft ain't comin'. It was Wozencraft arranged this big council and now, sudden like, he's too sick to travel."

Marvin leaned around, adjusted his saddle pack, leather creaking. "That's an excuse, you know. He's got his reasons, two reasons really, for not coming. First, the Indians aren't going to understand the U.S. district attorney's ruling that reservation land is outside federal jurisdiction."

"Guess he don't wanna be the one tells 'em killin' Indians ain't against the law where there ain't no law," Jim said, eyes on the horizon's distantly dancing heat shimmer.

"Essentially."

"Don't astonish me none." He let Girl have her head, relaxed the reins. Hill and dale the two of 'em, all these years. Horse could practically read his mind.

"And second, now that Harvey's been elected judge of Tulare County, he's the law here."

Jim knew what that meant. "Makin' prosecution hopeless," he said.

"Essentially."

"Wouldn't expect Harvey to convict himself of anythin' 'cept bein' a sterlin' citizen. Ain't gonna charge himself with murder, that much certain." He looked at Marvin. "Like to imagine it if'n I could, but I'm losin' my sense of humor."

Marvin pulled a bandana from his shirt pocket, mopped the back of his neck. "If I ever had one I left it in Boston when I abandoned a perfectly good law practice to come to California." He hesitated a moment, then laughed. "Wait, no, I did have an amusing experience a couple of years ago. Ludicrous. Did I ever mention that California's first legislature appointed me the state's superintendent of public instruction? I went to San Jose and found nothing there to take charge of. No schools, no money, no plans."

"Ain't much for knee-slappin' if'n that's your idea of a joke."

"Joke was on me. I don't recall saying it was a good one."

They rode in silence awhile before Marvin said, "Law school prepared me poorly for California's endless, senseless killing."

"Not much frolic lately."

"Harvey convincing the legislature to establish a new county so he could finally get himself a judgeship, might be a joke in there."

Jim felt heat rising from the road, the horses, the land lying weighted beneath a white sky. He tipped his hat back, looked up, a lazy motion catching his eye. Overhead, a distant spiral of buzzards. "Mighta been the only way to get shut of him."

"And then making Woods' old place a county seat," Marvin said. "That cabin ought to have been burned down after he was slaughtered in it. Indians flaying him alive, nailing his skin to a tree. Barbarous, the whole business."

"Weren't just Woods got killed," Jim said. "Thirteen men massacred is what I heard. Got the story from the Indians, no whites bein' left to talk. Happened same time as my men—Kennedy and them. December of 'fifty. Kaweahs sorta got enlisted by the Chauchilas, Potoyensees, all the tribes unitin' in that last go at gettin' white men outta their country."

"You'd think, or I do anyway, that a dozen men might have known better than to place themselves in unnecessary danger."

"Bad timin' is what it was. They left Mariposa with farmin' in mind. Took some cattle to the Four Creeks area, built theirselves that log cabin. Indians warned 'em they was trespassin' on their land. Gave 'em ten days to leave. Way I heard it, Woods and his friends was roundin' up their cattle, fixin' to go."

"What happened?"

"Missed the deadline."

"My god, Jim, they weren't all skinned alive!"

"Mostly shot with arrows while they was out collectin' up their stock. Woods got back to the cabin. Holed up there and shot seven Indians before runnin' outa bullets. Kaweahs gave him special attention for killin' so many of their people." He glanced at Marvin. "Don't s'pose you seen much killin' in the war with Mexico."

"I was with the Quartermaster Corps. This killing here, it's so god-damned capricious."

"Capricious? Ain't acquainted with the word."

"Unpredictable."

Jim laughed. "Capricious, eh? Slap that word on life itself, my friend. I ain't seen anythin' predictable in this life 'cept summer sun and winter rain since my momma last switched my backside." He looked at Marvin again. "Quartermaster, eh? You and me should start up a freightin' business. Plenty opportunities here, you know." He waved a hand at the landscape. "Look at this country! Grow anythin', I bet. All this water comin' down to irrigate it. Four Creeks gonna be farmland one day, you wait and see."

"And who is going to farm it?"

"I seen plenty pie vendors in San Francisco, organ grinders, steamboat runners, wharf rats, all eligible for improvement. Not opposed to farmin' myself now, you know. You seen how me and the Indians got crops comin' up on the reservation. Barley we planted in December got harvested in June. Kinda fancyin' myself a settled-down farmer these days, growin' beans and peas and such." He squinted his eyes against the harsh white light of August, like he could see his future if he fixed on it good.

The day progressed with them, sun gilding the west when they finally reached the rendezvous point. Patten hadn't waited for them. Not near Poole's, not at Poole's. Jim sat his horse, studied the mud edging the river flowing summer-low, green and lazy past Poole's trading post. "Mud all churned-up," he said to Marvin. "Horses done that, recent. Dragoons already gone across."

Marvin nodded. "I suppose Patten expected us sooner rather than later."

"Mighta left us a message with Poole." The single horse tied up outside the trading post switched its tail as they dismounted, tethered their horses, went inside.

At the sound of the door banging, Harvey looked up from the table where he sat drinking with Poole, and laughed. "Well, here we all are!"

Jim stared at Harvey, shook his head. Tarted up in his black frock coat —in this heat!— like some go-to-meetin' preacher.

Standing, jovial as a host greeting guests, Harvey said, "Well, not all of us. Patten *was* here, but we had a little talk, him and me, a little preliminary discussion, I'd say it was." He paused, nodding at Marvin with a satisfied smile, as if to say, 'we understand one another, don't we?' without having to waste breath on the obvious. "Took his men across the river to locate themselves a campsite."

No, not a preacher. A judge! Harvey the judge of Tulare County. Paradin' his importance. Goddamned fraud is what he was. Jim felt himself gettin' riled just seein' the sweatin' man's black coat and hearin' his slick, greased-up voice.

Poole asked, "Get you boys anything?"

Jim stared at Harvey. "Gettin' yourself up somethin' of a sweat, ain't you, Harvey? Kinda hot for you in that coat? That why you're sweatin'? Or you just anticipatin' gettin' hanged? Them dragoons ain't come to camp out, have theirselves a Sunday School picnic, you know. They come to arrest you for murder. You might just as well surrender now, you son of a bitch."

Felt good, just sayin' straight out what was what. Make the man sweat some more, plant a picture of a rope in the man's mind.

Harvey, face reddening, turned to Marvin. "No need to be troubled, none of us. This so-called council is nothing. Nothing at all."

Jim stared. Oily. Harvey's every word oily. And the man was still talkin', like the sound of his voice was good company. He just kept on talkin'. Words leakin' out his mouth like grease from fatback.

"Nothing for anyone to get any further concerned about anyway," Harvey was saying now, looking at Marvin like they were old friends. "Patten and me had a little talk. It all comes down to—how did we put it?" He paused, looked up, like maybe the word he wanted was written overhead, then grinned, looked back at Marvin. "Yes, an error in judgment. That's all, an error in judgment."

Jim felt his blood start to boil. Harvey grinnin' like he'd hung a joke in the air for everyone to admire. Like that damned French contortionist, doin' nothin' and actin' like it was somethin' and everybody lucky to be regardin' his amazin' self. Harvey, grinnin', satisfyin' himself with his own oily performance. And still talkin'.

"Yes, Commander Patten and I agreed what we have here is an error in judgment. That's all, nothing more than an error in judgment. His words, Patten's, not mine, by the way. Patten's."

Marvin shook his head. "Harvey, if that's the case, why not surrender, go on record, let the facts speak for themselves?"

"Well, that's one possibility, isn't it? But Patten understands how things are in these parts. You know, with the Indians. A regular gentleman, Patten." He paused again, let Patten's name hang in the air a moment, Jim noticed, like it was his own personal achievement.

"Regret Dr. Wozencraft won't be joining us," Harvey continued, casting a brief, dismissive look in Jim's direction. "A gentleman, Wozencraft." He jokingly punched Marvin's arm. "Like yourself, Marvin. Harvard man, aren't you, Marvin? Heard that. West Point, myself. Gentlemen understand one another, don't we?"

Jim exploded. "You sayin' I ain't no gentleman, Harvey?! That what you're sayin'?!"

Harvey slowly turned to him. Contempt, that was the look Jim saw on Harvey's face, in his half-closed eyes, his slick, sneering mouth.

"*Mister* Savage, you are no more a gentleman than your name declares."

Jim, rigid, heard himself very distinctly, very slowly, very deliberately, say, "*Mister* Harvey, I'm suggestin' you retract that charge." He saw, heard, "I will not" ooze from the man's mouth. And then he knew he could no more resist punchin' that mouth than water could keep from bein' wet. Heat scalded his thinking, blistered his vision. Harvey's existence was a blot on the land, and this day's sun goin' down would shine brighter comin' up tomorrow without Harvey under it. Jim felt blood flood hot into his face, his chest, his arms, his hands, his clenched hot hands. He was hot, boiling hot. He sensed himself expanding with heat, swelling, enlarging. He could no more contain himself than a fired cannon could contain its charge.

"Harvey, you're no gentleman! You're a goddamned murderin' son of a bitch!" And, faster than thought, his fist hit Harvey's sneering mouth.

Harvey bellowed, stumbled, fell.

Marvin shouted. "Hey!"

Harvey got to his feet. "Why, you—"

Jim hit him again.

Harvey groaned, went down. Then, slowly getting to his knees, his breath labored, he reached under his coat. Withdrew a pistol.

Jim saw it, reached for his own.

Marvin shouted, "Hold on, men! Hold on! This isn't the answer!"

Jim heard only the blood drumming loud in his head. He had his gun now, its metal heavy and hot in his sweat-slick hand. He threw himself at Harvey. They went down, scrabbling, grunting, yelling. A thud. What was that? Marvin in the middle now, trying to separate them, arms flailing.

Poole's voice, shouting. "Harvey! Hold on! Major Savage dropped his weapon!"

Marvin's voice. "Jim, here it is! I've got it! Over here!"

And then an explosion. Another. And another.

White. Bright...bright, bright white. No.... red. No....black....black. He could see... Harvey in that...black... coat....risin' up... How... was he doin' that? ....Harvey floatin'...up....driftin'.... distant...... smaller.... floor risin'....piece of floor.....peace......peace and peas.....green peas.....green.....peas.....thought she said... somethin'.....thought she... said.....thought she.....thought.........

The Indians were terribly excited at his death. Some of them reached the scene of the tragedy soon after it occurred. They threw themselves upon his body, uttering the most terrific cries, bathing their hands and faces in his blood....

—*San Francisco Daily Herald*
September 4, 1852

HUNCHED INTO HER CORNER, she bent her head, covered her ears against the wailing. Such wailing. Like a windstorm whipping through the store. Crying, lamenting. Wailing. She pressed her hands against her ears, not to hear. Not to know.

"Isabel."

Lewis's voice. Lewis's hands gentle on her hands. Taking her hands in his, urging her up, helping her stand. "Come with me, Isabel."

His hands taking hers, leading her. She followed. Followed out the store's door. Into the sorrow, into the wailing she tried not to hear. Into the sorrow she didn't want to know.

Under the oak, a wagon. White men, soldiers, miners, the farmer, the teacher. Mules unhitched, soldiers and white men talking low. Around the wagon Indians collecting, keening, wailing, crying, demanding to see.

Lewis leaving her, climbing up on the wagon. Taking the top off a long box.

Indians, so many wailing Indians. Surrounding the wagon. Surrounding her, absorbing her into their slow shuffling around the wagon. Touching the box, looking into it. Seeing. Weeping. Their collected grief rising, sending sorrow into the cloudless sky.

She looked into the box. She couldn't breathe. She stared, disbelieving. She knew him. Knew he would not, could not, be so still for so long. Soon he surely, suddenly, must sit up, stand, laugh. A frolic, he was having a frolic. He was Woochi, the clown, fooling the People. Fooling.

"Isabel." Lewis again, taking her arm, leading her away from the box, the wagon, the crying crowd. She hadn't believed, and Lewis had showed her, and now she had seen, and he was leading her away, and she was shaking her head, no. And so she stood apart now, watching and waiting. To see this new white medicine man wizard trick. Waiting for the Woochi trick. A new frolic.

The day advanced. More and more people coming. White men talking. Indians looking, seeing, wailing. She waited, watched, silent witness to a noisy stunned disbelief. She waited. Woochi trick.

More white people, talking in low voices, white men climbing into the wagon. Fitting the top to the box. Nailing the box closed. Hammer slamming. Each blow splintering the day like a pistol shot. And then stabbing, jabbing shovels biting into the hard, parched soil. A thin dust rising around the open earth mouth. She watched white men lift the box from the wagon, hand it down to waiting hands. Watched it carried to the gaping earth mouth. Saw it lowered. And then she knew. And forgot how to stand.

The long sad day grew gray. And still they came, sorrowing, crying, carrying baskets and blankets, gifts for their lost friend's last journey. Weeping, they piled branches over the sealed earth where the box lay swallowed.

Then, with night lighted by fire, they danced. They circled and circled, exclaiming disbelief, lamenting loss. They wept from fire-lighted faces, feet finding the ancient rhythm. She was among them, one of them, one of the People, abandoned, lost, crying to the stars, to Great Spirit, addressing grief with despair. And when they had no more strength for dancing, they wailed. And when they had no more voice for wailing, they danced.

Through her tears she saw faces she knew or should have known and couldn't remember. Who was the child, the young boy, weeping, clutching a white handkerchief to give the fire, crying out, "Why didn't he catch the bullets? Why didn't he catch the bullets?"

Why didn't he? Why didn't he? She briefly fastened a wispy thread of attention onto a familiar face. "Homut," the mouth on the face said, "I am Homut." Their eyes connected, and their hearts, their crying hearts. "We are doomed," the Homut mouth said. And because her own mouth had lost the ability, she spoke from the empty place inside, spoke the long-known silent truth: 'We were always doomed.' And they looked away from one another and continued woefully circling the fire and dancing the long dance.

Their collected endless sorrow filled the night, and the next day, the next night, and the day after that and the night after that.

Eventually flames dwindled, died. Lamenting mourners gathered ashes into their hands, lifted them up to the four directions—east, west, north, south. Released grief and ashes into the sky, to join the ancestors, to find Great Spirit.

Epilogue

A more inoffensive and harmless race of beings does not exist
on the face of the earth....

—J. Ross Browne
California Inspector of Indian Affairs

... the paintings of Bierstadt and the photographs of Wat-
kins...[gave] the people of the Atlantic some idea of the sublimity of the Yo Semite.

—Frederick Law Olmstead

The dead, the First People advised, leave the world reluctantly, linger in the company of those who loved them. She cropped her hair, smeared her face with pine pitch and ashes, marked herself for loss once more. The old-ways warning: beware, a widow. One to shun. Here go ghosts.

She believed in ghosts, saw them everywhere now. Possibly she was one of them. Did ghosts possess feet? She stared at her own, watched, wondering, as they walked slowly east, followed the old trails, into the mountains, toward home. Awani.

Awani.

In the old village she found a remnant band of Yosemites who'd hidden when Tredwell Moore and the Fort Miller soldiers came to punish them for the prospectors' deaths. She joined them, saying nothing, remaining a ghost. Even had she words, which she no longer did, what was there to say? What is done is done. Everyone scarred by loss now, everyone acquainted with ghosts. So many dead now, so many names not to speak.

When the women gathered manzanita berries for trading, she did, too. And when the little band crossed the mountain to the Monos, she followed. There she found Chief Teneiya and all the last sad people who had fled with him from the soldiers. No one chased them now. No one cared that Teneiya had taken refuge in this high desert, on the shore of this briny lake teeming with black flies.

But the Monos had little food to share, and she saw how they watched their cousins reduce that little to less, grow weary of hospitality, become querulous and cross. Chief Teneiya, too, grew fretful, repeatedly muttering, "We are few upon earth and soon shall be none. We are few upon earth and

227

soon shall be none." When melting snow permitted, he and his despairing people departed for Awani, traversing the ancient mountain pass west toward *pywe'ack*, beautiful lake of shining stones. *Pywe'ack*, granite landscape doubled in its depths, clouds floating on water twice blue with captured sky.

At the lake's edge she knelt, took its cold water up in cupped hands, drank from a reflection she barely recognized as hers. *Pywe'ack*. Here ghosts dwelt. She heard them. Heard a flute. Did she say so? Or imagine she had? Did she ask Tabuce if she heard the flute? Or imagine she had? Tabuce, who had also lost words, saying little except to Lutario, all of them dispirited, lamenting loss, fearing the future.

Several ill-tempered Monos followed them to *pywe'ack*, demanding, as in the old days, another hand game. They sat, played, the Monos blustering and boasting, the game growing aggressive with argument and shouts. She ignored the angry exchange. It was only a hand game disagreement, she supposed, not paying attention, listening for the flute. But hard words flew.

And then rocks followed words.

Reasons and causes, did they matter? In the end, the world was as it was, not as she thought it ought to be. The sun came up, stars came out, acorns fell, people died. A rock flew from an angry hand. Chief Teneiya fell. When he failed to rise, no one seemed astonished. Chief Teneiya, gone to the ancestors, another name not to speak. Another inglorious death affirming the world's unraveling.

Leaderless now and confused, the Awanichees lost connection to one another, to the land, to purpose. Some returned to the Monos. Others drifted south to the Tuolumnes, or wandered down the mountain to mining camps. For her, home remained Awani, and she forlornly continued west with the timid few remaining together. She counted, and they came to twenty. No one hunted them now, cared where they lived, or if they lived. Now undeniably defeated, they were free to resume the shreds left of their old life, to curl wormwood leaves into balls they hung from milkweed necklaces to prevent dreaming of the dead.

Where once they lived large, they now lived small. They fashioned cedar into shelters they furnished with digging sticks and fishing spears, let the earth provide. The past receded, fell away, replaced by daily existence, subsistence, a gradual acceptance that what was done was done. Women collected acorns, constructed *chuck'ah*s for storing the precious food in the old way. They ground the nuts, cooked the meal in baskets with heated rocks. They foraged for roots and berries, gathered grass seeds, wove baskets, and shrank from their memories.

She was one with this tattered rag of people whose home was Awani. When she tired, she slept. When she thirsted, she drank. When she hungered, she ate. The earth fed them sweet clover and sour sorrel in spring, roots and grass seeds and insects in their season.

When food grew scarce, they knew hunger. A few wandered down from the mountain to beg. Some returned with food to share. Some drank whiskey and it made their heads bad.

Chief Teneiya's ghost whispered with the wind, "Soon we will be none." Why she was still in the world ceased being a question to pose or answer. She simply was, and took a pale comfort in climbing the old canyon trail to recall lost happiness. She still sensed spirit within each boulder and tree and bend along the way. Her eyes still feasted on the panorama of the beautiful grassy valley surrounded by soaring granite and cascading waters. This place was still her home.

Despite the strangers, the invading strangers.

> Previously…whoever had occasion to kill one did not avoid it, and thought he had done a useful and praiseworthy deed. After having worked with them, side by side, during the entire summer…we judged them more favorably.
>
> —Jean-Nicholas Perlot
> September 1854

She watched them come, the white men. Miners with their mules and tools. No one dared resist, or think to stop them now. Such times had passed. Miners explored the valley, looked for gold wherever they chose, making the land theirs. Lutario gathered courage, approached the prospectors, offered himself as guide, willing to show where gold might be found, in exchange for whatever white men chose to pay or share. She avoided the invading white people, ignored their presence. When she saw them, she pretended she didn't. If they noticed her, she disappeared.

One day, on the trail to the river, she unexpectedly encountered a heavy-bearded white man in buckskins, rifle in one hand, rope in the other. She stopped, stared, transfixed. Forgot to disappear. Great Spirit surely had abandoned the People, turned their world inside out. How else to comprehend *uzu'mati* with a pack on its back like a mule, led on a rope by a white man.

"Don't be scared of her," the man in buckskins said. "Sweet as pie. A real lady. Lady Washington is what I call her. Knows her name, too." He smiled. "What's your name?"

Did she have a name? She couldn't recall, could only stare until she remembered to disappear. Grizzly bear tethered to a white man. Eagle tethered to a ladder. Signs, surely, the world was ending. Coyote must have forgotten, she thought, fleeing, forgot when he made the First People, to tell them they would all die. She should have known. The People's stories were filled with death.

She stopped to breathe again, and heard a meadowlark warble a reminder of the old story, how Coyote saw the first person die, and said, "I think I will make him get up." But Meadowlark said, "No, do not. There will be too many people."

Chief Teneiya's ghost: "Soon we will be none."

> [O]ur party ran onto an encampment of the wretched Yosemites…. Their ragged garments would not admit of even a surmise as to their quality or pattern… I told them that it was because of their treachery and dishonesty that they had been made to suffer, and then left them in their wretchedness.
> —Lafayette Bunnell
> 1855

Lutario, alarmed, hollered that white men were coming toward the village. Everyone collected to see. Half frightened, half curious, they waited. What were the white men doing, what did they want, these white men measuring the ground, marking the trees?

She recognized Doc. He didn't recognize her. Why would he? She turned away, embarrassed lest he might. She knew how she looked, how they all looked, covering themselves with rags and tatters of white people's cast-offs, knowing nakedness offended.

Doc. She remembered how *wawona*'s trees and Awani's beauty astonished him. So long gone those days. So many ghosts. But he was real, coming into the present from out of the past, trailing memories. Doc. Why was he here? What were these white men doing in Awani?

Lutario, ever curious, asked.

Surveying. A road. A white man's road. Into Awani.

The white men looked at them, disdain obvious. She remembered scorn from the store on the Mariposa, how the oily-voice man curled his lip, said "Oklahoma" like it was a bad word. Remembered San Francisco women appraising her from beneath their bonnets, wrinkling their noses. A bad smell.

Once she had been beautiful, daughter of a great chief, danced in deer-skin adorned with feathers. One of the People.

The days advanced. The surveyors intruded the teeth of saws into cedars, reducing tall trees into neatly piled logs they roofed with canvas from their tents. Taking Awani, making it theirs. They were staying. More would come. It was their way, to keep coming. She remembered the ships' masts erected like a forest in the harbor, abandoned evidence of white men coming and coming.

> Five claims have already been taken, and one frame house erected…. At no distant day this must become a place of great resort by people from all parts of the earth.
> —*California Farmer*
> November 7, 1856

She understood when Tobuce's cousins, Kos-sum and So-pin, left, hungry, desperate, hopeful of a better fate in the camps and towns below. They returned with five white men eager to see Awani, toured them through the valley to admire the towering granite and cascading waters. The visitors camped in the meadow. She heard them laughing in the night around their campfire.

The following summer the sightseers returned and brought their friends to see Awani's extraordinary sights. More came the year after that. Some in spring, more in summer, camping, laughing, in the meadow. Her meadow, where fragrance of sweet green clover, yellow lupine, and wild anise engulfed her with memories. She, too, once had laughed, laughed to happy shouts while holding a ball, been carried through tall grass, embraced.

Five years? six? since watching and waiting on the Mariposa, learning white men's words? Learning new ways one unaware winter in a trading post corner.

Watching and waiting. The beginning of vanishing.

Now she watched and waited on the Merced. Watched sightseers come into Awani, spread blankets for a picnic, admire the view and leave before frost filled the valley.

She knew one day they would stay.

And one day they did.

A tent. At first, only a big blue tent. Then a steady stream of pack mules. Then the thudding ax. Trees crashing. Saws rasping. Hammers pounding. It had begun, as she knew it must, another vanishing. She remembered San Francisco. Had the land by the bay been beautiful before white men buried it beneath planked roads and bricks, draped its hillsides with canvas shanties, dirtied its harbor with garbage?

Unable to ignore the intrusion, she and Tabuce, Lutario, all of them, gathered, silent observers, watched pines and cedars fall and a building rise, loom, a foreign thing of shakes and planks with cut-out eyes waiting for windows and doors. One floor, two. Would there be signboards? She had seen San Francisco. She recognized hotels.

And knew more must follow. More pack trains would come. More trees thunder to earth, branches breaking, ground shaking. One hotel would not be enough. White men, coming and coming, wanting more—more stores, more gold, more land. Never satisfied. How long before they reduced Awani into a white man's rancheria?

And who would know, then, that the People once lived here, played games on the meadow, told Coyote's stories, wove baskets, feasted and celebrated, danced like eagles, sang the acorn song?

How long?

> The Best Panorama of California is to be seen at Vance's Gallery, free of charge, in the exhibition of the fine stereoscopic views of Yosemite Falls and Valley…. Vance has duplicates for sale, at only $5 per dozen.
>
> —*Daily Alta California*
> May 19,1860

The white horse wearing a bell, leading the mules, was coming. Lutario and Tabuce and the others went to see what the Mexicans were bringing into Awani this trip. White people's necessities seemed endless: boxes of books and bolts of muslin, rolls of wallpaper, a clock, a rocking chair, crockery and cutlery, cooking pots and a stove to put them on, tables and chairs, a looking-glass, candles and carpets, windows and doors, brooms and brushes, wash-tubs and bedsteads, a plow; once even an entire wagon, in pieces, carried on the backs of the Mexicans' mules. And more: the steady stream of guests for the Hutchings hotel required jars of jams and jellies, bags of coffee beans, caddies of tea, crates of onions and potatoes, bottles of wine and brandy, tins of peaches, packets of pepper, barrels of flour and sacks of sugar.

She watched white people and their countless necessities coming and coming, wondered what her father would have thought of the long life he had urged for her. Fearing little but hunger, she silently spoke his name. Waited. His ghost had fled.

> Visitors to Yosemite Valley from Sacramento county can take
> Fisher & Co.'s Sacramento line…. easy Concord coaches, with
> reliable drivers… prompt to time of departure and arrival.
> —*California Farmer*
> July 26,1861

Eventually, as the years passed, she grew accustomed to inquisitive sightseers wandering from the hotels into what remained of the Awanichees' village. Chattering white women watched Tabuce weave baskets, watched her grind acorn. She was a curiosity indifferent to stares.

Tourists sometimes gave them coins. Occasionally, Tabuce sold a basket. Hutchings hired Lutario to tend his apple orchard, paid Lutario's cousin Tom to go weekly to Coulterville for mail. Tabuce's niece, Totuya, scrubbed visitors' clothes in a metal washtub behind the hotel.

The People had become useful.

> A LETTER from Paris states that Mr. Watkins' photographs of
> the magnificent scenes in the Yosemite Valley are on exhibition
> in that city, and eliciting high encomiums from the lovers of art.
> —*Marysville Daily Appeal*
> October 18, 1862

When the acorns failed to come three consecutive seasons, she weakened from eating bitter buckeye nuts. Florantha Sproat, mother of Hutchings' young wife, offered cornmeal muffins. And work.

She learned to sweep. What choice did she have? In memory, Victoria's voice recalling mission days: "We were never hungry."

She swept dirt from the hotel's rooms, ignored the guests. They ignored her. She was invisible, ghost woman sweeping. Hutchings had hung muslin from the rafters to divide one room from another. Voices floated through the curtains like sunlight: "Their baby girl, little Floy, so adorable—" … "If you're in San Francisco, on Clay Street, Mrs. Cole has the latest French fashions—" … "You must see Vernal Falls before you leave—" …

Hushed conversations drifting like dust: "Hutchings insisted he got to Yosemite Valley ahead of the park and had every right to buy an existing hotel—" … "Congress gave Yosemite to the people of California. Private property not allowed—" …"Says he'll take his case to the Supreme Court—"

To escape the voices, the invaders, she occasionally climbed the old trail. Beneath pines scattering shards of sunlight, she found refuge amid Awani's granite cliffs and boulders where *cho'lak*'s waters misted the breeze, where towering cedars scented the air.

One afternoon, sitting where Seethkil first told her the sad story of the lost arrow, hearing his ghost voice in her heart, a dog barked nearby. She turned. With his dog was the tall young carpenter Hutchings hired to replace muslin with wooden walls. She'd heard guests complain. They wanted walls their candles didn't dance their shadows through, walls that muffled voices.

SOMETHING NEW, SEND HOME THE NEW WORK
Entitled "Scenes of Wonder and Curiosity of California." Also, Views of San Francisco, and YOSEMITE VALLEY AND FALLS. For sale at A. ROSENDFIELD'S, No. 603 Montgomery street, S.F.
—*Daily Alta California*
September 27, 1863

The carpenter called to the dog, "Carlo. Carlo."

She remained motionless, invisible, her thoughts here, in this special place she and Seethkil had made their own. She silently spoke his name, invited his ghost to join her, to gaze with her, through her eyes, upon Awani's beauty, the land Great Spirit gave the People. Nearby, the creek danced lively waters over stones smoothed since time first gave spirit to granite, to whispering trees and soaring hawks.

And then, suddenly, unexpectedly, the dog was at her knee, panting, looking up at her with its large, sad dog eyes. She ignored it, ignored the present here, as she always did. In this place the present receded and the past rose from its ashes. She imagined Coyote planting sticks and feathers here, making the People.

She heard the carpenter call again. "Carlo." She ignored the intrusion, hearing instead the cry of the crane, *totau'kon,* building its nest atop the summit of the great rock. In memory she imagined bear cubs rescued by little inch worm. Ancient stories told by firelight, when foot-drummer drummed and shaman shook his rattle.

The Senate has passed Conness' bill to grant to the State of California the Yosemite Valley and the Mariposa Big Tree Grove.... a pleasure ground which, for beauty, sublimity and extent, will make all the princely parks of other lands dwindle into insignificance.
—*Sacramento Daily Union*
June 16,1864

A scampering squirrel stopped, chittered at the dog. The carpenter sat down nearby on a rocky outcrop. She watched him fold his arms around his knees, like her. Stare into the distance, like her. After a time, she heard him say, very low, very slow, "We are in the mountains, and the mountains are in us."

He was speaking to himself, not to her. She was not here, she was invisible, visiting a time long gone, a time peopled by ghosts. She was with Victoria, Victoria in her faded red calico skirt hiked to her knees, *metate* singing, bright bird eyes watching Anna's child crawling, learning the earth. She was with her father on a horse quietly following ancient trails sheltered by fragrant cedars, trails traveled since the First People walked the earth. José Jesús, the great chief, with her, his daughter, greeted by laughing children, their mothers offering good acorn soup cooked in baskets woven watertight. She was with Seethkil, laughing, running through meadow grass. With Seethkil, warm beneath a buffalo robe. With Seethkil, holding her close, watching storm clouds gather above *Tis-sa'-ack*, sky darkening. Snow falling.

She barely realized she'd answered, could answer, could speak, when the carpenter asked her the name of the mountain his people called Half Dome.

She must have spoken. Or did she imagine she had? But he was saying, "I'll remember that. *Tis-sa'-ack*." And then he said it again, softly, slowly, "*Tis-sa'-ack*."

How had she spoken? Her thoughts lived with ghosts, and soon she would join them. Soon the People would be gone, and one day no one would be left to say the names of the People's places, tell their stories. No one left to remember the stories or the People who told them, to remember that here Awani fed and sheltered them, here they danced and chanted and celebrated. No evidence would remain that the People once walked this earth, tasted the clover, greeted the sun. And when the People had all become ghosts, she supposed, sadly, Awani itself must follow, be swallowed, like the People, by the avalanche of white people coming and coming, carrying with them the clutter of their endless necessities, slaying the cedars for ships and houses, turning pines into piers. And no one to say no. Neither Coyote, nor the First People, had told how to be in the world without hope.

"*Hum-moo*," she said, half surprised she'd heard the carpenter's question, and answered it.

"And what is your name?" he asked.

Name? Did she possess a name? She was a ghost, untethering from the earth, disappearing with her disappearing world, to an Awani no more. Name? She looked over at him. Saw blue eyes. She remembered a ghost with blue eyes. A ghost with hair yellow as sunshine, eyes like sky. For a moment, she sensed his presence, felt his hand on her face.

Memories. Ghosts. She stared at her moccasins. Remembered. Remembered her mother's voice calling, remembered seeing a child's moccasins, her moccasins. Remembered the dream-time darkness, the barren landscape, remembered wondering where the People had gone. Remembered her mother's voice, calling from the dream-time.

"Di-shi," she said at last, watching clouds gather over the valley below, hearing the whispering of trees. "I am Di-shi."

"I'm John," he said. "John Muir."

In the distance a crane called.

Afterword

The first arrest in the county was that of Judge Harvey for the
killing of Major Savage, but nothing came of it.
—History of Tulare County

In 1854 Walter H. Harvey was appointed sergeant-at-arms of the California State Legislature. In 1861, having married California State Governor John Downey's daughter, he was appointed Commissioner of Emigration for the Port of San Francisco. He died in August of that year.

In 1855 Dr. Lewis Leach disinterred Jim Savage's remains and transferred them to the site of his store on the Fresno River. There a shaft about ten feet high, standing upon a pedestal, marked the spot where Savage then rested. According to the *History of Tulare County* (W. W Elliott & Co., 1883), the granite monument, weighing many tons and costing $800, "was shipped from Connecticut by water to Stockton and from there transported across the country by eight horses, and on a truck especially constructed. Great difficulty was found in placing the monument, owing to want of proper tackle." In 1973 the U.S. Army Corps of Engineers relocated the grave and monument above the waterline of the dam built to create Hensley Lake.

In 1859 the Fresno Reservation was officially abandoned following years of decline, its few remaining Chauchilas, Chukchansi, Pohonochee, and Potohowchi destitute and dying. Much of the reservation now lies beneath Hensley Lake, a popular water recreation area.

That year, 1859, Lafayette Bunnell published a brief account of the Mariposa Battalion in *Hutchings' California Magazine*: "How the Yo-Semite Valley was Discovered and Named." Although called "Doc" by many members of the expedition, Bunnell was not a certified physician. In 1861, having returned to Wisconsin, he enlisted in the Union Army where he served as a hospital steward and in 1864 was awarded an honorary medical degree. In 1880, "to correct existing errors relative to the Yosemite Valley," he published the first edition of *Discovery of the Yosemite and the Indian War Which Led to that Event.* In 1903, age 79, he died in Homer, Minnesota. The California Medical Association honored his contribution to Yosemite history with a plaque affixed to a large boulder near the eastern edge of Bridalveil Meadow.

On October 31, 1902, James Hutchings, aged 82, was killed while visiting Yosemite when his horse reared and threw him from his buggy.

In 1929, as Rebecca Solnit reports in *Savage Dreams: A Journey Into the Hidden Wars of the American West,* "the U.S. government finally decided to pay California's original inhabitants for the land that had been taken from them, at the rate of forty-seven cents an acre, minus all appropriations of goods made for all of the Indians of California since 1848....By 1950 disbursements of $150 to each individual had been issued, and a few similar sums were handed out until the 1970s, when the government satisfied itself it had bought California from its first peoples."

Acknowledgements

For providing encouragement and generously reading the manuscript for inconsistencies and infelicities, I thank Suzanne and Craig Sheumaker, Marilyn Snider, Liz Trupin-Tulli, and Gary Noy. Dave King provided invaluable editorial advice. To Joan Frantschuk goes sincere appreciation for the title, and for shepherding the ms through publication. I remain grateful.

I am most indebted to the writers, scholars, librarians, and historians whose work made this one possible, including the California Digital Newspaper Collection, the Yosemite Online Library, and the following sources:

Adventures of a Mountain Man: The Narrative of Zenas Leonard. Zenas Leonard. 1979

American Fur Trade of the Far West. Hiram M. Chittenden. 1902

American Odyssey: The Autobiography of a 19th-Century Scotsman. Robert Brownlee. 1892

Sam Brannan and the California Mormons. Paul Bailey. 1942

"The California Indian Treaty Myth." Harry Kelsey. *Southern California Quarterly,* Fall 1973

California's Agua Fria: The Early History of Mariposa County. Raymond F. Wood. 1954

California Indian Folklore. Frank F. Latta. 1936

Dawn of the World: Myths and Tales of the Miwok Indians of California. C. Hart Merriam. 1993

Destruction of California Indians. Robert F. Heizer, ed. 1974

Diary of John Augustus Sutter. 1932

Discovery of the Yosemite. Lafayette H. Bunnell. 1892

Early Days of San Francisco. John Henry Brown. 1949

Early History of Yosemite Valley California. Ralph S. Kuykendall. 1919

Early Recollections of the Mines, and a Description of the great Tulare valley. J. H. Carson. 1852

"Early Years in Yosemite." Carl P. Russell (Reminiscence of Stephen F. Grover). *California Historical Society Quarterly,* Vol. 5, No. 4, December 1926

The Eighteen Unratified Treaties of 1851–1852 between the California Indians and the United States Government. Robert F. Heizer, 1972

French Journalist in the California Gold Rush: The Letters of Etienne Derbec. Etienne Derbec. 1964

Geography and Dialects of the Miwok Indians. S.A. Barrett. 1908

Gold Seeker: Adventures of a Belgian Argonaut during the Gold Rush Years. Jean-Nicolas Perlot. 1985

Handbook of the Indians of California. A. L. Kroeber. 1925

Handbook of Yokuts Indians. Frank F. Latta. 1977

History of California, Vol. VI, 1848-1859. Hubert Howe Bancroft. 1886

History of Tulare County, California. 1891.

Indians, Franciscans, and Spanish Colonization: The Impact of the Mission System on California Indians. Robert H. Jackson. 1996

Indians and Indian Agents: The Origins of the Reservation System in California, 1849-1852. George Harwood Phillips. 1997

ACKNOWLEDGEMENTS

Indians and Intruders in Central California, 1769-1849. George Harwood Phillips. 1993

Indian Legends of Yosemite. Harriet Meuel. 1983

Indian Life at the Old Missions. Edith Buckland Webb. 1982

Indian Survival on the California Frontier. Albert L. Hurtado. 1988

Indians of the Yosemite Valley and Vicinity: Their History, Customs and Traditions. Galen Clarke. 1902

It Will Live Forever: Traditional Yosemite Acorn Preparation. Bev Ortiz. 1991

"Journal of George W. Barbour, May to October 1851." Alben W. Hoopes. *Southwestern Historical Quarterly*, Vol. 40, No. 2, October 1936

Languages, Territories and Names of California Indian Tribes. Robert F. Heizer. 1966

Last of the California Rangers. Jill L. Cossley-Batt. 1928

Legends of the Yosemite Miwok. Frank LaPena. 1993

Making of Yosemite: James Mason Hutchings and the Origin of America's Most Popular Park. Jen A.Huntley. 2014

Mariposa Indian War, 1850-1851: Diaries of Robert Eccleston; The California Gold Rush, Yosemite, and the High Sierra. C. Gregory Crampton, ed. 1957

Miwok Material Culture: Indian life of the Yosemite Region. S. A. Barrett and E. W. Gifford. 1933

Natural World of the California Indians. Robert F. Heizer and Albert B. Elsasser. 1980

Northern Sierra Miwok Dictionary. Catherine A. Callaghan. 1987

One Hundred Years in Yosemite. Carl P. Russell. 1947

Jim Savage and the Tulareno Indians. Annie R. Mitchell. 1957

Savage Dreams: A Journey into the Hidden Wars of the American West. Rebecca Solnit. 1994

Scenes of Wonder and Curiosity in California. James M. Hutchings. 1862

"The Secret Treaties with California's Indians." Larisa K. Miller. *Prologue*, Fall/Winter 2013

Seventy Five Years in California. William Heath Davis. 1929

Jedidiah Smith and the Opening of the West. Dale L. Morgan. 1953

Studies of California Indians. C. Hart Merriam, et al. 1955

John Sutter and a Wider West. Kenneth N. Owens, ed. 1994

The Tragedy of Tenaya: A Yosemite Indian Story. Allan Shields. 1974

Three Years in California: William Perkins' Journal of Life at Sonora, 1849-1852. William Perkins. 1964

Treaty Making and Treaty Rejection by the Federal Government in California, 1850–1852. George E. Anderson, W. H. Ellison, and Robert F. Heizer. 1978

Tribes of California. Stephen Powers. 1976

Sam Ward in the Gold Rush. Samuel Ward. 1949

Western Panorama, 1849-1875: The Travels, Writings and Influence of J. Ross Browne on the Pacific Coast. David Michael Goodman. 1965

What I Saw in California. Edwin Bryant. 1848

When the Great Spirit Died: The Destruction of the California Indians 1850-1860. William B. Secrest. 2002

ACKNOWLEDGEMENTS

"A White Medicine Man." James O'Meara. *The Californian*, February 1882; *Yosemite Nature Notes*, November 1951

Yosemite Indians. Elizabeth Godfrey. 1941

Yosemite: Its Discovery, Its Wonders and Its People. Margaret Sanborn. 1981

Made in the USA
Columbia, SC
01 September 2021